The DOG of the NORTH

Tim Stretton was born on the Isle of Wight in 1967.
A graduate in English and American Literature,
he now lives in West Sussex.

TIM STRETTON

The DOG *Of the* NORTH

Annals of Mondia

TOR

First published 2008 by Macmillan New Writing

First published in paperback 2009 by Tor
an imprint of Pan Macmillan Ltd
Pan Macmillan, 20 New Wharf Road, London N1 9RR
Basingstoke and Oxford
Associated companies throughout the world
www.panmacmillan.com

ISBN 978-0-330-46083-5

1 3 5 7 9 8 6 4 2

A CIP catalogue record for this book is available
from the British Library.

Typeset by Intype Libra Ltd
Printed and bound in the UK by CPI Mackays, Chatham ME5 8TD

For Sue and Danielle

Acknowledgements

Although there is only one name on the cover, many hands go into the making of a book. Patrick Dusoulier, Paul Rhoads and Steve Sherman all believed in *The Dog of the North* before it was published, and made many useful suggestions to the early drafts. Greg and Kate Mosse also provided technical advice, encouragement and the suggestion that I submit the book to Macmillan New Writing. At Macmillan, I'm indebted to my editor Will Atkins, both for having faith in the book in the first place, and for his invaluable editorial comments.

I'd like also to mention Jack Vance, for writing better than anyone else the kind of books I like to read – books that made me realize I wanted to be a writer too. For over a quarter of a century his writing has inspired and delighted in equal measure.

Finally I should say a big thank you to Sue and Danielle for accepting uncomplainingly the ruthlessness with which I've appropriated evenings and weekends in pursuit of my writing, the most unforgiving and demanding mistress of all.

Principal Characters

Arren	Son of Darrien
Beauceron	'The Dog of the North', brigand captain of Mettingloom
Brissio	Heir to the Winter Throne of Mettingloom, son of King Fanrolio
Coppercake	Tutor of mathematics and adviser to Lord Thaume
Cosetta	Companion to Lady Isola
Darrien	Captain of Lord Thaume's Guard
Davanzato	Under-Chamberlain to King Fanrolio
Eilla	Daughter of Croad's master mason Jandille
Fanrolio	Winter King of Mettingloom
Goccio	Knight of the Summer Court, Mettingloom
Guigot	Nephew of Lord Thaume
Isola	Daughter of Lord Sprang of Sey
Laertio	Heir to the Summer Throne of Mettingloom, son of King Tardolio
Langlan	Knight of Emmen, adviser to Lord Thaume
Monetto	Beauceron's lieutenant
Mongrissore	Legulier
Oricien	Son and heir to Lord Thaume

Panarre	Duke of Lynnoc; liege-lord of Lord Thaume
Pinch	Thaumaturge in the service of Lord Thaume
Raugier	Lord High Viator, Emmen
Siedra	Daughter of Lord Thaume
Tardolio	Summer King of Mettingloom
Thaume	Lord of Croad
Virnesto	Captain-General of the Winter Armies, Mettingloom

I

Croad

I

Captain Fleuraume peered back into the mist. His eyelashes were damp with the fog and his eyes not as keen as they once had been. 'How many do you see?' he asked Cornelis, the lookout.

'It's hard to tell in this light. Ten for certain, maybe more.'

Fleuraume frowned. 'There must be more than that.'

'If there are, they're keeping out of sight.'

Fleuraume turned in his saddle and gestured around him. With the sun only just over the horizon, the track ahead was visible for less than a hundred yards. The plain away to the west gleamed in an eerie reddish light as the sun came up, while the Ferrant Mountains to the east cast a heavy gloom.

'Look around you,' he said. 'They want to be seen. It wouldn't be hard to keep hidden in the mist.'

Cornelis shook his head. The cold of the mist leached into his chain mail and chilled the cotton shirt underneath. He wanted nothing more than to be warm in his bed – but it looked like he might have to fight to get there. He shivered, not simply from the cold.

'I'll send Webrecht and Ryckaert to join you,' Fleuraume said. 'I'll need to wake my lady.'

He spurred his gallumpher back up the column. After sending the two men back to reinforce Cornelis, he dismounted and leaped aboard the stout-coach. Inside, two bleary-eyed figures looked back at him.

'Good morning, Lady Isola, Lady Cosetta! I trust you slept well.'

Lady Cosetta appeared still to be enjoying her repose and made no response. Lady Isola scowled back at the captain.

'The rolling of the stout-coach does not make for a restful environment, Captain Fleuraume. Was it really necessary to continue through the night?'

'I'm afraid so, my lady. If the men we saw on the road yesterday were innocent, we would have left them behind overnight: my guards report they are still visible this morning. It is not unduly pessimistic to suggest they mean us no good.'

Lady Isola, whose lustrous dark hair and regular features hinted at an appealing appearance if she could be prevailed upon to smile, continued to frown. 'You are something of an old woman, sir, if you are discomfited by ten men on gallumphers, no matter how well armed. You command an escort of forty of Lord Oricien's best troops. You cannot seriously fear these men?'

Fleuraume bristled. The girl could be no more than twenty, whatever her birth. 'I did not say "fear", my lady. I am cautious for your safety, and the security of the valuables. If ten men permit themselves to be seen, how many more are hiding?'

Lady Isola sniffed. 'Your concern for my welfare does you credit, Captain. But surely they would have attacked under cover of darkness had they intended an immediate mischief. The Consorts preserve us, this is the Duchy of Lynnoc, man! Do you really expect brigands to molest Duke Trevarre's peace?'

'My lady, we are nearly at Croad. The northerners have been quiet of late, but the Dog has been known to venture this far south. He knows the lands around here well; he does not fear to operate so far from home.'

'Do not think to frighten me with tales of the Dog of the North,' said Lady Isola. 'I am travelling under the protection of Lord Oricien and Duke Trevarre: an outrage is inconceivable.'

Fleuraume dropped back to where Serjeant Ryckaert and the sentries kept watch. As the sun rose the mist began to fade, but there was no sign of more men. The group of around ten hovered on the boundary of visibility.

'Should we speed up, sir?' asked Webrecht. 'They are not moving quickly.'

'We cannot outrun them,' said Fleuraume.

'Perhaps we should chase them off,' suggested Ryckaert. 'We outnumber them four to one, and we are heavily enough armoured.'

Captain Fleuraume rubbed his chin. 'I am tempted, but I cannot leave the caravan unguarded. By midday we should be at the River Casalle: there is no way across but the bridge. We will see their strength then.'

Webrecht muttered to himself. 'If we get there . . .'

At mid-morning Lady Isola and Lady Cosetta emerged from the rear of their stout-coach to take a breakfast on the viewing platform. The autumn sun stood proudly in the sky and the mist had all but gone. Talk of brigands seemed feverish in such beautiful light, with the Ferrant Mountains now visible in all their glory to the right and the plains rolling away to their left. Lady Cosetta clambered to the roof of the stout-coach and looked back.

'Captain!' she called out. 'Are those the raiders?'

'Lady Cosetta! I must pray you to descend immediately!

The motion of the stout-coach will surely shake you to the ground!'

Cosetta, slender and athletic, slid back to the observation platform. 'I have heard nothing but brigands all morning. I wanted to see for myself what caused such alarm.'

One of the guards rode up to the captain from the rear of the column.

'Sir! They have raised their banner.'

The captain sat upright in his saddle. 'And?'

'A white wolf's head upon a scarlet field. They are the Dog's men.'

Fleuraume nodded. The confirmation did not seem a surprise. 'Ladies, please return to your carriage until I give you leave to emerge. There will be blood shed today.'

Lady Cosetta paled; Lady Isola gave a slight smile before eating the last mouthful of her sausage.

Fleuraume looked ahead to the River Casalle and its unique bridge, its wooden structure carved into an intricate griffon representing the House of Croad. The sooner they were across, the better. He ordered the postilions to bring the stout-coach up to its maximum speed and put the bulk of his men at the back of the column between the raiders and the stout-coach. The bridge was no more than ten minutes away and the road was clear. He had no choice but to run.

He dropped to the back of the caravan and saw dust rising in the distance. The raiders were starting their charge. Were there only ten of them? The Dog's troops were formidable, and they did not bind themselves by the rules of chivalry: but they were outnumbered nearly three to one, despite the men kept back to guard the stout-coach. If they wanted a fight, Fleuraume would give them one. Who could say, maybe the Dog of the North himself was among their number?

He heard a thrum of arrows. This was not knightly conduct, but it was to be expected. He saw a man near him go down, an arrow through his gorget. Fleuraume tightened his lips. If he captured the Dog, Oricien would hang him in the marketplace as his grandfather had done when he captured rebels. The Dog of the North would pay for his arrogance.

Suddenly the raiders wheeled their gallumphers about. Fleuraume's cavalry line was immaculate, but there was nothing opposing it. The raiders had peeled away to either side.

'Fight like men!' he called. 'Steel to steel!'

The raiders continued to remain out of skirmish range, while trying to pick off Fleuraume's men with arrows. The strategy was not effective; only two men had fallen in the first pass – and all the while the caravan drew closer to the safety of the bridge.

Up ahead, the fifteen men guarding the stout-coach saw the narrow wooden bridge come into view. Serjeant Ryckaert, who commanded the remaining men, rode out ahead of the caravan and looked down into the fast-flowing river. The bridge creaked beneath his gallumpher, but he knew it would bear the weight of the stout-coach. He had been this way many times before. There was no sign of any ambush. The captain had engaged the raiders and they no longer presented a threat. Thirty yards away lay the other bank. On that side of the river there was no place of concealment other than a copse a mile or so away: too far to represent a danger, even if the Dog had been able to deploy a sizeable force this close to Croad.

Ryckaert's orders were simple: cross the bridge with the caravan, and await Fleuraume's men on the other side. In the unlikely event that the Dog's men overcame Fleuraume, Ryckaert had the advantage of controlling the exit from the bridge: no matter how good the Dog's troops, they would not be able to deploy.

Ryckaert smiled to himself. He imagined himself stepping

into the ladies' stout-coach. 'Lady Isola, Lady Cosetta: I am pleased to report the emergency is over. You may wish to emerge and inspect the prisoners.'

Both ladies would favour him with an appreciative smile. The blonde Lady Cosetta, not so haughty as her companion, would give him that sideways look she could deploy to such devastating effect. 'You must tell me all about the battle once we are at Croad, Serjeant Ryckaert.'

He beckoned the stout-coach onto the bridge and watched as it came past him, allowing himself a nod of satisfaction as the noise of the wheels on the wooden bridge stopped: they were on the rutted track again, and he had carried out his orders. The stout-coach was across the river.

'Sir! Smoke! I see smoke!'

Ryckaert looked around. 'Where can smoke be coming from?'

'I can't tell! But it's everywhere!'

Ryckaert looked around him. He could see wisps of smoke too, and there was a smell . . . Suddenly he realized.

'The bridge is on fire!' he cried. 'Those treacherous dogs! Across, with me, now!'

Ryckaert could not imagine how the bridge could have been set alight, but what mattered was that he got his men across to the same side as the stout-coach. The bridge was dry wood and soon the flames were visible. His men were close to panic: soon they would be babbling of sorcery.

In half a minute all of his men – only fifteen, he thought – were across the bridge, which was now well and truly aflame. Webrecht called out: 'Look – down there!'

On the river bank, below the bridge, two figures clambered up to the land on the far side. Ryckaert could not pursue them because he was on the wrong side of the bridge, which was now impassable. Neither could he get word to

Fleuraume because all of his men were with him. Whatever the Dog had in mind, only Ryckaert's fifteen men remained to prevent it. From across the river, one of the incendiarists put a horn to his lips and blew a long mournful note. Someone, somewhere, was being summoned.

Ryckaert jumped aboard the stout-coach, in circumstances very different to those he had envisaged only a few moments before. Lady Cosetta appeared close to panic; Lady Isola possessed more sangfroid. 'You will simply have to fight the raiders off, Master Ryckaert.'

From the copse, Ryckaert looked out to see a group of mounted men emerging. He reckoned their strength at around thirty – close to a hopeless situation. He leaped down from the stout-coach and drew his men up in defensive formation against the river bank.

The attackers raised their wolf's-head standard. At some inaudible signal they began to charge. 'Follow me!' cried Ryckaert. There was no point in waiting for reinforcements who were trapped on the other side of the river. Lord Oricien's troops rode forward to meet the assault head-on.

Ryckaert charged straight for the centre of the enemy line. The raiders' armour did not sport surcoats or marks of rank, but the prime troops were normally in the middle of the line. He put his shield up and unsheathed his broadsword. His foe ducked out of the way and swung at Ryckaert as he charged past, catching his helmet. Ryckaert turned his gallumpher and prepared to charge again. From the side he felt a blow against his chain mail and he slipped from the gallumpher. There were now two mounted adversaries against him.

'Yield!' called one of the men. 'We want plunder, not corpses.'

Ryckaert lunged for the gallumpher's eyes with his sword; the gallumpher reared and threw the rider to the ground, where he lay stunned. Ryckaert stabbed at the gorget, which gave way, followed by a spurt of blood. The second rider cursed and spurred his gallumpher straight at Ryckaert, who jerked back with only a blow to the shoulder.

He knew he had no chance of remounting his own gallumpher. He looked around. Those of his men still fighting were alone, split apart by the raiders' charge; but most of them were disarmed on the ground, some of them ominously still.

He realized the rider before him would be able to mow him down at any point. Instead the man raised his visor, to reveal a square face frosted with an expression of contemptuous humour.

'Enough! Look around you, sir. Your men are dead or wounded. You cannot win. Don't throw your life away for folly.'

Ryckaert shook the blood from his sword. 'The last man to offer me quarter died. If you care to join him, I am waiting. Let us settle the matter through single combat.'

The rider sighed. 'I have you at a disadvantage; I am not about to relinquish it to pander to your whim of chivalry. Put up your sword, or die.'

Ryckaert looked around him. The rider was right. All of his men lay dead on the ground or disarmed. The raiders had already secured the stout-coach. His first command had ended in humiliating failure. Two of the raider's companions had ridden up; there was no way out.

'I am Master Ryckaert,' he said. 'Must I surrender to a raider?'

'You may prefer to die. Otherwise, put down your sword.'

Ryckaert looked up at the rider. In the implacable face he saw no choice. He turned the sword in his hand and offered the hilt to his conqueror.

The raider dismounted and removed his helmet to display more clearly keen blue eyes, a tightly compressed mouth and nondescript dust-coloured hair. He walked over to where his men had disarmed the surviving guards. 'How many, Monetto?'

'Four dead, eleven yielded.' The man called Monetto ran a hand through his sparse red hair and grinned. 'Plus, of course, the twenty or so on the other side of the river.'

'We need not concern ourselves with them, unless your feelings are hurt by unfriendly gestures.'

Monetto did not spare them a glance. 'What of our men?'

The raider shook his head. 'That fool Ryckaert killed Stolio. A waste of a good soldier's life. We will make sure his wife has his share. Everyone else on this side of the bridge survived. Let's see if the prize was worth the price. Have you been into the stout-coach yet?'

'Naturally not,' said Monetto. 'I defer to the privilege of rank.'

'Come with me, then. Dello can look after the prisoners. Do you think it's her, Monetto?'

Monetto pointed to the flag drooping from the roof of the stout-coach. 'Yellow and blue. It's the arms of Croad. Who else can it be?'

The raider gave a grim smile. 'I have waited a long time to renew our acquaintance. Too long, in fact.'

He leaped onto the viewing platform at the front of the coach. He was not surprised to find the door locked. 'Open up in there!' he called. 'Else I must damage this valuable carriage!'

A high voice came from within. 'A moment.'

The raider allowed himself a smile. After a brief interval he heard the lock turn. 'You may enter.'

He stepped into the coach. Before him stood a blonde woman, probably no more than twenty, startled as a rabbit. From the side he felt himself buffeted; he heard a metallic scraping at his gorget and a sudden pain in his ear. He grabbed the wrist and pulled his assailant to the ground. There was a clatter as the knife fell to the floor.

'Get up!' he said. 'Did you really think to injure me with your breakfast-knife?'

The woman on the floor merely looked up scornfully, her breast heaving and her eyes flashing. She looked at him a moment, stood and went to sit on the couch at the back of the compartment. Her companion went to join her.

The raider looked at them thoughtfully. 'I don't recognize either of you.'

The dark-haired girl said: 'I rarely – if ever – consort with brigands. Our lack of acquaintance should scarcely come as a surprise.'

'Are you the only ones here?'

'Of course. The stout-coach is cramped for two, let alone three.'

The raider stared at them. His clear blue eyes conveyed no emotion. 'You are not what I expected to find. Tell me your names.'

'You are a rude and impertinent fellow. I am Lady Isola, eldest daughter of Lord Sprang of Sey. My companion is Lady Cosetta, also of Sey. If you intend to molest us, please inform us now. I would observe that my father will pay a considerable ransom, particularly if I am returned undamaged.'

The raider frowned. Events were not turning out as he had planned.

'By what right do you fly the standard of Croad, if you come from Sey?'

Lady Isola said: 'I am betrothed to Lord Oricien of Croad.

I am travelling north to celebrate our nuptials. Lady Cosetta accompanies me as my attendant.'

The raider cursed softly. 'You are not the ladies I had expected to find. No matter: I am sure we can turn the situation to advantage – to mine, at least. Presumably you bring a handsome dowry? I doubt that Oricien would have consented to a match without one.'

Lady Isola pursed her lips and stared ahead.

'If you will not tell me, no doubt Lady Cosetta will,' he said, stepping over to where Cosetta was shrinking back into the couch. She was close to tears.

'Behind us,' she sniffed. 'There are jewels and plate. The coin was to be transported separately.'

'Good. Your compliance is encouraging. Since we are likely to be companions for some time, the sooner you accommodate yourselves to circumstances, the better matters will go. You will not be molested, either by me or my men. Our motives are purely mercenary.'

Lady Isola stood up and walked to the window of the carriage. 'Your bearing is not that of a brigand. You appear not only educated, but to speak with the accents of Emmen – of Croad, even.'

'We all follow our own Way, Lady Isola. My own circumstances, while perhaps of vulgar interest to you, are tedious to recount. You may know me as Beauceron. I am also known as the Dog of the North.'

Lady Cosetta shrieked. Lady Isola smiled quietly. 'In Sey your existence is believed to be apocryphal. Any rogue could make the claim.'

'Whether you believe me or not, my lady, I am your captor: call me Beauceron, the Dog or King Enguerran. Now, kindly gather up your effects. I will be setting light to the stout-coach before we move on. We have a long journey ahead.'

2

Croad

I

Arren's earliest memories were of people shouting his name in the streets. 'Long live Arren! Good health to Arren! Long live the King!' He was sitting on his father Darrien's shoulders in the sun, the market square thronged with folk cheering his name as a herald read out the King's decrees.

From his vantage high above the crowd he could see the parade of gallumphers as they trotted across the market square, a haze of dust kicked up by their hoofs in the summer heat. The crisp blue and green surcoats of the riders delighted him and his ears thrilled to the high clear call of the clarion.

He was too young to realize that more than one person could have the same name, or indeed that a person could have several names. When he asked why they were shouting his name, his father laughed.

His mother Ierwen reached up and chucked his cheek. 'It is not you they are calling for, my love. It is King Arren, away down in Emmen.'

Arren did not know what a king was. 'Why does a man in Emmen have the same name as me, Mama?'

'Why, we named you after good King Arren. It is good luck to name a son after the King.'

'What is the King? Why is everyone cheering?'

The royal party, which to Arren had been little more than a parade of gallumphers, passed out of view. Darrien lifted his son down from his broad shoulders. 'You know that I serve Lord Thaume in his Guards. Well, Lord Thaume, here in Croad, he serves King Arren in Emmen. The King rules all of us in Emmen.'

'And who does King Arren serve?'

'Why, the King serves nobody!' said Ierwen, stepping over a discarded flag. 'If he served anyone else, he would not be the King.'

'Can I be the King when I grow up?' asked Arren. 'I would like it if I did not have to serve. No one could make me eat turnip, and I could play with Eilla and Clottie all day.'

Darrien laughed. 'I am sure it is not all play being the King,' he said. 'Besides, you cannot be the King. Only his own family can do that. When good King Arren dies, his son Prince Jehan will be King after him. That is the way of kings.'

'But I have the same name as the King,' said Arren. 'Should I not be King before Jehan, who has a different name?'

'There are many boys called Arren,' said Ierwen. 'But the King has only one son, and it is he who will be King.'

2

The early years of Arren's childhood were unburdened with trouble, or with learning. His father was the Captain of Lord Thaume's Guard, and since raids from the North were frequent, he spent many of his nights and days on the city walls. Ierwen found Arren's younger brother Matten more demanding of her time, and Arren grew into an active and independent lad. His favourite playmates were Eilla, a dark-haired imp of a girl a year his junior, and her sister Clotara – Clottie – a further year younger and of more malleable temper. Matten often joined in their amusements.

The children were forbidden to play outside the city walls, and the strongest prohibition of all was that they were never to cross the bridge and venture into the Voyne, the small irregular town south of the river.

Eilla in particular harboured a special desire to explore the Voyne, largely as a result of the ban her father Jandille, the city's mason, had put on the area. The Voyne, outside of the city walls, housed those who did not have leave to enter the city, and those whose work kept them outside. This settlement had an air of impermanence, despite the inn which did a lively trade among visitors awaiting admittance to Croad.

One spring morning, Arren woke early and roused Eilla, Clottie and Matten. They ran down to the marketplace in the centre of the city, hooting and calling in their excitement. The sun was up and already the day promised heat to come. Arren loved market day, with its clamour of sights, smells and sounds. Traders came from far and wide, gallumphers pulling rattlejacks piled high with goods, and Arren always kept an eye out for the olive-skinned, almond-eyed men who made the journey north from Glount, and always brought the most exquisite goods to defray the cost of their journey. Jostling with them were the farmers from the nearby plains, filling the square with their livestock and produce. Booths cooked every kind of food, and Arren's mouth was always watering by the time he arrived in the square.

Eilla, who would now have been about nine years old, was always voluble on such expeditions. She had big dark eyes and could often charm the traders at the fish stalls into frying them up some fillets for their breakfast. There was a new lad on the fish stall today: a pimply lad of thirteen or so.

'Hello. Who are you?' said Eilla, looking downwards with a demure gaze. Arren hung back with Clottie and Matten.

'Haroust,' said the boy with a flush. Two other lads perched on a fish-crate beside the stall observing the scene.

'Where is Teppentile?' asked Eilla with a shy smile.

'Poorly,' said Haroust.

'Oh,' said Eilla. 'He had promised me breakfast if I came early this week. I am sure you will fry us some fish, good Haroust!'

Haroust's companions sniggered, and his face crimsoned. His voice was a squeaky crackle as he shouted 'Be off with you!' Eilla sloped away with her shoulders drooping.

'I know. We'll play raiders today,' she announced as they left Haroust's shrill curses behind them. 'You have to steal three things from three different booths. We'll make a feast of what we steal.'

'Eilla!' cried Matten. 'We'll be whipped if we're caught!'

'Do you think the raiders escape punishment when they are captured?' said Eilla with a curl of her lip. 'If you don't want to be whipped, don't get caught!'

She ducked into the crowd, to reappear with an apple in her hand. Arren followed Matten more sedately: there was every chance his brother would be caught.

As Arren followed Matten he managed to slide a lemon, all the way from Paladria, into his pocket while the stall-holder served a portly lady. A rare and precious find! As his attention moved towards a necklace on a nearby booth – not strictly suitable for lunch, but still – he was distracted by a yelp. 'Eilla! Help! Help!'

He turned to see a green-robed apothecary holding Clot-tie by the ear. 'Shut it, you little sneak! Steal my purge, would you! It's no use howling now! We'll see what the constable makes of this.'

Arren could not help thinking that Clottie, in attempting to steal a laxative, had not fully understood the point of the game. He looked around for Eilla. She looked back across at him, shrugged, and dipped something into her pocket. She had two items already, and slipped away from the apothecary and Clottie.

While the younger girl continued her wailing, Arren absent-mindedly slipped the necklace into his pocket. He heard a call of 'Hoy there!' and tried to shrink into the crowd. 'Get away with you there, boy!' called the constable, but it was a furtive and guilty-looking Matten who was the target of his suspicion. 'Get off home, now, son. I know your father and I'll be checking up tonight.'

Arren moved off at a tangent to the constable, pouching a loaf of bread as he went past. He had his three items – would Eilla be able to evade capture and get her third item? Arren made his way to their usual rendezvous, the entrance to the Temple of the Wheel. Some five minutes later, Eilla arrived, grinning.

'I've got my three!' declared Arren. 'What of you?'

'Animaxia take it! I've only got two,' said Eilla. 'But it isn't lunchtime yet. That fat old constable is driving all the children off the market. It looks like Clottie will get a whipping.'

'Matten escaped,' said Arren. 'So I win. Only I have three things.'

'Not so! I haven't finished yet. But you're scared to go back.'

'I am not. You're the one who's scared. I'm the King of the Raiders.'

'Are not! Prove it!'

16

'How? And anyway, I don't have to. I have my plunder already.'

Eilla clambered up onto the wall surrounding the temple gardens and sat kicking her legs against the stone. 'If you're really King of the Raiders, you have to take your booty back to your secret palace in the Voyne. You have to go over the bridge. We'll eat our lunch in The Patient Suitor's courtyard – if you dare!'

Arren squinted up at the wall into the sun. 'We aren't allowed across the bridge.'

Eilla sniffed. 'Some raider you are. If raiders only did as they were allowed, they wouldn't be raiders.'

'Well then! You must meet me there at midday – with all three items. Otherwise you're a coward and a sneak and no true knight.'

'How could I be a true knight? I'm a raider,' said Eilla, jumping back down from the wall. 'I'll see you in the court-yard at midday.'

And with that she scampered back off into the crowd.

It was easy to slip into the Voyne on market day. Arren walked out with some fishermen, always expecting the call of the Guards. But nobody noticed him as he slipped across the bridge. Soon he found himself in front of The Patient Suitor Inn.

The sign above the inn depicted a dejected-looking suitor staring into the middle distance at a fine lady on a fine horse. Arren thought he looked sullen rather than patient; he wouldn't like to be the lady once she'd agreed to marry him. Arren set himself to be equally patient until Eilla should arrive – providing she wasn't caught. Or did she intend to leave him there on his own to get into trouble sneaking back into the city? He wouldn't put it past her. He sat down at a table in the corner of the bustling courtyard.

Precisely as The Patient Suitor's bell chimed for midday, however, Eilla appeared on the cobbles. He could see that she had been successful in securing her third item of plunder; it would have been hard to miss: a live cow strolling at the end of a long rope. As the patrons thronging the courtyard eased aside, she led the cow over to the table.

'Eilla! What have you got?' said Arren, in mingled awe, bafflement and suspicion.

'What does it look like to you? In my house we call this a cow. I have three items. I am Queen of the Raiders. My items are better than yours, because they're bigger.'

'Where did you get it?' Arren nodded at the cow.

'I thought the King of the Raiders had to be intelligent. It was in the cattle pen at the market. I opened the gate, took hold of the rope and walked out. No one stopped me. Now we can have our feast. Look, an apple, a nice cheese, and a cow.'

Arren folded his arms and sat back. 'The cow doesn't count. You can't eat it.'

Eilla screwed her face up. 'Of course you can eat a cow. It's called beef.'

'You can't eat it now, stupid. It's alive.'

'Well then, what about milk? Find me a pail, and I'll milk it. Anyway, what have you got?'

Arren brought his items out and laid them on the smooth heavy wood beside Eilla's. 'First, a lemon. Rare and very tasty! Next, a crisp fresh loaf. Feel, it's still warm. Last, a necklace, with red and blue beads.'

'Ha! If you can't eat a cow, you surely can't eat a necklace. Although I'll have it anyway: it should go on the neck of the Raider Queen.'

Arren handed it over. At ten years old he had no sweetheart in mind to give it to. The only girls worth playing with were the ones who thought they were boys, like Eilla.

Eilla nonetheless displayed a feminine delicacy in arranging the trophy around her neck. 'Have you ever eaten a lemon, Arren?' she asked with a smile.

'Of course! My father is always bringing home titbits from Lord Thaume's castle. We've had oranges, lemons and limes, redders, all the fruits you could imagine.'

'And how do lemons and oranges differ?'

'You really are a stupid girl, Eilla. A lemon is yellow, an orange is orange. And redders are red.'

'I don't believe I've ever eaten a lemon. Will you show me how?'

'Of course.' Arren pulled out his pocket-knife and deftly removed the peel. A little knowledge could go a long way, and the lemon appeared identical in every respect except colour to the oranges Darrien often bought home. He carefully split the lemon into two equal portions, offering one to Eilla. 'Here, you just eat it now.'

Eilla weighed the lemon in her hand and looked at Arren. 'Do you eat it all in one? Or cut it into little pieces?'

'Oh! Some Raider Queen you are! Look! One mouthful – like this! Uuurgh! Ohhhh! Pah!'

'Arren! Dear me! Here, have mine too . . .'

By the time they returned to the city, with the cow in tow, and only partly fortified by a lunch of bread, cheese and apple, Arren suspected that trouble waited. Eilla had hidden the necklace away in her pocket: Arren wondered whether it was worth the whipping Jandille would give her.

Darrien and Jandille waited by the gate. Jandille grabbed Eilla by the hair and hauled her off home for punishment. Darrien said nothing, indicating his wishes with a jerk of his head.

They walked back from the gate to Darrien's cottage near the East Walls in silence. The crowds were gone. Once home,

Ierwen was waiting. Matten sat on a chair, his eyes red. He fidgeted and shot Arren a reproachful glance.

'Before I beat you, Arren, have you learned anything from today?'

'Yes, Father.'

'Good. Your wisdom has been earned with pain. I hope you consider it worthwhile. Do you care to share your learning?'

'Oranges and lemons look alike but taste different. Eilla is cleverer than I. It is as easy to steal a cow as a loaf. You always get caught in the end.'

'These points are all unarguable. Ierwen, I lack all appetite to beat the lad. You must do it.'

Ierwen gave a sigh and reached for the cane above the fireplace.

3

Croad

I

In the twilight Beauceron's party made its way along the rough trail leading into the foothills of the Ferrant Mountains, concealed by the scrubby trees on the slope as they moved upwards. As night fell, he called a halt at a clearing of modest expanse with the mountains at their backs.

In the darkness, Beauceron looked down into the Casalle valley at the blazing stout-coach. The flames, set against the starry sky, would draw attention away from his band, should anyone think to look up into the woods. His rabbit stew, fresh from the earth-oven, was given savour by mountain herbs, and from the exhilaration of the afternoon's raid. It was disappointing that Siedra had not been on the coach, but there were compensations.

He looked across to where Isola and Cosetta were picking at their stew.

'Eat up, ladies. This is as good as food gets in the wilds. We have the open road ahead and many adventures to come.'

Cosetta looked at the stew with a grimace. Isola said: 'Our appetites are understandably impaired. We are unclear as to your intentions, but it seems unlikely our wishes will be taken into account.'

'I have assured you that your chastity is safe.'

'You expect me to be grateful that your men have not violated me? I was on the way to my wedding! You have taken my future!' said Lady Isola, with spots of colour at her cheek.

Beauceron leaned back against a rock. 'It might be more accurate to say I have substituted one future for another. Your wedding will no doubt proceed, but at a later date. We will take you back to Mettingloom and ransom you there.'

'Mettingloom!' cried Cosetta. 'You cannot take us all the way into the Northern Reach!'

'I am returning there myself, with the treasure we have abstracted this afternoon.'

'Beauceron,' said Isola with an approach to a smile. 'Can you not simply take us to Croad? Lord Oricien will pay you a ransom on the spot, and you are spared the inconvenience of transporting us north, and then all the way back south.'

Beauceron laughed. 'I prefer to avoid the inconvenience of a noose around my neck. Croad and Mettingloom might not be at war, but I can assure you that if I fell into Oricien's power he would hang me. We will skirt Croad to the north, take the mountain pass and secure a ship from Hengis Port. In three weeks we will be in Mettingloom, ready to secure your release.'

Isola dropped her hunk of bread to the ground, her nostrils flaring. 'Dog!' she shouted, throwing her stew at Beauceron. 'You will live to regret treating Lady Isola of Sey in this fashion.'

Beauceron did not even need to lean aside, so wild was Isola's aim. He stood up, lifted the empty bowl from the ground, and passed it back to her. Before she could respond, he turned on his heel and walked away.

Early the next morning the party set off into the mountains. Lady Cosetta remained largely silent throughout the day;

Lady Isola set up a steady stream of imprecations, until Monetto, riding as their escort, threatened to gag her for the remainder of the journey.

On the second day the group rested for lunch in the high mountain pass which led from Lynnoc to the Northern Reach. Down in the valley below them was the city of Croad, compact and secure behind its walls. The air was becoming chill as they rose from the valley, and both ladies were wrapped in rough cloaks from Beauceron's store. Lady Cosetta's cloak had clearly been pierced by a sword, but if she had misgivings as to the fate of its previous owner she said nothing.

Beauceron settled to his bread and cheese, sitting on one of the flat stones strewn around the rocky pass. While he ate, Lady Isola approached and sat down. Lady Cosetta sidled up a few feet behind.

'Gentle Beauceron,' Isola said with an awkward smile. 'Can you not let us walk down into the valley to Croad? You already have my dowry.'

Monetto chuckled. Beauceron smilingly shook his head. 'You are asking me to give money away. I doubt my men would allow me to do so, even if I wished it.'

A sly smile crossed Isola's face. 'What if I gave my parole that Oricien would send on my ransom to Mettingloom if you released me now? He is a good and true lord, and would keep his word.'

'You are hardly in a position to bind the man who is not yet your husband. I am sure he would find good reason to avoid payment of the debt, or to ransom you at a lower value than I would set on you. Indeed, how can a man justly value his own betrothed?'

Isola pouted. Her dark eyes glared at Beauceron, who remained impassive. 'There must be some agreement we can reach consistent with both our dignities.'

'Perhaps there is, my lady,' said Beauceron. 'To assure myself that the ransom would be paid, you would need to leave an item of value.'

'I have no property except my clothes. You have taken the rest.'

Beauceron nodded. 'True, true. But what of this? I will let you walk down into Croad, to send your ransom on to Mettingloom: but you must leave Lady Cosetta. She will not be released until both ransoms are paid.'

'No!' cried Cosetta, the cheese falling from her rough wooden plate. 'You could not do that, Isola!'

Isola was silent. Beauceron looked at her a moment. 'Well, my lady? Is that "consistent with your dignity"?'

Lady Isola stood up, brushed her skirts. 'Very well. I am sorry, Cosetta, but better that one of us should reach civilization than neither of us. I will ensure Oricien compiles our ransom immediately.'

'Isola! You cannot leave me with these brutes!'

'Cosetta, it grieves me to leave you. But Beauceron's men have treated us as well as we could have expected. The circumstances are unfortunate but we must make the best of them. If Beauceron had offered to release you instead I should not have complained.'

Cosetta sank her head into her hands and sobbed. 'Please, please . . .'

Isola looked at her a moment and turned to Beauceron. 'I have eaten, and see no reason to tarry further. With your leave, I will depart immediately.'

Beauceron held up a hand. 'A moment, my lady. I merely outlined a hypothesis. The situation is unrealistic. I know Oricien of old: he is somewhat parsimonious, and he will not care a fig for Lady Cosetta's freedom. I simply wished to see how you would react.'

Isola scrambled to her feet as if to rush at Beauceron.

He languidly leaned aside as Monetto dragged her away. 'Nonetheless,' he continued, 'I am grateful for the favourable characterization of my conduct that you shared with Lady Cosetta.'

Isola continued to struggle with Monetto, her cheeks aflame and her hair hanging loose at her shoulders. 'Is there nothing that will compel you to release me?' she spat at Beauceron.

He shook his head. 'For reasons I will not bore you with, I bear Lord Oricien considerable ill-will. It may be that allowing him to marry such a shrew is punishment enough; but I am persuaded he will feel this double blow to his pride and his coffers more strongly. Kindly remount, my lady. We have many miles to cover before nightfall.'

Isola clambered aboard her gallumpher. Cosetta, who had already mounted, turned her back, and the two rode in silence for the remainder of the day.

2

After a journey of ten days, the party arrived at Hengis Port on the western coast of the wide plain known as Jehan's Steppe. The settlement consisted of a ramshackle agglomeration of low wooden buildings, hunched against the winds blowing in off the sea. Defences were unnecessary, for there was nothing to attack or to steal. The town was no more than a stopping place on the sea-road from the Emmenrule to Mettingloom. Beauceron's men camped outside the town until he could secure passage north. Eventually two rough cogs put in to port and Beauceron split his party between them.

The sea was grey and the sky a turbid off-white. Isola succumbed to seasickness and remained below deck; Cosetta preferred the fresh air. While the atmosphere was damp on the deck, no doubt it was preferable to being closeted with a fretful Isola.

On the second afternoon Cosetta approached Beauceron. They leaned against the starboard rail looking back towards the land as the terrain became ever more inhospitable.

'What can we expect at Mettingloom?' she asked from under the hood of her oilskin. The sea air had brought colour to her cheeks and she looked, for the first time, a lady of Sey.

Beauceron looked out over the rail. A gull swooped to pluck a fish from beneath the waves. 'There will be no indignity,' he said. 'Matters are normally settled in a few months. In that time your freedom will be circumscribed to an extent, but you will not be confined. You are ladies of rank.'

'Who will pay Lady Isola's ransom?'

'Why, her father, I should imagine. Lord Sprang is a wealthy man, and I do not propose to set an unreasonable fee.'

Cosetta brushed her hair out of her eyes in the breeze. 'No one will pay my ransom.'

Beauceron turned to look at her. A gull cried overhead. 'You are a lady. Surely your family will pay to see you home.'

Cosetta shook her head sadly. 'My father is Lord Coceillion. You may have heard of him.'

'I do not follow the doings of the Emmen nobility in detail.'

'His father, Lord Mosseillion, rebelled against King Alazian. He was attainted and our property was confiscated. When King Arren came to the throne he restored our seat but not our lands or money. My father is penniless. That is why he sent me north with Lady Isola. He had no money to give me a dowry.'

Beauceron rubbed his chin. 'Why did you not tell me this sooner?'

'I was worried that if you could not ransom me, you would use me ill instead. I saw how your men looked at us.'

'My men have been in the field all summer. Of course they will look at a woman who comes among them. But they answer to me, and they are disciplined. They have seen me hang men for rape.'

'I did not know how you would treat me if you knew there would be no ransom.'

Beauceron sighed. 'Shall I tell you?'

Cosetta looked at him with full eyes.

'I would have released you. You would have been no use to me, and I could have sent you to Croad: Oricien could then have instructed Lord Sprang to begin preparing Isola's ransom. Your silence has cost your freedom.'

Lady Cosetta began to cry. 'So will you release me once we get to Mettingloom?'

'It is not so simple. I will have to ask for a ransom for you; I would lose face otherwise, to have brought back a prisoner I could not ransom. And face is important in Mettingloom. I would not insult you by presenting you to society as my courtesan. Perhaps your father will be able to raise a mortgage on his castle, or Lord Sprang may even ransom the pair of you. I assure you, I will not ask for an unreasonable amount.'

Cosetta looked at him for a moment. 'I must go below,' she said. Beauceron watched her go, shook his head, and presently returned to his own cabin.

3

The sun made a fitful attempt at piercing the heavy grey overcast as the boat approached Mettingloom. Everyone was on deck as the city came into view, even Lady Isola, whose seasickness – Beauceron suspected – had become an excuse to avoid her captor's presence over the final days of the voyage.

Lady Cosetta let out a gasp. 'I had heard Mettingloom was remarkable,' she said. 'But I never imagined – this.'

'"The City in the Sea",' said Beauceron. 'Allow me to point out the main features. You see the little cluster of islets ahead, through the neck of the bay? That is where the customs men, or Pellagiers, conduct themselves. Then, rising from the sea over there, you see the Metropolia, that cluster of closely packed islets. They are linked by bridges, and instead of roads, there are waterways – the famous aquavias. That is where we find the King's palace, the Occonero. Over to the left you see Hiverno, the Winter King's residence. The Summer King's retreat, Printempi, is behind the Occonero and not visible.'

'And where will we be going?' asked Isola.

'I have apartments in the city. You will be my guests for a while.'

Lady Cosetta sighed. 'The city is unutterably beautiful. The light, and the red and blue roofs . . .'

'You should see it in full winter,' said Beauceron. 'The lagoon freezes over. You can walk from isle to isle, and the aquavias can be traversed on foot. The only people who complain are the boatmen, who have to put away their craft for the winter – and of course the Sun King.'

As they spoke, the cog made fast against a smartly varnished jetty. Two men in red coats and blue hats leaped aboard, nimble against the rocking of the boat.

The cog's captain stepped negligently over to the Pellagiers, who bowed respectfully.

'Good morning to you, sir. Do have cargo or passengers?'

'Good morning, gentlemen. I declare myself, Captain

Uzzo, my crew of eight, plus seven passengers and their goods.'

Beauceron interrupted. 'I should more accurately say, five passengers. The two ladies you see before you are my goods, as well as the chests I have stowed below.'

'I am nobody's—' began Lady Isola.

'Silence, woman!' said the first Pellagier. 'I see from the paperwork that this is correct. See here: under the schedule entitled "Spoils of War" is entered "Plate and Jewels", 70,000 florins, and "Ladies Isola and Cosetta", 55,000 florins. All is in order.'

'I am the daughter of Lord Sprang of Sey. I am no "spoil of war".'

'My schedule says otherwise. I have dealt with Beauceron on many occasions, and have never known his book-keeping to be at fault yet. Unlike many war-captains, I must say. Their record-keeping is invariably slapdash.'

Lady Isola looked at the Pellagier. 'My interest in accountancy is negligible at best. I am held against my will and demand immediate release.'

'Since Beauceron values you and your companion at 55,000 florins, that is unlikely. Captain Uzzo, cast off and proceed to Ruglatto.'

The cog lapped towards its new mooring. Beauceron and Monetto conferred at the bow.

'Have you decided what you're doing with the ladies?' asked Monetto.

Beauceron looked back down the boat to where Lady Isola was still expostulating with the Pellagier.

'We failed in our first objective,' he said. 'Siedra must have been travelling back to Croad. The ransom for the ladies will be useful, however, as will the plate.'

'Do you think Sprang and Coceillion will pay the

ransoms? My understanding is that Sprang is niggardly and Coceillion penurious.'

'We may need to be flexible.'

4

Beauceron took temporary lodgings for himself and the ladies at a tall inn of eccentric proportions, leaning to the east as if in supplication to the west wind whipping in off the sea. The rates were modest, and Beauceron used a tone of surly menace to extract a further discount.

'You will no doubt wish to refresh yourselves,' said Beauceron as he escorted the ladies to their new quarters. 'I regret that conditions over the past weeks have been primitive.'

Isola looked around her room. 'I cannot deny that hot water will be welcome.'

Beauceron sat down on a couch opposite the ladies. The curtains were faded and the fabric worn in places. Only the fastidious would notice the faint smell of cabbage from the adjacent kitchens. 'We must have an understanding,' he said. 'It is regrettable but true that you remain, for now, my guests.'

'Guests!' spat Isola.

'It is not my intention that your stay in Mettingloom will be undignified. I wish to allow you as much freedom as possible, and indeed escape from Mettingloom is all but impossible, especially in winter. I am your best – indeed your only – hope of a return to your homes. You need not concern yourselves with expenses, and I will arrange for you to be suitably housed. I would advise you to look upon this interlude as a kind of holiday.'

'You are a madman,' said Cosetta with quiet emphasis.

'This is the Northern Reach, and I am your prisoner. Talk of "holidays" is callow.'

'Lady Cosetta,' said Beauceron with a sigh. 'I understand – and indeed regret – your discomfort. But circumstances are as they are, and Mettingloom is a city of many attractions. You will be much in demand in society, and I profit nothing from cloistering you and having you pine away and die. Enjoy your celebrity, make the most of your adventure. You will both tell your grandchildren of your stay in Mettingloom.'

Isola shook her head. 'You do not have the remotest understanding of our situation.'

Beauceron leaned forward. 'Perhaps not. But I understand Mettingloom.' He stood up from the couch and bowed. 'I will return in two hours to escort you to dinner.'

5

The next morning Beauceron slung a bag over his shoulder and took passage on a wherry. It conveyed him around the Metropolia to set him down at the imposing square before the Occonero: for the duration of winter, the residence of Fanrolio, the Snow King.

Beauceron had always admired the cool elegance of the Occonero. Two pillars, slender yet grand, stood before him, marking the entrance to the central piazza. One column was topped by a stylized sun, the other by a moon: an orange banner fluttered from this latter pillar. The piazza was enclosed on three sides by buildings several storeys high, mullioned windows concealing who knew what secrets. Beauceron had been in Mettingloom for seven years and much of what went on behind the windows remained a mystery to him. At the right-hand side of the piazza stood the portion of the Occonero given over to the King of the Season's household. Beauceron hitched his bag over his shoulder and strode through the colonnade into this area. Much would depend on the next hour.

A guard in shining silver mail, with a black surcoat and a snowdrop scarab pinned to his breast, stepped forward to block his way with a halberd.

'What do you here?'

'I am Beauceron. I have an appointment with the Chamberlain.'

'The Chamberlain is indisposed.'

'Then take me to Davanzato. No doubt he still conducts business in Osvergario's absence.'

The guard grunted and motioned with his head for Beauceron to follow him. If the man recognized him he gave no sign of it.

Beauceron strode through the marbled walkway, a route he knew as well as the guard. Soon he found himself before a heavy wooden door, and two guards with the same snowdrop scarabs.

'It is customary to pay me a gratuity,' said his escort.

'I am not a slave to custom. Be thankful that I do not report your avarice to Davanzato.'

The man scowled and slunk back off down the corridor.

'Stand aside,' said Beauceron to the two door-guards. 'I am here to see Davanzato.'

One of the guards stepped forward. 'Davanzato may not want to see you.'

'Your attempt at surly menace is not intimidating. If I wished you harm, you would already be dead,' said Beauceron with a sharp smile.

From within the room came a voice. 'Send him in, Sicurano. This visit I am expecting.'

Beauceron pushed past the guard into the room. A fire

in the hearth and rich burgundy hangings softened the cold stone walls. A window looked out over the aquavias and a plush battlecat-pelt rug lay on the marble floor. At the far end of the long room sat a slender man in his early maturity, thick dark hair confined in a long tail behind his head. No expression creased the olive skin of his face.

'Beauceron,' he said.

'Davanzato,' said Beauceron with a minimal bow. 'You are kind to see me at such notice.'

Davanzato gestured to a couch exquisitely carved with innocent faces, and Beauceron moved to sit. Davanzato came out from behind his desk to sit on an adjacent chair.

'I await with interest, as ever, news of your doings,' said Davanzato. 'His Puissance has few more industrious commanders in the field – although you look a little tired.'

Beauceron made a dismissive gesture. 'A summer's campaign is always arduous. I ask for nothing better.'

Davanzato clapped his hands and a pretty young servant appeared. 'Theria, two glasses of langensnap, if you please. I take it you still enjoy a glass, Beauceron?'

'I would never decline your hospitality. You might think I was suspicious of poison.'

'Aha! The Dog of the North will never succumb to poison. Your destiny must be to die on the battlefield.'

'Lord Oricien has decreed that I shall die by the rope. He has built a gallows in the marketplace of Croad, and will not allow common felons to hang there: it cannot be used until I am there for its maiden voyage, so to speak. All of his preparations are in hand, with the exception of the honoured guest. Such laxity mars his thinking here as in so much else.'

'I feared for your safety this time. You were away long enough that there were those who said you were not coming back.'

33

'I am sure you knew better. I was delayed by the nature of our plunder; it required careful handling.'

'Plunder?' Davanzato leaned forward.

Beauceron smiled. He sipped at his glass of langensnap, feeling the cloying warmth slip down his throat. 'In fact, Davanzato, I have brought you a gift. I remembered your fondness for all things Sey.'

He took from his bag a candlestick of gold, inlaid with tiny rubies and intricate silver filigree, and handed it to Davanzato. 'I confess that I did not declare the item to the Pellagiers. They are scrupulous in their observance of the King's ordinances, but they do not always move with speed.'

Davanzato's black eyes gleamed. 'I can overlook your misdemeanour on this occasion. This is a delightful piece, and genuine Sey workmanship. There is none of the heaviness in the filigree one finds in the Emmen copies. This is a valuable and beautiful piece: I thank you.'

'Think nothing of it. I am always conscious of the great service you render to the Winter King, and show my appreciation accordingly.'

Davanzato inclined his head. 'Service is its own reward. If I might perform any small convenience for you, I should be glad to.'

Beauceron raised his hands in denial. 'I would not wish to impose upon your time or regard for me. Naturally I would like to see my prizes expedited by the Pellagiers, and my men and guests cleared to enter the Metropolia as soon as possible, but in this I wait my turn along with everyone else.'

'Nonsense, Beauceron! By lunchtime all will have leave to enter the city, and your prize will be cleared by sundown tomorrow. It is unthinkable that such a renowned commander must wait in line with the merchants of the

Briggantia.'

'I am grateful for your attention to such a trivial matter,' said Beauceron. 'I trust that His Puissance remains in good health.'

Davanzato nodded. 'His physician has prescribed a new regimen: he thrives. Indeed, I have not seen him so well for years.'

'Good! Perhaps the physician will have time to spare for Chamberlain Osvergario.'

'Ah,' said Davanzato softly. 'There the omens are not so favourable. He rarely leaves his bed, and if anything his condition worsens. I may be conducting his duties only temporarily, but there seems no end in sight to my labours.'

'Four years, I believe,' said Beauceron. 'A long time to toil at "temporary" duties.'

'Not quite four,' said Davanzato with a frown. 'Still, we must sacrifice ourselves where we must. What of your own plans?'

Beauceron sat back. 'My goals remain unaltered. I intend to advocate to His Puissance the wisdom of an assault upon Croad.'

'My dear Beauceron! King Fanrolio has considered this proposal in the past. He views it as a concept of valour and merit but alas impractical.'

'I believe that circumstances may have changed since last year. Perhaps you could arrange an audience.'

Davanzato smilingly shook his head. 'You will remember that his Council debated the matter last year. The Winter King is in no position to launch such a raid upon the territory of Emmen. Even General Virnesto considered the venture unwise. You will remember that, as a friend, I suggested you approach the Sun King.'

Beauceron chuckled. 'Davanzato! I hope you understand

me better than that. I wear the snowdrop badge, and I am Fanrolio's man. I would never approach King Tardolio.'

'The fact remains that the Summer King is better placed to put an army in the field. How much easier is campaigning in the summer. You cannot blame good King Fanrolio for husbanding our resources during the long dark winter months!'

'The situation has changed materially,' said Beauceron, setting his glass on the table and leaning forward. 'You can be assured that I will never desert my allegiance by offering my services to Tardolio. And this year I am in a position to finance the assault on Croad myself. I need only King Fanrolio's assent, and I will recruit, pay and lead the army. On securing the city, I will raise His Puissance's banner high over the marketplace. He will have secured a valuable prize at no cost to himself.'

Davanzato rubbed his chin. 'Finance the raid yourself? In the circumstances, your gift to me is perhaps not as princely as I had imagined – although still, of course, greatly appreciated.'

Beauceron bit back a smile as Davanzato took the bait. 'I have several similar items, which I might submit for your approval.'

'Be that as it may,' said Davanzato, 'Mettingloom is not at war with Emmen. Our relations with Lord Oricien, while not cordial, cause neither of us inconvenience, and to assault Croad must necessarily bring forth a reprisal from Duke Trevarre or even King Enguerran.'

'Let them try,' said Beauceron. 'If we hold Croad, we interdict passage to Jehan's Steppe. Enguerran could not supply an army along the eastern approach, and Trevarre's galleys would not get past Khadaspia. Take Croad, and we lock the door from the South.'

Davanzato shook his head. 'There are matters of policy

you do not understand. It is all very well to saddle up your gallumphers and ride south every summer to wreak whatever havoc you choose. King Fanrolio must deal not only with the princes of Emmen but the sordid manoeuvrings of the Sun King. Tardolio would look to turn such an event to his advantage.'

Beauceron crossed his legs. 'I yield to no one in my admiration for your command of the currents of policy,' he said. 'I simply ask the opportunity to petition His Puissance on the subject, if necessary before his Council. From simple regard for an old friend, I am sure you would want to raise the matter with him.'

'I make no promises,' said Davanzato. 'His Puissance's time is as precious and rare as any Sey jewel. You must display patience: in particular, you must avoid overt lobbying. Outside of this room, it will only hurt your cause. I still do not understand your lust to humble Croad.'

'That must remain my own affair,' said Beauceron. 'The King need only look to his own advantage.'

Davanzato made an emollient gesture. 'As you wish. The inscrutability of the Dog of the North is part of your mystique, I suppose. Is there any other way I can assist you?'

'There is one matter,' said Beauceron, pulling a paper from his breast pocket. 'I am glad to say it will profit both King Fanrolio and yourself.'

'Theria! More langensnap!'

'You may be aware that I have brought two guests back with me from Lynnoc.'

'I would be negligent to have overlooked the matter. Ladies of the Sey nobility, I believe.'

'Just so: Lady Isola, on her way to marry Lord Oricien, and her companion, Lady Cosetta.'

'The dowry you intend to use to finance your assault on Croad?'

'Just so.'

'Continue.'

'I believe a ransom of 45,000 florins for Lady Isola and 10,000 florins for Lady Cosetta is not unreasonable. Monetto has drawn up papers to that effect,' said Beauceron, passing them across to Davanzato.

'I wish you much happiness in your good fortune.'

'Ah no!' said Beauceron. 'These papers assign the ransom to King Fanrolio. I have also taken the liberty of appointing you the ransom agent.'

'Fifty-five thousand florins times fifteen per cent – over 8,000 florins. You have my full attention.'

'I feel sure that His Puissance will relish the chance to accept the parole of two such lovely ladies – and believe me, they are both lovely. Lady Isola is of spirited temperament, but she carries herself like a Sey battlecat. Lady Cosetta is fair and delicate. Both will be ornaments to His Puissance's court. And if I have been able to arrange matters in such a way that you profit too, well – all should share in good fortune, should they not?'

'Indeed they should, my dear Beauceron, indeed they should. I cannot, of course, make any promises as to the King's view of an assault on Croad, but you can be sure I will exert myself to the maximum practical extent.'

'I am glad to see your friendship take such concrete form. So often gratitude is expressed in fine words only, and when actions are looked for, they are not forthcoming. Your assurances are to be welcomed!'

Davanzato looked at Beauceron for a second. 'I have much to occupy the morning. I am sure you too have important affairs in hand.'

Beauceron rose and bowed. 'Let me know when you have arranged suitable accommodation for the ladies. For now, good day.'

A wherry loomed into a view. A matron was in the queue before him, but Beauceron had no time for niceties. He stepped across her and spoke briskly to the wherryman. 'Ruglatto, at your best speed!'

6

Beauceron took the wherry back to his apartments. He was pleased to see that they had been kept clean during his summer's absence, and he found that Isola and Cosetta had established themselves in the guest suite. Beauceron felt a twinge of disquiet at the interviews to come. He presented himself at their suite. The walls were plastered in a rich ochre, and softened with burgundy hangings. The Occonero could be seen in the distance from the large window.

'Good morning, my ladies. I trust you have been well cared for.'

Cosetta responded before Isola. 'Thank you, we have. Kainera has seen to our comfort, and our suite is very much to our liking.'

Beauceron was encouraged that Cosetta showed such good humour. Maybe the magic of Mettingloom was beginning to work its effect.

'I never imagined a brigand to command such an imposing residence,' said Isola. 'The rooms are airy and spacious, and the rugs and hangings show some taste.'

Beauceron smiled as he sat on the couch. 'I am only a brigand abroad, my lady. Mettingloom is my home, and I am a respectable man here. Brigandage is a prestigious calling in the city, and I am one of the best. But in Mettingloom I am Beauceron; only in Emmen am I the Dog of the North.'

'The light is excellent,' said Isola. 'The view over the

aquavias and out to sea is most stimulating. Will we be here long?'

Beauceron rubbed his chin. 'You will shortly be moving to new quarters: possibly as soon as tonight; and the new ones will be even more salubrious.'

Cosetta turned to face Beauceron. 'I had understood we were to stay with you until our ransoms were received.'

'It is customary for your sponsor to take responsibility for your bed and board. As of this morning, you have a new sponsor.'

Isola rose from her seat. 'You dog! One morning in the city and you have sold us!'

'Is this true?' cried Cosetta.

'In the strictest sense, no. I have transferred your custody, but not for any fee.'

'To whom?' asked Isola with ominous politeness.

'As of today, you are wards of King Fanrolio. He will negotiate with your fathers and secure your ransoms. The situation is to your advantage: Lords Sprang and Coceillion will feel no shame in dealing with His Puissance, and your status will be augmented while you are in Mettingloom.'

'You had mentioned freedom to move around the city,' said Cosetta. 'Does that still apply?'

'Providing you give your parole to His Puissance, there will be no difficulty. Indeed, I suspect he will be keen to show you off in society.'

Isola sat back on her couch. 'It is not pleasing to be treated as cattle, passed from sponsor to sponsor. I believe you had estimated our ransoms at 55,000 florins. I cannot believe you would give such a sum away, and can only assume we have been passed on to settle a debt, or for some non-financial consideration.'

'My motives must remain my own, Lady Isola. The simple truth is that in capturing you, you have become my prisoners, and I may dispose of you without reference to your feelings. In this case I have chosen to do so, although my assurance that the move is to your advantage can be relied upon.'

Isola tilted her head and looked at Beauceron. He could tell from the curl of her mouth that an expostulation was likely to occur.

At this point the maid Kainera interrupted them. 'Sir, a messenger from Under-Chamberlain Davanzato is here.'

Beauceron scowled. He had hoped to be able to placate the ladies before Davanzato got hold of them. 'Send him up.'

The messenger was a man of middle age and dignified mien. His doublet was a rich forest green and his white breeches sparkled with fresh laundering. 'The Under-Chamberlain sends his compliments. Lady Isola, Lady Cosetta.' He bowed. 'Under-Chamberlain Davanzato invites you to take supper with him tonight. He also begs that you will pack your belongings during the afternoon, that you may remove to the Winter Palace, Hiverno.'

Cosetta looked across at Beauceron uncertainly. 'I have not had the pleasure of Under-Chamberlain Davanzato's acquaintance.'

'Davanzato acts as the King's agent in the matter of your ransom,' said Beauceron. 'Therefore he takes responsibility for your welfare. Hiverno is the personal residence of King Fanrolio: you cannot help but be comfortable. Even in winter, the palace is warm. The King maintains a dimonetto to ensure the comfort of all.' He looked at the messenger. 'Does Davanzato's supper invitation extend to me?'

'The Under-Chamberlain considered that, on your first night in Metropolia, there would undoubtedly be matters requiring your attention. He did not wish to burden you further.'

Beauceron grinned. 'His thoughtfulness, as ever, is an example to all.'

The messenger bowed. 'I will return with a wherry for the ladies at eight bells.' He slipped from the room with scarcely a whisper.

'You will need to pack, my ladies. I will not detain you.'

'A moment,' said Isola, with a return of something like the hauteur of a lady of Sey. 'Our packing will be the work of moments, since you left us with no moveable goods. I would rather hear of Davanzato and your role for the remainder of our stay.'

'I no longer have a responsibility for you, Lady Isola. You are wards of the King, and Davanzato will look to your day-to-day comfort. I hope that we will meet again, since I find your company agreeable, and to a certain extent we will mix in similar circles.'

'You acquit yourself of responsibility very easily. The man who took me from my nuptials on a whim cannot then forget about us simply because he no longer anticipates revenues from our captivity.'

'On the contrary, Lady Isola, that is exactly how things must be. I took you hostage for financial reasons. For reasons that I do not care to explain, I do not expect to realize that investment. The only ties binding us are, potentially, those of friendship; and since I do not expect either of you to entertain any such feelings, our relationship is essentially at an end. I can only wish you good fortune and a swift return to your homes. It would be cant for me to offer my apologies for your abduction, since I cannot sincerely regret it. I wish you good day, my ladies.'

'Leave us now, dog!' cried Lady Isola, springing from her seat. 'You bitch-whelped—'

'Enough, Isola,' said Cosetta. 'He only means to rile us.'

Beauceron forbore from observing first that Lady Isola

42

could not compel him to quit his own apartments, and second that he was in the process of leaving anyway. With a dignified bow he turned and walked for the door. His hand on the knob, he turned back to face the ladies.

'Given your manifest – and understandable – hostility, I am under no obligation to give you advice, nor you to believe it to be in good faith. Nonetheless: you are to dine with Davanzato tonight. He is a man of high deportment who will no doubt aim to charm. I hope you will not be affronted if I tell you not to trust him for a second. He is a master of subtlety and indirection, and above all things he prizes his own advantage. He will ensure your welfare for his own self-interest, but beyond that he will care nothing for you.'

'You paint a pithy picture of your own character,' said Isola. 'We are swapping one rogue for another. I do not trust you, and neither do I intend to trust Under-Chamberlain Davanzato.'

'Very well,' said Beauceron. 'I merely offer you friendly advice.'

7

King Fanrolio sent Beauceron an invitation to a reception at the Occonero only two nights hence; Beauceron could not be sure if Davanzato's agency was involved. Beauceron's apartments in The Gills were nearby, and by stepping across the Emphyrian bridge he was able to walk directly to the palace. He had dressed himself every bit as carefully as he armoured himself before going into battle; which of course he was, in a sense. Black boots and breeches of good cut were paired with a dead-black cloak over a red waistcoat and white shirt. At his breast he wore the snowdrop sigil of the Winter King. A three-cornered hat sat on his head with a wolf's-head badge at the front; at his waist was a rapier with an iron handle wrapped in leather: a weapon of utility rather than decoration.

He looked over his shoulder as he crossed the bridge. A figure ducked into a booth with an alacrity Beauceron found suspicious. He shrugged: a man of note in Mettingloom could expect nothing else. Davanzato would undoubtedly be tracking his movements, although Beauceron doubted that his men were that inept.

Winter was beginning to close in, and despite his cloak Beauceron shivered against the chill. There was a faint crunch of ice underfoot, and he was pleased to reach the warmth of the Occonero. Fanrolio maintained a dimonetto here as at Hiverno.

Beauceron found himself escorted to the Flower Room, so named for the meticulously painted ceiling, covered with a thousand summer roses. It was not a room of high state, but informal, with chairs and couches arranged in pleasant randomness. He recognized most of the thirty or so guests: Davanzato was present, of course, with both Isola and Cosetta, arrayed in notable finery, close by. Neither seemed the worse for their change of abode. Cosetta greeted Beauceron with a half smile; Isola looked away.

He made his way over to the liveried footman standing by the dimonetto dispensing wine.

'Good evening, Prince Brissio, General Virnesto.'

Brissio, a stocky young man with a florid complexion and incongruous ringlets, took a sip from his goblet before acknowledging Beauceron with a loose nod. Virnesto, a trim figure with an upright martial bearing, briskly shook Beauceron's hand.

'I heard you were back,' he said. 'With plate and prisoners.'

Beauceron took a goblet with one hand and made a negligent gesture with the other.

'The "prisoners" strictly belong to King Fanrolio – and since I understand they have given their parole, it is a touch indelicate to use the term at all.'

Brissio set his goblet down with an audible thud. 'You are a fine fellow, to talk of delicacy when you spend all summer on the back of a gallumpher.' He turned so that his words were audible to Isola and Cosetta. 'I think it a poor display for a man who professes the ideals of chivalry to abduct two ladies – two beautiful ladies – from the security of their stout-coach.'

If either had heard the remark they did not show it.

'I would not lightly contradict the King's son, my lord, but I have never professed any chivalric conduct. I am a brigand, pure and simple. The calling has its detractors but I know no other.'

Brissio picked his goblet up and said to Virnesto: 'What do you make of this escapade?'

'Beyond a doubt, my lord, Beauceron is intrepid and audacious. His actions may not excite universal approval, but it cannot be denied that your father benefits from the terror that the Dog of the North evokes.'

Brissio drained his goblet and set it down heavily. 'If you will excuse me, General, I must introduce myself to the ladies.'

Beauceron took advantage of Brissio's departure to assess his surroundings. Mettingloom in winter could be chill, drear and inhospitable, but inside the Occonero there was only comfort. The vents of the dimonetto issued a soothing warmth, and the walls were plastered a quiet umber. Sconces flickered in the alcoves, and Beauceron felt compelled to remove his cloak against the heat. A footman came to take the cloak away. 'I must ask you to surrender your rapier, sir,' he said. 'His Puissance is on his way.'

Beauceron heard a fanfare in the corridor outside, and after a slight hesitation he gave the man his blade.

'All hail His Puissant Majesty, the Winter King of Mettingloom, the Northern Reach and Lynnoc: Fanrolio!'

Beauceron dropped to his knee along with the rest of the company as Fanrolio entered the room. He had forgotten the King's absurd claim to the Duchy of Lynnoc, stretching back three centuries through bastardy and the female line.

Fanrolio entered through the double doors and paused. 'Rise!' he said, in his scratchy voice. Davanzato claimed that the King's physician was having a positive effect, but looking at Fanrolio's drawn face and stooped bearing, Beauceron remained to be convinced. The King was only fifty, but could have passed for twenty years older.

'Welcome, all!' he continued. 'We have new guests among us tonight.' He moved towards a chair reserved for him by the warmth of the dimonetto, leaning on the arm of an attendant. Brissio made no move to help him. Reaching the seat, he sat with an almost audible creak. He beckoned to Isola.

'It gives me the greatest pleasure to introduce two ladies from the fair city of Sey who are my guests for the nonce. Lady Isola, the daughter of Lord Sprang, has the blood of Lynnoc in her veins: we are perhaps distant cousins, although her beauty would suggest otherwise.'

Beauceron did not find the witticism worthy of laughter, but he was in the minority. He leaned against the wall and sipped from his goblet.

'Her companion, Lady Cosetta, is no less beautiful, nor indeed any less amiable. We are grateful that they have chosen to winter among us.'

Isola shot Beauceron a bleak look from the corner of her

eye. Cosetta curtsied to the King, evidently deciding to make the best of the situation.

'These noble ladies accompanied none other than that most redoubtable of captains, Beauceron, known to his foes as the Dog of the North. A dog will always return to his home, and we are fortunate that this brave captain has chosen once again to make his home among us. Captain, we welcome you!'

Beauceron stood straight, then bowed. The courtesy cost Fanrolio nothing but there seemed no reason not to acknowledge it.

'For now,' Fanrolio continued, 'we know the partiality of young folk for dance. Minstrels! Play!'

4

Croad

I

Arren's unstructured way of life came to an end the summer he turned eleven. One evening, while Arren attempted to apply an armlock to Matten as they wrestled on the cold stone floor of Darrien's cottage, there was a knock at the door.

Ierwen sighed. 'Is there no peace? Even when you are home they cannot leave you alone.'

Darrien grunted and rose from his seat. 'It is probably Viator Dince to see why I have not been to Find the Way this week.'

Ierwen shook her head and some brown hair escaped from its bun. 'Is it too much to ask for a night's peace?'

Darrien opened the door, which gave directly on to the living area. 'Pray enter, my lord.'

Ierwen rose to her feet, for the visitor was none other than Lord Thaume. He was a tall, spare figure who carried himself with a self-contained gravity. Only the depth and animation of his dark eyes hinted at a vitality not immediately apparent. Ierwen curtsied as Lord Thaume bowed. 'Mistress Ierwen, I apologize for my intrusion. I had hoped to see Master Darrien at the castle today, but I find he was detained at the stables.'

48

Ierwen flushed. Lord Thaume was not a man who normally called at his inferiors' homes. 'Please sit down, my lord. Arren, Matten, away out the back now. Lord Thaume does not want to be vexed by your noise.'

Arren released Matten's arm and slid quietly back to the wall.

Lord Thaume sat and said: 'That will not be necessary. Indeed, it is about young Arren that I wished to speak.' He stretched his long legs out across the fireplace.

Ierwen's eyes widened. 'What has he been doing now? That Eilla is not involved again?'

Lord Thaume smiled. 'You need have no concerns, mistress. Arren is in no trouble – indeed, quite the contrary.'

Ierwen and Darrien were silent. They waited expectantly for Lord Thaume to continue. Arren himself looked on with a mixture of apprehension and curiosity. Lord Thaume always had a friendly word for him, and had once given him a copper royal.

'You will be aware that Arren and my son Oricien are of an age,' he said. 'One day, a day I hope is far in the future, Oricien will be Lord of Croad. Such is the melancholy passage of time, and the viators would tell us it is all for the best. Platitudes, if you ask me, but that's by the by.

'When Oricien becomes lord, there are two legacies I can give him: full coffers and good counsellors. Mistress Ierwen, I hope you are sensible of the reliance I place on your husband. As Captain of the Guard, he is my strong right hand.'

'I am glad to hear you say so, my lord. I would be even more delighted were his stipend to reflect that.'

Lord Thaume dismissed the point with a wave. 'A ruler has many calls upon his purse. But I would be happy to know that Oricien had a friend of his own age who might in turn become captain of his guard.'

'I am sure your son will always find Arren a loyal servant,' said Darrien.

'I wish to advance matters by taking Arren into my household,' said Lord Thaume abruptly. 'Oricien's education has been somewhat neglected and it is high time that a programme of preparation for his responsibilities began. I must of course educate Lord Guigot along the same lines, and I see no reason not to include Siedra in the programme: a degree of intellectual cultivation can only increase her prospects when she goes to court at Emmen. I propose that Arren should join them. I have already secured a number of excellent tutors.'

Arren could scarcely move in his amazement. He looked across at his father, who sat rubbing his chin.

'I am grateful for the thought your lordship has shown our lad,' said Ierwen with a trace of colour in her face. 'I am sorry that the course you suggest is not possible.'

'My dear lady! Why ever not?' said Lord Thaume, his eyebrows twitching.

'Yes, Ierwen, why not?' asked Darrien.

Ierwen set her jaw. 'Arren is our eldest son. We don't want to lose him. But he would not be happy in a great lord's household, begging your pardon, sir. We are simple people and we know our place. What good would it do Arren to learn the manners and appetites of lords and ladies, only to return here at the end of it, or to be dependent on your son's patronage? Arren's place is here with us. He will always be a loyal servant to the Lord of Croad, but not as some lordling.'

Lord Thaume scratched his chin. 'I hardly know what to say, mistress. In my folly I had never imagined that the idea might be objectionable to you.'

'Ignore my wife, my lord,' said Darrien. 'Arren leaves tonight, if it is your wish. Arren, run upstairs and pack your things.'

Ierwen began to cry and Arren soon joined her. 'Come now, lad,' said Lord Thaume with gruff courtesy. 'It is hard for you at first, but you shall come home on the feast days, and everyone will marvel how you have grown. The castle is no distance away, and you will see your mother all the time.'

Ierwen looked at her husband through swollen red eyes. 'You will regret this, Darrien. The lad will not come back as our son, mark my words.'

Darrien gave an uneasy laugh. 'Nonsense, woman! He will have learning in many fields and the friendship of the lord of the city. He will even be Captain of the Guard in his turn.'

Ierwen turned away. 'Do you understand nothing, Darrien? Will he come back ready to marry Eilla or Clottie, or will his head have been turned by longings for great ladies who will laugh in his face? How will he ever be satisfied with what he has?'

Arren's sniffling was brought to a halt by the ludicrous idea that he might marry Eilla or Clottie. Naturally he never intended to marry at all, but if he did, it would never be to such vexatious creatures.

Matten interrupted to ask: 'If Arren is going to be a great lord, may not I come too? I am much cleverer than Arren and more handsome besides!'

Arren scowled at his brother. If joining Lord Thaume's household meant he did not have to marry Eilla or Clottie, and put Matten in his place at the same time, it had to be a good idea. 'Let me gather my items, my lord!' he cried. 'I am ready.'

2

Arren followed the housemistress Eulalia into Lord Thaume's family dining room, a space panelled in dark wood, with a squat table at the centre, and an air of gloomy dignity. Arren was put in mind of Lord Thaume in the black robes he wore to administer justice each Consorts' Day. Around the walls were portraits, generally of armoured men brandishing swords from their gallumphers. A window commanded a view of the Pleasaunce, the family's exclusive gardens.

'I am sure you are hungry, Arren,' said Mistress Eulalia, her plump cheeks dimpling. 'Lord Thaume has ensured that the children waited so you need not dine alone.'

Arren peered out from behind Eulalia to survey the room before him and the three solemn children arrayed there.

'Well, children,' said Eulalia. 'Are you not going to greet Arren?'

From the head of the table, a wiry fair-headed lad of around Arren's own age rose and gave a precise bow. 'Welcome, Arren,' he said in a fluting tone. 'I am Lord Oricien.' He indicated a chair next to him. 'You will wish to sit.'

Arren knew Oricien by sight, but they had never spoken. 'Thank you,' he said in a small voice.

'This is my cousin Guigot—' Oricien continued, indicating a solid young man of twelve or thirteen, with keen black eyes partly obscured behind an unruly fringe.

'*Lord* Guigot. The son of Lord Borel.'

'And this is my sister, Lady Siedra.'

Arren's experience of girls was not extensive, but he instantly realized that here was a person different in kind to Eilla or Clottie, who were as happy as he to frolic in mud. Lady Siedra, perhaps ten years old, was attired in a gown of rich cream silk and her expression suggested she regarded mud and Arren in much the same light. She tilted her head to the side to the smallest perceptible extent and said: 'I am charmed to make your acquaintance.'

The three children sat down and Mistress Eulalia ushered Arren to the seat indicated by Oricien. 'Arren will be taking his meals and his lessons with you from now on,' she said. 'Lord Thaume will have told you as much.'

Guigot sniffed. 'Yes, although he has not explained the necessity. Lord Thaume does not take meals with his inferiors, and I fail to understand why we should do so.'

Oricien said: 'His father is a most valiant man. My father has said Arren is to be treated as a gentleman.'

'In that case,' said Guigot, 'why do we not take our meat with your father's fighting-cocks? They are nothing if not valiant.'

Mistress Eulalia rapped the table. 'Lord Guigot, I am sure you are all hungry. Lord Thaume has made his decision and that is that.'

Guigot shrugged. Siedra said: 'My father has said that Arren will be a valuable friend and counsellor to Oricien when he becomes Lord of Croad.'

'He needs no such counsellor,' said Guigot. 'I will be at his right hand, and the blood of Lord Gaucelis flows in both our veins.'

Oricien spoke quickly: 'The Lord of Croad can never have too many counsellors. I will welcome Arren's advice as I do Guigot's.'

As they spoke servants had slipped into the room on noiseless feet to array a series of dishes before them.

'Do not wait for us, Arren,' said Siedra with a sharp-toothed smile. 'Eat the stew while it is hot.'

Arren looked at the implements before him. Siedra's hands were below the table and gave no clue as to which might be the proper choice.

'The one to your right. It is called a spoon and retains the liquid while you convey it to your mouth,' she said in a voice of unvanquishable superiority.

'Although you may try the fork if you wish,' crowed Guigot.

'At home we use a hunk of bread,' said Arren.

Siedra merely raised an eyebrow while Guigot demonstrated the use of the spoon on his own stew. Oricien gave them an inscrutable look but said nothing.

Arren watched the group as they ate. Siedra, her golden hair brushed out and hanging loose to her waist, conveyed her food to her mouth with a delicacy so exaggerated as to be almost comical; it disappeared with scarcely a movement of her full red lips. Guigot seemed to care little for such refinement: the food was intended to assuage his hunger, and so it did with an avidity Arren found almost alarming. Oricien ate as he spoke, with a restrained and unobtrusive elegance.

After a while Arren settled into a routine which was not uncongenial. The schoolroom was light and airy on the top floor of the castle, overlooking the bustle of the town and the snow-capped Ferrant Mountains to the east. It was furnished with a spartan utility, desks and chairs of rough wood constructed with little concession to comfort or luxury. Around the walls were hung representations of the Consorts and other reminders of the Way of Harmony, silent encouragement to diligence and application.

Lord Thaume had decreed that his wards should be instructed in a wider range of disciplines than the norm, and Arren found himself forced to apply his attention to subjects he might have preferred to avoid. While 'Preparation for Combat', under the knight of Emmen, Sir Langlan, provided stimulation along with a complement of cuts and bruises, the lessons on 'Etiquette and Deportment', with the respectable Master Guiles, and 'Finding the Way of Harmony' under Viator Sleech remained at best tedious.

Arren remained indifferent to 'History and Literature', taught with a languid melancholy by the mysterious Lady

Cerisa, and the obscure realm of 'Mathematics', outlined by the earnest young scholar Master Coppercake.

'Why must we learn to push and pull numbers to our will?' Oricien asked Coppercake one morning. 'I have learned to multiply a sum by six, and today I learn to multiply it by seven. These rotes are worse than Sleech's Catechism of the Way!'

Coppercake, a tall slender man in his early twenties with neither birth nor fortune to commend him, merely laughed. 'Can anyone answer Lord Oricien's question? Lady Siedra, do you know why we turn our attention to such matters?'

'No, master,' said Siedra, who showed animation only in Guiles's and Cerisa's lessons.

Guigot interjected with a didactic shake of the finger. 'One day, through whatever quirk of fate, Oricien will be Lord of Croad. How will he be able to rule if he cannot work out whether his taxes balance his spending, or the size of the dowry he can give his daughter, or how many troops he can spare King Arren?'

Coppercake nodded in approval. 'Very good, Guigot. Mathematics is not a subject of dry rote and meaningless complexity: it is the most robust and practical of disciplines. Lady Siedra, I am sure Master Guiles has taught you it is impolite to yawn when someone is addressing you, and even to you mathematics has relevance and application. When you marry, your noble lord may make you a monthly allowance. How many new gowns will that afford you? Only mathematics will take you to the answer.'

Siedra briefly removed her attention from the world beyond the window. 'I will not marry a man who stints me such necessities.'

'And you, Arren. Can you see the value of our studies?'

'Yes, sir,' said Arren. 'A man who does not command the

revenues of a city must learn to weigh his florins with exactitude, or he will find he cannot afford to fill his belly.'

'Correct!' said Coppercake. 'Now that we all see the applications of the subject, we will turn our attention to multiplication by seven. You were all asked to learn the rote yesterday. Lady Siedra, what are eight sevens?'

'Fifty-four.'

'Guigot?'

'Fifty-six, sir.'

'Hmmph,' sniffed Siedra. 'Approximation is normally good enough.'

3

Lady Siedra was excused, for obvious reasons, from 'Preparation for Combat', but the three boys rushed to the lesson with unmatched enthusiasm. They scampered down the stairs, pushing and laughing, to where Sir Langlan awaited them in the muddy courtyard. Sir Langlan was something of a mystery to the children. He dressed with precision and flair, and carried the air of court about him.

'Good morning, young sirs!' called Sir Langlan. 'Today we have a double lesson, and Lady Siedra will be joining us for the latter part.'

'Are we having a mock tournament?' cried Arren. 'Are we fighting for the favour of the fair lady?'

Guigot snorted. 'We would need to find one for that to occur. I shall not be exerting myself to win Siedra's approval.'

'What do you mean by that?' said Oricien with a scowl, pushing his face into Guigot's.

'Enough, gentlemen,' said Sir Langlan, lounging on a wooden bench as if it were a court chaise. 'Lord Guigot, your cousins are worthy of greater respect. In any event, we are not conducting a tournament; this evening's programme will come as a surprise.

'Now, let us begin: Lord Guigot, which parts of the body are most important to a swordsman?'

'The head and the feet, sir. The feet must be nimble and the head still. All else follows from this.'

'Good, you remember the lesson. Today we are moving on to the rapier, where the Dictum of Head and Feet is most important of all. Lord Oricien, why do we learn the rapier when the broadsword is the weapon of war?'

Oricien furrowed his brow and looked at the ground before his eyes brightened.

'The rapier is the gentleman's weapon, sir. We use it for duels and other contests of honour.'

'In addition,' said Arren, 'if the rapier requires the most skill to master, other weapons will be simpler to learn.'

'Excellent, Arren. You and Oricien will fight first today. Oricien and Guigot must cool their resentments awhile.'

Guigot leaned against the wall and scowled. 'Why can Arren fight and I must watch? I am of higher birth than Arren and it is imperative that I learn immediate mastery of the gentleman's weapon.'

'Again, Lord Guigot, your sentiments do you no credit. All of you are taught alike, and Arren receives a gentleman's education as much as you. In addition, you can learn a great deal from observation.'

With that, Sir Langlan tossed Arren and Oricien wooden rapiers and made occasional comments as they lunged at each other. 'Arren, move your feet! You are a sitting target. Oricien, you must do more than parry!'

Arren surged forward with abandon, and Oricien was forced to give ground. But as he moved in to touch Oricien on the chest, he found his quarry gone, and felt a tap at his own ribs.

'Excellent, Oricien!' called Sir Langlan. 'Arren, you move only in a straight line. By using his feet, Oricien is able to step aside and in a single movement catch you. Why? Because your movements are predictable. Again, this time with Lord Guigot.'

Guigot presented Arren with a different challenge. He leaped into the attack from the outset, arms flailing and feet stamping. A year older and taller than Arren, his longer reach also presented problems. It was all Arren could do to keep him at bay.

The Dictum of Head and Feet, thought Arren. Guigot's feet may be moving, but so is his head. Arren essayed a sidestep as Oricien had done. Guigot continued his lunge, and as he attempted to pull back, overbalanced and fell to the ground. Arren placed his foot on Guigot's chest and his wooden rapier at his throat. 'You must yield, Lord Guigot.'

Guigot rolled aside and jumped up. He brushed the mud from his breeches with a disdainful hand. 'You were lucky that I fell over, boy.'

Sir Langlan said: 'On the contrary, Lord Guigot. Your head moved in circles. It is no wonder your balance is questionable. Arren showed a modicum of foot movement, and this was sufficient to topple you.'

Guigot scowled back at Sir Langlan and spat in the mud.

'Allow me to observe, Lord Guigot, that you exhibit a belligerent disposition. I am not Viator Sleech, to explain how this blocks your path to Harmony: but as your combat instructor, I will observe that those of contentious dispositions are more likely to find themselves duelling than those of milder temper. You, more than others, should therefore take care to ensure that your swordplay is beyond reproach.'

Once their lesson had finished, Siedra joined the boys, carrying herself with fastidious precision. Guigot was still sullen and uncommunicative, although Sir Langlan observed that his head had become more stable.

'Tonight we have a rare experience ahead,' said Sir Langlan as Arren looked on in anticipation. The knight was elegant in mustard pantaloons and shirt offset by a red cloak, his neat blond beard trimmed and perfumed. 'We shall be visiting a tavern, which should in itself prove educational, even before we take into account the display of the wondrous Illara.'

Arren was not convinced that Lord Thaume would view a visit to a bawdy tavern with approbation. He himself harboured no such concerns, and he ran on ahead with the others to reach the tavern in good time.

There were three taverns in Croad, and Arren wondered why Sir Langlan chose to take them to The Hanged Raider, which was not regarded as the best of them. As Sir Langlan pushed through the door, Arren looked into the gloom within while his nostrils recoiled from the sour smell of spirits.

'Oh!' cried Siedra. 'Why have we come here? The room smells poorly and there are rogues within.'

Guigot grinned. Oricien looked around with no obvious emotion.

'Sir Langlan!' said Bardo, the innkeep. 'Your custom is always welcome, particularly when you bring in new patrons. Beer for you, is it?'

'A long pint for me, small beer for the lady and gentlemen. Their palates require a little coarsening. We are not too late for Illara, I hope?'

Bardo poured the mugs of beer. 'Just in time, as it happens. She is loosening up out the back.'

'Is "loosening" the right word, Bardo?' said Sir Langlan, taking a long pull of his beer. 'Bring me a jug to top this up over to the corner table, and a jug of small beer too.'

Sir Langlan moved over to the corner table with a smooth motion, nodding and exchanging a few words with the other patrons as he did so. Arren could hear whispering as they walked past '—young Lord Oricien—' '—would Lord Thaume say—?' '—should know how his people live—'

Once in the gloom of the corner, attention soon left them. The table had an undefined stickiness and Arren was glad the dark precluded closer inspection. After a few minutes his nose became accustomed to the smells of the tavern. The 'small beer' tasted foul, however, and he made note never to move on to 'large beer'. Siedra had fastidiously set her mug aside after a single sip, while Guigot grimaced as he quaffed his mug in two gulps. 'Trenchant!' he announced. Oricien sipped his beer with visible distaste, but continued to drink it nonetheless.

Shortly after, Bardo scrambled on top of the bar: not a straightforward procedure, since he was not a lithe figure. 'May I have your attention please!' he called. 'I may say, without exaggeration, "lords, ladies and gentlemen", since we have all in attendance in addition to our normal clientele. Tonight I am honoured to present a remarkable spectacle for your delectation – one indeed suitable to set before any lord or lady of the city, or indeed King Arren himself!'

Arren felt himself an expert on the King's tastes by virtue of their shared name, and was sceptical that the venue would be likely to earn the King's favour.

'I set before you,' continued Bardo, inching dangerously close to the edge of the bar, 'Illara and her Dancing Bravos!'

Applause met the announcement, and even stamping on the boards from one corner of the room. From a room in the back of the tavern, four men in black pantaloons, loose white shirts and red sashes issued forth. Rapiers hung at their waists. These could only be the 'Dancing Bravos'. Then, after a suitable pause, appeared a woman in similar attire, although somewhat tighter at the haunch, waist and breast. Her red hair was confined in a fillet on top of her head. The hooting that went up from the crowd confirmed that this was Illara. Guigot attempted a wolf-whistle, but emitted only a squeak.

From beside the bar a musician began a jig on the fanfarillo. The Dancing Bravos pulled their rapiers from their sheaths and began to swirl them in complex patterns: Illara herself waved her arms and swayed in a dreamy rhythm. Imperceptibly she moved in towards the swords, seemingly oblivious. Arren became concerned that she might be endangering herself, but as he opened his mouth to call a warning, Oricien nudged him in the ribs. 'It's part of the act,' he hissed.

Soon Illara was leaping with abandon as the swords crisscrossed above, behind, below. How could anyone move with such precision? wondered Arren.

Faster and faster the fanfarillo played; faster and faster the rapiers whirled, and closer and closer to the leaping Illara. Then the music began to slow; Illara too slowed to match the rhythm. Eventually the fanfarillo ceased altogether. Illara came to a halt, bowed low to the ground, and threw her arms wide to the audience.

The crowd burst into applause, whistles and bellows of approval. Arren noticed that Sir Langlan raised his mug high towards Illara before tossing back its contents. Illara bowed again – seemingly directly to Sir Langlan – before skipping from the room, followed by the Dancing Bravos.

'Well, my lads – and Lady Siedra – what did you make of that?' asked Sir Langlan with a beam.

'Most decorative,' exclaimed Guigot with a leer. 'When I am older I shall take a lady like Illara as my mistress.'

Sir Langlan raised his eyebrows. 'You are young for such thoughts,' he said eventually. 'In truth Illara would be a poor consort for one of your pedigree.'

'You appeared to take great pleasure in her performance,' said Guigot.

'I would not recommend you to follow my conduct or morals. Oricien, Arren, I would hope your observations are more elevated.'

Oricien rubbed his chin in a gesture reminiscent of his father. 'I enjoyed the music of the fanfarillo,' he said. 'The dance was also exciting. I will recommend to my father that she be invited to play in his hall.'

Sir Langlan paused in refilling his mug. 'I am not sure the entertainment is entirely to Lord Thaume's approval. He is a broad-minded man, but Lady Jilka is less flexible. But come now, we have seen enough for the evening, and I must return you to Mistress Eulalia or risk her tongue.'

'No! Let us stay a little longer,' said Siedra. 'I am not sure of Illara's breeding but the dancing was surely worth our attention – and look, she is returning for an encore.'

'We have seen enough for tonight. We have all enjoyed the performance and there will be much to discuss at tomorrow's lesson for the young gentlemen.'

Guigot chuckled.

Siedra narrowed her eyes. 'I doubt that my father has given his consent to our excursion.' Her eyes reflected the light from the wall sconces. 'Were he to learn that you had taken us to a low tavern, drunk copious beer and even forced it upon us, it would surely go ill with you, Sir Langlan. I think we will stay to watch Illara's encore.'

Sir Langlan's mouth gaped like a fish. He waved a hand in dismissal. 'As you will, Lady Siedra. Do not blame me if the encore is not to your liking.'

Siedra sat back, her arms folded in satisfaction, and

tossed her hair. Illara once again gyrated to an air from the fanfarillo, this time in slower measure. To Arren's amazement she divested herself of her sash, then pulled at her belt, causing her pantaloons to fall away; before pulling her shirt back and thrusting her chest out.

Illara was in her underclothes, although they did not closely resemble the ones Arren had seen on his sisters. Releasing her hair from its fillet, and holding out her arms, she advanced towards Sir Langlan, soon to sit in his lap, before removing her final garments with a dextrous gesture.

Arren was at once thrilled and horrified. He turned his head away while continuing to peer out of the corner of his eye. Guigot scurried under the table as Illara reached forward to stroke his cheek. Oricien sat rapt, staring at Illara's breasts, less than a foot in front of him.

Laughing, Illara sprang to her feet and drifted to another table. Siedra shrieked 'Harlot!' and ran for the door. 'My father will hear of this!'

Sir Langlan sat back in his seat with a heavy movement, mechanically draining his mug.

'Come, lads,' he said, rising swiftly if unsteadily to his feet. 'We had best ensure that Lady Siedra has not come to mishap. We will discuss the value of tonight's lesson tomorrow. Lord Guigot, you may emerge and join us.'

5

The first lesson the next day was 'Preparation for Combat' with Sir Langlan. Siedra was not present – instead she had extra 'Etiquette and Deportment' with Master Guiles – which Arren could not help but think was for the best.

Sir Langlan's complexion was pale as he met the three

boys on the courtyard. 'Well, gentlemen: I hope you found last night's display educational.'

'Yes, Sir Langlan,' said Arren. 'Although I am not clear as to your purpose in taking us.'

'Oricien? Guigot? Are you more perceptive than Arren?'

After a pause Guigot said: 'We must all learn to drink beer and assess a woman in due course. I assume you intended our education to begin last night.'

'Incorrect,' snapped Sir Langlan. 'The visit was directly relevant to your combat studies. How do you think Illara managed to avoid injury in the sword dance?'

'Head and feet!' exclaimed Oricien. 'Her head was still but her feet were nimble.'

'Just so,' said Sir Langlan with a broad smile. 'The event was not entirely wasted. Illara would no doubt prove indifferent with the rapier, but her footwork puts the three of you to shame. Lord Guigot, would you care to share the point you have just made to Arren?'

'I merely remarked that Illara would not prove indifferent to my rapier, Sir Langlan.'

'Your attempt at wit is misconceived, and sits poorly with your timidity when she approached you last night. If you wish to talk like a man, you must also act like one.'

From the centre of the courtyard boomed a voice: 'How very well said, Sir Langlan.'

Arren looked in dismay to see Lady Jilka, wife to Lord Thaume and mother of Oricien, advancing towards them. She was red of hair and keen of nose, and Arren knew that the fear she struck into him was not unique. Sir Langlan was in for a difficult engagement, and his footwork would be unlikely to save him, unless he used it to take to his heels.

'Lady Siedra has informed me of last night's unauthorized expedition. Lord Thaume is keen to hear your explanation, as am I.'

Sir Langlan gave a tight grin. Arren could see guards around the courtyard watching. 'I thought to provide the children with a memorable lesson. The boys – in particular Guigot and Arren – are deficient in their footwork. I looked to provide them with a powerful example of the value of smoothly moving feet.'

Lady Jilka paused a moment to pick the hem of her cream charmeuse dress from the mud of the courtyard. 'Your "powerful example" was a visit to a bordello?'

'The Hanged Raider is not the most elevated of establishments, my lady, but I would not characterize it as a bordello. As it happens, the lads witnessed a rare display of virtuosity and Lord Oricien in particular readily absorbed the lesson.'

'This does not explain,' said Lady Jilka with a touch of ice, 'how not only the boys but my daughter were exposed to a vulgar flaunting of the private parts, or compelled to drink beer.'

'Aha, my lady—'

'Well?'

'I acceded to Lady Siedra's wish to enjoy more of Illara's artistry, and no one was as surprised as me as to the scope of her accomplishments. As to the beer, the tavern was hot and I did not wish the children to go thirsty. I ensured that none of them drank to excess.'

Lady Jilka pursed her lips. 'They may not: but you, not for the first time, surely did. You can be sure that Lord Thaume will hear of this. In the meantime, you will all accompany me – yes, you as well, Arren! – as we go to the marketplace.'

Some ten minutes later Arren stood with the others at the front of a large crowd which had assembled. A crude set of stocks had been brought out, and Arren saw to his dismay that Illara had been fixed within, her hands above her head and her nimble feet also pinioned. She was stripped to the waist, with a placard on her torso proclaiming 'Shameless, Brazen, Immoral'. Lady Jilka nodded with evident satisfaction. Arren was confused as to why the display of her breasts was praiseworthy in this context, when it had been so reprehensible the previous night; but he forbore from raising the topic with Lady Jilka.

'Sir Langlan!' said Lady Jilka. 'Let the lads observe the lesson for a while, and then return them to their studies. I myself have business at the Viatory, but we will speak later.'

'Yes, my lady.'

On Lady Jilka's departure Sir Langlan walked up to Illara. Arren could not hear what he said, but Illara's oath in reply was clearly discernible, as was the spittle she launched to accompany it. Sir Langlan returned to his charges. 'Come, lads, we have much to do today.'

As the boys trudged through the drizzle back to the castle, Arren felt a tug on his sleeve. 'Arren! Wait there!'

He looked around. 'Eilla! What are you doing here?'

'It is market day. I am getting goods for my mother.'

Arren inspected Eilla more closely. It was several months since he had seen her, and in the excitement and bustle of his new life he had scarcely given her a thought. She had grown, he thought. Now she was nearly as tall as him, and her dark hair hung longer to her shoulders. She was beginning to look feminine, or perhaps the sight of Illara had made such things more obvious.

He hung back from the group as they walked on ahead.

'Are you allowed out?' she asked. 'Surely you cannot stay in the castle all the time.'

'We have lessons every day,' he said. 'But Viator Sleech allows us to go to the Viatory when we choose, because Lady Jilka says accomplishments are worthless if our feet are not

66

on the Way of Harmony. I don't go often because Viator Goor who takes the services is tedious and smells badly. But we are allowed to go to the Viatory by ourselves.'

Eilla's eyes lit up. 'So could you slip out to the Viatory and then not go?'

'I suppose I could,' said Arren, sucking in his lip.

'We go to the Temple of the Wheel,' said Eilla, her eyes shining with something of her old self. 'My father says the viators are wicked parasites. I don't care about the viators or the Wheel, but I am allowed to go to the Temple when I choose. Can you get out on Dinksday evening?'

'I think so,' said Arren.

'Good! Meet me by the North Gate at six bells,' she said. 'I have much to tell you . . .'

6

To Arren's disappointment, Sir Langlan excused himself from lessons for the remainder of the day, and instead a double lesson on 'The Way of Harmony' with Viator Sleech followed. Siedra joined the lesson with a marked lack of enthusiasm.

Viator Sleech was a thin, elderly man with an earnest manner. His black robe was rather too long and dragged on the ground as he walked. Guigot often followed close behind in the hope of stepping on it. However, Sleech's devotion to the Way of Harmony was undeniable. There was little misbehaviour in his lessons, partly because the children forbore from rousing him to doctrinal excess, and more importantly because he reported their transgressions to Lady Jilka, to their eventual dismay. 'Today,' he said, 'we will consider recent events from the perspective of the Way. First, however, we will review yesterday's teachings on the Harmonic Elixir. Arren, what is the Elixir?'

'It is the bounty of Hissen and Animaxia, uniting the essence of both, Viator.' Arren picked at his nails: the subject held little interest for him.

'Good. Siedra, when do the viators distribute the Elixir?'

'On the Feast Days, Viator.'

'Very good. And Guigot, how do the people use the Elixir?'

'They fill their lanterns with the Elixir and it burns with the Pure Light of Harmony—'

'Excellent, Guigot, excellent! Your inattention in class is illusory!' Sleech's sharp nose sawed the air with approval.

'—in addition,' continued Guigot, 'in times of siege or invasion it is ignited and poured from the walls onto the heads of attackers.'

Sleech frowned. 'While this is true in the most literal sense, it forms no part of our doctrine. At times expediency requires the lord of the city to act in haste. Never let it be said that the Consorts endorse such profane use of the Elixir.'

'No doubt they would prefer the city to be overrun,' said Guigot with a smirk.

'The contingency is remote,' said Sleech. 'It is many generations since an army has besieged the walls of Croad, Hissen be praised. Now, as to Sir Langlan: in taking you to a low tavern last night, was he motivated by Hissen or Animaxia? Oricien?'

'Animaxia represents Noise, Excess and the Female Principle, Viator. His conduct therefore represented Animaxia.'

'Good! Siedra, was this a move towards Harmony or Disharmony?'

'Sir Langlan already has an excess of Animaxian ether, Viator. Therefore he moved towards Disharmony.'

'And Arren, how should he move towards Harmony?'

Arren sat up straight in his seat and pulled his gaze away from the window. 'He should embrace Hissen, Viator. At the Viatory he will be guided towards Harmonic conduct.'

'Excellent! Excellent! I shall have a sound report to make to her ladyship! Guigot, if Sir Langlan does not follow this course, what will follow?'

Guigot snorted and leaned his chair back at a precipitous angle. 'Your Catechism would have me say that he will approach Equilibrium, where he will become mired, forever bereft of Harmony. But at the Temple of the Wheel, Jandille told me that the Doctrine of Equilibrium was heresy and existed only to provide employment for the viators.'

'Impious youth!' bellowed Viator Sleech, in a voice much larger than his person. 'This cannot be tolerated. For Lord Thaume's nephew to visit the Temple of the Wheel and spout its doctrines to a Viator of the Way!'

'Jandille said that the world naturally tends towards Harmony. Equilibrium was invented by the viators to ensure that folk would not find Harmony by themselves.'

Sleech's face darkened. Arren became concerned at the possibility of an apoplexy. 'You parrot the beliefs of the Wheel, based on the teachings of the so-called martyr Golleay. Every King of Emmen has denounced the teachings as heresy, and Golleay was broken on the wheel for good reason. I have said before to Lady Jilka that Lord Thaume is too tolerant in allowing the Wheel to flourish in Croad. Now his own nephew proclaims the word of Golleay.'

Oricien rose from his seat. 'You take much upon yourself, old man, to condemn the rule of Lord Thaume,' he said. 'Your robes will not save you from the whips or the stocks.'

'I speak only with the voice of Harmony!' cried Sleech in a ringing voice, spittle spraying from his lips. 'King Arren has spoken against the Wheel, and the Consorts have proclaimed it a heresy – yet Lord Thaume allows a Temple of the Wheel to flourish in his city. I will speak against any man who permits the Wheel to be worshipped. Golleay was broken for good reason, I say. Lady Jilka will hear of this!'

Guigot smirked. 'Let her. Your endless catechisms bore me. Even timid Oricien threatens you. We have heard enough of your cant.'

Siedra sniggered. Arren looked on. Sleech's lessons were tedious, and his doctrines difficult to master, but he had the ear of Lady Jilka. They had not heard the last of the matter.

7

That night all four children were summoned to Lord Thaume's chambers. From behind his heavy desk he looked up with a dark face. In passing, Arren noticed the spartan aspect of the room. There was not a picture of an ancestor to be seen.

'Sit down,' he said briskly. 'Lady Jilka has brought me reports that I have not enjoyed hearing. Last night you consorted with rogues and harlots in a low tavern; today you mocked and abused Viator Sleech. I intend to impose punishments. Tomorrow you will also be making the acquaintance of a new tutor.'

'Is Viator Sleech to leave us?' asked Guigot with a smirk.

'Whatever punishments I decree, yours will be the heaviest, Guigot,' said Lord Thaume. 'Your guilt has been the most manifest. Viator Sleech has, at the express request of Lady Jilka and myself, consented to stay and continue your education, which most clearly is needed. You will meet your new tutor soon.'

'Oricien, I understand the spirit behind your remarks to Viator Sleech. Your sentiments in themselves were not blameworthy, but Viator Sleech represents the Way of Harmony, and his person deserves respect. Siedra, Arren, your behaviour was not in itself at fault, but you contributed to the atmosphere in which it took place.

'Guigot, you are to have six lashes of the whip; Oricien, three lashes. Siedra and Arren, you are to eat only bread and water for the next week, in which you will be joined by Guigot and Oricien. The four of you will apologize in person to Viator Sleech. I will administer the whippings myself at dawn. That will be all.'

8

As Arren settled in to life at the castle, time began to pass more quickly. He made good progress with his lessons, especially combat and mathematics. Relations between Oricien and Guigot worsened, and Arren, who had hoped to befriend Guigot as another outsider, found himself rebuffed at every turn. Oricien proved less hostile and the two boys began to drill together outside of lessons. Siedra remained suspicious of Arren's low birth, but as her detestation for Guigot grew she became more willing to treat Arren with civility. On occasion he was also able to slip out, ostensibly to the Viatory, and meet Eilla.

The new tutor Lord Thaume had brought in was called Master Pinch. To the children's wonder he was to teach them thaumaturgy.

'Well, then,' he said on the morning they were introduced, 'who can tell me what thaumaturgy is?'

Arren looked at Master Pinch in amazement. Rather than standing in front of the class, he leaned against the windowsill with his arms crossed in a quizzical pose. Only his blue eyes, sleepy yet wary, hinted at concealed powers. His plentiful hair was moon-white but his face was unlined, neither young nor old. Was he thirty, sixty, a thousand? Arren could not tell.

Guigot raised his hand. 'It is the working of marvels, miracles and magic. It is abominated by the viators.'

Pinch smiled. 'You are correct in the first point,' he said in a soft voice with an accent Arren could not place. 'As to the second, opinions differ. Some hold that the thaumaturge can never approach Harmony, by virtue of his activities, others that he may achieve Harmony the same as any other man: with toil, good luck and the intervention of the viators. I myself never trouble to think about the matter. Do not tell the viators I said so, but the most important thing is for a man to have food in his belly. If he starves to death, what then of Harmony?'

Guigot grinned.

'Is a thaumaturge a magician?' asked Siedra.

'Yes and no. "Magic" most specifically refers to manipulation of the Unseen Dimensions. A thaumaturge who cannot perform at least some such manipulations is a poor fellow, a charlatan or mountebank.' He unfolded his arms and paced the room. 'But many of the effects a thaumaturge employs require no magic at all. You see this locket, Lady Siedra?'

'It is the twin to the one I wear at my neck!'

'Wrong, my lady.'

Siedra gasped. Her hand went to her neck and found her locket gone.

'Strictly speaking,' said Pinch, 'that was not magic. Using techniques I will not outline, I was able to remove the item by directing your attention elsewhere.'

Oricien looked up. 'Surely this was not thaumaturgy, but common theft. Footpads in the marketplace achieve as much.'

'Just so. If I could only do such tricks, I would be no thaumaturge. In fact, I could have achieved the same end through a simple cantrap, which is more the kind of sorcery you would expect.'

'Why did you not do so, then?' asked Oricien.

'Simple. The manipulation of the Unseen Dimensions is not without cost. The exercise of the skill is draining, and if I can achieve a similar effect through other means, I will do so. There is a valuable lesson for you all in this, which I hope you are able to see.'

'Will you teach us actual, practical thaumaturgy?' asked Guigot, leaning forward in his seat.

Pinch chuckled. 'Such a course would be inadvisable, even if feasible, which it is not. The essential gift of thaumaturgy cannot be learned, although it can be trained if the subject has a latency.'

'Perhaps,' said Siedra, 'one or more of us has a latent gift.'

'You do not,' said Master Pinch. 'I can assure you of that. I can, and will, teach you some of the charlatan's tricks, legerdemain and the like. But you will never be thaumaturges.'

9

The reason for Master Pinch's presence became apparent as the weeks unfolded. The sporadic war with the Northern Reach was entering an active phase. Lord Thaume had received intelligence that Tardolio, the young Summer King of Mettingloom, was planning an assault on Croad. Lord Thaume had sent to his overlord, Duke Panarre of Lynnoc, for assistance, but he thought also to hedge his bets by engaging the services of a thaumaturge. In this he was wise, since Panarre declined to send troops to Thaume's assistance. He compensated by sending his good wishes and sage advice: 'Do not be affrighted by rumours from the North. They are as common as flatulence, and as enduring. In the unlikely event of attack, these dogs will scatter at the sight of cold steel.'

Lord Thaume read Panarre's letter to his council and threw it down. 'He wishes Croad to come under attack,' he said. 'Then King Arren must supply him with troops and money to defend us, and he will gain glory without the need to exert or impoverish himself. Do any of you disagree?'

He looked around the room, panelled in that gloomy dignity which was his hallmark. His advisers comprised Master Pinch, Darrien as Captain of the Guard, Sir Langlan and Thaume's cousin Sir Artingaume. A more formal body existed, but Lord Thaume disdained the military advice of the traders and guildsmen who comprised it. He had also taken to bringing Oricien, Guigot and Arren to his deliberations, that they might begin to learn the business of statecraft.

Pinch responded to Lord Thaume's assessment. 'You cannot look to Lynnoc for succour,' he said. 'In the circumstances you are limited to looking to your walls, and you may wish to consider some form of negotiation with Tardolio.'

'Never!' said Sir Langlan. 'It is inconceivable that we should treat with brigands.'

'They are only brigands once they enter Emmen,' said Pinch. 'The time to negotiate is now, before an assault is launched. Why do you not approach the Winter King? The way to deal with Mettingloom has always been simple, if you would follow it: play off the Summer and Winter Kings against each other. Fanrolio has no appetite for a protracted war.'

Sir Artingaume, bluff and gruff, shook his head. 'You have forgotten, Master Pinch, if you ever knew, that the northmen killed Lord Thaume's father. You were invited to offer us your skills of sorcery, not your counsels of defeat.'

Master Pinch gave the bland smile that Arren saw so often

in lessons when one of his pupils had stumbled into fallacy or error.

'I cannot imagine, Sir Artingaume, that I was engaged to smite the northmen with a bolt from the Unseen Dimension. The number of thaumaturges capable of such an act is limited, and almost by definition, anyone with the capacity to do so would not be interested in such petty affairs. My involvement in events is more casual than you imagine.'

'Gentlemen,' said Lord Thaume, 'we need not bicker. Artingaume, Master Pinch is able to offer advice and useful information from his recent visit to Mettingloom. On occasion he can use the lesser thaumaturgical arts to help us. Let us be content with that.'

Sir Langlan cleared his throat. 'On more practical matters,' he said, 'are we concerned that Tardolio can hurt us? If he sends a host, what then? Let him pass Jehan's Steppe. He will only come to our walls, which he surely cannot take.'

'I would prefer to avoid a siege,' said Lord Thaume. 'Last year's harvest was not good, and I do not want to lose this year's because we cannot leave the city to garner it. I should not like to be reliant on Duke Panarre's assistance, which may well come too late to prove efficacious.'

'Do you mean, then, to take the field?' said Sir Artingaume. 'A vigorous policy would be to assemble a host and interdict the passage of Jehan's Steppe.'

'I hope that diplomacy bears fruit,' said Lord Thaume. 'I intend to dispatch an emissary to the Winter King proposing a treaty to end the war – wait, Artingaume – but I am not hopeful. At the same time we must mobilize our forces and march on Jehan's Steppe. The northmen are more likely to prove amiable if they see our steel.'

Sir Artingaume nodded in satisfaction. 'This is true statesmanship.'

Lord Thaume turned to the end of the table where

Oricien, Guigot and Arren sat. 'Lads, the day must come when we are all blooded in war. That day has arrived. We march in a month: the three of you will come with us. Sir Langlan says you are ready.'

Arren looked across to Darrien, who had sat quietly following the debate. He nodded at his son. 'It is time,' he said, 'although I do not relish telling your mother.'

10

Arren took the first opportunity to slip out and find Eilla. They had discovered an unoccupied building belonging to the wealthy vintner Foulque, and here they met to exchange tidings.

'There will be war with the North, and Lord Thaume is taking me with him,' said Arren.

Eilla was sitting on Foulque's red chaise, her muddy shoes dirtying the fabric. She looked down at her skirts. The late afternoon sunlight slanted in low through the window, casting one eye into relief. 'Are you sure? And why so delighted?'

'Master Pinch says that Tardolio plans an assault on Croad, and Lord Thaume means to march against him on Jehan's Steppe.'

'And what does Master Pinch know? He is a thaumaturge, not a general. You seem in a great hurry to get yourself killed.'

'I am sixteen, old enough to fight and to be a man. Sir Langlan says I am ready for war.'

'If you say. But don't expect me to rejoice.'

'Not even if I win renown and come back "Sir Arren"?'

'I will rejoice if you come back, knight or no knight. Perhaps I could dress as a boy and sneak along as your page.'

Arren surveyed her figure. 'Eilla, you could no longer pass for a boy.'

'Fah!'

'You are out of spirits today.'

'Nothing is like it was when we were young,' she said, drawing her knees up to her chest and leaning against the arm of the chaise. 'Do you remember when we used to play raiders? We did whatever we wanted, and the worst that could happen was that our fathers would beat us. Now you're off to fight real raiders, my father is threatened with attainder . . .'

'Attainder? Why would anyone attaint Jandille?'

Eilla gave a weak smile. 'Our family has always followed the Wheel.'

'So what? Half the families of Croad follow the Wheel. Lord Thaume does not care.'

'Maybe not, but Lady Jilka does. She is most orthodox, and close to the viators.'

Arren stepped across to lean on the window-ledge next to her chaise. He could sense the warmth of her body a few inches away. She had never used to confide in him like this. 'Lady Jilka does not rule Croad.'

'Lady Jilka is not going to war. And they say that the Consorts have challenged Thaume's Statement of Orthodoxy.'

'I don't understand what that means,' said Arren.

'Doesn't Viator Sleech teach you anything? Every city has a Statement of Orthodoxy, issued by the Consorts, signifying that it follows the Way of Harmony. The Consorts can revoke the Statement and depose the ruler.'

'King Arren would never allow Lord Thaume to be deposed.'

Eilla shook her head. 'Never be sure. The viators have great power, particularly at court in Emmen. It is best for Thaume that his Statement of Orthodoxy is not challenged.

They say he may make an example of some the Spokes of the Wheel, and my father is foremost among them. Why do they care so much? It is all nonsense.'

Arren wanted to take her hand – but this was Eilla. It seemed no time since they had been wrestling in the dirt together, but now he was conscious of something new in their relationship, part constraint, part – he could not define what else. However much he wanted to comfort Eilla, touching her like that would be flowing downriver; he would not be able to go back against the current. He scratched his chin.

'Eilla,' he said eventually. 'You must trust Lord Thaume. He is a good man, and a just lord. He will not allow the Wheel to be persecuted.'

Eilla gave a half-smile. 'I only hope you are right, Arren. There are times of change ahead.'

Arren looked back into her eyes. He could feel the cool sweetness of her breath on his face. 'Some changes are good, Eilla. Don't fear for Jandille, and don't fear for me.'

Eilla jerked her head away. 'You are a boy, Arren. You know nothing and you control nothing!'

'Eilla! I am trying to—'

'What are you trying to do? Impress me with your mature wisdom? You are skipping in delight in going to war to get yourself killed, telling me of Lord Thaume's plans as if you are his closest counsellor, explaining his policies of religious tolerance, and you know nothing about anything!'

Arren was taken aback by Eilla's vehemence. 'I didn't have to tell you anything. I thought you'd be happy that I'd got my chance for glory and I thought you'd want to know that the northmen were on their way. I should be at the Viatory, but I've come to see you instead.'

'How noble of you to spare a few minutes for the peasant girl Eilla and her ignorance. Well, you needn't have concerned yourself. You are puffed up with your own importance now that you associate with Lord Thaume and his children and learn your swordplay with that sot Sir Langlan. Your opinion is of no interest to me. I once had a friend called Arren but he went to the castle and never came back.'

She jumped on the couch and ran from the room, tears gleaming on her cheeks. Arren looked after her in bafflement. If he had ever doubted that she had become a woman, this would have confirmed it.

The next weeks were packed with preparations for war, and he was involved at all levels: Arren had no scope to reflect on his quarrel with Eilla. One morning he sat on Lord Thaume's war counsels; in the afternoon he was measured for his own suit of mail. And he, Oricien and Guigot drilled, drilled, drilled. Sir Langlan was a hard taskmaster.

'Oricien!' he called late one afternoon. 'Do you think the northmen will give you quarter because you are tired?'

'No, sir.'

'Then why do you sit on your arse while Guigot and Arren continue to fence? We must work hard now to make war easier.' Oricien nodded and rose to his feet. 'Good! Now let's see you use the broadsword as if you mean it!'

Lord Thaume had been watching the practice from the walls; now he came down to the courtyard. 'Take a rest, lads. I must confer with Sir Langlan.'

Arren gratefully set his sword down and sat with his back against the wall. It was a warm spring day and the combination of armour and exertion was making him sweat profusely. The ballads Lady Cerisa made them learn had not painted the practice of valour as so coarse. Idly he listened to the snatches of conversation from Lord Thaume and Sir Langlan.

'Are they ready?'

Sir Langlan looked over his shoulder to ensure he was not being overheard. Arren feigned stupor.

'Some are readier than others,' said Sir Langlan. 'Guigot is if anything too ready. He is strong and fast for his age, and he practises like a demon. His basic skills are excellent, and he needs only the seasoning of real warfare. You know the darkness in his soul; my fear is that on the battlefield he will prove cruel. You will need to use him carefully.'

'Oricien? Arren?'

'Arren has not the ferocity of Guigot, but he learns fast. I only have to tell him things once, and he makes good decisions. He is his father's son, and he is never beaten. He will be a credit to you and Darrien, I think.'

'What of my own son, Langlan?'

Sir Langlan flicked a twig aside with his foot. 'I wish we fought in a year's time. Every lad outgrows his strength at some point, and Oricien's height outstrips his muscle. He lacks force, but I do not doubt his courage.'

'I cannot leave him at home while I take the other two. He is my only son, but I must take the risk. Unless I leave all three at home . . .'

Sir Langlan shook his head. 'You cannot leave Guigot behind. He already feels that you do not do justice to his birth. I could not answer for his conduct if he were left behind while your army marches north. They must all go, my lord.'

Lord Thaume scratched his chin. 'You are right, of course. All three are green: I will put them in the flanks.'

'Have you decided your dispositions?' asked Sir Langlan after a pause.

Lord Thaume stood straight. 'I have. Darrien will command the right flank; Artingaume the left. You will command the centre and the cavalry, and I will command the reserve. I will put the lads in Artingaume's wing.'

Even through half-closed eyes Arren could see the gleam in Sir Langlan's. 'You really mean to give me the cavalry?'

'You are a knight of Emmen, Langlan. If I trust you to teach my son to fight, I trust you with my cavalry. King Arren may not value your merits, but be assured that I do.'

'Thank you, my lord. We shall sweep Tardolio from the field.'

I I

The date for departure was set; Lord Thaume announced that Lady Jilka would be his Regent in his absence, an aspect of the war which did not meet with universal approval. The viators regarded events with equanimity, for Lady Jilka was a strong patroness. Arren thought of Jandille and his fears, and resolved to find Eilla before he departed.

They had been accustomed to meet after supper on Kabbelsday, each waiting in the house of Foulque for the other to appear. Arren had missed the two previous weeks since their quarrel, and he wondered whether Eilla would be there this time. By the time the next Kabbelsday came around, the army would have marched. He realized that he had to see her before he left. Who knew what could happen on the battlefield? Sometimes a life could be both Harmonious and brief.

That Kabbelsday, however, supper was extended beyond its normal span. The housemistress Eulalia often invited one or more of the tutors to eat with their pupils to improve their deportment and conversation, and tonight not only had Master Pinch been invited but tedious Viator Sleech and, even worse, Master Guiles, whose attention to the minutiae of etiquette was unrivalled.

81

'Lord Guigot,' he called in a fluting voice. 'Do I see your elbows grazing the table linen?'

Guigot grimaced and drew his arms into his side. Arren had heard Oricien hint to him last week that Lord Thaume considered leaving him at home. Since that moment Guigot had shown unusual deference to his tutors, even the detested Sleech and Guiles.

Arren was usually able to deal with their prolixity with composure, but tonight he was impatient to be gone. What if Eilla thought he was not coming, and chose not to wait? What if she had not come at all?

'Arren,' said Viator Sleech, 'I was speaking to you.'

'My apologies, Viator. My mind was occupied.'

'Understandable enough,' said Pinch with a twinkle. 'The lad is off to war next week. Who knows, perhaps he is contemplating his progress along the Way of Harmony.'

'He would learn more from listening to a viator,' said Sleech. 'Such introspection smacks of the Wheel.'

'Really, Sleech,' said Pinch, setting his bread down on the cloth. 'Can the boy not show some apprehension over his first battle without you accusing him of heresy?'

'With all due respect,' said Arren, 'I have displayed no apprehension. I welcome battle, as do all men of true heart.'

'Well said!' declared Oricien. 'We are all true subjects of King Arren and look to acquit ourselves with honour.'

'We are not men until we have the blood of a foe on our swords,' said Guigot.

'Hmm,' said Master Guiles. 'The true knight does not dwell with relish on the gory aspects of battle. When occasion demands, he slays his foe with courage and vigour, but also with regret. He most certainly does not brag and boast of his prowess with the blade, or dwell on the crude mechanics of the act.'

Guigot managed to look angry and crestfallen at once. Pinch interjected:

'Have you ever fought a battle, Master Guiles? Have you slain a foe with regret?'

Master Guiles dabbed at his lips with his napkin. 'One need not be a fish to appreciate the sea, Master Pinch, and in any event I am unclear as to your own martial history.'

Pinch smiled. 'I freely admit that I have never participated in a battle, nor did I ever intend to. Nonetheless, Lord Thaume has requested my presence and I shall travel north, even if only as a spectator. Perhaps you might be prevailed upon to accompany us?'

Guiles blinked his watery pale eyes slowly. 'That would not be seemly. I have duties here in Croad, particularly in regard to Lady Siedra's education.'

Siedra looked up from her plate, where she had been absentmindedly pursuing some undercooked turnip. 'Please do not detain yourself on my account, Master Guiles. You have taught us that the first rule of etiquette is consideration for the feelings of others. I hope I have been an apt pupil, and the last thing I should wish would be to deny you the richness of experience,' she said with an expression of innocent modesty.

Oricien nearly stifled a giggle. 'Sir, the road north might lie upon the Way of Harmony. As I would expect, my sister does not insist upon her privileges. She has a generous heart, well schooled by you.'

Guiles peered at Oricien through half-closed eyes. 'My value to Lord Thaume in the field would be negligible at best, while I can never spend too much time helping Lady Siedra to prepare for court.'

'You underestimate your value,' said Guigot. 'You must be on hand to guide Lord Thaume in the gracious acceptance of Tardolio's surrender.'

'The matter is settled,' snapped Guiles. 'I remain at Croad to continue my duties. Why do you not attempt to persuade Viator Sleech to make the journey?'

Sleech beamed. 'No such attempt is necessary. I am already resolved to travel north with Lord Thaume's army. Many folk will need assistance in finding Harmony as they lie on the field of battle.'

Master Guiles's lessons in deportment must be having some effect, thought Arren, for there were no audible groans at the thought of Sleech's sermonising accompanying them to, and beyond, battle. Guigot's cough might charitably have been attributed to gristle stuck in his throat, while Oricien's expression could have arisen from gastric discomfort.

The time weighed heavily on Arren. Viator Sleech interrupted the dessert course with a homily on the Humble Tailor and the Proud Knight – a person of mean origins might achieve Harmony more easily than a gentleman who denied the intercessory power of the viators – and Master Guiles took Guigot to task for passing wind with unseemly relish. Eventually the meal concluded and Arren was the first to leap from his seat.

'Arren!' called Master Guiles. 'Is this really the way of the gentleman? Lady Siedra is to your left – how is she to regard your bounding from her company with such haste?'

Arren bowed. 'My apologies, Siedra.'

Siedra smiled and flicked her hair from her eyes, a gesture she had been practising a great deal of late. 'I take no offence, Arren. I know how eager you are to visit the Viatory before bed.'

'Really?' said Viator Sleech. 'I myself am stepping across to the Viatory. Perhaps you would care to accompany me through the dark streets.'

Siedra sniggered. Arren said: 'Ordinarily I would be honoured, but I find an unpleasant griping of the guts which I must attend to on the instant. I would show Viator Sleech no honour in sharing such delicate pangs. I feel sure that Guigot would make a more suitable companion.'

With this he scampered from the room. He could hear Master Guiles saying: 'Arren's conduct is worthy of censure. First, he has insulted the good Viator Sleech; second he impugns the capacity of the cook; and third he lies poorly.'

But Arren was out of the room and free. A rebuke on the morrow from Master Guiles was a small price to pay.

12

It was a still night with only a sliver of moon. Arren made his way through the streets of the Old Town. Everyone knew that raiders were on the way, and with faulty if understandable logic, locked their doors and their shutters early.

Arren loved the city when it was deserted. He padded through the market square, normally thronged with people. Tonight even the gallows was empty: the cutpurse Lord Thaume had hanged last week had putrefied with a rapidity which made the credulous whisper of omens and portents, and Thaume had ordered the corpse cut down before more adverse comment was heard.

He slipped down the alleyway between two houses into the communal vegetable garden shared by the several houses on the plot. He looked around for Foulque's deserted house. It would be embarrassing, and potentially dangerous, to enter the wrong one. At this time of night, all the houses were dark, but his eyes had become accustomed to the gloom and he was able to pick his way past a familiar cluster of thunderberry bushes.

Foulque's house appeared secure to a casual inspection, particularly in the dark, but Arren knew better. He snaked his arm into a gap between two planks and reached around for the boss he knew was there. On finding it, he pulled his hand back to release the catch. The door swung open a fraction with a creak. Widening the gap as little as possible he slipped inside the house.

Foulque had inherited the house from a creditor who had become so drunk on Foulque's fine Garganet wines that he had fallen down a well in the night and drowned before anyone realized he was gone. He had died in debt to Foulque for the very case of wine which had caused his death, and Foulque had wasted no time in claiming the house in settlement. He had never subsequently lived there, having a much smarter residence near the Viatory. Already an air of decrepitude began to hang over it, and a thick film of dust coated the worn furnishings. At night the house was not so much unsettling as cheerless.

'Eilla!' he called softly. 'Are you there?'

There was no reply. Had she come at all? He was later than usual, and even if she had been here, she could not have been confident that he would come. How would he see her before he left for war?

He sat on a knobbly chair to consider his options. He could go to her house and ask for her; he had known her father Jandille since he was a boy. He realized that her good opinion still mattered to him. For all his courtly training and elevated deportment, he had never been happier than when he scampered in the streets with her, Clottie and Matten. If he respected Master Sleech he would have asked him what this meant for his journey towards Harmony.

Upstairs he heard a scraping. Rats were already at work in the house. Eilla would surely not have thought to wait for him upstairs; by unspoken convention they had never gone so far from the exit. He felt a prickling at his neck. He would not be able to rest until he had investigated. He would quickly check around and then return to the castle. He would work out how to find Eilla tomorrow.

Taking the steps two at a time, stumbling in the dark, Arren made his way up the stairs.

5

Mettingloom

At King Fanrolio's command, the musicians around the ballroom set up a leisurely air. These dances were designed to facilitate conversation rather than exercise. Dancing was essentially a foppish activity, not suited to the military temperament, and Beauceron saw General Virnesto scowling as he looked for a chair; but Beauceron had always enjoyed it. He could glide with a slow and easy rhythm and carried himself to advantage. If a suitable partner presented herself he would be happy to step out.

He noticed that Davanzato had swiftly secured Lady Isola's company. The room was not awash with women who combined youth, beauty and crisp deportment, and Beauceron disdained to dance with inferior materials. He resolved to wait the dance out until a partner like Lady Letteria or Lady Romina became available. He looked around to notice Prince Brissio's eyes lingering on Lady Cosetta hungrily. Her rich new gown of russet and burgundy set off her blonde hair. Presumably Davanzato, as her ransom agent, had provided it.

Cosetta was no longer any of his concern, but she could not profit from closer association with the loutish Prince Brissio. 'Lady Cosetta,' he called. 'Would you do me the honour?'

Cosetta turned away from Brissio and inclined her head. 'Why not?' she said with an approach to a smile. Brissio shot Beauceron a glance which he ignored: time to worry about his cloddish antagonism later.

'I trust you are settling in well to your new surroundings, Lady Cosetta,' he said as they began their stately dance.

'I cannot believe you are befriending me after all that you have done,' said Cosetta without heat. Beauceron thought her eyes most becoming.

'The past is the past, Lady Cosetta. For good or ill, we cannot change it. I am glad to see you embracing your new circumstances.'

She leaned forward and Beauceron caught a whiff of subtle fragrance. He deftly steered them out of the path of a less agile couple. 'In truth,' she said, 'I am not dissatisfied with events. I was travelling to Croad to be a penniless companion in an unfamiliar city. Here, it seems, I am esteemed on my own merits, under the protection of the King. This may not be the life I would have chosen, but I do not expect either my father or Lord Sprang to ransom me. I find myself cast on my wits, and I do not fear the matter as I thought.'

She smiled for the first time in Beauceron's experience; an expression that transformed her face. Never anything less than comely, now she was beautiful. How had he failed to notice before?

The music drew to its stately conclusion and Beauceron took her hand to lead her to the upholstered chairs at the side of the room. 'I am not a man to divulge my thoughts lightly,' he said with a smile. 'When I have done so in the past, I am invariably described as a monomaniac.'

'I do not claim to understand your thoughts, Beauceron; and indeed I have no particular desire to. You have brought me into captivity, and if that captivity is less oppressive than I had feared, that is no reason to thank you. You have never treated me with anything other than calculation and indifference.'

Beauceron handed her a goblet and inclined his head. 'I will not magnify my offence by specious denials. I have subordinated a great deal to achieve my goals, and that has included your own convenience. But I may say that dancing here with you now, feeling the warmth of your person in my arms, my indifference seems inexplicable, and I heartily repent of it.'

Cosetta bit her lip against a laugh. 'You kidnap me, subject me to every privation, give me away; and then you act as if nothing had happened and, if I am not mistaken, attempt to seduce me. You have a short memory.'

Beauceron shrugged and sipped his own drink. 'Whatever my faults, a short memory is not one of them. I forget nothing, and remember old slights as if they were yesterday. As to seduction, such matters take two, and for now I merely attempt to secure your good opinion.'

Now Cosetta laughed openly. 'You have some way to go. I may allow you to visit me in due course, but only because I admire your complete shamelessness. Listen, here is the Bocarillo and I must secure a new partner.'

Beauceron stood to hand her from her seat and turned away as she engaged another young man's attention. He moved away with a smile, looking around for Lady Letteria. His attention distracted, he bumped into the man beside him.

'Excuse me, sir.'

'I shall not,' said the man. 'Do you not recognize me?'

Beauceron constrained his attention to the thin resentful countenance before him. 'Albizzo.'

'Just so, and your offences exceed a moment of clumsiness. We must discuss my sister.'

Beauceron frowned. 'How is Etheria?' he asked in a flat voice. He lifted his goblet from the table.

'Well might you ask, sir,' said Albizzo with an expression simultaneously sneering and self-pitying. 'You might have displayed similar concern for her welfare before you debauched her.'

Albizzo's voice was shrill, and heads turned to look at them. 'Albizzo, you only demean yourself ranting before the King.'

'I demand satisfaction of you, sir. You must apologize – as you observe, before the King – or face my wrath.'

'Your wrath?' Beauceron raised an eyebrow.

'Do not provoke me. Our family has held land in this city for generations. Etheria could have hoped for a good marriage before you defiled her.' Spots of colour stood out on Albizzo's cheeks.

'Must you transact your business in this way? I did not force your sister; she was, in fact, all too willing. If your family commands the respect you suggest, I cannot imagine her marriage prospects materially blighted.'

'Dog! Who would want a woman with a character compromised by a natural child?'

Beauceron set his goblet down. 'A child?'

'Yes, sir. You left her with a bastard and not a thought for her welfare. It is late now to affect concern.'

'You mistake me, Albizzo. I care nothing for Etheria and less for her brat. She assured me with some babble of phases of the moon that the event you describe could not occur; more, it seems, to comfort herself than me, for I was indifferent throughout.'

'You are despicable. I can tell you now the child did not survive his birth one hour; and I intend that you should meet your son within the same period. You will fight me now, and may you find Harmony.'

'Do not be a fool, Albizzo. If you declare a duel to the

death, be sure you are prepared for the outcome. Let us leave the matter aside.'

'Not just a seducer but a coward too? I should have known that the boasts of the Dog of the North were hollow. I am glad the King has seen you for what you are.' He turned away.

'Enough, Albizzo. If you challenge me, I must respond. That is why I give you a chance to withdraw.'

Albizzo stepped so close that their noses almost touched. Beauceron could see that he was in trim condition, and his eyes glittered with a manic intensity.

'Then I challenge you, Beauceron. We will fight this very night with the weapon of your choosing: the rapier, the broadsword, the knife, or hands. And it shall be to the death.'

Beauceron shrugged. 'As you wish. I choose the rapier. If this is how you wish to achieve Harmony, I am on hand to help you.'

Fanrolio rose from his seat. 'Come now, gentlemen, can you not be reconciled?' he said in a wavering voice.

Albizzo and Beauceron turned to the King and bent the knee. 'Your Puissance,' said Albizzo, 'if you command it, I shall of course withdraw my challenge, but the insult to my sister remains grave. I beg you will not command me to forswear my honour.'

Fanrolio turned to Beauceron with rheumy eye. 'Beauceron, your conduct does not appear beyond reproach.'

'Your Puissance, events happened as they did. It is futile to wish them otherwise. The good Albizzo has impugned my honour and my courage before this august group. If he challenges me I must respond.'

Fanrolio thought for a moment. Davanzato whispered in his ear.

'Very well,' said Fanrolio. 'Albizzo is within his rights to demand satisfaction, and I will not tarnish his honour by demanding he withdraws his challenge. You may fight, but outside. It is forbidden to draw steel in my presence.' He beckoned to a liveried attendant. 'Bring their arms and escort them to the courtyard. Name your seconds.'

Albizzo smiled. 'I call on Massaio.' From the side of the room a trim man in a bright green cloak stepped forward, making a bow. 'I am honoured, friend.'

Beauceron had no obvious second to hand. Monetto was the usual choice but Beauceron was not sure where he was spending the evening. With a faint smile, he said: 'I call on General Virnesto.'

Virnesto stepped forward. He was beginning to thicken around the middle, and his hair was now more grey than black, but he radiated martial competence.

'Really, Beauceron,' said Virnesto. 'We are hardly so intimate that I am your natural second.'

Beauceron bowed. 'You are my comrade in arms: did we not range Jehan's Steppe together? By custom you may not refuse me.'

Virnesto shook his head and scowled. 'Indeed I may not, but I am vexed to leave the warmth of the dimonetto on such a night. It is an inconvenience.'

'Albizzo will soon be facing the inconvenience of death. Your own vexation is minor in the context.'

'Very well,' said Virnesto. 'The sooner we start, the sooner we finish.'

The attendant had brought the rapiers out, and the combatants belted them on and strode from the hall.

In the courtyard the moon was full. The ground had a thin skimming of ice, and Beauceron's breath misted as he exhaled. He took off his cloak and waistcoat; Albizzo did the same. They bowed to each other, and went to stand ten paces apart. It was too late for apologies now.

'Fight!' called Massaio.

They circled cautiously, blades outstretched. Beauceron was concerned about the slippery footing: he was confident he was the better swordsman, but he needed to be on his feet to show it. Albizzo had planned the event, and no doubt had been training extensively.

Beauceron stepped briskly forward, feinted and lunged. Albizzo swayed to the side, parried effortlessly and counter-attacked. Even as Beauceron slipped he noted that Albizzo was moving with a sure-footed certainty. His planning had obviously extended to his footwear: his ribbed soles would give him an advantage over Beauceron's everyday boots.

Beauceron recovered his slip and pushed Albizzo's blade aside. The trick with the shoes was not strictly honourable, but he could not call for a halt in mid-duel. He stepped carefully into the offensive. Head and feet, he thought. All swordplay began with the head and feet. As Albizzo parried him he slid to the side, with the centre of the courtyard to his back; Albizzo's back was now facing the wall and Beauceron aimed to force him back. But Albizzo came skipping forward, launching an assault studded with feints and lunges. This was crisp swordplay, the result of extensive practice and a good master. Beauceron parried a lunge an inch from his throat: he was getting slack. Albizzo might be a duellist but he was no soldier: Beauceron kicked out to gain a moment's respite. Albizzo was ready for the move, feinted right and lunged left. Beauceron jerked aside but he felt a sting in his ribs: Albizzo had bloodied him.

Beauceron looked up and caught Albizzo's eye. It gleamed with a crazed intensity, but the passion was suppressed in the swordplay. There was none of the carelessness of the fanatic in his work.

In the moonlight and the glimmer of the torches the blood on Beauceron's shirt looked black. It could only encourage Albizzo, although Beauceron judged the wound superficial.

Albizzo lunged again, this time disdaining a feint. He was keen to finish the fight. Beauceron stumbled aside and let out a groan. *Let him think I am sorely hurt.* He gave ground in the face of Albizzo's assault. As Albizzo chased him, Beauceron let his foot slide from under him on the ice. He lay on his side in the dirt and Albizzo leaped forward for the kill.

But as he made his killing stroke, Beauceron continued his roll on the ground, using his momentum to push him upright. Albizzo overstretched in following the movement, and Beauceron twisted to catch him under the ribcage. Albizzo staggered back in astonishment, blood pumping from his chest. Beauceron stood watching in disappointment. He had hoped to spit Albizzo's heart directly.

Albizzo composed himself with an effort. He wrenched his sword into a defensive position. Then he swayed. 'No,' he said thickly. 'Is this Harmony?' He fell forward to the ground, his blade slipping from his hand and clattering to the cobbles.

Beauceron stood some distance away, watching the pool of blood mingle with the ice melting from the heat of Albizzo's body. He had seen death before; and he saw it now. Massaio stepped forward, knelt, and turned Albizzo over, looked into his eyes and felt his pulse. He shook his head.

'Beauceron is the winner. His honour is vindicated,' said Virnesto.

Massaio stood up. 'You killed a better man than yourself today.'

Beauceron said nothing. He felt nothing but weariness. He sheathed his rapier and walked over to Albizzo's body. After inspecting the corpse's feet, he pulled one of Albizzo's boots off. He banged it against the ground; slush fell from the treads. He laid the boot sideways on Albizzo's chest so that everyone could see the ridged sole.

'Take your better man and bury him,' he said to Massaio.

He turned and walked out of the courtyard with the moon at his back.

2

Beauceron allowed himself the luxury of a lie-in the next morning. An apothecary had applied a poultice to his wound and he felt disinclined for exertion. He rose stiffly from his bed and opened the shutters. The aquavias glowered with winter darkness and there were a few flakes of snow settling on the paths. The wind insinuated itself around the casement and he wrapped his cloak around his thin shirt. Against the chill he thought of the Summer King.

He had been tempted several times to take his proposals to Tardolio. The Summer King lacked Fanrolio's timidity and might be thought more favourable to the idea of an assault on Croad. But ever since Beauceron had come into Mettingloom he had been Fanrolio's man: his contacts and influence were all in the court of the Winter King. Tardolio must be suspicious of any overture from one of Fanrolio's captains, and Fanrolio would have him killed at the slightest suspicion that Beauceron was courting the Sun – and Davanzato's intelligencers would find out soon enough. For all its superficial appeal, the idea was impractical.

From downstairs he heard the tinkle of the guest bell, and then the heavy tread of Kainera on the stairs. 'Lady Isola requests the pleasure of your company, sir.'

Beauceron raised his eyebrows. He did not remember having a visiting relationship with her. Perhaps she meant to stab him, or worse, to upbraid him again.

'Send her in, Kainera. And see if you can get some more heat from the fire.'

Kainera poked ineffectually at the hearth before disappearing downstairs. Beauceron reached for breeches, boots and a jacket. He heard a much lighter tread on the stairs and then Lady Isola stood before him.

'My lady,' he said, still pulling a boot on. 'I am honoured by your attention, and charmed by your loveliness.'

Davanzato had certainly ensured she would dress as a lady during her stay in the North. Her cloak of deep red covered an exquisite aquamarine silk dress decorated with the battlecat emblem of Sey. The winter air had brought a flush to her cheeks and her dark eyes shone from the exertion. Beauceron also noticed that she did not have a knife obviously about her person. Was this indeed simply a social call?

Isola merely returned an arch look. 'Cosetta said that you flirted with her. Your brazenness is almost admirable.'

'All experience is valuable, my lady. "While we live, we learn." Please, be comfortable. This was once your home, if only for a night.'

Isola sat on the couch with schooled precision. 'I came to assess your health. I understand you took a wound last night.'

'A scratch,' said Beauceron with a smirk. 'Albizzo, inevitably, was more seriously dealt with. I am gratified – if puzzled – by your solicitude.'

Kainera appeared with hot drinks and Isola sipped calmly at her steaming cup.

'My betrothed has promised to hang you in the market square at Croad,' she said. 'I would hate for circumstances to deny him the opportunity.'

'I am comforted to know that your concern has a rational basis,' said Beauceron. 'I am able to present both good and bad tidings. The good news is that I plan to stand, after a long absence, in the centre of Croad. Hissen willing, the day is not too far distant. The worse news, certainly for Lord

Oricien, is that I do not plan to put my neck in his noose; although he is welcome to try.'

Isola sat and drank her tea for a while. 'Davanzato says that you harbour an insane resentment against Croad, and think only of its humiliation. Since I am to marry its ruler, I am curious as to your motives.'

'I warned you that Davanzato is untrustworthy,' he said. 'He is not a casual gossip, and if he imparts information it is for the purposes of influencing your opinion. It is no secret that I have advised the Winter King to assault Croad, but I am not the first captain to have had the idea. Lord Oricien's father had to deal with a similar invasion.'

'But Davanzato says there is something personal, deep within you, that impels you to such desires. You show no interest in taking Jeis or Slent.'

'Neither city is readily accessible from Mettingloom. Only a buffoon would attempt such an assault.'

'So you do mean to attack Croad? Are you mad?'

'On the contrary. Croad may be walled but Oricien can rely on little help from Emmen or Glount. King Enguerran is a belligerent young man, and his Immaculates are unmatched for valour, but he is more concerned with the South than the North. He thinks to wrest Vasi Vasar from King Ingomer. Croad might as well not exist for him.'

'Why then has Croad not fallen to the North before?'

Beauceron drained his tea with a flourish. 'Allow me some secrets,' he said. 'Soon you will return to Croad and report this conversation to Oricien. So far he learns only that factions within Mettingloom wish to attack Croad – hardly news. But were I to list the weaknesses of his defences I would only allow him to regroup.'

'I am no closer to understanding your motives.'

'It is not my intention that you should,' he said, rising

from his seat. 'I must pay a number of calls, including Davan-zato. May I escort you to the Occonero?'

Isola rose as well; Beauceron passed her cloak and for an instant their hands brushed and Isola coloured. 'That would be kind. Davanzato has allowed me no money for the wherry.'

Thirty minutes later they arrived at Davanzato's offices. The Under-Chamberlain was disengaged and they were ushered in to the parlour. Davanzato rose from his seat. 'My lady! Beauceron! I am charmed to see you both, especi-ally on such cordial terms.'

'Lady Isola is adamant that I should remain safe from harm until such time as Oricien should capture and hang me. I find her candour refreshing.'

Isola removed her cloak and sat down. Davanzato said: 'A degree of resentment is understandable in the circum-stances.'

'Your generous spirit does you credit, Davanzato,' said Beauceron. 'The viators would give praise at your approach to Harmony. Imagine their delight were you to show your sympathy in a more concrete way – for instance, by waiving your commission and thereby reducing the ransoms the ladies' sponsors must pay.'

Davanzato looked sourly at Beauceron. 'I cannot imagine that Lady Isola is deceived by your sophistry into believing that anyone other than yourself is responsible for her predica-ment.'

Beauceron shrugged. 'It was never my intention to do so. We must all take the consequences of our actions – or indeed, inactions.'

'Inactions?'

'I had no specific examples in mind. I merely spoke in a general sense. While I am here, perhaps I might arrange a time for my audience with His Puissance.'

Davanzato shot Isola a sideways glance, his brown eyes flashing. 'You imagine that I have no other duties but to see to your convenience.'

'On my return to Mettingloom I offered you proofs of my regard for your person. It is common for folk of friendly feelings to do each other a good turn.'

'Your observations are boorish in the extreme. It is impolite to refer to your cordial feelings in this crass commercial manner, and even more so when one of the "proofs of your regard" sits beside you.'

'I cannot imagine how you arrived at the conclusion that I had "given" you Lady Isola, a woman of dignity and worth. She was not my property to give you. You will remember that I petitioned the King to collect her ransom, and out of friendship offered you the chance to secure the agent's fee. My gift, if it can be so described, was the commission, rather than Lady Isola herself.'

Isola stood up. 'I am not some chattel that you can bargain among yourselves for petty advantage. I am a lady of Sey and I expect to be treated as such. You are both as bad as each other, except that Beauceron is somewhat worse.'

She snatched her cloak and swept from the room.

'I am glad that Lady Isola has formed such a rapid assessment of your merits, Beauceron.'

'You gain nothing by antagonizing me. I have shown you great favour since my return. To date I see no sign of it being reciprocated. Have you attempted to arrange an audience for me with the King?'

'Frankly? Since your project is an impractical fanfaronade, I saw no point in wasting my time or His Puissance's.'

Beauceron gave a measured nod. 'In that case you will have no objection to returning the items of plate I gave you, or indeed reimbursing me the 8,000 florins agent's fee I have forgone. A man with your reputation for probity would not wish to have it bruited about, however unfairly, that he took gifts for services he had no intention of performing.'

Davanzato looked at Beauceron with cold eyes. 'You are over-hasty. His Puissance will be consulting me on his diary after supper tonight. We may yet be able to arrange an audience.'

Beauceron rose and bowed. 'I will wait to hear from you,' he said as he left the room.

3

Beauceron took a wherry to the Armamentary, sandwiched between the dockyard and Fanrolio's private palace, Hiverno. He presented himself at the gate. 'Where will I find General Virnesto?'

The guard consulted his schedule. 'The General is next door at the docks reviewing a new pinetto.'

'Thank you. I will find him there.'

He stepped next door into the dockyard, immediately to find Virnesto in conversation with a shipwright who was explaining the merits of his new craft, which bobbed on the blue-black sea. A cruel wind dragged their cloaks almost to the horizontal.

'She is fast, seaworthy. She will run with the wind faster than a cog and can even outrun a galley.'

'Hmph,' said Virnesto. 'And in a calm? If I had a fleet of these off Garganet and the wind died? Their galleys would cut us to pieces in an hour. If you cannot deliver me a ship which can outrun a galley in a calm – presumably with oars – then do not waste my time. Your pinetto is as much use as a gelded bull: it's too light to fight and too heavy to row. Bring me a new design within the month.'

Beauceron grinned. 'Still trying to beat the Garganet navy?'

Virnesto turned and ran a hand through his hair. 'Beauceron! I thought you might be resting today.'

'I am too hardy to be worried by a nick.'

'You should be more careful,' said Virnesto. 'Sooner or later you will get yourself killed.'

Beauceron shrugged. 'We all have our foibles. I yearn to take Croad; you have not given up your dream of trouncing the Garganet navy.'

'The circumstances are not similar,' said Virnesto, leading Beauceron out to the sea wall at the front of the dockyard. The lagoon stretched away before them, grey and pettish. 'I have no lust for war – at least, not your sort. A spot of raiding in the summer; well, why not? But a deliberate, purposeful assault on a fortified city that we do not want and could not hold? I cannot understand your enthusiasm.'

'Maybe you are getting old, Virnesto.'

'Or maybe just wiser. I remember you arriving in Mettingloom. You were a hothead then, and you remain one to this day,' said Virnesto with an easy smile.

'I know how to hold a grudge. It is one of the marks of true nobility.'

Virnesto's mouth twitched. 'If that is so, you will be King of all Mondia one day.'

'For now, I have a difficulty.'

'The situation cannot be unusual for you. Last night you escaped a pointless death by a whisker, and you have those two Emmenrule ladies baying for your blood.'

'My concern is much simpler: Davanzato.'

'Ah.'

Beauceron leaned on the sea wall and looked southwest. At the limit of his vision he could see the Ferrant Mountains: on the far side of the range lay Emmen.

'I have – of course – bribed Davanzato liberally. The fact remains that he lacks enthusiasm for the venture. He will neither raise the matter with Fanrolio nor allow me to.'

'There is no profit for him in a war. Trade with Mettingloom would decline, to his detriment, since he skims a percentage from the Pellagiers' revenues. Not, I think, that Fanrolio would support your scheme in any event.'

'I cannot understand,' said Beauceron as the wavelets lapped against the dock wall, 'why there is so much resistance to the idea. When I was a child in the Emmenrule, all folk talked of was the terror of raiders from the North. Now I am one of them, and the raiders are too timid to leave their fires and dimonettoes.'

Virnesto reached into the pocket of his cloak and pulled out a handful of sour-nuts mixed with dried redders. He offered some to Beauceron and said: 'It is not that simple now, and it was not then. Fanrolio is the Winter King, and the winter is not the campaigning season. When did a Winter King last launch an invasion? The Snow King's job is to look to the defences, to build and to plan.'

Beauceron ate the last of the nuts and brushed the dust from his hands. 'I can take it that you will not advocate the plan to Fanrolio?'

Virnesto opened his hands wide. 'I never said that I would, and nor did I take a bribe to do so. I see no benefit to Mettingloom in your programme, regardless of the advantages to yourself. If you wish to convert Davanzato to your cause, you must appeal either to his self-interest or his fears – preferably both.'

With that he turned on his heel and walked off towards his barracks. Beauceron was left looking out over the sea towards the enemy over the horizon.

4

In Mettingloom, the days turned into weeks and the weeks into months. Winter held the city in its grip; the aquavias froze over and the wherries were put away. Beauceron was no closer to an audience with Fanrolio, and now he was no longer paying his men, he knew they would be sinking into dissipation. Once the time came to assault Croad they would have become indolent and slack.

Beauceron presented himself at the suite on the upper storey of Hiverno, where Isola maintained her small household.

'I am not sure if her ladyship is at home to visitors,' said the maid, Dortensia. 'Under-Chamberlain Davanzato has already gone away disappointed.'

'I am not Under-Chamberlain Davanzato,' said Beauceron with a grimace. 'I should hate that confusion to occur.'

Dortensia went away and returned after a lengthy pause. 'Her ladyship will see you,' she said with a curious expression that seemed to mingle disdain and anticipation.

He walked through the double doors into the small but expensively furnished salon. 'My lady! How do I find you today?'

Isola turned away from the window where she had been looking out over the frozen lagoon. Her eyes were reddened and moist.

'You are the man I hate most in the world,' she hissed. 'You have ruined me.'

'Isola, we have discussed before how you only hurt yourself by repining.'

'I will be in Mettingloom for ever,' she said softly. 'I will never see the sun again.'

'You exaggerate, my lady. The sunshine may be rare in winter, but it is all the more precious when it breaks through.'

Since she seemed disinclined to offer him a drink, he helped himself from the flagon of langensnap, pouring one for Isola as he did so. 'Your sufferings will soon be over,' he said.

She reached into her breast and drew out a letter, torn and ragged from handling.

'This is from Davanzato. My father will not pay my ransom.'

Beauceron glanced at the crabbed hand on the page. 'It is a negotiating ploy,' he said.

'No,' she said, dabbing at her nose with a kerchief. 'He says that since he has paid my dowry, and I was kidnapped within the county of Croad, I am Oricien's responsibility, and he is responsible for my ransom.'

'The position is extreme, although it may be defensible. I am not an expert on betrothal law.'

'Davanzato then asked Oricien to pay. Since he had not received the dowry, he refused, saying that my father must pay both ransom and dowry.'

'The positions are not compatible,' said Beauceron as he sipped his langensnap. 'No doubt the court at Emmen would rule one way or the other, although the case would be time-consuming. You must be patient.'

Isola flung her glass into the fire. 'Do you not understand? Neither of them wants me! My father, and the man I was going to marry, and they are fighting to be rid of me. And you are the one who took my dowry!'

Beauceron jabbed at the fire with a poker, as much to keep it out of Isola's hands as for any other reason. 'I needed the money. I did not imagine that you would not command a ransom. I sympathize with your plight.'

Isola stepped over to him and looked into his eyes. 'You

did not realize what would happen to me. I know you meant me no harm; you protected me and kept your men from violating me. You are not a bad man – can you not restore my dowry? Oricien would then pay my ransom.'

Beauceron broke her gaze. 'That is not possible. You imagine an intimacy between us which does not and has never existed. You owe me no particular thanks for any forbearance. While I may enjoy your company, my use for you has always been commercial. Your dowry allows me many possibilities.'

Isola slapped half-heartedly at him; Beauceron took both her wrists in one hand.

'Possibilities!' she spat. 'You mean your precious invasion of Croad. Have you no eyes? Davanzato will never permit it. A child could see as much.'

Beauceron poured another glass of langensnap for her and led her to sit on the couch. 'Drink that.'

He sat on a chair out of her immediate reach.

She drained the glass in a single motion. 'Did you hear me? Davanzato will never let you take an army to Croad.'

'Davanzato is not the King.'

'He might as well be. It seems the Chamberlain will never recover, so he controls access to Fanrolio. You would do better in persuading Tardolio.'

'The option is not practical. And although it comes from your mouth I hear Davanzato's voice.'

'Pah! I hate Davanzato as much as I hate you. He has used me throughout while pretending to be a concerned friend. And he will not drop one florin of the commission he is owed. He will learn that fifteen per cent of nothing is nothing.'

'No doubt that does not increase his regard for me.'

'I do not care what he thinks of you. Ideally you would both kill each other.'

Beauceron crossed his legs. 'I did not come here to give

you advice, and I have nothing to gain from doing so. Nonetheless: it is important to make a distinction between the past and the future. In the past, I kidnapped you and took your dowry. At the time you were understandably vexed with me. Understand that hating me cannot help you. I am no longer able to harm you; I may even be able to help you, in a limited sense, although clearly that help cannot be financial. Forget the past, calculate where your advantage lies for the future, and act on that basis.'

Isola began to laugh, gently at first and then with increasing abandon. Soon she was howling with laughter and tears.

'My counsel was not intended to be humorous.'

'They say you are the least forgiving man alive, that you are gnawed with hatred of Croad, that the lord of the city gelded you, that every normal feeling and principle has been perverted and subverted to your lust for revenge.'

Beauceron rubbed his cheek. 'I do not recognize the portrait. I most certainly have not been gelded. "Revenge" is an emotive term. I nurture a resentment proportional to a long-ago event, and would gladly see those who injured me suffer just penalty.'

'How, then, do you differ from me in hating those who have taken my life?'

'My programme is rational and constructive. Every day I take steps to bring it about. In so doing I give myself useful occupation. Were I of religious bent I would argue that I advance along the Way of Harmony. Your own bitterness, if I may say so, has become directed inwards rather than put to constructive use. You are unlikely to benefit from such an approach.'

Isola rose from her seat. 'Your arrogance is breathtaking! You allow yourself to nurture grudges in the name of "Harmony" while I am told to see sense and accustom myself to my daily humiliation of owing my bread to Davanzato. I should even look upon you in a friendly light! Be assured that I do not. Kindly leave immediately.'

Beauceron bowed. 'As you wish, my lady.'

As he turned and left the room, Isola was already filling her glass with another measure of langensnap.

5

On leaving Isola, Beauceron resolved to pay a call on Cosetta. She had taken an apartment overlooking the Grand Aquavia in the Metropolia, a respectable address.

When he arrived at the apartment, Cosetta was fastening herself into a dress in preparation for a ball that evening. It sagged loose at the front and Beauceron made an effort to look elsewhere.

'I am honoured to see you, Beauceron,' she said, 'although, as you see, time presses. Please, help yourself to refreshments if you choose.'

Beauceron sat and looked around the apartment. It was spacious and airy, the couches and tables tricked out with fashionable gildings.

'I have just come from the Lady Isola,' he said. 'She has received some bad news about her ransom.'

'I have not seen her for several days,' said Cosetta. 'I have had many affairs to occupy me. I take it that Sprang is declining to pay.'

'Not just Sprang – Oricien also. They are arguing over whose responsibility she is.'

Cosetta pursed her lips. 'Better that she should learn Oricien's character before she marries him. A man who is parsimonious in such circumstances is unlikely to prove an open-handed husband.'

'She does not take quite that view. And Oricien is not so

much parsimonious as proud. He worries that Sprang is trying to play him for a fool. I do not know which of them has the right of it.'

'That is scarcely the point,' said Cosetta.

'Isola said much the same.'

Cosetta gave a half-smile which could have meant anything. 'Here, can you tie my dress at the back? It is so difficult without a maid.'

Beauceron stepped across and tied the red fabric to cover her exposed back. Her skin had the limpid purity of the mountain source of the Emmen. It would be stimulating to see more of it. He returned to his seat, and Cosetta sat and faced him.

'I am surprised that you have not been more in Isola's company,' he said. 'Indeed I am surprised that you no longer share an apartment.'

Cosetta shrugged. 'Neither of us was drawing comfort from the other. Isola was always expecting her ransom to arrive; I merely hoped for mine, and resolved to make plans in case it did not. In this I was wise, for my father's refusal arrived yesterday.'

'Cosetta! I am sorry.'

Cosetta's eyes flashed for a moment. '"Sorry"? Is that polite sympathy, or do you regret kidnapping me and setting a price on my head? The two are very different.'

Beauceron gave a rueful grin. 'I find it unproductive to regret past actions, since they cannot be undone. There are no meaningful amends I can make, so you will have to accept my remark as expressing formal, if sincere, sympathy.'

Cosetta laughed. 'You are wonderfully free of hypocrisy, Beauceron. You kidnapped me for gain and you hold to your purpose with firmness and vigour. But you never pretend otherwise. Davanzato oozed sympathy and consideration when he received the letter. "If there was anything I could do for your suffering" . . . Does he think I am a child, not to realize that he is profiting from the situation?'

'You should be careful, Cosetta. Davanzato is a dangerous man. He has the ear of the King, and he is ruthless when crossed.'

Cosetta shrugged. 'He is more interested in Isola. The commission on my ransom is only 1,500 florins, and he has never expected to gain it in any event. Isola is worth rather more to him. That is another reason why I left the apartment.'

'Do not make an enemy of him.'

'He knows better than to trifle with me. How do you think these apartments are paid for?'

'I have wondered ever since I have known of them,' said Beauceron.

'Prince Brissio maintains them. Do you remember the night we danced? Brissio was most jealous. After the duel he escorted me back to my apartment in Hiverno. I owe you some gratitude for piquing his attention in that way.'

'You and Prince Brissio are—'

'No indeed!' laughed Cosetta. 'A man of that stamp does not prize favours once they are yielded to him. I keep him in a frenzy of anticipation. He does not realize it, but he enjoys the situation more than if he possessed me every night. Clod that he is, he has some imagination, even if of a base sort.'

Beauceron looked sideways at her. 'Again I must warn you to be careful.'

Cosetta laughed again. 'You may speak with authority of the treacherous currents of Fanrolio's court, but where dealing with a man like Brissio is concerned I have nothing to learn from you. Indeed, perhaps I should ask him to hire me a maid . . .'

'You are dealing with circumstances differently from Lady Isola.'

'Isola is always expecting to go home tomorrow, so she never plans for events here. I hope we are both redeemed soon but I should hate to rely on the prospect.'

Beauceron paused a moment. 'I wonder how much influence Brissio has with his father.'

Cosetta smiled. 'Do not even consider what you are implying. First, I have no reason to help you; second, I do not wish to become embroiled in making Brissio a rival to Davanzato; and third, if Brissio had the influence you suggest, he would use it to thwart rather than help you.'

'He has confided as much to you?'

'We have other things to discuss than our sentiments towards you, Beauceron. Nonetheless, he is envious of your accomplishments, both on the battlefields and as a duellist. He suspects that I entertain a partiality for you – as if such a thing could be countenanced in the circumstances – and this does not prompt warm feelings in his breast either.'

'I care nothing for Brissio's feelings towards me. Since he is neither able nor willing to help me I will not pursue the matter further.'

'There is also the point that I am unwilling to help you.'

Beauceron smiled. 'If I ever needed your help, Cosetta, I am confident that one way or another I would be able to secure it.'

Cosetta narrowed her eyes. 'I think, Beauceron, that we shall never know.'

6

Beauceron left Cosetta's apartment and immediately saw the man who had been following him, standing on the frozen aquavia pretending to read a religious tract. Beauceron walked slowly but purposefully out on the Grand Aquavia and thence to the frozen lagoon. A walk of forty-five minutes or so brought him to the nondescript waterside tavern where Monetto was to be found in the afternoons.

'You are early today,' said Monetto. 'Will you take beer?'

'On this occasion, no,' said Beauceron. 'I am weary of being followed. I think we shall take some more deliberate action.'

Monetto nodded, draining his mug as he rose. 'My rooms are nearby. They will do as well as anywhere.'

'You know what he looks like?'

'Of course. I have seen him too.'

Beauceron stepped back out into the street, pulling his cloak around him, for the wind was now in his face. He walked back in the direction he had come, past the man who had been following him. Once he had got far enough to be sure that his pursuer would be in motion, he turned and walked back towards the tavern. The man had nowhere else to go and looked around in confusion. Before he could reach any conclusion, he found his way blocked by Monetto.

'Come, friend,' said Monetto. 'You have been keen to make Beauceron's acquaintance, if a little shy. I will introduce you.'

'Ah – you – you mistake me, sir. I merely take the air on this glorious afternoon.'

Monetto stepped closer and leaned into the man. 'Do you feel my knife?'

'Ah – yes. There is no cause—'

'There will not be if you do as I say. Follow me – don't tell me you don't know how. Beauceron will be behind us to make sure you do not try to slip off. Then the three of us will become better acquainted. What is there to worry about?'

In a few minutes they were in a lodging house in a low part of town. Monetto led them up a narrow twisting flight of stairs to the garret where he made his home.

'Is this really where you live?' asked Beauceron, for the room was cramped and the light indifferent under the midwinter sky.

Monetto shrugged. 'I have no taste for luxury,' he said, 'and I can keep an eye on the men. They are less inclined to dissipation if they know I am on hand.'

The third man stood smirking in the doorway. The room was not large enough to accommodate three in comfort.

'You, inside,' said Beauceron. 'Who are you?'

The man sat down in the least worn of the three chairs.

'My name is Nissac,' he said. 'I would have volunteered as much without this charade.'

'I intend some more searching questions,' said Beauceron. 'Monetto, do you keep rope?'

'Enough,' replied Monetto.

'Whatever purpose you have for rope, it will not be necessary,' said Nissac. 'I merely wish to make a proposition.'

Monetto added a log to the fire. 'You have an unconventional way of transacting your business,' he said.

Nissac crossed his legs. 'I felt it necessary to understand the circumstances, given the delicate nature of my commission,' he said. 'Rash conduct impresses no one.'

'You have not begun well,' said Beauceron, leaning against the wall. 'Already I am unfavourably impressed with your pertness and your smart manners.'

'Maybe you will be more impressed when you hear what I have to offer,' he said. 'You, Monetto, do you keep beer? I am somewhat thirsty.'

Beauceron stepped forward and smacked Nissac around the ears. 'Monetto, bind this insolent clown.'

Monetto made rapid work of the knots. Nissac struggled against the ropes and let out an oath.

'Now,' said Beauceron, 'we shall hear your "proposition".'

'You treat me with little dignity. I am attached to the court of King Tardolio,' he said, 'although like yourself I hail from Emmen.'

'You know nothing of my origins, poltroon.'

'Very well,' said Nissac. 'I will be blunt, since it seems questions of etiquette are wasted on you. His Puissance King Tardolio is interested in your planned assault on Croad. He wishes to discuss the matter with you.'

Beauceron laughed. 'Tardolio has failed once in such an undertaking. I hear nothing to suggest he intends to repeat the attempt.'

'If you will forgive me, you are a peerless commander in the field, but a plain man. The workings of the royal mind must always be mysterious to you.'

'I understand that Tardolio no longer wishes to take Croad. The business of garrisoning it bores him, and he does not wish to defend a siege of Mettingloom should Enguerran venture north. Do you tell me this has changed?'

Nissac's eyes gleamed. 'Exactly so. His defeat last time he ventured south still rankles. It is well for the Winter King to sit within his walls and look to defence of the city, but the Sun King needs to display boldness and enterprise. He thinks Lord Oricien weak, and wishes to try him in the field. Can you not see yourself as one of King Tardolio's mighty war captains, leading a company of proud knights? Will you not at least talk to King Tardolio?'

Beauceron paused. 'I am always at liberty to attend to His Puissance's pleasure. However, I would not wish to waste his time or mine discussing the topic you suggest. I am King Fanrolio's bannerman, and such a discussion would be in contravention of my allegiance.'

Nissac swallowed. 'Will you not at least consider it? Think of the advantages of starting your assault in the summer and interdicting Oricien's harvest. How much more convenient than leaving before the flowers bloom to avoid Tardolio's ban – and that is in the unlikely event that Fanrolio allows the invasion to proceed.'

Beauceron stepped away from the wall and stood to his full height. He looked down into Nissac's face.

'Monetto, untie Nissac. He is free to return to Tardolio's palace.'

Nissac rubbed at his wrists after Monetto had untied him. He stood to face Beauceron. 'What am I to say to King Tardolio?'

Beauceron smiled. 'What you always intended to say: nothing. You may proceed directly to Davanzato and tell him I am insulted by this farce. Did he think to convince me with a reed such as you?'

Nissac coloured. 'You – things are not as you suggest. I am Tardolio's man. I have never met Under-Chamberlain Davanzato.'

'Since you believe me a fellow countryman, take my advice. A career as an intelligencer is not for you. If Tardolio finds out your game, you will not outlive the night: and I intend to write to Tardolio this evening, unless you have anything to say which will change my mind.'

Nissac drooped. 'Matters are as you suggest,' he said. 'Davanzato approached me through an intermediary, offering a good sum of money to establish whether you would consider treating with Tardolio.'

'A vindictive man would tell not only Tardolio but Davanzato of your duplicity and ineptitude: it would be interesting to see which of them dealt with you first. Despite popular belief, I am no such man. Make your report to Davanzato in whatever way you see fit, but be sure never to cross my path again. I will not be so forbearing next time.'

7

Beauceron sat with Monetto nursing a mug of indifferent beer in a shabby tavern near Monetto's lodgings. A few poxed doxies sat around in the shadows where their imperfections would be less manifest. Beauceron ignored any attempt to catch his eye.

'Events are not going to plan,' he said. 'Essentially I have made no progress since we returned.'

Monetto stared into his mug. 'Did you expect facile success? We might have expected Davanzato to be implacable.'

'Davanzato is a pragmatist, and avaricious. It is a question of balancing his advantages and helping him to see that the invasion is in his interests. His opposition is factitious.'

'You think he is not opposed to the invasion?' asked Monetto.

'He would prefer it not to happen, since it can only upset the equilibrium from which he profits; but it is a front to induce me to offer him a larger bribe.'

'It was perhaps a mistake to give him the ladies so early.'

Beauceron shrugged and drained his mug. 'More beer!' he called. 'The strategy was not flawed,' he said. 'A rapid and unexpected access of cash could only have ensured his good will, and maintaining the ladies at my expense was something I wished to avoid. I could not have foreseen that neither Sprang nor Oricien would pay Isola's ransom.'

'What will happen to them?'

'I cannot say,' said Beauceron. 'Cosetta is proving resourceful. She seems to be planning to stay here.'

'And Isola?'

Beauceron shook his head. 'She is not dealing with captivity well. If I am honest, I have come to regret kidnapping her. It has brought me no benefit and undeserved woe on the lady.'

Monetto grinned. 'Does your regret extend to furnishing her ransom yourself? The figure is set at 45,000 florins, and no doubt Fanrolio is open to offers.'

Beauceron sipped at his beer. 'My regret is perhaps more abstract than you suggest. After my expenses, I cleared only 50,000 florins from the summer's campaigning, and I need that to finance Croad. The quixotic gesture you propose is impractical.'

'I merely outlined a possibility,' said Monetto. 'I wished to test the tenor of your "regret".'

Beauceron laughed. 'You have done so with skill and economy.'

'As much as anything, you are punishing her for not being Siedra.'

Beauceron was silent for a moment. 'I admit when we captured the stout-coach, it seemed it could only have been Siedra inside: the Croad standard flying above it, our intelligence that she was travelling back to the city. It all added up.'

'The evidence was only circumstantial,' said Monetto. 'You allowed your emotions to colour your judgement. It is not Isola's fault she was not Siedra.'

With a grimace, Beauceron said: 'You are right, of course. But she represented ready money, both in her person and her dowry. Next time, it will be Siedra. When we take Croad, she will be there along with Oricien. It will be sweeter to encounter them together as Oricien makes his surrender.'

'That is some way in the future. We are not yet sure of leaving Mettingloom at all.'

'Virnesto suggested that the way to deal with Davanzato is to play on his fear. That strategy I have not yet explored, but he is not as invulnerable as he likes to think.'

Monetto sat back in his seat and swallowed the last of his beer. 'You need to consider why you are doing this, and whether you still need to.'

Beauceron did not move, but his eyes swung to Monetto's face. 'Are you suggesting I give up the assault on Croad?'

'I am suggesting that you ask yourself whether you will benefit from it.'

'That you of all people should ask it . . . you were there. You know why I have to do this.'

'No. I know why you want to. The only compulsion comes from within you.'

'Think of it as seeking Harmony.'

'I cannot imagine that you do. And even if you do, the obvious path is not always the Way. Consider, you are a wealthy man: there can be few wealthier captains in Mettingloom than you. You could buy an estate shoreside if you wished. You could even go to Garganet or Gammerling if you chose not to stay here.'

Beauceron shook his head. 'I thought you understood. How can there be rest for me, knowing that I have left undone my duty of vengeance? They took everything from me.'

'Did they? You have more now, however you measure it, than you could have expected if you had stayed where you were.'

Beauceron looked into Monetto's face. 'They took much which was mine by right. I will not rest until I have restitution or vengeance.'

'Restitution is hardly possible.'

'Then vengeance it must be.'

8

During the winter, Davanzato lived at the Occonero, and he had little occasion to venture out from its comfort and security. Nonetheless, he sometimes found it necessary to transact business he did not care to delegate, and it was at such a moment that Beauceron intercepted him. The afternoon was chill and Davanzato picked his way along the aquavia with care. Beauceron moved with a silkier precision.

'Good afternoon, Davanzato! A pleasant surprise.'

Davanzato looked out from under his muffler. 'Beauceron,' he said without enthusiasm. 'Pressing matters of state do not allow me to dally, if you will excuse me.'

'Step in out of the cold a moment. The wind is icy today – it is whipping down from Niente and unless we run to the extravagance of battlecat cloaks nothing will keep it out. Look, here is an inn.'

Davanzato scowled at Beauceron. 'I do not have time for your nonsense. No doubt you wish me to update you on your audience with Fanrolio. I will save you the inconvenience: there is no progress to date. If you wish to discuss the matter further, make an appointment to see me as anyone else would.'

Beauceron raised his hands in denial. 'I was not intending so crude an inquiry. I merely wished a few moments of your time, and ideally not in the street. By the way, your friend Nissac sends his regards.'

'Very well, if I must,' said Davanzato after a pause. 'I hope you will not detain me too long. I have more business to attend to.'

'Let us hope that Chamberlain Osvergario is back on his feet soon,' said Beauceron.

They stepped inside the inn – a gloomy space where both furniture and clientele mouldered the winter away – to be met by a fug of heat from the hearth. Beauceron held up his hand for two glasses of langensnap.

'How are Isola and Cosetta?' asked Beauceron as they waited for the drinks to arrive.

'I cannot imagine this is why you diverted me from state business.'

'It takes time to savour a glass of langensnap. A little conversation avoids awkward silences.'

'Frankly, the ladies are the bane of my existence. Cosetta has moved out of the Occonero altogether, taking expensive apartments on the Metropolia. Isola plagues me every day for news of her ransom, and holds me responsible for its delay – as if I could influence her father. You may have observed that for all her graceful carriage she nurtures a shrewish disposition.'

'Cosetta's apartment is no burden to you; I understand Prince Brissio pays the lease.'

'How do you know that?'

'She told me herself. Do not try to invoke sympathy for your expenses, at least as far as Cosetta goes.'

Davanzato said, 'I may inadvertently have misled you. My real vexation is that Brissio becomes involved in my affairs at all, since he now takes an interest in Cosetta. I would not have expected a lady of Sey to be such a trollop.'

'Cosetta assures me nothing improper has occurred.'

'And you believe her?' said Davanzato with a raised eyebrow. 'I took you for a man of sceptical temperament.'

'I found her reasoning compelling, although I will not share it with you, since you are so oppressed by business. I have more sympathy with you in the matter of Lady Isola.'

'I begin to doubt that her ransom will be forthcoming. Fanrolio will not lower himself to bargain with Sprang or Oricien, so she remains in my charge, at my expense, indefinitely. This gift from you has not proved bountiful.'

A surly pot-girl appeared and set the crude glasses down with a thud. Beauceron sent her away with a scowl and no gratuity.

'It was well-intentioned,' said Beauceron. 'However, since the favour I expected has not been forthcoming, I see a certain justice in the situation.'

Davanzato said nothing as he sipped his langensnap. 'I thought you were not going to press me for news of my progress. It is not simply a matter of arranging an audience with His Puissance, which would be the work of minutes. The delicacy lies in ensuring the King takes an appropriate view of your proposals,' he said. 'There is little point in an audience which leads to the rejection of your schemes.'

'I do not intend to press you,' said Beauceron cheerfully. 'You will tell me whatever you see fit. I will merely outline my views. I spent an afternoon with Nissac yesterday, for reasons you understand. I was inconvenienced and irritated by the matter; and the episode justifiably led me to question your motives and intentions. When I consider that no audience, nor even a hint of one, with King Fanrolio has been forthcoming, can you wonder why I question whether my approach has been the correct one? I have treated you with good faith and generosity, but my seeds have not borne fruit. Perhaps it is time for me to consider another method.'

'You interest me. Perhaps you intend to storm the Occonero with your band of brigands; maybe you will make smoke signals from a wherry; conceivably you will take the risk of approaching King Tardolio. Maybe you will even set up an outcry at the Midwinter Ball. Please keep me apprised of any progress you may make.'

'None of these tactics was in my mind. I thought rather to convince you that the balance of advantage to yourself lay in facilitating the audience. The farmer who owns a stubborn gallumpher first tries to persuade it with a carrot; if the beast is still intractable, he belabours it with a stick. Both farmer and gallumpher prefer the carrot, but on occasion the stick remains necessary.'

'I hope you are not characterizing me as a farm gallumpher.'

'I merely used a metaphor which from a certain angle

bears some resemblance to our own transaction. You are no more a farm animal than I am a farmer.'

'In that case your meaning escapes me.'

'It is simply this. I have expended effort and money in securing your good will. To date both appear to have been wasted. I am known as the Dog of the North for a reason: I have a justified reputation for harsh and bloody violence. I would not wish you to learn why, but equally I do not wish to forgo my audience with the King.'

Davanzato calmly finished his langensnap and stood up. 'I am disappointed that you think me not only craven but a fool. I would only be cowed by your threats if I were of a nervous disposition and giddy enough to think you would carry them out. Since my only use to you is as a live and func-tioning Under-Chamberlain, I may yet sleep easily in my bed. Good afternoon to you, Beauceron.'

He wrapped his cloak around his shoulders and pushed open the tavern door to allow entry to a gust of icy air. Beauceron looked after him and beckoned the pot-girl for another glass of langensnap.

6

Croad

I

As Arren reached the top of the stairs, he heard a sound like an intake of breath, suddenly choked off. Could there be someone up here? In the dark, concealment would not be difficult. The first chamber he looked into was empty. His foot creaked on the floorboard as he moved towards the second. He pushed open the door. Moonlight struggled through the grimed windowpane. On the bed, curiously contorted, lay Eilla.

'Look out!' she cried, and Arren was aware of a movement to the side of him. From behind the door an arm reached out and buffeted Arren on the head. He staggered even as he threw himself to the side.

'What—' he began, before a kick snapped into his kneecap. He turned awkwardly to face his assailant. In the moonlight he caught the glimmer of a knife blade.

'Enough, young wolf,' said the figure. Arren recognized the voice. It was the vintner Foulque, the owner of the house.

'Foulque? What is going on?'

'I might ask you what you are doing in my house.'

'Why is Eilla on your bed?'

'Ha ha! Are you so innocent?'

Arren grimaced. Foulque was corpulent and not enamoured of washing.

'Arren! He was trying to force me!' called Eilla from the bed. 'He hurt my stomach.'

Arren stepped closer to Foulque, heedless of the knife. 'Tell me what has happened here,' he said. 'You cannot frighten me with talk of trespass.'

Foulque shrugged. His face glistened with a patina of sweat. 'The girl thought to use my house. I was happy for her to do so, if she paid an appropriate fee.'

'Have you hurt her, you fat dungsack?'

'There's no call for that, just because Thaume has taken you from that slattern of a mother.'

'I think we shall all go to the guardhouse, and let them decide what to make of events. Lord Thaume's penalty for rape is gelding or the rope, depending on his humour. Which is your preference?'

'There's no need for that, lad. It's late. Get back to your bed. If the wench wants to come with you, she can.'

Arren tensed his shoulders. 'After what you have tried to do, you suggest we simply forget the matter?'

Foulque leered and moved between Arren and the door.

'I have the knife. You appear unarmed. Now, run along, before we discuss gelding once more.'

Arren turned away, his arms outstretched.

'Arren!' shouted Eilla. 'No!' as Foulque swung the knife at his back.

But Arren was ready. He ducked under the blow he had invited and punched hard into Foulque's ample gut. Foulque gasped but continued to move towards Arren. With his knife arm Foulque struck at Arren's back, but Arren twisted away. Foulque stood panting as Arren skipped back out of range. He knew he was faster and nimbler than the vintner, but Foulque was strong and heavy – and armed.

'Eilla!' he called. 'Get out – go to the guardhouse.'

Eilla slipped from the bed, crouching in obvious discomfort. Foulque stepped towards her, and reached to grab her neck with his free hand. Arren slipped under the knife arm as Eilla brought her knee up into his groin.

Foulque let out a surprisingly high-pitched cry as he buffeted Eilla's head. She fell stunned to the floor, but Arren was inside the sweep of the knife. This time he hacked at Foulque's fleshy neck with the side of his hand; as the vintner recoiled Arren brought the heel of his hand up into the base of Foulque's nose with all his force. Foulque fell back, blood and mucus bubbling. His head smacked against the bed pillar and he fell to the floor. Arren stamped on his wrist, which gave a satisfying *crack!*, and knelt on Foulque's neck. The knife fell from nerveless fingers to lie on the floor.

Eilla had dragged herself to a sitting position. Arren looked across at her and put his full weight on his knee. Foulque thrashed and croaked. His eyes bulged and his cheeks took on a purple flush.

'Arren, no,' said Eilla, putting a hand on his shoulder. 'Don't kill him.'

'Why not?' hissed Arren. 'Thaume will.'

'Then let Thaume's justice act for us all. There is no need for vengeance. He didn't – you arrived just in time.'

Arren relaxed his pressure on Foulque's neck. 'Can you run to the guardhouse? My father is on duty tonight.'

Eilla nodded.

'Good,' said Arren. 'We shall have Lord Thaume's justice tomorrow. Do you hear me, Foulque? We shall have Lord Thaume's justice. May it be more merciful than mine would be.'

Foulque disdained to reply; or perhaps did not yet command the power of speech. In any event he kept his thoughts to himself.

At sunrise the next morning Lord Thaume was roused from his bed to sit in judgement on the merchant Foulque. He convened an immediate court in the marketplace. If Foulque was not of a sanguine disposition, the immediate proximity of the gallows would be sure to give him pause for thought. The low morning sun struggled through the low cloud with a grey lassitude and cast grotesquely exaggerated shadows.

The square rapidly filled with city folk. Foulque was not popular for his haughty ways or the price of his wines.

His hands were bound and a tether around his neck was held by Darrien. His nose was swollen and askew, both eyes black. His right hand hung within the tether. Lord Thaume sat in his black robes, behind an oak table brought from the castle for the purpose and set on a platform. To one side sat Lady Jilka, to the other Viator Sleech.

'Foulque,' he said. 'I am the true lord of this city, and in that capacity I sit in judgement. I may if needful call upon the counsel of my wife and the Way. Do you recognize my authority?'

Foulque bowed his head. 'I do, my lord,' he said in a scratchy voice.

'Good,' said Lord Thaume briskly. 'You stand accused of attempting to rape Eilla, the daughter of mason Jandille, as attested by Eilla herself, and Arren, the son of Darrien. In addition you are held to have assaulted Arren with a knife with purpose malign. Do you declare your guilt?'

Foulque pushed his head forward. 'I do not, my lord. Both were trespassing in my house, and looking to sequester my goods.'

'Eilla? Arren? Do you have anything to say to this?'

Arren stepped forward to stand before the platform.

'Foulque lies, my lord. Eilla and I were accustomed to meet in the house, which lay empty. We were friends before I came into your household, and thought to keep in touch.'

'Then why did you not come the last time, or the time before that?' asked Foulque. 'Eilla remained in the house by herself, seeking to inventory my goods. Last night you were on hand to remove the items, until thwarted by my vigilance. I regret only that I did not bring the matter to your attention sooner, my lord.'

Lord Thaume frowned at Foulque. 'You were aware of Eilla's presence on previous weeks, and yet you did nothing?'

Foulque licked his lips. 'I was unaware of her purpose until she arrived with Arren last night. It was only by my intervention that a great theft was averted.'

'Your story is implausible in several aspects,' said Lord Thaume. 'First, Arren has learned combat at the side of Sir Langlan. If he had wished to incapacitate you and remove your goods, he would have found no difficulty in doing so. Instead, he chose to inform my guards. Second, you are notorious for demanding the intercession of my guards at the slightest provocation: it is not conceivable that you would have lain in wait to settle this matter yourself without inviting my guards to be on hand. Third, my wife has examined Eilla's injuries. They are of a personal nature, and are not consistent with any account you have given of the event. Do you have any observations before I render my judgement?'

'What of Arren and Eilla? By their own account they are guilty of trespass.'

Lord Thaume nodded. 'True. Arren, I fine you ten florins; Eilla, five. These sums are to be paid to Foulque within the week.'

'But—' began Arren.

'Enough,' said Lord Thaume. 'Now we move to Foulque. You are manifestly guilty of the crime. These are times of war, and I do not have the leisure or the inclination for a protracted legal process. There are but two penalties for rape, or its attempt: gelding and the gallows. If anyone wishes to argue for one penalty or the other, now is the time to do so.'

Foulque spoke up, his face ashen. 'I reject and object most strongly to either sentence.'

'I anticipated such an objection,' said Lord Thaume. 'Naturally I discountenance it. Eilla, you are the victim of this offence. Do you ask for clemency?'

Eilla, prim in her best white dress, looked at Lord Thaume with dumbstruck fascination. Silent tears ran down her cheeks.

'My lord,' said Lady Jilka. 'Foulque is regular in his attendance at the Viatory and in his alms. He has no previous history of such acts.'

Lord Thaume shot his wife a look of incomprehension. 'His religious beliefs magnify rather than ameliorate his offence. He might have been expected to adhere more strongly to the Way as a result, and his conduct cannot possibly be seen in that light. As to his previous history, since the penalty for rape is death or gelding, it is hard to imagine how a repeat offence might occur.'

Foulque looked around, but no one met his eye.

'In addition,' continued Lord Thaume, 'the age and virginity of the victim weigh heavily against you.'

'Virginity!' croaked Foulque. 'That one is no virgin!'

Lord Thaume looked at him through narrowed eyes. 'If I had any doubts as to your fate, they would now be at an end. You shall die on the tree, as soon the noose can be affixed. I myself shall haul upon the rope. Do you have any final statement?'

Foulque looked back at Lord Thaume in silence. From his throat came a choking sound.

'No? Viator Sleech, perhaps you would care to address the crowd while Darrien attends to the noose.'

Sleech rose from his seat beside Lord Thaume.

'I am often asked at such times,' he said in his soft querulous voice, 'how the First Doctrine can be held to be true in these circumstances. It tells us that all human life tends towards Harmony, and yet a man is to be hanged for a most heinous crime. How, then, can Foulque's life be seen moving towards Harmony?'

Foulque, struggling as Darrien's men attempted to slip the noose over his neck, appeared uninterested in this ontological nicety.

'The answer, of course,' continued Sleech, picking at the hem of his robe, 'is that even at this last moment, Foulque may become conscious of his errors, and achieve one final moment of Harmony. Indeed this may be seen as the purest journey to Harmony of all.'

Sleech paused expectantly and looked down at Foulque. The hint was lost, however, and Foulque did not evince a sudden access of Harmony. Sleech cleared his throat and continued.

'In most cases,' he said, 'this desired event does not happen. What is proved, instead, is that we are all lost without the intercession of the viators. The man who not only attends the Viatory, but listens to the viator, will find the Way of Harmony greatly smoothed. If two farmers are bringing their wagons to market, which arrives sooner? The one who must drag his cart through the mud of the North Road, or who glides across the smooth South Road? So it is with the Way of Harmony. Foulque may not achieve Harmony himself, but his example, if it brings one more of you to the Viatory, nonetheless supports the First Doctrine by bringing other lives to Harmony.'

Sleech nodded in satisfaction and sat down. After a pause, Lady Jilka responded: 'Well said, sir,' and applauded politely.

Meanwhile Foulque was dragged up the steps – no easy task in view of his bulk – with the noose around his neck. Lord Thaume, Darrien and several of the guards pulled with coordinated vigour on the rope, and Foulque was hauled aloft. The opportunity to offer any response to Sleech's conclusions was for ever lost.

Lord Thaume stepped down from the platform and walked over to Arren and Eilla. 'This is a disagreeable affair,' he said. 'Arren, your conduct has been foolish and you are fortunate matters have ended so well. If you wish to say your farewells to Eilla you must do so this afternoon. Tomorrow we march north.'

3

Arren led Eilla back to Lord Thaume's castle and they slipped into the Pleasaunce, the cultivated wilderness abutting the West Walls which was enclosed and reserved for the use of Lord Thaume and his family. Eilla was silent during the walk and Arren was disinclined to break her reverie.

Inside the Pleasaunce she began to show a little more animation. 'I like it here,' she said with a weak smile.

Arren sat with his back against an oak tree. 'In truth, only Lord Thaume's family are entitled to enjoy it. Strictly speaking that excludes the pair of us.'

Eilla sat on the ground beside him, her arms holding her knees against her chest. She grinned with something like her old spirit. 'I have been in here many times: the walls are not maintained as they should be.'

Arren looked at her. 'Had I known your negligence of status we could have met here throughout.'

Eilla's smile vanished. 'Much would have been avoided had we done so.'

'The events are behind us now. I must of necessity look ahead, and you should do so too.'

'Is it so easy to dismiss the death of a man?'

'Surely you have no sympathy for Foulque? Lord Thaume would not have hanged him so swiftly if he had not been convinced of his evil.'

Eilla thought a moment. Her dark eyes searched the ground for answers. 'No. But I should have. He died through my testimony. I don't feel guilty that he died – but I should, shouldn't I?'

'You know I would have killed him last night, without a pang.'

She turned her eyes to his face. 'You are trained for war. You cannot afford scruples. But that does not stop me questioning my own conduct.'

'That is what comes of following the Wheel,' said Arren with a half-smile. 'If you followed the Way, the viators would tell you to forget the matter. The Wheel's emphasis on introspection is unhelpful.'

Eilla did not smile. 'We do follow the Way, Arren. We just follow it in our own fashion. I had no idea you were become the theologian.'

Now Arren laughed. 'Never think it! Sleech is a tedious canting hypocrite, and I have no more intention of modelling my conduct on his precepts than on Sir Langlan's – rather less, in fact, since Sir Langlan at least derives some pleasure from his vices. But the Way is here to make our lives easier, so why torture yourself with conscience?'

Eilla lay back on the grass and looked up to the sky. 'I do not devote great attention to the matter,' she said. 'But it is difficult to look on last night with equanimity.'

'The matter is simple,' said Arren. 'Foulque attempted an

outrage. In this Lord Thaume agreed, and dispensed field justice.'

She stretched out and rolled on her side to look at Arren. 'No doubt you are right. And I have never thanked you for saving me.'

Arren shrugged. 'The circumstances left me little choice. I could hardly leave Foulque to work his will.'

'But he had a knife.'

'And not the faintest concept of how to use it. For three years I have learned every kind of chivalrous combat, and several less honourable. If he had killed me I would have deserved it.'

'I thought you were not coming,' she said in a quiet voice. 'You were so late, and you had not come the weeks before.'

Arren looked into her eyes. 'Did you come every week?'

'Of course. I had said that I would.'

'But we quarrelled last time.'

'I quarrel with Clottie every day. We have been friends for so long, Arren, in a sense we are like brother and sister. Quarrels will never change that.'

Arren thought for a moment. 'Brother and sister?'

'Well, in a sense. I cannot believe you are going tomorrow,' she said. 'Look at the buds on the trees. They are nearly in bloom, but by the time they flower, you will be marching north under Lord Thaume's banner. Are you afraid?'

'Afraid! Tardolio shows great presumption in bringing his host south. He must be chastised.'

'I did not ask whether it was right to defend Croad against Tardolio – how could it be otherwise? I asked about your feelings.'

Arren was puzzled. 'I have no choice in the matter. If I trouble to think, I am conscious only of eagerness to begin. I should like to be back in the city for the Midsummer Fair.'

Eilla reached out and took his hand. 'Be careful, Arren.

This is not a game. We are not playing at raiders now. These are real raiders with real swords.'

'It is the raiders who should beware,' said Arren with a confidence he did not think to examine.

'I must go,' she said. 'My father will want to be assured that I am unhurt.' She skipped to her feet and kissed him fleetingly on the cheek. Arren watched her as the sunlight dappled her dress and she dwindled into the distance.

I might never see you again, he thought, wondering as he did so where the notion had come from.

4

The sun was barely up the next morning when Lord Thaume rode out of Croad at the head of his army. He was flanked on one side by his cousin Sir Artingaume, on the other by Oricien. Arren marched some way back in Sir Artingaume's company, with Guigot alongside him. Oricien would rejoin the company once they were out of sight of the city.

As they marched out through the North Gate, Arren looked back over his shoulder. The walls were packed with folk watching them on their way. Lady Jilka, wearing Lord Thaume's scarlet ceremonial robe to indicate her regency, sat on her strider looking impassively ahead. Beside her were Master Guiles and Lady Cerisa. Arren's eyes were drawn to the path atop the city walls: he saw standing alone on a tower Eilla's figure watching the troops as they marched out of the gate.

The army was not as large as Lord Thaume had hoped. Duke Panarre had sent no troops from Glount, and he had been forced to leave before his additional request had even reached King Arren at Emmen. Nonetheless, to Arren's eyes the force looked as grand and glorious a host as had ever been assembled. The cavalry rode in martial formation at the front of the column, both riders and gallumphers gaily arrayed in canary-yellow surcoats. The yellow and blue banner of Croad rode at the front of all, and as the sun came up it reflected off the knights' helmets. Who could stand against such a force?

By the time the army stopped for lunch, some eleven miles further on, Arren was not so convinced of the glory of warfare. His new boots pinched his feet abominably, and the city of Croad was not yet out of view. His mail felt heavier than he expected and chafed against his shoulders, despite the cotton undershirt Ierwen had given him.

Oricien, now back with his squadron and on foot, chewed his bread with deliberation. If he was feeling qualms, he kept them to himself. Guigot, meanwhile, evinced a sunny good humour. Arren had never seen Guigot light-hearted before, but he seemed in no way discommoded by the distance they had covered or the discomfort of their equipment.

'Eat up, Arren!' he said. 'Tardolio will never be vanquished on an empty stomach. I aim to ensure my strength is at its maximum when the raiders come in view.'

The lads had been assigned to the care of Serjeant Fleuraume, a wiry veteran of many campaigns. He did not interpret his duties as including excessive deference to his charges.

'Guigot is right, lads,' he said. 'An army marches on its stomach, and this is where we have the advantage over Tardolio. He has brought his army by ship as far as Hengis Port, and then disembarked them on Jehan's Steppe. He cannot hope to keep them fed in the way that we can, for we can send food up from Croad whenever we choose.'

'Why then, in that case,' asked Arren, 'do we not have more appetizing victuals?'

'If it was fine foods you wanted, you could have stayed behind with Lady Jilka,' said Fleuraume. 'You will find little pampering on the battlefield.'

'Viator Sleech eats well enough,' said Oricien. 'I do not notice Master Pinch stinting himself, and even Master Coppercake appeared to be tucking into a roast fowl when I walked past.'

Fleuraume shook his head wryly. 'You have much to learn, lord's son or not. Coppercake is quartermaster for the duration of our campaign; you must expect him to divert the best food for himself. And Sleech is a viator – have you ever seen one of them go hungry? He says he must keep up his strength for when he Finds the Way with the soldiers who call at his coach. Pinch simply finds himself in the right place at the right time, since he travels in the following stout-coach.'

Oricien frowned. 'This is not right. Sleech, Coppercake and Pinch do not fight, but they eat the best food. And yet we must throw our bodies before the enemy on a diet of bread and cheese.'

Fleuraume grinned. 'That is the first rule of army life: the less a man contributes to the fray, the more he eats. You must get used to it.'

5

By the time the army camped at nightfall Arren was ready for immediate sleep, but Fleuraume had assigned him cook's duties. Two men from the squadron – farmers in normal life – had caught rabbits, and Arren superintended a stew bulked with potatoes issued by Coppercake. After supper Lord Thaume summoned them to his own tent. Outside on the ground sat the lord with his war captains, arrayed around the fire. The featureless steppe stretched away in all directions, both Croad and Tardolio's army lost in the magnificent emptiness.

'Now we are away from Croad we can think with a clear head,' said Lord Thaume. 'Pinch, are you able to divine the whereabouts of Tardolio's force?'

Pinch looked into the fire as if he had not heard, but eventually he said: 'I have conjured a dimonetto of the least potent sort to scour the countryside. My powers are weak on such matters, but I have compelled it to a kind of truth. The dimonetto tells me that the host is to the north—'

'That is scarcely news,' said Sir Artingaume with a harsh bark of laughter. 'I should be surprised to hear they are to the south.'

'—but the Steppe is barren terrain. It is unable to tell me more precise geographical information. It can, however, estimate with exactitude the size of Tardolio's army. This news is not good, since he has about three thousand men – half as large again as our own force.'

'What of the composition of the forces? How many are cavalry?' said Sir Artingaume, running a hand through his short grey hair.

'The dimonetto conveyed no such exact information. The Unseen Dimensions are rather different to our own. The distinction between cavalry and infantry is lost upon it.'

Sir Artingaume stood, grimacing as he shook the stiffness from his legs. 'Do you still command the dimonetto?'

'It is pent within my stout-coach by magic. I may use it again tomorrow.'

'Bring it forth now, that we may interrogate it.'

Pinch shook his head. 'That would not be advisable. The being requires careful handling. I can communicate with it only with difficulty; restraining it is even more taxing.'

Sir Artingaume scowled. 'It has seen Tardolio's army.

There is much information it could provide if only the correct questions were asked.'

'If I sent a bird north to assess Tardolio's strength, would you expect interrogation to be productive? The dimonetto is no larger than a bird and probably less intelligent.'

Sir Artingaume tipped the dregs of his stew into the fire and looked down to where Pinch reclined on the ground. 'Could you not secure the services of a more useful dimon? A more intelligent and tractable being could furnish valuable information.'

'If you wish to make such an attempt, Sir Artingaume, do not allow me to stop you. I find my reserves much depleted from bringing forth this dimonetto. I could not summon a more powerful beast without oversetting my reason. In your case, the potential losses are less significant.'

Sir Artingaume eventually discerned Pinch's meaning. 'I meant no offence, although I wonder why Lord Thaume did not secure a more potent thaumaturge.'

Pinch raised his eyebrows. 'I can think of five, perhaps six, thaumaturges who could summon and control a modest dimon without destroying their minds. They would find this war at best trivial, at worst incomprehensible. I myself agreed to assist Lord Thaume largely from ennui, which reflects poorly on me.'

'Enough,' said Lord Thaume. 'We are grateful for the information you have gleaned, Master Pinch. To know the size of the enemy force is valuable knowledge. We must consider where to force battle.'

Darrien spoke up. 'In a sense the terrain is irrelevant. Jehan's Steppe is flat: there are few defensible positions. There are no hills we can defend, no rivers to put at our backs.'

'True,' said Lord Thaume. 'Can you draw any conclusions?'

'We should not push on too far. The further Tardolio must come to meet us, the more his lines are stretched, and the harder he will find it to feed his men. Conversely, the closer we remain to Croad, the more easily we can maintain our supplies.'

'If Tardolio should defeat us too near to Croad, he can advance upon the city before we can regroup,' said Sir Langlan.

Sir Artingaume gave a croak of outrage. 'Defeat! This is not credible! You must apologize to Lord Thaume on the instant!'

Sir Langlan drained his goblet. 'We are outnumbered. If we do not fight well, we lose,' he said. 'Lord Thaume would be a fool to think victory assured.'

'Sir Langlan is right, up to a point,' said Darrien. 'But if we are beaten, Croad would not fall in a day. We have supplies within the city, and our walls are strong. Unless Tardolio destroys us in a single engagement, he must besiege the city while defending his rear. I say we fortify here. We know where Tardolio is going: let us wait for him.'

Lord Thaume was silent while he thought over the views of his captains. 'Let Tardolio come to us,' he said. 'We will dig in here. Oricien, tomorrow you will learn the life of the labourer.'

6

Arren had found the discussion interesting, although he did not look forward to digging ditches on the morrow. He was more stimulated by the thought that Master Pinch had a dimonetto pent within his stout-coach. What harm could it do to take a peek? Pinch himself had characterized the being as ineffectual, but any dimonetto was better than none. What a story he would have to tell Eilla if he examined the dimonetto!

While the captains debated the best means of fortifying their surroundings, Arren slipped away into the dark. Master Pinch's stout-coach was identifiable by the lightning-bolt standard flapping feebly above it in the moonlight. Was there really a dimonetto within?

Arren noted with surprise that there were no guards outside the stout-coach. Pinch had said that the dimonetto was 'pent', whatever that meant, but this was negligent conduct.

The stout-coach had small windows set high, and Arren could not see within. Looking over his shoulder to ensure he was not observed, he clambered onto one of the wheels, which brought him closer to the window. He leaned across, one hand on the roof, and by stretching his neck was able to reach the bottom quadrant of the window.

He peered through. Nothing out of the ordinary was evident. His night-vision was good, but there was no cage, no rope, simply a plain couch, a chaise and various chests and robes. Where, then, was the dimonetto?

He pushed further on his toes against the wheel's rim to afford himself a better view. Was that a flash of movement? Stretching too far, Arren slipped and crashed to the ground, landing heavily on his elbow. He stood up and brushed the dust from his shirt. Even if he had caught a glimpse of the dimonetto, it was not enough to make a proper report to Eilla on his return. What if there were no dimonetto at all? The information it had provided could easily have been fabricated, and none of it was in any way controversial or surprising. Pinch had always stressed that most magical effects could be achieved through charlatanry, and that indeed this was usually the best course. No wonder he had seen nothing through the window, and that Pinch had been unwilling to submit the dimonetto to inspection! He liked

Master Pinch – he did not have the hypocrisy of Viator Sleech, or the arid sarcasms of Master Guiles – but nonetheless this matter should be drawn to Lord Thaume's attention.

He set off back towards the war council. Unbidden, the image of Foulque swinging from the town gallows came to his mind. Lord Thaume was on the whole a fair and just lord, but he tended towards the arbitrary in his exercise of justice. It seemed unlikely that he would hang Master Pinch, but Arren felt that he should at least verify the facts before apprising Lord Thaume.

He turned back towards the stout-coach. Pinch did not even have the door closed; instead a heavy burgundy curtain was drawn across the entrance, with a white lightning-bolt embroidered. This would hardly be likely to hinder a hypothetical dimonetto's escape, he thought.

With a deep breath he pulled back the curtain. Inside the coach all was as it had appeared through the window. The air inside seemed a little filmy, his perceptions dulled. An effect of the moonlight . . .

He stepped across the portal into the coach: he would have much to explain should Pinch return now. His eye was drawn to the chaise where Pinch presumably relaxed. Was there something underneath it? He dropped to the floor and peered into the shadow. As he looked into the gloom he heard a noise he could not identify. There was something under there! He was conscious of the rapid beating of his heart. Foolish to be afraid of a noise, which could easily come from a rodent.

Clack-clack-clack.

From under the chaise crawled – something. It was brownish in colour; it had wings; and it was about the size of a pigeon – but it was no bird. Its skin was leathery, it appeared to have at least four wings, with four legs terminating in clawed paws. The head was not unlike an eagle's, with a cruel beak and malevolent golden eyes. Perhaps Pinch was not so mendacious after all . . .

Clack-clack-clack. The noise was the scratch of the creature's claws on the wooden floor. The dimonetto advanced towards him, its eyes level with Arren's as he lay prone on the floor facing it. It looked into his eyes with an expression Arren had no hope of deciphering. He told himself this was a dimonetto of no force, less intelligent than a bird, and he had found it hiding under the chaise. It was probably more alarmed than he was. And somehow Pinch had it 'pent by magic' – perhaps the symbols on the curtain.

The dimonetto opened its beak. *Arkh! Arkh! Arkh!*

It leaped into the air, flapped its wings and skipped across Arren's back to the doorway. In no way inconvenienced by whatever method Pinch had used to bind it, it flew unsteadily out into the camp.

Arren scampered out after it. 'Come back!' he called, conscious as he did so that this was a foolish thing to say. 'Master Pinch! The dimonetto has escaped!'

The dimonetto appeared unsure what do with its new freedom. It circled above the stout-coach croaking with an unpleasant timbre. Pinch ran with a waddling gait, Lord Thaume at his back.

'What have you done, boy?' shouted Pinch. 'Have you let it out?'

'I only wanted to look,' mumbled Arren.

'Fool!' Pinch ran into his coach. The dimonetto ceased its croaking, settled to the ground and scampered under the nearest coach, which happened to be Viator Sleech's.

Pinch emerged with what looked like a crystal in his hand. '*Hnorr hnapp hnopp*,' he said, or something similar. Beads of sweat were standing out on his forehead.

'*Fnurr fnapp fnopp*. Return to your cave.'

The dimonetto appeared disinclined to leave the sanctuary of Viator Sleech's coach.

'You, Arren,' said Pinch. 'Drag it out.'

'But sir!' said Arren.

Lord Thaume said: 'You released it. You bring it back.'

Recognizing the justice of Lord Thaume's judgement, Arren dropped to the ground and crawled under the coach. The dimonetto's eyes gleamed in the darkness as it backed against the far wheel. Arren wriggled further under the coach and reached out. *Arkh!* called the dimonetto and bit Arren's hand. He cursed but managed to get his hands around it. The dimonetto was warm to the touch – in fact it was actively and uncomfortably hot.

'Pull me out!' he called, waving his feet, which protruded from underneath the coach. He felt hands grasping his ankles and he was dragged into the camp and hauled erect.

'Hold it still!' commanded Pinch.

'It's hot!'

'Of course it's hot – it's a dimonetto. Hold still!'

Arren did as he was told.

Pinch touched the crystal to the dimonetto's head. It glowed with a pulsing blue radiance. '*Avato!*' he cried. Arren felt a puckering sensation on his palms and then a sense of lightness. The dimonetto was gone.

Arren looked at Pinch, his hands throbbing. Pinch was drained of all colour, his face as white as his hair. The irises of his grey eyes were barely visible against the whites.

'We will discuss this tomorrow,' said Lord Thaume. 'Arren, you have disappointed me.'

Darrien said: 'You are my son, but Lord Thaume's subject. I hope he punishes you well.'

Arren looked at the ground.

Pinch said: 'The lad's hands will be burnt. The dimonetto carried some of the energy of the Unseen Dimensions with it.

There is a salve in my coach which is effective. See that it is applied to the burns.'

With that, Pinch crashed to the ground in a swoon. The cost of dispersing the dimonetto had been considerable.

7

The next morning Lord Thaume made his way through the mists to arrive at Arren's squadron, accompanied by Master Pinch and Sir Artingaume, who was Arren's commander. The pain from Arren's hands had ensured he passed a poor night's sleep, and he hunched disconsolately before his tent.

'Take the bandages off,' said Pinch. 'I would examine the wounds.'

Oricien unwrapped the linen. After a brief examination Pinch announced himself satisfied.

'I am sorry, Master Pinch,' said Arren. 'I was curious to see what a dimonetto looked like.'

Pinch gave a wan smile. 'You need only have asked.'

'I did not bring you to be curious,' said Lord Thaume. 'You are here to learn warfare, not thaumaturgy. I take it the dimonetto is gone, Pinch.'

Master Pinch nodded. 'I had no option but to disperse it. It would have been complex to bring it once more under control. We do not have the option of using it again today.'

Sir Artingaume shot Arren a baleful glance.

'How was the dimonetto pent, Master Pinch?' asked Arren. 'I noticed no obvious restraint, and it escaped at the first opportunity.'

'You have done enough damage with your curiosity, boy,' growled Sir Artingaume. 'Such questions suggest you have not learned your lesson.'

Guigot strolled back in from his morning visit to the

latrine trench. 'Arren is incorrigible,' he said, stretching the last of the night's sleep away. 'But I am sure we are all interested in this aspect of thaumaturgy.'

'Let the lads indulge their curiosity,' said Pinch. 'There is little enough of it about, and a spirit of inquiry is the root of all true wisdom. Lord Thaume's army would be valiant if composed of five thousand Sir Artingaumes, but his city would be the poorer as a result.'

Lord Thaume compressed his lips against a smile. 'Arren has paid a high price for his curiosity. Why should he not have the answers?'

Master Pinch paused to collect his thoughts. 'You may have noticed, Arren, that the air in the stout-coach was different in nature to that outside: thick and heavy. That is the air of the Unseen Dimension, held by a charm in my stout-coach. In entering the coach you burst the bubble, and the spell maintaining it. It allowed the dimonetto the opportunity and incentive to escape.'

'You will forgive me, Master Pinch,' said Oricien, 'but I was mindful of your lessons on thaumaturgy and misdirection. I half-suspected that the dimonetto did not exist.'

'Then Arren has, unwittingly at least, worked to my credit, since no one can now doubt its veracity. Nonetheless, I do not wish to have my integrity questioned or my stout-coach violated, and the lad must be punished.'

Arren looked quizzically at Oricien. He had shown none of his doubts last night. Events might have gone better if they had investigated the dimonetto together.

'I have already instructed Serjeant Fleuraume in Arren's punishment,' said Lord Thaume. 'Arren, it was always my intention that you should provide an intelligent counsellor for Oricien when he comes to rule, but you must develop greater judgement in when to exercise your spirit of inquiry.'

'Yes, my lord,' he said, bowing as Lord Thaume turned on his heel and went about his business.

'Arren!' called Fleuraume, 'there are many pots requiring washing. Lord Thaume tells me Pinch has salved your hands, and you will be experiencing domestic duties for a while. My own jerkin has popped a seam; once the pots are clean you will turn your attention to its repair.'

Arren's head drooped but he said nothing. The sooner the breakfast pots were begun, the sooner they were finished.

8

A dimonetto summoned for obscure purposes, flying high before the moon, would perhaps have seen little difference between the two hosts encamped below it. The press of human affairs would have interested it not at all, and it would have seen in the huddled postures around the campfires none of the fears so ineptly concealed by the men of the North and South. On Jehan's Steppe they camped; on the morrow they would meet.

Lord Thaume carried out the traditional general's task of wandering among his men throughout the night, assessing their mood and heartening them where necessary. When he returned to his tent dawn was only a couple of hours away. On impulse he got up and walked across to Serjeant Fleuraume's squadron, where there was little sleep. He sat down by the fire between Fleuraume and Oricien, where Arren and Guigot were also warming themselves.

'I remember my first battle,' said Lord Thaume. 'My father Lord Gaucelis had answered King Arren's call to chastise King Gundovald in Gammerling. We fought on the shores of Lake Vasi and we were beaten in two hours.'

'That is scarcely a promising portent, my lord,' said

Fleuraume, poking at the embers. 'Should you not be telling us of your victories?'

'The outcome of the battle is only indirectly relevant. King Arren was ill-advised to fight, and his defeat prevented a lengthy and unnecessary war. He has learned wisdom since, including the important precept "Only fight when you must." I still remember my feelings the night before the battle: like you, lads, I could not sleep. But once the battle came I was not afraid: I did not have time to be. I killed my first man, then another and another. By the end I was not counting. Our wing, which my father commanded, was not beaten. Indeed, we had almost broken through when Arren called for terms. Lord Gaucelis was a fine commander.'

'Are you telling us we should not be afraid?' asked Guigot, the fire reflecting in his eyes.

'The very opposite,' said Lord Thaume. 'I am telling you that fear is natural, and that come tomorrow morning you will find courage and not know where it has come from.'

'I am not afraid to start with,' said Guigot. 'I only anticipate the chance to show my prowess. My own father was at the Battle of Lake Vasi, and King Arren knighted him on the field.'

'If you have no fear, I envy you, Guigot, although perhaps I pity you as well. And yes, I remember Lord Borel's valour that day. His helm was dinted in the first pass, and he had a sore cut to the scalp, but no one fought better.'

'He fought better than you, my lord?' asked Guigot with a queer smile.

Lord Thaume looked at him. 'Of course, for the King knighted him.'

'I am surprised you admit it so freely, my lord.'

'My valour is my own, and I fought well that day. I do not diminish my own achievements by acknowledging Lord

Borel's. Do not forget he was my brother as well as your father.'

'I never forget it for a moment, my lord,' said Guigot with a smile that had nothing agreeable in it. He poked a stick into the fire, provoking a flurry of sparks.

'He has been dead these past thirteen years, Guigot, as has my own father. Much has happened since, and we must concentrate on our own deeds on the morrow.'

'Perhaps such a sentiment comes more easily when you have known your father, my lord.'

'Nothing can bring Lord Borel back, Guigot. Tomorrow you become a man in your own right.'

Guigot pursed his lips and nodded. 'As you say, my lord.'

'Oricien, you are quiet,' said Lord Thaume.

'I am thinking of what must come,' Oricien said, pulling his gaze away from the fire. 'Sir Langlan encourages a period of calm reflection at this time, since there is no more preparation to be done.'

'You, too, are allowed fear. Do not be fooled by Guigot's assurance. None of us has repose tonight.'

'I am not afraid, Father. How could the heir of Croad fear to defend his city?'

'The same as any other man,' said Lord Thaume. 'We all advance along the Way, and the path is dark.'

Guigot interjected: 'You will tell us Viator Sleech's homily of the Humble Tailor and the Proud Knight next.'

'Guigot, I allow you a degree of latitude tonight because we fight tomorrow, and whatever you say, no man is himself before his first battle,' said Lord Thaume softly. 'Nonetheless—' this with a touch of steel '—I am your lord and your uncle. I will not tolerate disrespect.'

Guigot said nothing.

'I myself do not attend the Viatory as much as I should, and perhaps do not give due weight to Sleech's sermons.

There are those who draw comfort from the Way at such times, and for a fact Viator Sleech's stout-coach is busy tonight. And of course there are those who would sooner hang themselves than take counsel from the viators, is that not so, Fleuraume?'

Fleuraume grinned. 'Indeed it is, my lord. I am not the only man to follow the Wheel here – I reckon fully one man in four of your army has seen the light.'

'That may be an exaggeration,' said Lord Thaume, 'but a man may choose his path along the Way as he sees fit, for he has but one life. Do not tell Viator Sleech I said so!'

Fleuraume chuckled.

'I have something to ask of you, Serjeant,' said Lord Thaume. 'Oricien, Guigot, Arren: all are well-drilled and valiant, but they cannot imagine what tomorrow will be like. I would regard it as a personal favour were you to keep an eye on them.'

'I would do the same for any new recruit, my lord.'

'And lads, the three of you must look out for each other. A man alone in battle dies in minutes, no matter how many comrades he has around him.' Lord Thaume stood. 'Arren, would you care to step aside with me a moment?'

'Yes, my lord,' said Arren, puzzled. They made their way to a secluded part of camp.

'You are not the only man whose father will be fighting alongside him tomorrow. You will not have time to worry about him, and he will not have time to worry about you.'

'No, my lord.'

'I must tell you that I have given Darrien the most dangerous assignment tomorrow. Tardolio's men clearly outnumber us, but we have a slight advantage in cavalry. I wish to make that advantage larger. Darrien will command the right wing, which will be made up mostly of pikemen. I must make that wing the weakest part of our line, because

I wish Tardolio to try to break it. If he smashes the right wing, he can attack our centre from the side. So I am tempting him to throw his cavalry against Darrien.'

Arren swallowed. It had never occurred to him that a soldier as experienced as Darrien could be endangered.

'Darrien is the man I trust the most to hold the pikemen together. If he can scatter the cavalry that Tardolio throws at him, Sir Langlan will have a clear advantage in deploying my cavalry. If the pikemen are routed, the flanks of the centre will be unprotected.'

Lord Thaume did not need to say that the centre was where Arren's squadron would be fighting.

'Sometimes a commander must give an order which puts valued comrades in grave danger. I have had to give such an order to your father. I do so because I would rather entrust our safety to Darrien than to any other man in Croad, including Sir Artingaume. Whatever happens tomorrow, remember that.'

'You think he will be killed, my lord.'

'Do not misunderstand me, Arren. Our victory tomorrow depends on the pikemen holding, and I hope Darrien will be there to lead them throughout. What I am saying is that, even if I knew he would be killed, I would still give him the order.'

'Yes, my lord.'

'Sometimes the fighting is the easy part, Arren. Fight well tomorrow.'

9

By the time the sun came up, both Thaume and Tardolio were busy deploying their forces. The steppe was flat and feature-less: there was no terrain to give advantage. Thaume's men were arrayed behind a series of ditches intended to slow

Tardolio's cavalry, but the ditches were few, since Thaume did not wish to impede the free play of his own superior riders.

Thaume had deployed his infantry in the centre of his line, under the command of Sir Artingaume. Serjeant Fleuraume's squadron, including Oricien, Guigot and Arren, was towards the front of the 'arrowhead' formation. To the right was the small group of pikemen commanded by Darrien, positioned both to tempt and to destroy Tardolio's cavalry. To the left, under Sir Langlan, was Lord Thaume's own cavalry, although Thaume himself commanded the rearguard, made up of both cavalry and infantry: these troops Lord Thaume could commit to the battle where they were most needed.

Tardolio's army comprised a sizeable block of infantry in the centre with two smaller blocks on either wing. He had split his cavalry into two squadrons separating the infantry blocks. He took a risk by splitting his cavalry, the price he paid for being able to bring at least some of his riders to bear quickly at any point on the field.

Arren's view in the infantry arrowhead was limited by the press of bodies around him. He could see the lilac and gold sunburst banners of Tardolio's forces snapping in the strong steppe winds, and the huge mass of his infantry in front of them. He was no longer conscious of the weight of his mail armour, his helmet, his longsword or his shield: he felt distanced from physical sensation altogether. It was scarcely possible to believe that battle was about to begin. He could be dead in minutes, although the thought did not seem real. Beside him Guigot stared into the distance, a grim smile on his face. Oricien, taller than either of them, peered ahead over the infantrymen in front.

Ba-da-ba-da! The sound of the horn from Tardolio's herald. Away to his right he saw infantry marching, cavalry under a pink banner trotting forward on gallumphers of enormous dimension. They were heading for Darrien's pike-men.

Ahead of him was Sir Artingaume, perched high on his own gallumpher. 'Steady now, lads!' he called. 'Patience – they'll be here soon enough.'

Arren could see the infantry breaking into a run ahead of them, charging straight for their position. One moment they seemed infinitely distant, the size of the toy soldiers he had once played with; the next they were on top of the Croad infantry, howling with possessed fury.

A man in front of him fell. Instinctively Arren raised his shield with his left arm, hacked with his right. The attacker fell to the ground; Oricien next to him put his sword through the man's neck. Another came, with no armour. Arren drove his sword through the leather jerkin and out of the man's back.

He glanced across at Guigot, who seemed paralysed, whether by indecision, fear or simple incomprehension of the scene unfolding. 'Guigot!' called Fleuraume. 'Guigot!'

Guigot seemed uncomprehending as a huge Northman surged towards him with a mace raised. Fleuraume leaped forward, flung himself and his sword under the killing stroke, and drove the sword up under the ribcage. With a grunt the Northman coughed blood, and slumped. Fleuraume with-drew his sword, smacked Guigot hard on the helmet with the hilt. 'Fight, you fool!'

Guigot shook his head to clear the blow and seemed to come alive. He charged forward into the melee, pushing Northmen away with his shield, hacking them with his sword. Arren could hear his great cries of rage even as he held off his own adversaries.

Arren could not tell how long this phase of the battle lasted. Men fell around him – Northmen and Croadasque –

but still they kept coming. *Shield – parry – slash*. So it went, time after time. *Shield – parry – slash. Shield – parry – slash*. The more Northmen fell, the more came on. Arren's yellow surcoat was soaked with blood; his eyes stung with it. Some of the blood was his, dripping from his forehead, but he could not tell how he had come by the injury.

He saw Sir Artingaume on his gallumpher charge over to the right of the infantry line. 'Cavalry! Cavalry!' he called. 'Look to the right!'

Even as Arren clattered his sword into an opponent's shield, he knew that cavalry attacking from the right was the worst outcome. Not only did it mean that the infantry was attacked on two fronts – including by cavalry, which it was not equipped to resist – but that Darrien's pikemen must have been defeated.

He heard the sound behind him of the herald's horn. 'Lord Thaume!' went up the cry. He had committed his reserve to protect the infantry's flank and fight off Tardolio's cavalry.

Sir Artingaume raised his sword above his head. 'To me! To me!' he cried as a cluster of foot soldiers gathered around him. Fleuraume beckoned his own squadron, and, tripping over the corpses and wounded, Arren made his way across the field with the Serjeant. He did not understand why they were all but turning their backs on Tardolio's infantry which had been occupying them for so long.

Thaume's cavalry met Tardolio's with a crash. Arren realized that Tardolio's was outnumbered – had Darrien inflicted heavy casualties on it? From somewhere – Arren could not tell where – went up the cry 'Sir Langlan! Sir Langlan!' The main force of the Croadasque cavalry was in action, perhaps scattering the very infantry Arren's squadron had been fighting.

Tardolio's cavalry was now in great difficulty. Thaume

was attacking it from the flank, and Artingaume's infantry was barring its way. The gallumphers could not deploy properly because of the press of infantry around them. This was a true melee.

Arren saw Sir Artingaume pulled from his gallumpher, or perhaps the beast had been killed under him. He struggled to his feet, flung himself into the press of Tardolio's infantry, then he was lost from view. A few feet away Oricien and Guigot were fighting side by side, Guigot swinging his sword with muscular relish, Oricien employing the careful footwork and swordplay Sir Langlan had drilled into them.

Arren felt a clang on his helmet. He fell stunned to the ground, but the soldier next to him drove off his assailant as he moved in for the kill. In that curious battlefield dynamic Arren had already noticed, the fighting surged away from him for no discernible reason and he was left lying alone on the ground. As he pulled himself erect he saw Oricien charging after a fleeing foe: he tripped on the boot of a wounded Croadasque and fell sprawling to the ground. The impact knocked the helmet from his head and he lay exposed. Guigot moved across instinctively. A Northman saw Oricien struggling to get up, and dashed at him, sword upraised. Guigot had ample time to interpose himself and fight the man off, but he simply stared ahead.

'No!' cried Arren, although no one could hear and he was too far away to intervene. But from nowhere Fleuraume appeared and brought the Northman crashing to the ground. Oricien pulled himself to his feet and set his helmet back on his head.

Arren looked around to see where he was most needed. Then the cry went up: 'Rout!'

Tardolio's army was fleeing. The infantry had turned tail and was running with no discipline at all back to its own lines – only to meet the wall of Sir Langlan's cavalry. By the time

Arren had caught up with the fighting, it was all over. Tardolio's herald had sounded the mournful note of surrender. His army – what was left of it – sat on the ground, its weapons lying where they fell.

Lord Thaume had won the Battle of Jehan's Steppe.

10

That evening Arren learned the full story of the battle, which, immersed as he had been in a single portion of it, he had not comprehended at the time. Tardolio had thrown a large force of cavalry and infantry against Darrien's pikemen, and although Darrien's wing was eventually forced from the field, it had inflicted merciless losses on Tardolio's men. By the time they turned their attention to Sir Artingaume's infantry in the centre, they were all but fatally weakened. Once Lord Thaume chose to lead his cavalry reserve against them, the issue was decided: Tardolio's advance force was destroyed.

At the same time Tardolio had led the main force of his infantry and the remainder of his cavalry against Sir Artingaume's centre. This was the assault in which Arren had been engaged. Sir Langlan had waited until the last moment to commit the main Croadasque cavalry, but when he did, Tardolio paid the price for splitting his own riders, for Sir Langlan annihilated the remainder of Tardolio's cavalry. Sir Langlan was then in position to attack the flanks of Tardolio's advancing infantry. This was the point at which the battle became a rout.

Tardolio himself escaped in no very gallant fashion, slipping away with his personal guard after the surrender had been sounded. Lord Thaume kept a number of high-ranking prisoners for ransom, and sent others back to Tardolio with his demands.

Casualties had been heavy on both sides. Virtually all of Tardolio's cavalry had been killed, and his infantry had fared little better. Thaume's casualties had been highest among Darrien's pikemen – although Darrien himself sustained nothing worse than a gashed neck – and Sir Artingaume's infantry. Sir Artingaume himself had fallen in the press of battle. It was a victory achieved at high price, but Thaume had achieved his goal: Tardolio's army had been destroyed utterly. It would be many years before Mettingloom had the capacity or the desire to mount a full-scale assault upon Croad.

11

Arren sat by the campfire wincing as Fleuraume stitched the wound above his eye. 'If I stitch it now, it will not scar later,' he said. 'I am sure you want to look your best for the young ladies.'

Arren tried to grin but the effort was too much for him. He had expected battle to be glorious, especially when it ended in victory. He had not had time for fear, and by any standards he knew he had acquitted himself well, so why did he feel such a pervasive gloom? His friends had all survived the battle, and not only was his father safe, but a hero too.

The death of Sir Artingaume was a shock, of course. He had fought in the forefront of the battle with his men, heartening them throughout. With his gruff manner and impatience with both ceremony and fools he had commanded respect and affection, but Arren knew his own disenchant-ment went deeper than bereavement alone.

'Serjeant, do you remember when you saved Oricien?' he asked. 'Ouch!'

'Sorry,' said Fleuraume unapologetically. 'Hold still one moment. Which occasion do you refer to?'

'At the end, when he tripped and his helmet came off.'

'Ah, yes.'

'Guigot could have saved him, but he didn't. He just stood and watched.'

With his head held still for the stitching, he could not see Fleuraume's face. Eventually Fleuraume said: 'It can be hard to tell on the battlefield. Sometimes a man's attention is elsewhere.'

'You told us to look after each other.'

Fleuraume stood back from Arren's face to examine the stitches. 'You should be careful what you say, Arren. Guigot will be an important man: do not traduce him unless you can prove it.'

'You saw what happened. So did Oricien.'

'Oricien was lying on his front. He saw nothing. Me, I just saw that one of my men needed succour.'

'You won't do anything about it?'

'What happens on the battlefield stays there. If you want me to tell Lord Thaume that Guigot tried to get Oricien killed, I won't do it. There are other interpretations of what happened.'

'Such as?'

'When you've been in the battles I've been in, you realize things are often not as they seem.'

Arren thanked Fleuraume for his attentions and wandered back over to the main camp. Guigot was explaining to anyone who would listen the range of strokes he had employed and his estimate of the number of foes he had killed. Oricien was sitting with a half-smile away to the side of the squadron. Arren went and sat beside him.

'You did well today, Oricien.'

'I survived, and I did not run away,' he said. 'But good

Sir Artingaume is dead, a man who gave brave and honest service to my father.'

'Croad is safe,' said Arren. 'Tardolio will think twice before coming back.'

Oricien gave a strained laugh. 'By the time they return, I myself may be Lord of Croad. You fought well today; I hope one day you will succeed your father as Captain of the Guard.'

'The walls of Croad are strong,' said Arren. 'If Duke Panarre had sent troops and supplies instead of fine words, we need never have left the city. When you are Lord of Croad, it is more important to have powerful friends than good troops.'

Oricien looked at him. 'That is an unorthodox view.'

'I do not claim to have originated it. I heard it first from Master Pinch, but it is good sense.'

Oricien pursed his lips. 'It is of a piece with Pinch's charlatanry. Why do magic when you can perform a sleight? Why fight when someone else can do it for you? Why summon a powerful dimon when you can use a pitiful dimonetto?'

A soft voice from behind them said: 'An interesting perspective, young Oricien.'

'Master Pinch!'

Pinch sat down beside them with an inscrutable smile.

'Your father has secured a great victory today, Oricien. Indeed, more comprehensive than he might have expected. But look around you at the corpses on the field. Look over there – they are breaking up their pikes. Do you know why?'

'No, Master Pinch.'

'There is no wood on the steppes. They are turning their pikes into firewood for Sir Artingaume's funeral pyre.'

Oricien looked at the ground.

'I would not criticize Lord Thaume in any way. He has

proven himself an excellent battlefield commander, and he inspires great loyalty in his subjects and his troops.'

'But?' asked Arren.

'He will wonder as he lies in his tent tonight whether he might have spent time in the past showing greater friendship to Duke Panarre. King Arren and Emmen are far away. Thaume is an intelligent man. He will not make the same mistake twice.'

'What do you mean?' asked Oricien.

'If I were your sister, I would be turning my attention immediately to the customs of the court of Duke Panarre at Glount. She is yet young for marriage, but not for betrothal.'

'Siedra cannot go to Glount! She is but a girl.'

'She is fifteen years old, and has already flowered, if the rumours are to be believed. I can assure you that your father will already have scrutinized the Register of Nobility.'

Oricien was pensive. 'Things are changing. Sir Artingaume dead, me a warrior, Siedra betrothed. I do not know what is to come.'

Master Pinch looked at Oricien, not unkindly. 'Human affairs are fragile, mutable. You have become a man today, Oricien. Not because you killed others on the battlefield: that was merely the press of circumstance. You are a man because you realize that things do not stay the same. To the child's mind, the world is unchanging. It is a sobering moment to learn that certainty is an illusion.'

Pinch got up and walked over to where the soldiers were building Sir Artingaume's funeral pyre. Oricien stayed staring into the fire and did not notice when Arren rose and went to look for his father.

7

Mettingloom

I

One morning Beauceron received an invitation from Cosetta to join him for lunch at her apartments, as if she were the great lady of the city and he the impecunious hostage. He admired her spirit, and sent an immediate acceptance.

He looked out of his window onto the aquavia to assess the weather. There was a brave winter sunshine, enough to light the city, if not to bring warmth. Icicles hung from the eaves of the houses across the aquavia and sparkled in the sunlight. Soon it would be spring, he thought with a frown: once King Tardolio reascended the throne, six months would be wasted until Fanrolio once again held power.

He put the thought to the back of his mind and selected an outfit appropriate to lunch at a respectable salon. His breeches were umber, fitted at the calf, his shirt a jaunty cerulean. His dark blue cloak was fringed with battlecat fur. The only elements of his outfit which did not bespeak the man about town were his supple and well-worn winter boots and the dull handle of his rapier. He remembered one young buck who had commissioned a rapier with a jewelled hilt and a blade chased with gold. It had been made by a jeweller rather than a swordsmith, and had snapped clean in two during the first pass. Beauceron, who had happened to be his opponent, had merely sliced the waistband of the young man's trousers, glad that it had not been a duel to the death: it would not have helped his reputation to have been forced to kill an unarmed man. Beauceron was sure that the dandy would never again confuse decoration and utility.

It was not a long walk to Cosetta's apartments, and Beauceron enjoyed the clear crisp conditions as he stepped along the paths and bridges leading him to his destination. He was immediately ushered into Cosetta's reception chamber.

'Lady Cosetta! You look as beautiful as ever.'

Cosetta inclined her head. 'We have an adage in Sey: "Silver tongue, iron heart." I am sure it is inapplicable here.'

'You are a tyrant, my lady, to array yourself in such finery and then disdain the compliments you must inevitably attract.'

Her dress of deep burgundy trimmed with rich orange was of the finest velvet, and revealed a wide expanse of skin around her collarbone. This was not intended – at least not primarily – to titillate: rather, a dress which exposed flesh in the winter was advertising that its wearer was affluent enough to be able to afford the warmth of a dimonetto. Prince Brissio was a generous patron – or an infatuated one.

'A woman is allowed such inconsistency,' said Cosetta, her cheeks dimpling. 'Laria, some tea please,' she called, and a young maid appeared.

'Your establishment has expanded,' said Beauceron. 'Not just a dimonetto, but a maid.'

'It is so difficult to entertain without someone like Laria to help me,' she said. 'And Brissio recognizes that a woman brought up in Sey has little tolerance for this cold. A dimonetto is a necessity.'

Beauceron walked over to the hearth where the dimonetto sat, tangible heat issuing through the wrought vents.

'I have always been tempted to take the apparatus apart,' said Beauceron, 'to see if there really is a dimonetto within. It would be an expensive experiment to buy my own, and I have never dared make the attempt at the Occonero.'

'So you propose to dismantle my dimonetto?' said Cosetta. 'Quite aside from how I should explain matters to Prince Brissio, I value the warmth. Your curiosity must wait for another day. Besides, if there is not a dimonetto inside, from where does the heat arrive?'

Beauceron nodded at the justice of the observation. 'I am at a loss for any more compelling explanation. They say that the dimonettoes are unwilling to come forth from the Unseen Dimensions.'

'Naturally,' said Cosetta with a hint of sharpness. 'Which of us likes captivity?'

Beauceron contented himself with a half-smile.

Cosetta continued. 'My wonder has always been reserved for the thaumaturges who summon the dimonettoes. To have such power, and to use it for such a trivial purpose.'

'My understanding is that the difficulty of summoning dimons increases proportionately to their size. The thaumaturge who can call forth a dimonetto suitable for furnishing domestic heat commands no great power; he may enjoy the acclaim that comes from mastering such a glamorous skill.'

'I had no idea you were so learned in thaumaturgy, Beauceron. I am coming to think you are not the rude brigand of Isola's invective. Next time Fanrolio decrees a summoning, perhaps we shall attend together.'

Beauceron sipped at the tea Laria had brought. 'In my position I find it helpful to cultivate an air of mystery. If you wish to consider me a great scholar – perhaps even a clandestine thaumaturge – in secret, it does me no harm for you to do so.'

'Your lieutenant is called Monetto. I take it that the name is assumed,' said Cosetta as she sipped her own tea.

Beauceron laughed. 'Of course. There is no great wit to it – it is simply the result of his red hair: it's short for "dimonetto". He did not choose the name; it was bestowed upon him.'

'By you?'

'No, indeed. He once served another captain. "Brigands", as you characterize them, are fluid in their allegiances.'

'I take it that all men, when they come north from the Emmenrule or Garganet or Gammerling, take a new name.'

'It is not obligatory, but it is customary. Most such folk are driven north unwillingly, and have reason to begin anew. Some have more sinister reasons for concealing their identities.'

Cosetta set her cup down. 'What of the name Beauceron?'

'It is not the name I came north with. In the old language of Mettingloom it means literally "Dog of the North".'

'I wonder at your real identity. When you wish, you display a certain refinement.'

'If I use a name I was not born with, there is a reason,' said Beauceron. 'Naturally I do not intend to hark back to the past now.'

'Your obsession with Croad is not the attitude of a man who thinks only of the future.'

'We all have our dreams, Lady Cosetta. It would be impertinent of me to grub yours out in conversation, and I am sure you would show no less respect for mine.'

At this point Laria stepped into the room. 'Madam, Sir Goccio is here and wishes to know if you are in residence.'

'Of course, Laria, send him up!'

Cosetta turned to Beauceron with a smile. 'I am popular today. Have you met Sir Goccio?'

'I am acquainted with him by reputation,' said Beauceron. 'We could scarcely expect to be intimates, since he is a liege-man of King Tardolio.'

'Fah! All the while I maintain my own salon I will have no truck with such folderol.'

'I wonder how Prince Brissio would view your stance.'

'I have never asked his opinion on the matter, and I do not intend to do so now.'

Into the room stepped a tall, slender man attired all in black. He bowed low to Cosetta, and more modestly to Beauceron. 'Lady Cosetta! I am delighted to find you at home.'

Cosetta inclined her head. 'You are always welcome, Sir Goccio. I am fortunate to entertain two such noble paladins in my apartments. Laria, more tea, on the instant! Please allow me to present the famed captain, Beauceron.'

Sir Goccio came forward and shook hands. 'I am honoured to meet you, sir. And indeed there are matters I would discuss with you. Your daring exploits are well-known, even in Tardolio's court. And of course, every gentlemen of Metting-loom is in your debt for bringing the lovely Lady Cosetta to the city.'

Silver tongue, iron heart, thought Beauceron, although Cosetta forbore from making the remark this time.

'Your own prowess is well-known, Sir Goccio. Did you not take service for a season with King Ingomer?'

'You are too kind, sir. In truth, I found myself embar-rassed by creditors, and found it expedient to spend a while in Gammerling. I was favourably impressed with both realm and King.'

'Yes, King Ingomer is held to be more subtle and flexible

than his father, not that this would prove difficult. I trust your difficulties are now over.'

Sir Goccio dismissed them with a wave of his hand. 'They were trivial in nature. I had managed to secure some valuables from the Emmenrule, and they became ensnared in the maze of the Pellagiers' bureaucracy. As a result I found myself short of ready cash. I thought it best to leave the scene for a period.'

Beauceron nodded. 'The Pellagiers can be obstructive if one does not know how to deal with them. I am fortunate in that my use to Under-Chamberlain Davanzato induces him to speed matters along.'

'Ah, Davanzato. Tardolio's Chamberlain Urbizzo is perhaps less flexible.'

'Sir Goccio, Beauceron, I did not invite you here to discuss the Pellagiers,' said Cosetta, her reproof tempered by a twinkling of the eyes.

Beauceron bowed. 'My apologies, Lady Cosetta. We forget that plunder is not an endlessly fascinating subject.'

'Sir Goccio, you will of course stay to lunch?' said Cosetta.

'I should be delighted. I would stay if only to enjoy the warmth of your dimonetto and your person.'

Beauceron found such compliments over-studied, but Sir Goccio was a knight of some renown, and no doubt understood the form of such things better than he.

'Shall we repair to the front parlour?' said Cosetta. 'The view over the aquavia across to the Occonero is unsurpassed.'

As they rose, Laria entered again. 'My lady, Prince Brissio is downstairs and requests your company.'

Cosetta made a moue. 'Oh, this is bothersome! I can hardly deny him admittance to my apartments in the circumstances, but no doubt he will be vexed to find I have company.'

'Do not worry on that account,' said Beauceron. 'I am eager to learn the business Sir Goccio has with me. We will leave at once.'

'Regrettably Beauceron is right,' said Sir Goccio. 'This visit has been all too short, but I console myself that I will see you at the Midwinter Ball, if not before.'

Beauceron heard a heavy clumping on the stairs.

'Cosetta? Do you keep me waiting! I have had a most vexing morning going over treasury records with my father! I have no desire to learn book-keeping!'

The door crashed open, and in stepped Prince Brissio, resplendent in a red cape trimmed with cloth-of-gold, a brilliant white shirt and deep maroon breeches and boots.

'Oh! I had not realized you were entertaining!' said Brissio with a choleric cast to his face. He flung himself down on the couch. 'I had hoped for some light diversion.'

'We are just leaving, my lord,' said Beauceron with a bow. 'I was merely making a brief social call.'

Brissio glowered. 'And who is your friend?'He peered at Sir Goccio's cloak. 'Is that a sunflower sigil I see?'

'Sir Goccio, at your service,' accompanied by a bow.

'Goccio . . . Goccio . . . a knight of King Tardolio.'

'Just so, sir. I was delighted to receive an invitation from Lady Cosetta.'

Brissio turned his gaze to Cosetta. 'You invited a knight of Tardolio to wait upon you?'

'Indeed I did. In Sey it is considered good manners to invite new acquaintance to one's home, bringing honour to both.'

'You are not in Sey now, my lady.'

'I am well aware of that, sir. No doubt Beauceron can explain the circumstances by which this came about.'

Brissio's heavy brows almost met as he frowned. 'I meant that in Sey one does not have two separate courts. It is a breach of etiquette and a grave embarrassment for the heir to the Winter Throne to be invited to a salon with a knight of the Summer Court.'

'There need be no embarrassment,' said Cosetta, 'since I did not invite you today. If you choose to appear unannounced you cannot complain at the company I keep. You may remedy the situation by departing, if you choose.'

Brissio leaped from his seat. Beauceron could see that he wanted to tell Cosetta that he paid for the apartments and could visit when he liked; but he retained just enough composure to recognize this as inadvisable. Sir Goccio's polished manners came to the rescue.

'Please do not leave on my account, my lord. As Beauceron said, we have business elsewhere.' He bowed again to Brissio and Cosetta, and stepped gracefully from the room.

Beauceron also bowed, but he gave Cosetta a look of sharp meaning. The matter had clearly been staged from first to last. He realized that he should be irritated at being used as Cosetta's cat's paw, but he felt only a sardonic amusement.

'I hope to make your acquaintance again soon, my lady,' he said. 'Prince Brissio, my apologies for disturbing your afternoon.' He turned and followed Sir Goccio from the room.

2

Beauceron followed Sir Goccio down the stairs and out onto the path running alongside the frozen aquavia. A bird scrabbled for purchase on the smooth surface

'I think we have been used,' said Sir Goccio with a grin as he pulled his cloak around his shoulders. 'Cosetta has

Brissio on a string. Naturally as a Knight of the Summer Court I am not heartbroken to see Brissio cutting such a pitiful figure.'

'I may be Fanrolio's liegeman, but I admit my admiration for his son is somewhat constrained,' said Beauceron. 'If he is a laughing stock, he has only himself to blame.'

'One day Brissio will be the Winter King,' said Sir Goccio. 'Will you not find it difficult to serve a man you do not respect?'

'There is always employment for a man with my skills. Perhaps I too will take service with King Ingomer.'

'Come, let us walk.'

After a few minutes of silence Sir Goccio said: 'My father fought at the Battle of Jehan's Steppe. Indeed, he was killed there. I had broken my leg falling from a gallumpher, and I stayed at home. I was furious, for it would have been my first battle. As it happened, it saved my life.'

'I am sorry for your losses; but Jehan's Steppe was long ago.'

'To Tardolio, it was yesterday. He did not just lose; he was humiliated. It has profoundly influenced his policies, and does so to this day. He sends raids south, but nothing which constitutes an army. Most of the damage to northern Emmen comes from brigands like yourself.'

'I prefer the term "raider", but I take your point – although you are telling me nothing new.'

'You have been advocating the idea of an invasion of Croad with Fanrolio for several years; with very indifferent success, as far as I can tell.'

'I am confident that Fanrolio will eventually agree to my proposals.'

'I am equally confident that he will not,' said Sir Goccio with a smile. 'But what if I suggested that King Tardolio was prepared to sponsor the expedition?'

Beauceron laughed. 'The notion is risible.'

Sir Goccio inclined his head in polite inquiry.

'Little more than a week ago, I was approached by a member of the Summer Court with a similar proposal. He proved to be an agent of Under-Chamberlain Davanzato, seeking to entrap me in treasonous discourse with Tardolio.'

'Amusing, I agree, but Davanzato's clumsy stratagem surely does not invalidate any arrangement we might reach.'

'Indeed not. However, I remain sceptical.'

'May I take it that you have no objection in principle to riding under the Sunflower Banner? After all, you are a foreigner; your service to one King or another is essentially a matter of pragmatism.'

Beauceron grimaced. 'It is fruitless to speculate on the question, since Tardolio's aversion to the scheme is manifest.'

'Allow me to be a better judge of His Puissance's thoughts than you. The Battle of Jehan's Steppe was the defining moment of his life. The Summer King by tradition is vigorous, aggressive; tormenting and terrorizing the folk of Emmen, harrowing their dreams. Tardolio is conscious of this, and thinks of his own legacy.'

'Continue.'

'Jehan's Steppe is the one battle he has ever fought. It is not how he wishes to be remembered.'

'Naturally not.'

'He has been considering – not openly, but considering nonetheless – how matters might be righted. He lost the Battle of Jehan's Steppe, but if he learns from that . . .'

'And what lessons might he learn?'

'Are the men of Mettingloom less valiant than those of Croad? Of course not. Tardolio has reached the conclusion that he lost at Jehan's Steppe because he split his cavalry; Thaume, of course, kept his together under that sot Langlan. Think of the architects of Croad's victory.'

The wind had abated but Beauceron shivered under his cloak. 'Thaume's commanders were uniformly excellent, if the "Song of the North" is to be believed.'

'Just so, and think of this: Lord Thaume is dead; Sir Artingaume fell on the field; Darrien who commanded the cursed pikemen is dead. Only Sir Langlan survives, and he is old for battle.'

Beauceron grimaced. 'Time moves on.'

'It would be wrong to attribute the word "fear" to a man as valiant as Tardolio; but he always was conscious of Thaume's stature as a commander, and he did not wish to take arms against him. Lord Oricien is untried.'

'Oricien has more steel than you think, when he has no choice but to use it.'

'The facts are these. Tardolio does not wish to die with Jehan's Steppe unavenged; and he believes he can beat Oricien. Surely you see your opportunity?'

'Does he not fear Duke Trevarre, or even King Enguerran? Oricien is better at building alliances than his father.'

'If we beat Oricien in the field, Croad will fall before Enguerran can arrive, and Trevarre is more interested in his catamites than his liegemen.'

Beauceron said nothing.

'All Tardolio needs is a commander. He needs to be persuaded that the scheme is feasible. You and I know it is. You have planned the invasion a hundred times. Put your proposals to His Puissance! He will make you Captain-General Beauceron.'

'I need time to consider what you have said. My allegiance to King Fanrolio may not be in the blood, but nonetheless I swore to give him good service. It is unlikely he would regard plotting with Tardolio in this light.'

'We are still in winter,' said Sir Goccio. 'I will see you,

perhaps at Cosetta's, to learn how your inner debate pro-
gresses. But do not wait too long.'

Sir Goccio turned at the next bridge and hurried away.
Beauceron was left alone with his thoughts looking across the
aquavia to the Occonero.

3

Back at his house, Beauceron pondered his conversation
with Sir Goccio over a goblet of red wine. He had no particular reason to trust the knight, although those parts of
his story amenable to verification were reasonable enough.
Nevertheless, it would be as well to learn a little more of
the man before he made his interest more manifest. This
might present a problem: his contacts in the Summer Court
were limited, although he had campaigned under Tardolio's
banner on occasions in the past. He would have Monetto
look into the man's background.

He was conscious of a vague mistrust of Sir Goccio. Intu-
ition was on the whole not a useful guide – presumably
Tardolio's own intuitions had led him to Jehan's Steppe – but
a degree of prudence was a worthwhile precaution. The fact
that he had approached Beauceron with the selfsame scheme
which Davanzato had dreamed up to ensnare him using
Nissac should not be held against Sir Goccio. It was further
proof of Davanzato's clairvoyant nose for intrigue. He would
not hold his position without it, Beauceron supposed.

His attempts at working on Davanzato directly could not
be characterized as anything other than complete failure. His
bribes might as well have been thrown into the aquavia, and
his threats had been called for the feeble bluff they were. He
had to accept that, face to face, he was no match for Davanzato in the matter of intrigue.

He decided to call on Isola, who was as acquainted with Davanzato's movements as anyone, and made his way to the Hiverno, where he was shown to Isola's apartments.

'My lady,' he said with a bow, on being admitted to her presence.

Isola rose languidly from her chaise, her dress of fine umber silk rustling, and gave Beauceron her hand to kiss. 'I am honoured,' she said in a voice faintly slurred. 'A visit from the gallant Captain Beauceron.'

This was not a good start, thought Beauceron. Isola in this humour was not capable of constructive discourse.

'I am conscious I have neglected you recently, my lady. I saw Lady Cosetta only at lunchtime and thought I would wait upon you.'

Isola sniffed. 'You manage more than I do. I have not seen Cosetta for over a week.'

'Lady Cosetta has many affairs to detain her,' said Beauceron. 'You are aware that she has been taken up by Prince Brissio.'

'Naturally, since he insisted on calling on her at all hours of the day and night while Cosetta resided with me. In that sense it was a relief when she moved out.'

'Have you not considered taking apartments away from the Hiverno, my lady? It cannot be congenial to loiter around the palace all day.'

Isola gave Beauceron an incredulous look. 'You are the agency – the sole agency – by which I find myself a prisoner in the Hiverno. Now you attempt to show solicitude. You cannot imagine a greater statement of my abasement than that I almost feel grateful for your attention. My only visitor in a normal day is Davanzato, generally to harangue me on how best to induce my father to pay up. Does he not realize that if I knew, I would be the first to tell him?'

'Does he oppress you greatly?'

'I have come to understand his character better than I would like,' she said. 'I regret ever saying that you were worse than he. There is at least a grandeur – perverted as it is – in your schemes. Davanzato cares only for money and power.'

This was accompanied with an arch look from under her lashes. Unlike Cosetta, thought Beauceron, Isola was not a natural flirt; she had never needed to be.

'I am grateful for the approach to a compliment,' he said. 'Perverted grandeur is better than none at all.'

'I will admit that these are the worst days of my life,' said Isola. 'I can never forget that they arise through your agency, but my confinement is so unnatural that—'

'My lady, I have long counselled you to put the past behind you. However few friends you have in Mettingloom, you will always find me among them.'

Isola blinked rapidly. 'I do not know what to do.' She seemed on the verge of tears.

Beauceron was moved in spite of himself – not so much in sympathy as horror. Was this what he had reduced proud and haughty Lady Isola to? Cosetta moved on with scarcely a look back, while Isola sank lower and lower.

'I feel a degree of responsibility for your circumstances,' said Beauceron, with what he felt was a frank and easy magnanimity. 'Davanzato is perhaps not the best guardian for you.'

The colour rose in Isola's cheeks. *Good, at least she can still be angry.*

'"A degree of responsibility"? I cannot see what is more direct than kidnap.'

Beauceron made a mollifying gesture. An Isola so broken in spirit should be more amenable to his influence.

'I have a proposal for you, my lady.'

Isola's eyes narrowed and her cheeks coloured further. 'I

am accustomed to such language from Davanzato,' she said in a precise voice. 'I had hoped for better from you, although you have fallen short of every expectation I might have of a gentleman.'

'Davanzato has importuned you?' said Beauceron with a startled glance. 'How would he hope to return you for ransom once he had debauched you?'

'He said that by the time my condition came to light the money would be locked in his coffers. He revolts and disgusts every fibre of my being.'

'I assure you, my lady – and I hope it is apparent from my shock and horror – that I had no such purpose in mind. I had hoped we might exchange favours of much smaller currency.'

Isola seemed to brighten. 'You interest me.'

'It is clear that these quarters are not wholesome for you. I propose that you return, temporarily, under my roof as my guest until such time as we can find you your own apartments.'

A look of something like hope came into Isola's eyes. 'You would do that for me? You know I cannot pay?'

Beauceron forced a shamefaced smile to his face. 'Seventy thousand florins go a long way. I feel sure we can arrange a suitable establishment for you.'

Isola caught herself before her enthusiasm became too manifest. 'You mentioned a corresponding favour.'

'The Midwinter Ball is but a fortnight away,' he said. 'As occasions in Mettingloom go, it is not without stimulation, since it is attended by both Winter and Summer Courts. I find myself without an escort, and I hoped you would honour me with your company.'

Isola looked at Beauceron with a blank expression. He was not sure whether she would revile him for kidnapping her and then proposing to escort her to the Ball, or collapse in pathetic gratitude. The former would at least show spirit.

A thousand expressions fleeted across her face, each too brief to read. He began to see how she might have been in normal circumstances.

'You are most generous,' she said. 'I am sure a captain of your renown has no difficulty in attracting a surfeit of suitable partners.' She again essayed the arch look which made him want to cry out in irritation.

Beauceron was surprised; his feelings were approaching shame. Hypocritical nonsense! She was worth 70,000 florins to him as a prisoner, however wretched, and if he truly repented of his actions the restitution was in his own hands.

'My lady, there is no one in Mettingloom I would rather have on my arm as I am presented to the Winter and Summer Kings. If you are not already engaged, I would be honoured by your company.'

Isola gave a harsh laugh. 'Already engaged? Davanzato's wooing does not extend to such matters, and the nobility of Mettingloom does not see me as a suitable partner.'

'I think it would do you good, my lady. You should be seen in society; it would raise your spirits.'

Isola's mouth kinked. 'What would raise my spirits is – I am sorry, I am graceless when you are only showing me kindness.'

'I will send a cariolo for you tomorrow,' he said. 'I am sure we can arrange also a new gown for the event.'

Beauceron rose to leave. Isola took his hand in both of hers. 'Thank you,' she said. 'Whatever has happened in the past, I am grateful for your conduct today.'

'I never intended you should suffer like this, my lady. Lord Sprang is wealthy – what is 45,000 florins? I never thought he would cavil.'

Isola dropped his hand. 'Neither did I, sir. If it is an

unpleasant shock to you, imagine its effect on me. Now go, please, or you will see me as I do not wish to be seen.'

Beauceron bowed. 'Until tomorrow, my lady.'

As he left, he thought to hear the catch of tears.

4

The social centrepiece of the winter was the Midwinter Ball, hosted by the Winter King in the Occonero, with the Summer King a guest of honour. Only the Midwinter and Midsummer Balls offered the two courts the chance to mingle, and by popular repute intrigue and passion seethed.

Beauceron viewed the event as an opportunity to speak with Tardolio's entourage in a way not obviously treasonous. If Tardolio was interested in invading Croad, he would find some way of making it known.

Lady Isola was in a febrile humour. She had seemed much happier since she had taken rooms within Beauceron's house, and her new gown, dyed a rich deep chocolate, served only to lift her spirits further.

Beauceron broke with his normal habit of walking to the Occonero and ordered a cariolo, which conveyed them via a circuitous route along the Grand Aquavia. Snow had settled on the ice and the wheels of the cariolo swished as they went along.

Isola looked out of the window, her expression rapt. What an unfathomable woman she was! Tonight she was mellow in humour, the spite normally so prominent in her character offset by resignation at her circumstances. Beauceron hoped to effect a reconciliation between her and Davanzato; she would learn little of use if they were not on speaking terms.

As the cariolo rolled up to the courtyard at the Occonero,

Isola looked away from the window. 'I cannot believe I am here,' she said. 'Only a season ago I was a girl preparing for my wedding. I could never have imagined what would happen.'

Her face was expressionless, her tone unreadable.

'In truth, my lady, I am not certain you would have enjoyed Croad. Lord Oricien has little taste for extravagance.'

'You sound very well acquainted with Lord Oricien.'

'"Acquaintance" is a broad term. I understand his character well, I suppose.'

'Look!' cried Isola, pointing from the window. In the centre of the courtyard was a fire of a bright blue colour, reaching high into the sky.

'Thaumaturgy,' said Beauceron. 'It seems Fanrolio has spared no expense.'

Beauceron leaped from the cariolo and held out a hand to help Isola down.

'Thank you,' she said, with an inclination of her head. Beauceron could feel the warmth of her hand through her glove. Once she was on the ground he held out his arm, and she linked hers through it.

They stepped past the guards, who nodded respectfully to Beauceron, and into the majestic hall. Every inch of the stone walls was covered with exquisite tapestries, intended to take the chill off the room. Dimonettoes of good size stood in every corner. At the far end of the room sat King Fanrolio, almost lost on the golden throne. At his side stood Prince Brissio; Lady Cosetta was nowhere in evidence.

Beauceron led Isola onto the long purple rug which stretched up to throne. 'Come, my lady,' he said. 'We must be presented to the King.'

'We have already met,' said Isola. 'I am surprised you have forgotten: it was the night you killed Albizzo.'

'That was merely a soirée,' said Beauceron. 'This is a formal ball. You have not met the King until you are introduced at such an event.'

Isola gave a quick crooked smile. 'When I was a girl,' she said, 'I always dreamed of being presented to the King, so in a sense my girlish fantasy is coming true.'

Beauceron looked at her.

'The only difference,' she continued with a twitch of her chin, 'is that I imagined it would be the King of Emmen.'

Isola broke away to curtsy at the feet of King Fanrolio, for they had arrived at the throne. Beauceron dropped to one knee.

From behind the throne stepped Davanzato: Beauceron might have expected him to be on hand.

'Your Puissance, you will remember Lady Isola, of the fair city of Sey in Emmen; and the gallant Beauceron, who is well-known to you.'

'My lady, you are most welcome,' said Fanrolio, his eyes watering in the warm room. 'You are under my protection. I pray you will make the most of your opportunity to enjoy Mettingloom. I understand that Beauceron is providing you with sustenance.'

'Yes, Your Puissance. He has been every inch the gentleman, if one ignores the circumstances under which we became acquainted.'

'When you reach my age, my dear, you will realize that such forgetfulness can be the best policy. Beauceron, you have our gratitude for looking after our guest, and indeed for bringing her to our city.'

Beauceron bowed. 'I had hoped at your convenience, Your Puissance, to discuss matters with regard to Emmen, going beyond the comfort of the young ladies.'

Fanrolio knitted his brows. 'I am always happy to hear

the thoughts of such a respected captain,' he said. 'See Davanzato and he will arrange an appointment.'

Davanzato's eyes glittered as he looked at Beauceron. 'I will arrange for it to happen as soon as practical, Your Puissance. There are many folk who press for your attention, and I must arrange them in the order that best suits your needs.'

'Yes, just so, Davanzato. You intrude upon my attention less than Osvergario, and I am sure you will find the right time for my audience with Beauceron.'

'Indeed I shall, Your Puissance,' said Davanzato, with a pregnant glance at Beauceron. 'Beauceron may be assured of an audience at exactly the appropriate moment.'

Beauceron's heart sank low. 'Surely a formal appointment is not necessary,' he said in a jocular tone. 'I might outline the essence of my business in two minutes.'

'Really, Beauceron,' said Davanzato. 'Look behind you – there are many folk crowding to be presented to His Puissance: he is scarcely at liberty to gossip with you, however he might incline. Come now, step aside and present your compliments to Prince Brissio.'

Brissio inclined his head with a smile on his snub-nosed face. 'My lady, Beauceron; good evening. I am happy to see you, Lady Isola.'

'And I you, my lord.'

Brissio, his eyes bulging and dressed in a tight greenish-brown frock coat, resembled nothing so much as a giant toad.

'Beauceron, these days I never see you away from the company of a beautiful woman. Tonight Lady Isola, the other day Lady Cosetta. It is unorthodox to secure such company by kidnap, but that is the way of the great captains, I suppose.'

'I see no duress on Lady Isola's face, my lord. We all have

our methods of securing the approval of those we wish to please. I myself have offered Lady Isola the use of my house, such as it is. In this I was inspired by your own generosity in furnishing Lady Cosetta with apartments. I am surprised not to see her this evening.'

Brissio took a pull at his goblet. 'My squire Thivalto escorts her; it would not be seemly for her to be seen on a prince's arm at the Midsummer Ball; so says my royal father.'

Beauceron grinned. Evidently Fanrolio had put his foot down; he did not want his son and heir in public thrall to a foreign adventuress. Inwardly he raised his cup to Cosetta.

'No doubt I shall see her during the course of the evening,' said Beauceron. 'I hope that you are equally fortunate.'

Brissio's smile slipped a little. *She does have you on a string*, thought Beauceron.

From the back of the hall came the call of trumpets. It was the 'Royalticar', played at the approach of the King. Since Fanrolio was already present, it could only signal the arrival of the Summer King.

'All hail to their Puissant Majesties, the Summer King of Mettingloom, the Northern Reach and Lynnoc, King Tardolio and his royal Queen Sassantia!'

The doors swung wide and Beauceron sensed as much as saw a column stretching way back across the courtyard. Tardolio had, it seemed, brought his entire court. A rush of cold air invested the hall.

Tardolio at this time was about forty-five years of age, carrying his height and increasing bulk with regal authority. His ultramarine robes were embroidered with sunbursts and his eyes glittered in the torchlight. Was this a man with the spirit to assault Croad? wondered Beauceron. As usual, he looked every inch the warrior king with his great sword hanging by his side.

Beauceron's eyes moved to Queen Sassantia – once, he remembered, an ordinary lady of Garganet, thinking of Cosetta – and Prince Laertio and Princess Agalina. They were the embodiment of a royal family, tall and straight, super-abundant with vigour. Beauceron thought of twisted King Fanrolio and his degenerate son, all that remained of the Winter House.

Tardolio advanced along the ceremonial rug. Kneeling before Fanrolio, he unbuckled his sword and laid it at the Winter King's feet. Fanrolio descended from his throne and raised Tardolio to his feet, kissing him on both cheeks. 'Take back your sword, Your Puissance. For tonight there are two kings.' Tardolio bowed and kissed Fanrolio's hands. The ceremonial over, Tardolio repaired to the quarter of the room set aside for his use, including a throne set carefully at a lower level than Fanrolio's.

'Minstrels!' called Fanrolio in what passed for a firm voice. 'The night is young! Play!'

Beauceron turned to Isola. 'Would you do me the honour, my lady?'

Isola half-smiled. 'I should be delighted.'

As they performed a pavane, Beauceron turned his thoughts to Tardolio: the Summer King's attitude would determine his plans to a great extent. He was conscious, though, of the warmth of Isola against him as they danced. She moved with a supple elegance, indeed hardly seeming to move at all. She was a most engaging partner, and he decided to set aside King Tardolio for a while; after all, as Fanrolio had said, the evening was young.

'Are you thirsty?' he asked when the first dance was over. 'Perhaps I might fetch you a tuttleberry wine?'

'You are attentive,' said Isola with a smile. The exertion had brought a flush of colour to her cheek.

Beauceron took this for assent and made his way to a

refreshment table. A man jostled his back, and he turned to see Sir Goccio.

'My apologies, Captain,' said Sir Goccio.

'Think nothing of the matter, sir.'

'I must press you for your answer on the question we discussed soon,' said Sir Goccio. 'The spring is nearer than you think. There are many preparations to make.'

'In good time, Sir Goccio. I may assess His Puissance's mood for myself tonight.'

Sir Goccio slopped a little wine from his goblet. 'I would not advise that. Tardolio has no intent to discuss matters of state this evening, certainly not those which might be regarded as treasonous to his host.'

Beauceron gave him a sceptical glance. 'What other purpose could Tardolio have for coming than intrigue?'

'You are a cynical fellow. You can see all you need: look at Tardolio and his tall son Laertio; compare them with the Winter House. You would think Fanrolio old enough to be Tardolio's father: in fact he is but seven years his senior.'

'What you ask of me is not straightforward, Sir Goccio. Allow me to decide matters in my own way.'

'Beauceron!' called a voice from his left: Davanzato. 'I did not realize that you and Sir Goccio were acquainted.'

Beauceron sprang back. 'Only in the most casual sense. We became acquainted at Lady Cosetta's salon.'

Davanzato nodded. 'Naturally, it is easier for a foreigner to maintain links with both courts. My own acquaintance in the Summer Court is negligible.'

'Do not overstate my familiarity with the Printempi,' said Beauceron. 'My relations with Sir Goccio are of the most cursory nature.'

Davanzato bowed fractionally. 'I would not dream of regarding your word as anything other than scrupulously accurate.'

Sir Goccio said: 'Under-Chamberlain Davanzato, you should not attach significance to a casual conversation at the Midwinter Ball. On this of all evenings, surely intercourse between our courts is permissible. Even you and I might converse with cordiality, did we but consider it agreeable.'

Davanzato reached for two glasses of sherbet from the table. 'I am grateful to you for your insight, Sir Goccio. If you will excuse me, I intend to offer refreshment to Lady Isola.'

Beauceron raised his eyebrows. He doubted that Isola would welcome the attention, but he was not minded to intervene. A measure of cordiality between Isola and Davanzato could only make his life easier.

Sir Goccio mopped his brow with a lace kerchief as Davanzato moved away. The room was warm, with torches burning at close intervals and abundant dimonettoes nearby, but Beauceron knew this was not the only reason.

'You should not have approached me tonight,' said Beauceron. 'Davanzato has the most keen perceptions.'

Sir Goccio tossed back a goblet of rum. 'He knows nothing. He is fishing.'

'Do you believe that?' asked Beauceron.

'I hope you show greater initiative on the battlefield. You cannot cower in the corner every time Davanzato approaches. What is his power? A knife in an alley would settle him in a moment.' His eyes shone with a strange gleam.

'Do not think I have not been tempted,' said Beauceron. 'He hates and fears me, and Mettingloom would be a safer place without him, but the fact is that I need his intervention; and he is not friendless. There are too many who depend upon him for their advancement.' He paused. 'Although if you are minded to take independent action, do not let me deter you.'

Sir Goccio reached for another goblet. 'I would not buy

his life with my own,' he said. 'One way or another, he will come to a bad end. It is simply a matter of patience. For now, we should part. I will wait on you in due course.'

5

Beauceron was well enough known to King Tardolio that he thought it not unreasonable to present his compliments. Surely Tardolio would give some subtle indication of his thoughts. He began to make his way over to the corner of the room where the Summer King was holding court.

Beauceron pressed through the throng and found himself drawn aside by a middle-aged man with a bald pate and self-important air: Urbizzo, the King's Chamberlain.

'Captain Beauceron, I believe.'

'You know me well, Urbizzo.'

'Not as well as you might think. You are hardly a familiar of our court, and neither should I imagine you would wish to be.'

'I have campaigned under the Sunflower Banner. I merely thought to present my compliments to His Puissance.'

'King Fanrolio licensed your previous campaigns. My sources suggest you are considering less formal activities. If I were you, I would be more discreet; and indeed I should reconsider my position altogether.'

'The hospitality of your court is much lessened, Urbizzo, if a man may not present his compliments to the Summer King at the Midwinter Ball.'

Urbizzo sniffed. 'His Puissance cannot give audience to everyone. My commission this evening is to weed out riff-raff: a category in which I emphatically place yourself.'

Another voice, strong and well-modulated: 'What goes here, Urbizzo?'

'My lord! I was keeping undesirables away from your father.'

The newcomer looked at both for a moment. '"Undesirables"? Beauceron is the only commander of spirit in the Winter Court – or the Summer for that matter.'

Urbizzo flushed. 'I only follow the instructions of your father the King.'

'Go and chase undesirables elsewhere. I will deal with Beauceron.'

With poor grace Urbizzo sidled away.

'Now, Beauceron, perhaps you will tell me why you are so eager to see my father,' said Prince Laertio, a model of understated elegance in an indigo doublet and cerulean cape. His almond-shaped grey eyes took in the surroundings with almost imperceptible movements. Tall, with a slender muscularity, he looked everything Prince Brissio was not.

Beauceron bowed. 'It is as I suggested to Urbizzo. I wished to pay my compliments to His Puissance.'

Laertio clapped him on the arm. 'We have ranged the northern steppes together, Beauceron. I know you too well for that. Now, the truth.'

Beauceron shrugged. 'I hardly know how to answer, especially given the implication that I lie in my throat.'

'Beauceron! Do not be so prickly. I have heard interesting rumours, to the effect that Fanrolio has forbidden your assault on Croad, and that you intend to approach my father.'

'Such a course would be treasonous.'

'So it would. You are not known as a scrupulous man.'

Beauceron's mouth twitched. 'Perhaps not. I am, however, a cautious one.'

'Let us step outside a while.'

'The night is cold, my lord.'

'You may prefer to discuss treasons in here.'

'I do not wish to discuss treasons at all.'

'Oblige me nonetheless. The air is stuffy, is it not? Dimon-ettoes are all very well, but any effect carried to excess must cloy.'

The crowd stepped respectfully aside at Laertio's approach and soon they were out in that courtyard where, Beauceron reflected, he had killed Albizzo less than a season ago. It paid to tread carefully in Mettingloom.

'Now we can talk like men, not fussy old women like Urbizzo and Davanzato,' said Laertio.

'You give me little incentive for frankness.'

'Come,' said Laertio with a laugh. 'I care nothing if you betray Fanrolio: quite the contrary, in fact.'

'I have never given any such indication.'

Laertio exhaled slowly, his breath a mighty cloud of condensation in front of him.

'I have agents the city over, as a man in my position must. More than one tells me that you are losing patience with Fan-rolio, and plan to approach my father. Somebody has told you my father looks favourably on the idea, or you would not take the risk. I would know the truth, Beauceron.'

'You seem to know much already, my lord. My testimony would add little.'

'You do not deny it, then?'

Beauceron smiled. 'Since you are not disposed to believe me, I will not waste my time.'

'Let me be candid with you. My understanding is that my father is completely, implacably opposed to the idea of a raid upon Croad, for reasons we both understand. If you know differently, I am interested to know how.'

'You ask for information I cannot give.'

Laertio rubbed his hands against the cold. 'I myself am not hostile to your raid. On the contrary, I support it with vigour. Were I King, as I could be tomorrow, I would launch the assault, and demand your own presence.'

'You are not the King, my lord. Your father looks to enjoy excellent health; he could live another twenty years.'

'Men die. All men die.' He looked into Beauceron's face without expression.

'I am unclear as to your meaning.'

'As you wish. If I were King, preparations for your assault would begin immediately. As matters stand, both Summer and Winter Kings oppose you. If I were you, I would be looking for ways in which I might alter prevailing conditions in either – or both – courts. They say "Everything comes to those who wait." Men of action know it for craven falsehood.'

Beauceron stared up at the top of the Viatory's tower outlined against the clear winter sky. 'What you are suggesting makes the treason you accuse me of less than nothing. Regicide, parricide . . .'

Laertio held up his hands. 'I suggested nothing, Beauceron. Our interests may coincide, but only under certain circumstances. Perhaps, as a token of our potential understanding, you might wish to tell how you have come to believe my father's attitude has changed.'

'I gain nothing thereby. Either your father is hostile to the raid or he is not. I must verify the matter for myself.'

'I verify it for you: his position is unchanged. Consider your advantage where you can take it, Beauceron.'

From behind them came a high clear voice: 'Beauceron! Are you ignoring me?'

Beauceron thought guiltily of Lady Isola, whom he had left to Davanzato's mercies, but the voice came from Lady Cosetta.

'My lady! I thought you were the companion of Sir Thivalto.'

'That tedious buffoon! What little interest I had in the breeding of gallumphers was exhausted within the first minutes of our acquaintance, but he would not take the hint. Who is your friend?'

'My lady, may I present Prince Laertio, lord and heir to the Sunflower Throne. My lord, Lady Cosetta of Sey.'

Cosetta dimpled and blushed as she curtsied; Laertio gave an answering bow with stately gravity.

'My, but you are well-connected, Beauceron!' said Cosetta. 'And Prince Laertio is even more handsome than Prince Brissio!'

'Such is the consensus,' said Beauceron with a smile. 'No doubt Brissio has other advantages.'

'You are well acquainted with Prince Brissio, my lady?'

Cosetta made a gesture of demurral. 'I would not go so far, my lord. His father holds me for ransom, and he is kind enough to look to my welfare.'

'Ransom? But of course, you are one of the ladies Beauceron kidnapped in Emmen! Beauceron, we all have reason to be grateful to you.'

Beauceron gave a sour smile.

'You must tell me of conditions in Sey, my lady,' said Laertio. 'I have never been more than a few miles inside the Emmenrule. Are all the ladies as comely as yourself?'

'My lord, you are shameless!' said Cosetta, her hand going to her throat. 'Are all the princes of Mettingloom so fair-spoken?'

'My lord; my lady; will you excuse me,' said Beauceron. 'I am conscious I have left Lady Isola unattended.'

Neither seemed to notice his presence, so Beauceron quietly walked away, leaving Cosetta to her conquest of the man who only two minutes before had been calmly plotting to murder his father.

Although he had only been outside for a few minutes, the atmosphere within the Great Hall had become more louche in his absence. Laertio had all but promised him his support in return for backing a coup against King Tardolio – a coup which could only end in the King's death. He owed Tardolio nothing and the idea was not one to reject out of hand. Laertio deserved credit for initiative, which argued that he might be prepared to launch an assault on Croad. But Laertio was clearly a dangerous, ruthless man, and one unlikely to be constrained by promises once they became inconvenient. Were he to murder Tardolio, his hold on the Summer Throne would, initially at least, be tenuous. Would he be prepared to send troops south at a time when he would need them to buttress his position at home? Or perhaps he might feel that such a distraction would draw attention away from his monstrous crime?

Beauceron had no moral objection to what Laertio was proposing. Arguably Fanrolio would approve of the scheme if he knew about it. The real difficulties arose from the reliability of Laertio as an associate. If Tardolio was willing to back the raid, Beauceron had no need to support Laertio. Could not Laertio act without Beauceron? The idea was conceivable, but Beauceron was under no illusions that his reputation as the most effective and ruthless captain in Mettingloom made him the ideal associate in such a scheme. He shook his head in frustration: the matter was becoming more complex.

'Where have you been?'

Beauceron turned to see the flushed face – and hear the shrill tones – of a clearly vexed Lady Isola.

'I was waylaid by Prince Laertio,' he said. 'Princes are impatient of delay.'

Isola's cheeks had a red flush. 'I imagined you were my escort. Instead, you bring me here, dance once, leave me with Davanzato and disappear to pursue your obsession.'

'It is in the nature of these events that one converses with a variety of folk. As to my "obsession", you may be sure that Prince Laertio is no part of its fulfilment. I am King Fanrolio's man.'

Isola made a swatting gesture – exaggerated, it seemed, by the wine she had drunk – indicating the matter of Beauceron's allegiance was of no interest to her.

'What is truly galling,' she said, 'is that under normal circumstances I would not even consider accompanying you to a ball. You are of a stamp more suited to be my steward, or even my linen-master.'

'My lady, you are shouting.'

'I am not!' she shouted.

'As you wish; but you are making your points with excessive vehemence.'

'It is only what is warranted by your conduct,' she said in a near-whisper, evidently intended to convince Beauceron she had not been shouting in the first place.

'Perhaps we should take a seat, my lady.'

'Do not touch me, servant!'

Beauceron assessed her coolly. 'Davanzato!' he called. 'Lady Isola is unwell. Perhaps you might find a cool and quiet ante-room for her.'

Davanzato appeared. 'With pleasure,' he said with a smirk.

'Thank you,' said Beauceron. 'And if I find that you have mistreated her, it will go the worse for you.'

Davanzato pushed his chin out. 'So you may dream, Beauceron.'

He watched Davanzato lead Isola away to some more secluded place. He was well rid of her, in this humour. How had she become drunk so quickly? In his experience, females and alcohol were best kept apart. Cosetta had more sense than to make such an exhibition of herself, he reflected.

He turned at the blundering approach of Prince Brissio. Some men should also be kept away from alcohol, he decided.

'Have you seen Cosetta?' Brissio said roughly.

'Yes, she – that is, no, I have not.'

'Which is it to be: yes or no?'

Beauceron feigned thought. 'No. Is she not with Sir Thivalto?'

'Apparently not. The old fool was talking to her about breeding techniques and she wandered off. He cannot understand why.'

Beauceron raised an eyebrow. 'Breeding?'

Brissio looked at him through bloodshot eyes. 'There is no call for your lewdness.'

'You mistake me, sir. If I were you, I would find the Lady Cosetta soon. She is a personable young lady.'

Brissio stumbled off and Beauceron helped himself to more wine. The evening had by almost any reckoning been a failure on all levels; his recent strictures on alcohol need not apply to himself.

7

Beauceron awoke early the next morning, despite having reached his bed only in the small hours. He had not found sleep easy to come by. The thin sunlight seeped around the heavy curtains and reluctantly he rolled out of his bed and walked over to the ewer, only to find the water frozen. There would be a fire in his parlour but he was not yet ready to face the world.

He sat at his rough desk and pulled some parchment and a stylus from the drawer. Briefly he noted his options and the corresponding advantages of each. Inaction was one possibility, which he instantly discounted. Pursuing his schemes with King Fanrolio could at least be carried out openly, and he was familiar with the Winter Armies; but he must contend with the hostility of Davanzato and the privations of a winter campaign. On the other hand, working with either Laertio or Sir Goccio embroiled him in dangerous treasons.

He considered what he had written. It appeared to comprehend all the factors. His plans with Fanrolio were no further advanced than when he had returned, and unless Davanzato could be in some way neutralized he saw little prospect of improvement. This left him with the choice of using either Sir Goccio or Laertio. Here the decision came down to which perception of Tardolio's attitude was the more accurate: Laertio represented him as implacably and irreversibly opposed to the invasion, while for Sir Goccio he nurtured the desire for revenge, a position with which Beauceron had an instinctive sympathy.

It seemed unlikely that he would be able to establish Tardolio's views for himself. If he was so well guarded at the Midwinter Ball, where intercourse between the courts was encouraged, access would be all but impossible at any other time.

If he pursued Sir Goccio's scheme and its assumptions proved flawed, he was not precluded from conspiring with Laertio; whereas if he followed Laertio's proposal from the outset, the option to side with Sir Goccio was for ever lost, and potentially he forfeited the advantage of a supportive king. When he added in his profound mistrust of Laertio, the question was surely decided. Monetto's research into

Sir Goccio's circumstances had revealed nothing he did not already know: a respected knight with a good battlefield reputation and many debts – in other words, a soldier like many in Mettingloom.

Snatching up his stylus, he penned a rapid note to Sir Goccio:

> Meet me at the docks at six bells. The merits of your proposals are now apparent.

He sealed the note with his wolf's-head sigil and took it down to the parlour along with the paper he had prepared that morning. The latter item he cast into the fire, and gave the note to Kainera to deliver. He felt his uncertainty and perplexity lift. He had chosen a course, and it was now down to his force and guile to make it the correct one.

He heard movement from Isola's suite below. He did not relish the idea of an interview, but there was no way of leaving which did not pass her apartments.

The door opened and Isola entered, her toilette not completed with its normal meticulousness. 'Good morning, Beauceron,' she said stiffly.

'Good morning, my lady. Kainera, kindly arrange tisane for us.'

Kainera bowed and departed.

'Your conduct last night was not to my liking, Beauceron,' said Isola levelly. 'Your attention to my person was deficient.'

'I can only apologize,' said Beauceron. 'Important matters of state occupied my time, and Prince Laertio detained me awhile.'

'The "matter of state" to which you refer is, of course, the capture of Croad.'

Beauceron shrugged. 'That is no secret. This is Mettingloom, and our ways are somewhat different to those of Emmen. I neither need nor desire your approval.'

'That is fortunate.'

After a pause, Isola said: 'Prince Laertio seemed greatly interested in Cosetta.'

'She is a lady of considerable charm.'

'She does not appear to be finding her captivity onerous.'

'No doubt she would argue she is making the best of her situation. Her prospects for ransom are not as good as yours. She may be here indefinitely.'

Isola uttered a shriek of near-hysterical laughter. 'My prospects of ransom "good"! I am caught in a stand-off between the two most parsimonious men alive.'

'Sooner or later Fanrolio will reduce your ransom, possibly to a token amount. Your father or Oricien will then see the value of paying.'

Isola sniffed. 'This sordid arrangement does not give me confidence in my own attractions.'

'It is said that as a youth, Oricien offered to take Lady Helisette of Glount without a dowry. His father was not amused. Oricien has learned much since.'

'My father settled a most generous dowry.'

'Oricien is unwilling to expend it on your ransom. His position is understandable.'

'My father is unwilling to pay my dowry twice. That too is understandable.'

Beauceron sipped his tisane. 'You see, then, that the question of your ransom is not related to your own charms. Two proud men are concerned for their treasuries and their concepts of justice.'

Isola beamed. 'You are right!' she said. 'I had never seen it in that light before.'

'Good! Are we friends again?'

'I was not aware we ever had been.'

Beauceron shrugged. 'The offer is there. Consider the facility with which Cosetta makes new alliances in the city.'

Isola tilted her chin in her characteristic gesture of disdain. 'I am not sure I like Cosetta's way of making friends.'

8

Beauceron was early for his evening rendezvous. In the short midwinter days the sun had already been set for two hours, and the night was moonless. A cruel wind snapped down from the north, insinuating its way under his cloak and into his shirt. There was no sign of anyone else. If Sir Goccio was early, he at least had the wit to keep himself hidden.

Nearby a bell tolled three times, then three more. Sir Goccio should now be on hand; and as if the thought had summoned him, the knight slipped from some place of concealment, all but invisible in black cloak and breeches.

Beauceron bowed. 'You are prompt; such efficiency is commendable.'

Sir Goccio's mouth twitched upwards. 'In the circumstances I thought it prudent to follow instructions. I take it you have come to a decision.'

Beauceron nodded crisply. 'I am ready to throw my lot in with Tardolio. Events at Hiverno proceed ever slower.'

Sir Goccio gave a quick nod. 'You had no real choice. Is it too soon to begin planning? Or do you require time to accustom yourself to your new allegiance?'

'I have made any necessary adjustments,' said Beauceron. 'Such decisions are not taken lightly.'

'Good. Let us seal matters over a mug of ale. You will probably not be familiar with The Ill-Favoured Loon – a tavern patronized by Tardolio's men.'

'Might that not be an unnecessarily overt statement?' asked Beauceron.

'You are like a timid old maid. Once Tardolio begins to raise an army your new status will become apparent. Without your sponsorship things will go much more slowly. I assumed you would not wish to wait until Tardolio's reascendance? We can achieve much in a month.'

'You are asking me to make an explicit and public commitment to Tardolio tonight?'

'Why not? Sooner is always better than later.'

'I will not survive until the spring. Davanzato's assassins will find me out as I wait.'

Sir Goccio stroked his beard. 'Davanzato's elimination is not part of the plan; although we could make it so.'

'The thoroughness of your preparations is not impressive. I am content to work with Tardolio, but my public involvement must wait until the reascendance. If the army does not leave on the first day of spring it is no loss.'

'I took you for a larger man, Beauceron.'

'It seems you took me for a stupid one. I have expressed my sympathy with your aims, and my willingness to lead an army: I have never said I would parade through the streets in a Sunflower smock.'

'That is your final word?'

'Until you have something more persuasive to say to me.'

'So be it,' said Sir Goccio. He removed a glove and put his fingers to his mouth, to give a lusty whistle. 'I am sorry, Beauceron.'

From a nearby building issued a squadron of soldiers in white uniforms set off with purple cloaks: the Royal Winter Guard. Behind them strolled Davanzato. 'Take him,' he said in a soft voice. 'Sir Goccio, you have done well.'

Sir Goccio twitched his head. 'He would not go to The

Ill-Favoured Loon; but he agreed to lead Tardolio's army. I will swear it on my honour.'

Beauceron stood motionless as his arms were tied behind his back. 'Your honour, Sir Goccio? That will carry great weight at trial, you poxed knave.'

Sir Goccio looked away. 'I did not want to do it.'

'We always have a choice.'

Davanzato stepped forward to stare into Beauceron's face. 'That we do, Beauceron. I await with interest how you will defend yours in front of His Puissance. We will proceed now to the Darkstone, where you will be lodged for a while.'

'I demand my full rights.'

'And you shall have them. His Puissance will be most scrupulous in ensuring you have a fair trial. Such a proud captain deserves no less.'

8

Croad

I

It was a smaller army which limped back into Croad than had set out a month earlier. Lord Thaume regretted the loss of so many good men – particularly his cousin Sir Artingaume – but he had achieved his purpose. Tardolio had been sent back to Mettingloom nursing wounds to his pride and his army which would take many years to heal.

Thaume had no taste for spectacle, but he rode ahead of his men along the road to the North Gate, with his prisoners walking in chains behind him. Standing on the wall above the Gate was Lady Jilka, with a black cloak over chain mail and a longsword hanging in a scabbard at her waist. This too was theatre, for Lord Thaume had sent riders ahead to bring the tidings of his victory.

As the gates were flung wide and the soldiers entered the city, Arren looked around for the faces he would recognize: his brother Matten, his mother Ierwen, and Eilla and Clottie. None was immediately visible, and he was conscious of a sense of anticlimax.

The army marched through the streets of the city, dust thrown up by the tramp of its boots, through the inner walls, across the bridge and ultimately into the courtyard of Lord Thaume's castle.

'Go and dump your gear in your quarters,' said Serjeant Fleuraume. 'Lord Thaume intends to address the people in half an hour.'

Lord Thaume ascended to the platform where Arren last remembered him passing sentence of death on Foulque. How long ago that seemed, and how many men had died since. The death of Foulque now seemed inconsequential; no doubt Foulque himself would have taken a different view.

Lord Thaume let the cheers die down. He had not changed out of his armour, and his yellow surcoat was torn and stained. He looked every inch the warrior prince.

'I bring you a great victory!' he called. 'We left this city to fight a great foe, and we have sent that foe back to his lair to lick his wounds – and grievous wounds they are. It will be many years before we see Tardolio again.'

More cheers.

'There is much to be proud of. My son Lord Oricien and my nephew Lord Guigot fought for the first time, and fought well. My Captain of the Guard, Darrien, fought with especial valour. Only King Arren may make knights, otherwise I should have knighted him in the field. I owed him much before the battle; now I owe him even more. Darrien, step forth!'

Arren cheered with the rest of the crowd as Darrien ascended the platform to join Lord Thaume, who embraced him as a brother and kissed his cheek. Sir Darrien! How that would sound. At the front of the crowd Arren saw his mother weeping with pride and embracing a reluctant Matten. He winked at his brother, who merely scowled back.

Darrien stepped back down off the platform and went over to join Ierwen as Lord Thaume continued his oration.

'We owe a great debt to the brave Emmen knight, Sir Langlan. Not only has he taught my son combat with such success, but he led the cavalry charge which routed Tardolio's attack. Sir Langlan, step this way!'

Sir Langlan ambled up to the platform, bowing casually to Lord Thaume and the crowd. Unlike Lord Thaume, his war-gear was immaculate. Arren thought that he looked the pattern of chivalry. Away from low taverns like The Hanged Man, and with occupations suitable to a knight, he had grown in stature. He embraced Lord Thaume and departed the platform to rapturous cheers from the crowd.

'No war is without cost,' said Lord Thaume, lowering his voice, 'and I must give you the ill tidings that my noble cousin Sir Artingaume fell in valiant defence of our city. He led our foot soldiers with the selfless courage we had come to expect. Our city has known no more valiant warrior. I decree a statue of this great knight will be erected where all can see it: I will discuss the matter with Master Jandille in due course.'

The crowd fell silent, a sullen, resentful brooding. It could not have been shock at the death of Sir Artingaume, since this had been known well in advance. Had it been the mention of Jandille? Arren had not seen him since he had returned – nor Eilla or Clottie for that matter. He felt a pang of alarm.

'Despite our grievous losses, we have returned to the city unbroken and unbowed. You will see in the square before you we have a number of noble prisoners from Mettingloom, not including King Tardolio, who had the grace neither to fall with his army nor to surrender with it. Nonetheless, the prisoners we have here represent a considerable boon, and it falls to me to decide their fate.'

Arren was conscious of Master Pinch sliding up beside him. 'Let us hope he has learned statesmanship,' said Pinch softly.

The thirty or so prisoners looked up at Lord Thaume;

some apprehensive, some affecting disdain for the proceedings.

'The last time such prisoners were brought into Croad,' continued Lord Thaume, 'my father Lord Gaucelis hanged them as brigands from the very gallows in this square.'

Master Pinch looked on, his expression as inscrutable as ever.

'The temptation to do the same here is strong,' said Thaume. 'However, my father's rashness led not only to his own death, but that of my brother Lord Borel, and nearly ended my own life. My nephew Guigot was left orphaned by the death of Lord Borel. The price of those hangings was high, since it led to the war we fight to this day.

'My judgement today is different. My army has destroyed that of Mettingloom. The war is over. On receipt of suitable ransoms from King Tardolio, you may return to your homes. There will never be amity between Croad and Mettingloom while Tardolio remains on the Summer Throne, but we need not show hostility. I have won a great victory; I will not squander it with harshness in my triumph. Darrien, see to it that the prisoners are comfortably lodged, using a minimum of necessary restraint.'

Master Pinch nodded. 'He has shown true wisdom. He could have avenged his father in a moment, and paid for the rest of his life.'

Lord Thaume called for wine; the day was growing warm, and the dust of the trail lay in his throat. He continued his oration.

'The battle was not fought solely on Jehan's Steppe,' he said. 'There have been privations in Croad too, and seasoned judgement necessary to ensure the smooth running of the city. I pay tribute here to my staunch wife, Lady Jilka, who has ruled the city with wisdom and restraint in my absence.'

Arren again noticed the sudden change in atmosphere as

when Jandille had been mentioned. Lady Jilka stepped up to the platform to embrace her husband, her red hair pent at the back of her head, her black cloak and breeches rustling as she walked. The crowd fell silent.

Even Lord Thaume, flushed with his triumph, noticed the change. He looked around. 'Jilka?' he said quietly.

Lady Jilka stuck her chin out. 'This might better be discussed in our chambers, my lord. Not all of my decrees have proved popular.'

Lord Thaume looked intently into her face. 'There is more to this than the simple exercise of justice. Will you tell me what has happened?'

'Not here, my lord,' she said with a hint of supplication.

'What decree can you have made which you are not prepared to defend in public to the lord of the city and your husband?'

Jilka shook her head, whether in defiance or resignation Arren could not tell.

'A number of decrees irked some folk,' said Jilka. 'I imagine the one which is causing this muttering is closing the Temple.'

'Muttering' understated the noise coming from the throng in the square. Lord Thaume looked intently into his wife's face.

'My lord?'

'Would you care to tell me exactly what you mean by "closing the Temple"?'

'The matter is simple enough,' said Lady Jilka. 'The Consorts and the viators teach us that the Wheel is a wicked heresy. Those who follow the Wheel depart from the Way of Harmony. King Arren himself has banned such practices. In my trust as ruler of Croad, however temporary, I found it necessary to bring these misguided folk back to the Way. As a result I promulgated a decree anathematizing the Wheel, banning its worship, and closing the Temple. It is of course sealed with your own sigil.'

Lord Thaume's face darkened. The crowd, as if sensing their conversation, had fallen silent.

'In thirteen years as the ruler of Croad I had seen no need to take these steps. You felt it necessary within a month?'

'We must each Follow the Way according to our own dictates.'

'No doubt you took counsel from the viators?'

'Of course. To settle such matters of doctrine and conscience myself would have been impious, indeed it would have smacked of the Wheel.'

'Viator Sleech has been inclined to take a pragmatic stance on such matters, an attitude I have much appreciated.'

'Viator Sleech was absent in the North with you, my lord.'

'From whom, then, have you taken counsel?'

'I have relied primarily on Viator Dince.'

Lord Thaume nodded grimly. 'And Viator Dince explicitly approved your decree?'

'Just so. In fact, he drafted it.'

'And where is Viator Dince now? He should be here to welcome his lord.'

'Ah – I – I believe he is in the Viatory, my lord, ready to give succour where it may be needed.'

'Who will fetch me Viator Dince?' said Lord Thaume in a quiet but penetrating voice. 'He has much to explain.'

The crowd burst into hubbub. There was no shortage of volunteers.

'Serjeant Fleuraume, go with them to ensure there is no outrage. Viator Dince is to be whipped in the square, and I want him fully aware of the fact.'

A great roar of approval went up from the crowd, many of whom stormed off to the Viatory. Arren wondered how many people in Croad followed the Wheel, and how many simply hated Lady Jilka.

'My lord,' implored Jilka, sinking to her knees. 'Consider what you propose. To drag an honoured viator from the sanctuary of the Viatory, to abuse his person, how can this be the Way?'

'Be assured, my lady, I take this action only because it is inappropriate to visit it upon yourself. Viator Dince must bear your punishment and his own.'

'My lord—'

'Silence! I return from the greatest victory ever won on the field of battle by a Croadasque army, paid for in blood, much of it belonging to those who followed the Wheel. I find that you have outlawed their hallowed practices. Was this what they fought and died for?'

Lady Jilka's voice fell almost to a whisper. 'It is heresy, my lord.'

'In that case, Serjeant Fleuraume is a heretic. Our son says Fleuraume saved his life on the battlefield: our only son. If allowing men like that to worship at the Temple secures their loyalty, it is a small price to pay.'

Jilka stood upright. 'No one could love Oricien more than I. I would repay the good Fleuraume in the best fashion I knew how – by bringing him to the Way of Harmony.'

Lord Thaume stepped down from the platform. 'I have heard enough. Return to your chambers. I will see you later.'

2

Arren turned to Oricien and Guigot. 'Shall we go? I have no love for Viator Dince, but neither do I wish to see him whipped.'

Oricien made a gesture of acquiescence. 'I would like to see Siedra, in any event.'

Guigot laughed. 'You have girlish stomachs. We all know that Dince is a prating hypocrite. Nothing will give me greater pleasure than to see him thrashed and hear his howls. The viators are parasites.'

'As you wish,' said Oricien with disdain. 'No doubt his howls will be audible from the castle. Come, Arren.'

Arren was conscious as they stepped through the streets that they were met with new deference. No longer were they pranksome lads; now they had defended Croad with their bodies.

The guards saluted as they turned into the courtyard. Oricien set them at ease with a negligent gesture.

'Where is Siedra?' he asked, and was directed to the family's private quarters overlooking the Pleasaunce. He knocked and walked in, Arren in tow.

'Siedra!' he cried, embracing her. 'How you have grown.'

Arren thought to see tears in her eyes as she flung her arms around her brother. 'You have only been gone a month! I was so worried for you,' she said. 'But our father sent back a letter saying how bravely you had fought.' She noticed Arren. 'Lord Thaume also commended your valour, Arren. And he said your father saved the day.'

Arren bowed. 'It was my father's duty to fight for lord and city.'

'Don't be so stuffy, Arren! He could have run away. I am sure I should have done. So could you.'

'There was little real choice,' said Arren. 'We were surrounded by Tardolio's men. It was not feasible to ask them to excuse us as we quit the field.'

'You speak like Sir Langlan,' she said, tossing her hair. 'You act as if the greatest feats of valour were simply achieved to stave off boredom. Dear Oricien, surely you will admit to courage and fortitude.'

Oricien gave a rueful smile. 'If we dwelled on the horror we would never fight again,' he said. 'We were part of Serjeant Fleuraume's squadron, and we did as he said. He was far more intimidating than all Tardolio's men.'

'Where is Guigot? How did he fight?'

Arren glanced at Oricien.

'Guigot fought well,' said Oricien. 'As you might expect, he displayed a bloodthirsty ethic.'

'Guigot has much anger,' said Arren. 'Now he also knows how to use a sword. He will wreak much destruction before he is done.'

'As long as he fights for his lord, it matters little,' said Oricien.

He will never fight for you, thought Arren. And you would never want him at your side.

'At this instant,' said Arren, 'he is in the market square, waiting for your father to whip Viator Dince.'

Siedra paled a little. 'Whip – the viator?'

'Just so,' said Arren. 'Lord Thaume has not relished your mother's decree to close the Temple, and holds Dince to blame.'

Siedra affected a nonchalant shrug. 'He should have known better, and my mother too for that matter. Dince deserves whatever punishment he gets, even what Jandille got. Let my father whip him. He will not be so proud again.'

Arren's palms felt clammy. 'What "punishment"? What has happened to Master Jandille?'

'I thought you knew. When you spoke about my mother closing the Temple.'

'That's all I know, that Dince drafted a decree and Jilka sealed it.'

'The Gollains – is that not what the followers of the

Wheel call themselves? – did not take kindly to the decree, of course. Dince should have seen that they would not simply give up their worship. Some of the Elders went to the Temple on the day of the decree to defy it. Master Jandille was at their head.'

'What happened?' asked Arren, his heart pounding.

'My mother told them they contravened the will of Lord Thaume and wilfully departed from the Way. They were to disperse at once, and if they valued Harmony, to visit the Viatory and beg forgiveness for their impiety. Jandille asked to see the decree. When he had read it, he said that he would not accept it until he had had it from Lord Thaume himself. My mother said that it had Lord Thaume's seal on it, and did he propose to defy his lord?

'Jandille ripped the decree in half and said again that until Lord Thaume presented it to him it was no decree.'

Oricien frowned. 'In this he was incorrect, whatever the provocation. Lady Jilka acted with Regent's authority.'

'But to outlaw the Wheel!' said Arren.

'The Wheel is already outlawed,' said Oricien. 'My father chooses to allow the Gollains to worship, but he disobeys the King in doing so.'

'What happened after, Siedra?' asked Arren.

'Viator Dince said that in destroying the decree he had struck the person of his lord, which is treason. He said that the penalty was death.'

'Death – for ripping a piece of paper?'

'My mother said that was too harsh. Jandille was a good man and should be given the chance to find the Way of Harmony. Viator Dince found this idea compelling. He recommended instead that, since Jandille had struck the person of his lord, that he should lose the hand which had offended. They took him to the square and cut off his right hand on the spot.'

'Siedra!' gasped Arren. 'He is the city's master mason – how can he work with one hand?'

'Viator Dince said—'

'I have heard enough of Viator Dince for today. What happened to Jandille, and his family?'

'He has a brother with a farm on the Southlands. They left the city to go and live there. My mother was glad to see them go, for the people were sorely angry at the treatment of Master Jandille. No doubt they are there now.'

'Enough!' said Arren. 'I need a gallumpher, now. I must find them.'

'Wait, Arren,' said Siedra. 'Lord Thaume will surely pardon him and recall him to the city.'

'And will our father give him a new hand?' said Oricien. 'I am going to join Guigot to see Viator Dince whipped. I hope he is flayed to the bone!'

3

The ramshackle farm of Canille, Jandille's brother, was no great distance from the city walls and Arren found it without difficulty. As he had ridden out through the streets of Croad he had heard the cries of Viator Dince, and on some deep level taken satisfaction; but he knew that things were too far awry to set straight with a flogging.

He dismounted from his gallumpher and tethered it to a fence. 'Hoi there!' he called to a youth of about Arren's own age. 'Is this the farm of Canille?'

'Who wants to know?' scowled the youth, squinting into the sun which silhouetted Arren's figure.

'I come from the war,' he said. 'My name is Arren.'

'Chandry?' came a voice from within a barn. 'Who is there?'

'One of Thaume's lackeys,' said young Chandry, scowling at the ground.

Arren, who was still in his surcoat and chainmail, admired the lad's pluck.

'Send him away! I want nothing from the city.'

Arren recognized the voice. 'Master Jandille! It is Arren!'

There was silence, and a figure appeared from the barn and walked across the yard. He looked into Arren's face, and after a pause embraced him.

'My, but you are the soldier, Arren. Hissen guard you.'

'I had heard . . .' said Arren, unsure how to broach the subject.

'About this?' said Jandille, holding up his bandaged stump. 'The exquisite mercy of Lady Jilka.'

'I do not follow the Wheel,' said Arren, 'but this is monstrous. Lady Jilka must have taken leave of her senses.'

'Do not let her hear you, lad. Her temper does not grow more forgiving with age.' Pigs squealed out of sight as they took their meal.

'Lord Thaume was enraged. He has returned to the city today and has had Viator Dince whipped.'

Jandille's eyes glimmered briefly. 'It resolves nothing. The Temple is closed, and my hand is . . .'

'I am sure Lord Thaume will pardon you. He has never been hostile to the Wheel.'

Jandille shook his head. 'I will not return to the city. I can never sculpt with one hand; even on the farm, there are few tasks I can perform with credit. I would not wish to receive a pension from Lord Croad; if I must accept charity, let it at least be from my own family.'

'You are a hero in the town, sir, even among those who do not follow the Wheel.'

'You have been at the wars, lad. Maybe you realize now that it is no great thing to be a hero.'

'The experience was not what I had expected. No doubt Tardolio's expectations have also been altered.'

'You have not come to see me, I am sure,' said Jandille, with an approach to a smile. 'The girls are over in Wanish Copse, looking for mushrooms. Why do you not go over and see them?'

With a bow Arren set off to walk into the woods. The interview with Jandille had been uncomfortable, as he had expected.

'Eilla! Clottie!' he called as he stepped into the copse. Out of the sun, the air was chill even at midday.

'Who is there?' came a high voice, with a tremor of uncertainty. From behind a tree came Clottie.

'Why, Arren! With sword and mail,' she cried. 'You look quite the soldier.'

Arren thought she looked thin and pinched. Her eyes were furtive. Lady Jilka's justice had not maimed Jandille alone.

'He *is* a soldier, you fool.'

Arren turned. 'Eilla!' he said.

Eilla ran a hand through her thick dark hair, now hacked roughly at her shoulders. Arren saw the same wariness in her eyes.

'Eilla, I have so much to tell you,' he said. 'But I think you must have more to tell me.'

She gave a bitter laugh and set her basket down on the ground. 'We have had our own war,' she said, 'and our own casualties.'

'I have heard,' he said. 'And I have spoken to your father.'

Eilla shrugged. 'He brought it on himself,' she said, her moist eyes belying her casual tone. 'Why did he give Jilka and Dince the excuse? Now we will all rot on the farm for ever. Canille already wants me to marry Chandry: the event will not take place. Clottie may have him if she wishes.'

A spark kindled in her eye. This was the Eilla he recognized.

'Does Canille not have a second son?' asked Arren.

'He does not, and he could have a hundred and it would make no difference. I would not marry my cousin: such things are unnatural. I have no wish for a five-headed baby, nor a husband who views an annual bath as freakish decadence. Clottie is younger and her views may not be so fixed.'

'Clottie will not be marrying Chandry either,' interjected Clottie, wrinkling her snub nose. 'My father says I am too young to think on such things.'

'They say that Lady Siedra will be packed off to Glount to find a husband,' said Arren. 'Lord Thaume will need to appease Duke Panarre. She is only Clottie's age.'

'That is called diplomacy,' said Eilla. 'It means you have to marry a man you have never met to keep happy another man you have never met.'

Arren frowned. 'Conceivably so, although Master Guiles does not represent it in that way.'

'There is no diplomacy involved in my marrying Chandry, nor in Clottie doing so, for that matter,' said Eilla. 'No one will fight a war because I refuse to marry a cousin who reeks of cow. I shall choose my own husband, or have none at all. Such is the privilege of peasantry, and I would not change places with Lady Siedra if you gave me the city of Glount as my dowry.'

'Come, have a mushroom,' said Clottie. 'We are both agog to hear how you came by the wound on your head, and how many Northmen you slew.'

Arren's anecdotes stretched into the late afternoon, and the sun made a tentative attempt to force its rays under the canopy of branches. Eventually a glowering Chandry was sent to find them, for his mother required the mushrooms for the evening's stew.

'I should have thought a great warrior had better things to do than waste the afternoon boasting to girls,' he said, his underlip drooping sullenly.

Arren had noticed that warriors as renowned as Sir Langlan appeared to do little else, but in this case jealousy was clearly at work. Did Chandry prefer Eilla or Clottie? he wondered. He did not appear promising husband material, but in this opinions might differ – although not in the case of his cousins.

'I must return to the castle,' said Arren. 'Chandry, I am sure you can see your cousins safely back to the farm.'

Chandry shot him a look of detestation. Arren could understand it: the limit of Chandry's ambitions would be to marry one of these girls and inherit the farm, while before him stood a lad his own age in Lord Thaume's livery who had been to war and could keep the girls on tenterhooks. Arren felt a flash of guilt for his condescension, but Chandry would not meet his eye, and the opportunity for cordiality was past.

4

By the time Arren returned to the castle, he was late for dinner. Lord Thaume had deferred his plans to host a banquet for the city's worthies, and the smaller group he invited instead, comprising little more than his household, rattled in the Great Hall like peas in a bladder. An atmosphere of pervasive gloom filled the remainder of the space. An artist had been at work rapidly, and pride of place on the wall was given to a martial scene entitled 'The Triumph of Lord Thaume', but Thaume paid it no mind and his guests followed his lead.

'You are late,' said Lord Thaume as Arren sneaked into the place reserved for him between Oricien and Siedra.

'I am sorry, my lord. I was in the countryside and did not notice the time.'

Lord Thaume frowned. 'The countryside?'

'I think he was visiting Master Jandille,' said Pinch quietly. An immediate tension went around the great table. Lady Jilka, at the far end, looked magisterially ahead.

After a pause Lord Thaume said: 'Yes, commendable, Arren. How did you find him?'

Arren swallowed. There was no safe answer to this. 'In truth, sir, his mood was not high. His hand—' Arren paused. 'Recent events have weighed upon his spirit.'

Lord Thaume nodded. 'Understandable. The man was a fine mason. I would do something for him.'

'My lord, I would be inclined to wait awhile. His present disposition—'

Darrien interjected: 'Do not contradict Lord Thaume, Arren.'

'This is not to be borne!' cried Lady Jilka. 'To have every raggle-taggle boy telling his lord how to rule his own realm.'

Lord Thaume pushed his bowl aside. 'Jilka, it is you who go too far. Arren is giving me honest counsel; counsel which would not have been necessary if you had not acted so pre-cipitately. And he is a boy no longer.'

Lady Jilka's jaw dropped. 'My lord—'

'Silence! You have said more than enough for today.'

Guigot, opposite Siedra, smirked. Arren looked guiltily into his soup.

Master Guiles rose from his seat. 'My lord, if I might be permitted to raise a toast to the safe return of you and your troops, the proud victory you have achieved, and the memory of those sons of Croad who have not returned.'

'Hear hear!' called Sir Langlan, his words echoing around the hall. *Hear hear, hear hear.*

'Well spoken,' said Darrien.

Arren had never previously appreciated the use of a Master of Etiquette, but on this occasion he had saved the day. Guiles raised his goblet and led the others in a toast.

Lord Thaume rose and bowed. 'I thank you, sir. Tonight we have an empty place at the table, that of the good Sir Artingaume. Let us keep him in mind.'

The meal was correspondingly sombre throughout. Arren would normally have enjoyed the soup prepared from Paladrian tomatoes grown under glass, but tonight he scarcely tasted it. The prime calf that had been slaughtered for the occasion went largely unappreciated, although Guigot did not stint himself.

'How is Viator Dince, my lord?' asked Guigot as they waited for the pears in brandy to arrive for the final course. 'When I observed the skin flayed from his back, his condition appeared unpromising.'

Lord Thaume frowned. 'This is not a matter for the dinner table, Guigot. There are ladies present.'

'I merely expressed concern for his welfare. He is an old man, and frail.' His face was as unreadable as a snake's.

'Your solicitude does you credit, Lord Guigot,' said Master Guiles. 'However, in the circumstances the matter should perhaps not be pursued. If you remain concerned for him tomorrow, I am sure he would welcome a visit in his quarters.'

'I understand that he is not in his quarters, but the infirmary,' said Guigot. 'The apothecary mentioned the possibility of gangrene.'

'Guigot!' thundered Lord Thaume. 'Did I not command your silence?'

'My apologies, sir.'

'My lord,' said Lady Jilka, 'your punishment can only have been just and merited. Surely you do not scruple to discuss it?'

'I am surprised that you prolong discussion of the unpleasant matter in the circumstances.'

Jilka gave a half-smile. 'Presumably you acted as you did for edification rather than punishment. I for one did not fully understand the lesson, since Viator Dince simply pronounced on the Way of Harmony, as is his trust.'

'Jilka, you insist on provoking me. We will hear no more of the subject tonight. If you require spiritual guidance, I suggest you commune with Viator Sleech after dinner.'

At the end of the meal, Lord Thaume set down his napkin and spoke with deliberation. 'For various reasons, this has not been the homecoming that I anticipated. It is also to be shorter than I had originally intended,' he said.

'How so, my lord?' asked Sir Langlan.

Lord Thaume reached out a letter. 'I have an invitation from Duke Panarre to visit Glount,' he said. 'I do not feel it prudent to refuse the request of my overlord.'

Sir Langlan snorted. 'This is the man who declined to send a single man to defend the city. He does not deserve our attention.'

'I understand your sentiments, Langlan; but I have neglected to secure the Duke's good opinion, and we have all suffered as a result. We shall be leaving for Glount the day after tomorrow.'

'"We"?' asked Lady Jilka softly.

'It is time that Oricien and Siedra were seen abroad. Oricien is a fine warrior, and soon I must present him at Emmen itself; while Siedra is not too young to command attention.'

'And who will rule in your absence, my lord?' asked Darrien, his eyes straying towards Jilka.

'Arrangements during my last absence were not satisfactory in every respect,' said Lord Thaume. 'Nonetheless, Lady Jilka retains my full confidence.'

'My lord—' began Viator Sleech.

'However,' continued Lord Thaume, 'my lady's presence is essential in Glount to introduce Siedra into society. The regency should have fallen to Sir Artingaume. On this occasion I will ask Sir Langlan to rule with my voice.'

'Will you not need me in Glount, my lord?'

'I need you more here, Langlan. I propose to take only a small retinue. Guigot, you too shall come with us. There may be many opportunities for a lad of your birth and spirit.'

Guigot's expression was midway between a smirk and a sneer. If Thaume noticed, he affected ignorance.

'Master Guiles, your presence will be invaluable, and Lady Cerisa, you will act as a companion for my wife and daughter.'

'What of Arren, sir?' asked Oricien.

Lord Thaume rubbed his chin. 'Ah, yes, Arren. His mother would like to see him, no doubt, Darrien?'

Guigot and Siedra giggled.

'He is in your household now, my lord,' said Darrien.

'Oricien, if you would like to take Arren as a companion, you may do so.'

'Thank you, father.'

And so Arren's destiny was settled without his being put to the inconvenience of expressing an opinion. Since he had never seen the sea, he was not disposed to complain.

The day after next, Lord Thaume rode again out of the city, once more at the head of the column. This time Lady Jilka rode beside him, dressed in her martial clothing. If cordiality existed between them it was disguised, perhaps for reasons of protocol. Mounted on a fine strider was Oricien, with Siedra and Guigot immediately behind them. Arren was further back, riding alongside Coppercake, who was a native of Glount, and whose mathematical skills Lord Thaume felt likely to be necessary. Master Pinch was not present: in the way of thaumaturges, he had slipped off into the night, to return at his own convenience.

The journey south, through the rolling hills of the Duchy of Lynnoc, was uneventful, and a week later they rode into the city of Glount, the seat of Duke Panarre.

5

Glount had been the seat of the Dukes of Lynnoc for a thousand years. One of the oldest cities of Mondia, squeezed between the Penitent Hills and the sea, it had long been a centre of commerce. If Croad was a poor cousin to Emmen, Glount was an older uncle, steeped in every vice and abomination concealed under a veneer of urbanity. The Dukes of Lynnoc embodied the essence of their city, and could trace their lineage back to its foundation with only a minimum of creative genealogy. A powerful independent city for six centuries until its fall to the first King Jehan, it had taken its absorption into the Emmenrule with scarcely a blink. Things went on as they had always done, and while the King away in Emmen might wield a nominal authority, to the folk and rulers of Glount, matters went on as they had always done.

These matters included the homage of the Lords of Croad, for Lynnoc had long held sway to the North. The Duke of Lynnoc's claim to be the overlord of Croad was recognized in Emmen, and at irregular intervals the Lord of Croad must present himself in the city to swear fealty for his lands.

It was this which brought Lord Thaume south only weeks

after his victory at Jehan's Steppe. Duke Panarre had learned that Thaume intended to exact ransoms from the captured nobility of Mettingloom, and summoned him south that a suitable tribute to himself might be negotiated. Lord Thaume, who normally would have ignored such a demand, felt bound to accede on this occasion as the price of introducing his children into the court at Glount. The time approached when a marriage would need to be arranged for Siedra: ideally to Panarre's eldest son Trevarre, although other expedients might be necessary. Panarre would be likely to raise the question of uniting his lackwitted daughter Klaera with Oricien, a prospect which could only be resisted most strongly. It was not out of the question that Guigot could be offered in this context, although Thaume could already hear the imprecations from his nephew should he raise the topic.

Arren had heard much of Glount, and expected anticlimax, but he was impressed in spite of himself at his first sight of the city. It was hidden away behind three hills, each topped by a castle – La Bastia, Castella and Fortessa – and appeared cramped against the shore from the high perspective of the traveller looking down. Ships teemed in the sheltered horseshoe of the bay, some the distinctive cogs of the North, more galleys from Garganet and Gammerling. Even from this distance, the place teemed with a visible vitality. Away to the east, the River Lynnoc bustled down to the sea, with the palace of Duke Panarre set against it.

Coppercake was riding alongside Arren. 'Glount. I hope you are prepared.'

'How could it be otherwise, Master Coppercake? All I have heard for the past week are your tales of how the citizens spend their days mulcting each other of coin, and their nights engaged in debauchery of every dye.'

Coppercake chuckled. 'I may have exaggerated a little, or at least glossed over the mundanities. But if you wonder at my facility with mathematics, it is because you learn it early in Glount, or you are rooked.'

'We will not be visiting the city, at least not immediately,' said Lady Cerisa. 'Lord Thaume intends us to proceed directly to the palace.'

'Perhaps for the best,' said Arren. 'I do not care to be rooked on my first day.'

'I am keen to visit the Molo,' said Lady Cerisa. 'It is where *The Masque of Louison and Eleanora* reaches its tragic conclusion.'

Arren had found *The Masque* – a tale of lovers thwarted by destiny, improbable coincidence and a large measure of their own stupidity – a vapid experience, but Lady Cerisa had insisted they spend a tedious two weeks watching and discussing the play. He had no desire to explore the matter further during his sojourn in Glount. Conceivably Siedra could be persuaded to accompany Lady Cerisa on her visit to the Molo.

Master Guiles rode back from the head of the column. 'We are approaching the gate. Full decorum is in order. You may find the folk of Glount somewhat haughty. Do not bridle at their inspection; they will take it as a sign of low breeding, and mock you the more. At the palace matters should proceed with greater punctilio.'

'I would add my own advice,' said Coppercake. 'Do not part with coin under any circumstances. You can be assured that the seeming bargain is not. If you are offered a house for a single florin, you may guarantee it is haunted, cursed, or worse. You should not undertake any transaction without my guidance.'

The party drew up outside the eastern gate of the city. The walls reached high above them, the towers grasping for the sky above. Glount had only once fallen to invasion, and that through treachery rather than assault.

Lord Thaume dismounted from his strider and approached the gate on foot. With the hilt of his sword he banged three times on the great doors. 'I am Thaume of Croad,' he called. 'I am come at the command of my overlord, good Duke Panarre of Lynnoc. May I gain admittance?'

From the gatehouse issued a squadron of ten or so soldiers, immaculately attired in uniforms of forest green, the sleeves slashed to reveal a lighter green which also coloured their four-cornered hats.

'You are welcome to our city, my lord. I will call upon the seneschal.'

One of the guards returned to the gatehouse, returning with a man of late maturity, his sober black coat and breeches given life by a scarlet neckcloth and hat.

'Lord Thaume, you are welcome. It has been too long since you were in our city.'

'Seneschal Tourmi, I am of course delighted to be here. I confess myself surprised that Duke Panarre is not here to take my obeisance.'

'Regrettably the Duke is otherwise occupied. Many affairs of state press upon him. He will greet you at the banquet in your honour tonight. Now, please enter our city. The Cavalieres will escort you to the palace.'

Lord Thaume remounted his strider and rode into the city, followed in precise order by Lady Jilka, Oricien, Siedra and Guigot. The other members of the party followed in a more random configuration.

Some twenty Cavalieres, in the same green uniforms as their comrades, led Lord Thaume's entourage through the streets. Master Guiles sniffed as he rode alongside Arren. 'Things go ill here,' he said. 'There are two clear breaches of protocol already.'

'How so?' asked Arren. These matters were generally tedious, but he was coming to realize that much lay below the surface of such niceties. If he was to be insulted, it would be useful at least to know it.

'First,' said Master Guiles with a didactic nod, 'Duke Panarre did not greet us himself. In certain circumstances this is permissible, but he should at least have sent a member of his family in his stead. Tourmi would only have been appropriate had our party been led by Sir Langlan or a person of similar stature. Second, a guard of twenty Cavalieres is disparagingly small. The Lord of a great city such as Croad should command a hundred, or even more.'

'What does Duke Panarre mean by such discourtesy?' asked Lady Cerisa. 'Lord Thaume is coming to make good homage.'

Coppercake laughed. 'Panarre may be a grand lord,' he said, 'but he has the blood of Glount running in his veins. He is concerned to ensure financial advantage over Thaume.'

'I fail to understand,' said Arren.

'Panarre wishes to take a share of the ransoms Thaume will gain from Jehan's Steppe. He intends to put him in his place from the outset. If rumours are to be believed, he also wishes to marry a daughter to Oricien or Guigot: in this case he will wish to minimize the dowry he has to pay.'

Lady Cerisa frowned. 'Should not a duke be too proud to dicker in this way?'

'You have much to learn about Glount, my lady,' said Coppercake. 'In the eyes of his people Panarre gains merit by such ploys. You cannot imagine that Lord Thaume has brought me to the city for my conversation or my red hair: I am here to count his fingers to ensure none has been purloined.'

6

The evening saw the promised banquet in Duke Panarre's palace, an imposing structure of marble chased with gold; gardens and grounds rolling over many acres. Arren could hear the sea crashing against the shore in the background, and the air had a fresh crispness he had never known in Croad.

The diners were arrayed over two tables. At the intricately carved Ducal Table, spread with rich damask, sat Duke Panarre and his lady Fourette beside Lord Thaume and Lady Jilka. In the places of honour next to them were their various connections: Panarre's sons Trevarre and Dinarre and his daughters Helisette, Genevieva and the lackwitted Klaera, plus Oricien, Siedra and Guigot. To his surprise, Arren was placed at the same table, even if at its foot.

The second table, with Seneschal Tourmi at the head, was for servants of greater or lesser stature, including Masters Guiles and Coppercake and the former Serjeant Fleuraume, now a captain in his own right.

As soon as everyone had taken their places and the minstrels had ceased their lays, Duke Panarre stood and raised his hand for silence. A man of late maturity, he had an easy confidence that held the attention. His cheeks were the veined purple of the habitual drinker; his lips full, red and moist. He carried off an outfit of scarlet and cerulean velvet without embarrassment.

'Lord Thaume, you are most welcome to my city,' he said. 'It has been too long since you graced us with your wisdom and counsel. I could never have imagined that young Oricien and Siedra would grow so fast, so strong and so handsome. If this matter is apparent to me, imagine the impact it has made on my children, ha ha! Lady Jilka, your beauty is unimpaired by the passing years: would that time were as kind to us all! Tales of your legendary piety have reached us—' Lord Thaume could not repress a grimace, as Panarre seemed to notice '—and it seems unfair to the rest of us that such pulchritude, wisdom and humility should be united in one person.'

Lady Jilka inclined her head to the most fractional extent possible.

'All will wish to hear the story of your great victory at Jehan's Steppe – would that I had been able to be there myself at the head of a mighty force of Cavalieres – but tonight I pray that you submit yourselves to the hospitality of our city. Some say we are sybarites, given over only to our own pleasures. Such caricatures are the work of envious minds, but none can deny that when we apply ourselves to festivity we are not without talent or imagination. Frivolity is a serious business, if I might be permitted a quibble. Lord Thaume, Lady Jilka, and your companions: I hope your visit to Glount is a memorable one.'

Duke Panarre sat down with a dramatic sweep, brushing his scarlet cloak aside when it threatened to become entangled with his person. At the other table Arren saw Guiles and Coppercake whispering; trying to calculate, he thought, the number of slights and insults buried in Panarre's speech.

Lord Thaume rose from his seat. In contrast to Panarre, he was dressed in ascetic black from head to toe.

'My lord, I am grateful for your fulsome welcome to your city and your palace. It is indeed all too long since the cares of Croad have allowed me to leave the city behind. Ever since my accession, careful vigilance has been necessary against the men of the North, all the more so because of the small number of troops at my disposal. It is only with the check to King Tardolio's warlike ambitions that I feel able to leave Croad in the hands of a capable lieutenant. Like yourself, I am astonished to find your children so grown. Indeed, Lords Trevarre and Dinarre are now young men, even if they still await the chance to show the world their martial prowess. Such fine young men will make bold and brave husbands to certain fortunate ladies of the future. As to your trio of beautiful daughters, I have no words adequate. Reports of Lady Helisette's comeliness are not exaggerated, and Lady Genevieva displays even greater elegance and grace than might be expected from her illustrious pedigree. Lady Klaera is fortunate to have such a family to care for her needs, and perhaps in time may even find a husband among the minor gentry.

'I see the footmen descending with the first course, and all folk of good sense will wish to apply themselves to your repast rather than to my words, so I do not have time to praise Duchess Fourette as she deserves. One need only to look at the five remarkable fruits of her womb to know how to assess her worth. Sir and madam, I thank you for your welcome and hospitality.'

As he sat down, Master Guiles nodded in satisfaction. Lord Thaume had shown that he was not cowed by Panarre's innuendoes. This was war, if not as overt as Jehan's Steppe.

Arren lost track of the number of courses. He had never realized there were so many ways to prepare potatoes, or that beef could be garnished with lemons and redders, or how many different wines the slopes of Lynnoc produced. He was seated between two mature ladies, who favoured him with little attention, until the point where the wine took hold, and one began to simper at him most alarmingly. The appetites of Glount were notorious, but Lady Sybille must have been at least fifty, and corpulent to boot. Master Guiles had not provided instruction in dealing with such situations.

During the meal he took the opportunity to appraise Duke Panarre's children. Trevarre took his attire most seriously, and his costume had more lace than most of the ladies present. His every utterance was grand and dramatic, accompanied with gestures so extravagant that Arren feared for the wine flasks on the table. When the conversation moved away from the topics that interested him – which appeared to be few – he pouted until such time as he could wrest attention back to himself. Guigot appeared simultaneously repelled and fascinated. He loosened his own garments and seemed to be doing everything possible to create a slovenly impression, despite reproving glances from his uncle and aunt.

Young Lord Dinarre had sharp regular features and plentiful dark hair. His clothes were rich without showiness, and he had a ready wit and smile which he deployed upon Siedra. Arren recalled that he had a reputation for cruelty, and he saw in the rich sensuous lips he had inherited from his father signs of a vicious disposition.

Arren was more favourably impressed with the ladies. Lady Helisette, as the eldest daughter of the Duke of Lynnoc, was one of the great prizes of the Emmenrule, and nature had endowed her with a beauty and vivacity to make the most of it. Oricien seemed enthralled by her curling golden hair and innocent blue eyes. A stern critic might have observed that her conversation tended towards the vapid, but Oricien appeared ready to overlook the fault. Arren remembered that Master Guiles had rated the chances of a match as minimal, but Oricien seemed nothing daunted.

Lady Genevieva had not the instant and captivating beauty of her elder sister. Nonetheless she impressed Arren with her quiet intelligence and good humour, and her attention to Lady Klaera, for whom eating a meal of many courses without embarrassment was a significant achievement.

At last the final course appeared, accompanied by a strong, sweet, dense wine which at once thrilled and repelled: rather like Glount itself, thought Arren. Duke Panarre led a toast to his guests and suggested that Lord Thaume might wish to join him and sample together some pleasures not suitable for mixed company. The other guests, seemingly, were at their own devices.

Arren, whose head was fuddled from the wine, and had little appetite for further food or conversation, offered his polite farewells and retired to his chambers.

9

Mettingloom

No building called the Darkstone was likely to promote the soul's ease, and Mettingloom's most notorious prison lived up – or down – to its sombre name. It was not designed for the rabble: only political prisoners, or those accused of the most serious crimes, found accommodation there. The island on which it stood jutted up from the lagoon in summer, and in winter was surrounded by a sheet of ice and snow. Escape, in any event only a theoretical possibility, would have required a lengthy swim in the summer; in the winter the escapee would have to negotiate the holes in the ice concealed beneath the snow, with a mistake meaning a fatal plunge into the chill waters below.

It was here that Beauceron found himself brought immediately after his arrest. Escape was not an immediate prospect. Intrigue had brought him here, and it would have to take him out again. As a well-known prisoner, he had a cell which was, if not luxurious, better than most of the other inmates enjoyed. He had a proper bed, a chair and a desk, and windows which closed. He would hardly be growing fat on good living, but at least he would not freeze to death.

The gaoler, a seasoned professional named Tintazzo,

agreed to take letters to various destinations at Beauceron's request. It was apparent that he was indeed to have at least an appearance of a proper trial. Essentially the evidence would come down to his word against Sir Goccio's, since there was little if any direct proof. However, he knew that Davanzato would be sure to have paid witnesses, and since the King was the final arbiter of the case, he could not expect the benefit of the doubt. An acquittal was unlikely without some external intervention. Now was the time to find out who his friends were.

Beauceron was allowed no visitors over the next three days, but on the fourth morning Tintazzo appeared accompanied by Monetto. Beauceron thought that he had probably had more sleep than his lieutenant.

'Be of good cheer,' he said as Tintazzo made his way out. 'I am not dead yet.'

Monetto sat down and withdrew various papers. 'The auguries are not good. You are accused of high treason against Fanrolio, by virtue of conspiring with Sir Goccio to raise an army against the Winter King's command.'

Beauceron nodded. 'The charge is hard to rebut, in that it is true. The only real witness, however, is Sir Goccio. I am unclear as to the niceties of the law: is he too not guilty of treason?'

'I have been researching the question overnight. His crime is petty treason, because he is not Fanrolio's man. You are accused of grand treason, conspiracy against a King to whom you have sworn fealty. Both are serious offences, but yours considerably more so.'

'Sir Goccio's status as a witness must therefore be questionable.'

'Davanzato has offered him a reduced sentence in return for cooperation. He does not intend to present you with a similar opportunity. In addition, there are further witnesses.'

Beauceron raised his eyebrows. 'They can only be paid informants. I discussed the subject with no one but Sir Goccio.'

Monetto flicked through his papers. 'There are various of Sir Goccio's associates. I assume they have been bribed to support their master's story. Most worrying of all, Lady Isola is to be called as a witness. Think carefully: have you had any treasonable conversation with her?'

'Most emphatically not. Do you think I would discuss such affairs with a woman, particularly one who nurtures such hostility?'

'I imagine not, although such a comely person must have considerable wiles. You have not always been wise where ladies are concerned.'

'I have never allowed such dalliances to retard my plans, and I have not started now. Am I to understand that Davanzato intends to prosecute the case himself?'

'Just so. As Under-Chamberlain it is not just his right but his duty to do so.'

'He has clearly been planning this for some time. I can only assume that Fanrolio is more amenable to my scheme than Davanzato had told me; otherwise why would he take the risk of destroying me? He is not a man for unnecessary risk.'

'The Bill of Trial seeks not only your execution – naturally – but the attainder of your goods. As the prosecutor he would be entitled to one-quarter of the proceeds. Even a less avaricious man might be tempted.'

'No doubt he has promised Isola it will pay off her ransom.'

'She cannot trust him?'

'She is desperate, and her judgement is overset by events. What has she to lose? She owes me no loyalty; quite the reverse.'

'I have taken the liberty of engaging a legulier, one Mon-grissore. Neither you nor I have the necessary knowledge to mount your defence. He is outside, if you wish to see him.'

'What kind of man is he?'

Monetto grimaced. 'He knows his business; and he puts a high value on his services. Meet him for yourself, reach your own judgement.'

Beauceron nodded. 'Fetch him.'

Master Mongrissore was a man of late middle age, scanty white hair flying in all directions. Commanding as his fees might have been, they were not spent on his wardrobe, which consisted of a threadbare black suit; nor did they appear to finance gourmandizing, for Mongrissore was rake-thin. Beauceron's initial impression was not favourable, and he looked askance at Monetto.

Mongrissore pulled out of a valise tucked under his arm a jumble of documents. He resembled the legal papers among which he spent his days. His skin had the dry waxy pallor of parchment; his untidy black suit rustled with a papery susurration when he moved; his small keen black eyes were like inkspots staining the margins of a page.

Mongrissore shook hands with greater firmness than his appearance might have implied. 'Gratified to meet you, sir. We have much to cover, since Davanzato is pressing for an immediate trial. I must assess your own state: what of your bowels?'

'Bowels?'

Mongrissore clucked. 'Regularity, man! Are you a five-a-day man, or once a week? You have a costive look.'

'I fail to see the relevance of this line of inquiry.'

'A skilled observer can learn more of a man from his bowels than from his eyes. I admit I am no coprognostic, but a little knowledge may go a long way.'

'If you must know, my bowels move with daily regularity.'

'And has this changed during your incarceration?'

'No. Is this germane to my defence?'

Mongrissore scratched his chin, which appeared not to have been shaved that day.

'I dislike explaining my reasonings, but you are clearly a man who will be satisfied with nothing less. The regularity of your movements, even under such difficult circumstances, argues for a phlegmatic constitution. You are unlikely to panic under questioning, and I can plan my defence on the basis that you can testify if needs be. I learn also that you are impatient, truculent, untrusting.'

'All this from negligible information as to my digestion?'

'The latter inferences I have drawn from your demeanour. Let me say that your situation is unpromising. Davanzato is a keen opponent, and his evidence is strong. You will have to show a far greater faith in my judgement if you are to escape the noose.'

'The "strong" evidence you refer to is fabricated.'

'You must disabuse yourself of the notion that truth has any part to play in these proceedings. A treason trial concerns what can be proved, not what is true: there is often considerable divergence between the two. What is true, of course, cannot always be proved; but in law, that which is proved may not always be true.'

'I have not employed you for a lecture on jurisprudence, nor for commonplace epigrams. Your role is simple: to secure my acquittal.'

Mongrissore nodded. 'Are you guilty?'

Beauceron raised his eyebrows.

'I have no scruples of any sort,' said Mongrissore. 'I do not care one way or the other; however, my job is easier if I know whether I am obscuring the truth or revealing it.'

'In a limited, technical sense, I imagine I am guilty. I had allowed Sir Goccio to believe that I supported his proposal to raise an army against Croad, and that I would lead it.'

'And to whom have you communicated this knowledge?'

'Other than yourself and Monetto, only to Sir Goccio himself.'

Mongrissore nodded. 'Davanzato has depositions not just from Sir Goccio but also fourteen of his men, who claim a detailed plan was worked out at The Ill-Favoured Loon tavern; and from Lady Isola, who deposes that you had expressed your dissatisfaction with King Fanrolio and your consequent intention to change your allegiance to King Tardolio.'

Beauceron poured himself a beaker of water. 'These allegations are uniformly false. I may be guilty of the treason described but there is no evidence.'

'Good, very good.'

Beauceron frowned. 'I fail to see how the prospect of my being convicted on false testimony is "very good".'

'That is why I am the legulier and you the hapless accused. We can now spend our time undermining the witnesses involved. Any information you can provide me which will call into question the motives of Sir Goccio, Lady Isola and most importantly Under-Chamberlain Davanzato will help us all.'

'Monetto has a wealth of such facts to hand.'

Monetto gave a quiet smile. 'The only difficulties will come in marshalling them,' he said.

2

'All hail His Puissant Majesty, the Winter King of Mettingloom, the Northern Reaches and Lynnoc: Fanrolio!'

Beauceron, already seated at a bench in the private judicial chamber alongside Mongrissore, craned his head as the King was announced. On Fanrolio's attitude much would depend. Today he was bedecked in his judicial robes of white and black. It was a treason trial, and by convention all those present were dressed only in monochrome. The only colour in the chamber was the ruddy wood of the benches and table, and a sprawl of jauntily coloured folios in front of Mongrissore.

The judicial chamber was not large: it needed only to accommodate the accused – Beauceron and Sir Goccio – Mongrissore, the prosecutor Davanzato and his assistants, the two Lords of Equity, and of course the King. The panelled walls were varnished to a high sheen and the ceiling painted a matt black, with stars picked out in white. The dark ceiling lowered oppressively and seemed to force Beauceron down onto his bench. He shook his head to clear the impression: the furnishings' effects were deliberate and calculated, and he could not afford to succumb to them.

Fanrolio seated himself with infinite care on the silvered throne. Beauceron idly wondered if the monarch suffered from haemorrhoids, such was the deliberation with which he placed his fundament.

'This is a melancholy day,' said the King in his customary quavering voice. 'To find a noble knight of the Sunflower and our own Captain Beauceron brought before us in this way. Under-Chamberlain Davanzato, you have marshalled the evidence: would you care to present it?'

Davanzato rose and bowed. He cut a dashing figure with his black robes set against his olive skin. His dark eyes flashed with diligence.

'Your Puissance, I thank you. It gives me no pleasure to outline treasons against your person. The sooner the disagreeable matter is concluded, the best for all. I hope that the accused will favour us in this matter by swiftly declaring their guilt, so that a due and proportionate sentence can be handed down. For reasons which will become apparent, I lay my charges first against Sir Goccio, Knight of the Sunflower.

'Sir Goccio, it is my contention that you have conspired to commit the act of petty treason against your just sovereign King Fanrolio, in concert with the low-born rogue Beauceron, once of the Emmenrule, and a sworn man of our King. Your allegiance, sir, as we all know, is to King Tardolio. Nonetheless, like every subject of this realm, you owe duty, obedience and loyalty to the King of the Season, regardless of any other oath you may have sworn. The penalty for the crime of petty treason is death, subject only to His Puissance's mercy. What have you to say?'

Sir Goccio rose from his bench. Unlike Beauceron, he had chosen to appear without a legulier. He bowed to the King, the Lords of Equity and finally to Davanzato.

'Before this court and before the King, I freely and humbly admit my guilt,' he said. 'I was approached by Captain Beauceron with a proposal that I should act as an intermediary between himself and King Tardolio, with the purpose of raising an army against the city of Croad. This I did willingly, but foolishly.'

'Were you aware,' asked Davanzato in a neutral voice, 'that in assisting Captain Beauceron to evade his oath of service to King Fanrolio, you committed a petty treason?'

Sir Goccio bowed his head. 'Sir, I was. My enthusiasm for battle, for glory, for Mettingloom, caused me to overlook my duty. With my comrades and Captain Beauceron, we drew up battle plans from The Ill-Favoured Loon, a tavern known for its allegiance to the Sunflower cause.'

'A melancholy tale,' said Davanzato, 'and one of a brave man, seduced from what was right and true by the silver tongue of a foreign rogue who played upon your good instincts. Although I prosecute this case, I recommend mercy to my lords and to Your Puissance. Guilt is incontrovertible; only the penalty remains to be fixed.'

Mongrissore coughed. 'Excuse me, good sirs,' he said, rising. Beauceron looked sideways. Mongrissore had not expressed any previous intention to intervene in this trial. Not for the first time Beauceron felt that Mongrissore's appearance was not in his favour. His patched suit was the only one Beauceron had ever seen him wear; although at least today he had honoured court and King with a shave.

Fanrolio blinked rheumily. Ulrado, the Lord of Equity from the Summer Court, fixed Mongrissore with a stern glance. 'This is not your case, Legulier.'

'Your pardon, my lord. However, Sir Goccio's testimony is pertinent to the case in which I am retained. It is more seemly to tackle such points as they arise.'

'This is most irregular,' said Gionardo, the Winter Court's corpulent Lord of Equity.

'Let us not stand upon legalisms,' said Fanrolio querulously. 'Let us have the facts. Legulier Mongrissore, ask such questions as you have.'

'Your Puissance, I thank you. Sir Goccio, you testified that Captain Beauceron approached you to act as an intermediary with the Summer King.'

Sir Goccio looked around. 'I did, sir.'

'Did you do so?'

'I do not understand.'

'Come, the question is simple. You must need sharp wits to be a conspirator. Did you in fact speak to His Puissance as Beauceron had requested?'

'Ah – no.'

'You did not speak to His Puissance on the topic?'

'No, sir.' This with greater firmness. 'You cannot imagine

that King Tardolio had any part in plotting against the Winter King.'

'I imagine nothing, Sir Goccio. We have established an important fact: King Tardolio was not aware of your scheme?'

'No, sir.'

'You plotted, with Captain Beauceron and fourteen others, to raise the Summer Army – King Tardolio's Summer Army – without the King's knowledge?'

'Yes, sir,' mumbled Sir Goccio.

'A curious act. Would you say you are well connected with the King?'

'I am his sworn knight, sir.'

Mongrissore nodded. 'I believe there are over eighty Knights of the Summer Court.'

'I have never counted them, sir,' said Sir Goccio with a drooping mouth.

'You may take my word for it. Do you imagine the King has eighty intimate counsellors?'

'No, sir.'

'I therefore remain to be convinced of the level of influence you maintain. How many times, in the past year, have you spoken to His Puissance?'

There was a pause.

'Are you counting to a high number, Sir Goccio? Twenty, a hundred? An approximation will suffice.'

'Once, sir.'

Mongrissore barked with laughter. 'I am sorry, Sir Goccio, I misheard you. I thought you said "once".'

Sir Goccio's shoulders sagged. 'So I did, sir.'

'You have spoken to the King once in the past year. At least you will easily be able to recall the occasion for us.'

Sir Goccio had given up any pretence of spirit. 'It was to renew my oath, sir.'

'Let me clarify this for my lords' benefit: Captain Beauceron approached you to use your great influence with the King to put in train plans for a mighty Summer Army. This influence, in fact, consisted merely in renewing your oath. Instead you said nothing at all to the King – who may well not even know who you are – and plotted merrily away without the slightest reference to events at the Summer Court.'

'You put an unfavourable construction on events.'

'I would be interested to know how one could favourably construe an acknowledged case of petty treason.'

'The fact remains that Beauceron engaged in a treasonous act! My motivations are not to the point.'

'No, indeed. Your veracity, however, is very much to the point, and when the time comes to weigh Beauceron's guilt, your inconsistent, muddled, implausible and frankly mendacious testimony will be in the forefront of our minds. My lords, I thank you for your indulgence.'

Mongrissore sat down and made a cryptic scribble on his pad. Beauceron looked at him with new respect. He had with great ease made Sir Goccio into a liar and a fool.

Davanzato rose from his bench. 'We are all grateful, I am sure, for Legulier Mongrissore's masterly proof of the guilt of a man who had already admitted his crimes. Had I known this lucrative profession required so little rigour I myself might have followed this path. Be that as it may, Sir Goccio has humbly and fully confessed his act of petty treason. His penitence is obvious, and it remains only to set the penalty. I call not for the death of this repentant knight, but a sizeable fine, perhaps in the region of 3,000 florins. My lords?'

Lord Gionardo scowled. 'You speak lightly of treason. I vote for hanging and attainder.'

Lord Ulrado shook his head. 'I am shamed that a Knight of the Sunflower should so forget himself. Nonetheless, the true guilt lies elsewhere. Your Puissance, a great king is one who knows where to show mercy.'

Fanrolio's head rolled from side to side. 'Under-Chamberlain Davanzato is a man of seasoned judgement, despite his youth. Sir Goccio, I note your guilt and your repentance. I commute the sentence of death to a fine of 3,500 florins. You are discharged, although I believe you must remain as a witness in our next case.'

3

Beauceron returned heartened to his cell. Mongrissore had effectively demolished Sir Goccio's credibility as a witness. He was sure, though, that Davanzato would not so easily give up.

Tintazzo had made no difficulty about furnishing Beauceron with meals of a good standard in return for a suitable consideration. Tonight the fare was half a roast fowl basted in its own juices, potatoes herb-roasted and a selection of winter vegetables. A crisp white wine complemented the dish to perfection, and Beauceron, who disdained mealtime chatter, decided that his incarceration was not without its benefits.

After dinner Tintazzo appeared with an unexpected visitor whose face was concealed under a black hood: Prince Laertio.

'My lord,' said Beauceron. 'I am honoured, if surprised.'

Laertio seated himself on the couch with a grin and stretched out. 'You are a foolish man, Beauceron. I had offered you a much better option than the one you chose.'

'Hindsight would appear to have vindicated you, although I am not without hope in this case.'

Laertio raised his eyebrows. 'I see little basis for

optimism. Your man Mongrissore proved Sir Goccio a fool and knave today: there will not have been a man in the room who did not know that already.'

'Davanzato intended his testimony to be the central strand of his case.'

Laertio reached for the wine flask. 'And so it shall. Do you think either of the Lords of Equity is favourably disposed towards you?'

'I had not considered the question.'

'I am, of course, well acquainted with Lord Ulrado. Given what I told you about my father's aversion to the invasion – which you chose to disbelieve – you cannot imagine he will wish to see you freed. And Gionardo will be keen to punish the slight against his King.'

'The Lords of Equity do not make the final judgement.'

Laertio gave a crooked smile. 'You have seen Fanrolio. Can you envisage him overturning the counsel of his Lords of Equity and his Under-Chamberlain?'

Beauceron took a gloomy pull at his goblet. 'Mongrissore is a resourceful man.'

'He is not a thaumaturge, which is what your situation requires.'

'I assume your leisure is not so extensive as to permit you to waste an evening taunting me. Do you have a concrete reason for being here?'

'We discussed certain eventualities at the Midwinter Ball,' said Laertio. 'The scenario I outlined remains attractive to me.'

'Were I free,' said Beauceron, 'I might take a more favourable view myself.'

'The Darkstone is not impregnable,' said Laertio. 'I might be inclined to exert myself if I knew there would be a return.'

Beauceron gave a sour smile. 'Such talk is easy. You will

forgive me if I do not base my hopes around such an eventuality.'

Laertio shrugged. 'As long as I am convinced of your support for my cause, all will be well. In addition, the Lady Cosetta would be loath to see you come to harm.'

Beauceron raised his eyebrows. 'Now you do surprise me.'

'She is a lady of unusual vivacity and refinement. The way in which she has dealt with her circumstances impresses me, and in so far as I am able, I indulge her whims. She regards you, perversely, as the architect of her current fortunes.'

'I will not enquire as to the nature of your intimacy.'

Laertio grinned. 'Perhaps you should not. For now, I bid you good evening.'

Beauceron lay on his bed and stared ahead for an hour after Laertio had gone. Nothing he had heard made him view the Prince as anything other than the most capricious and unreliable of associates. Beauceron was not a sentimental man, and persuasive as Cosetta might be, she would never be able to induce him to act against his own interests.

4

The next days went as expected for Beauceron. He was charged with grand treason against his sworn king, and Davanzato demanded from the outset execution and attainder of his goods as sanctioned under the Old Law of Treasons and Malfeaties. Before Davanzato dared to bring Sir Goccio forward again, all fourteen associate witnesses were called. Legulier Mongrissore once more exposed the implausibilities and inconsistencies of his account.

'Very well,' said Mongrissore at the end of his questioning. 'I cannot make your mendacity any plainer to the court.

You are free to leave with whatever honour you think you retain.'

Sir Goccio returned to his chair with a heavy tread. He had not looked at Beauceron throughout the trial; now, his ordeal over, he flicked a surreptitious glance: part guilt, part regret, part shame. Beauceron returned an unwavering gaze. He felt no sympathy for the Sunflower Knight: according to Monetto's researches, he had allowed himself to be bought for an agreement from Davanzato to settle his 3,000-florin debts. Even here, Davanzato had proved false, for the fine of 3,500 florins imposed by Fanrolio had more than wiped out his gains. But by then it was too late for Sir Goccio to go back. Once again Davanzato had skipped clear of his obligations.

King Fanrolio rose. 'We have had a long morning; we shall now repair to lunch.' The room emptied, only Mongrissore and Beauceron, who was not free to leave, being left behind.

'What do you think?' asked Beauceron.

Mongrissore gave an expressive gesture. 'We have done what we can. The testimony of Sir Goccio and his associates is revealed as lie piled on lie. If Fanrolio retains an open mind, Davanzato has proved nothing, regardless of what the Lords of Equity may advise.'

Beauceron nodded slowly. 'Optimism would seem premature.'

Mongrissore smoothed his unruly hair. 'Optimism is always called for, particularly in adverse circumstances. Where is the merit of a positive approach when the sun is already shining? In any event, this afternoon we have Lady Isola; her testimony may make a great impression on the King.'

'It is motivated by spite.'

'We shall see. She will be able to manipulate an old man's

sympathy; but her temper is uncertain. Here is an area for me to probe.'

'I ask you to be candid, Mongrissore: is there any hope of an acquittal?'

Mongrissore tidied the shamble of papers on the desk before him. 'The evidence is weak, but the political currents are strong. I have a further expedient, which I do not wish to use unless I must. It exposes you to danger I would prefer to avoid. If events are adverse, I will nonetheless deploy it.'

'Your expedient is?'

Mongrissore stroked his chin. 'There is no profit to explore it in advance. If we need it, we will use it.'

And with that, Beauceron had to be satisfied. Mongrissore was not a man to be coerced into revealing his secrets.

5

Immediately after lunch, Davanzato with great ceremony called Lady Isola into the chamber. Her white dress set her dark hair and eyes off to great advantage, and Beauceron thought gloomily of how innocent an impression she would make upon King Fanrolio.

Davanzato rose from his seat. 'My lady, your graciousness in consenting to appear before us is much appreciated. We well recognize your unfortunate circumstances.'

Lady Isola looked down at her feet.

'My lady, you were at one time resident in Beauceron's house?' asked Davanzato.

'I was, sir,' said Isola in a clear high voice.

'What were your feelings towards him at this time?'

'I naturally resented the fact that he had kidnapped me. I was grateful, however, for his offer of accommodation.'

'And what of Beauceron's feelings towards you?'

Isola flushed. 'I cannot say, sir. I surmised that he felt guilt at having kidnapped me.'

Davanzato nodded. 'And how, indeed, could he not? While you lived under the same roof, did he confide in you?'

'Not in general, sir. However, he nurtured a powerful desire to lead an army against Croad. This frequently formed the basis of his conversation.'

'He even referred to himself as a "monomaniac"?'

'Yes, sir.'

'Did he apprise you of the progress of his scheme?'

'Yes, almost daily.' Beauceron remained impassive as she risked a side-glance.

'His original scheme was to persuade King Fanrolio to award him the command of a large army?'

'Yes, sir.'

'How did his programme advance?'

'Not well, sir. He felt that His Puissance was not in favour of the scheme, nor his advisers.'

'In this he was correct,' said Davanzato with a grim smile. 'Surely a man as resourceful as Beauceron had an alternative approach?'

Lady Isola bit her lip. Once again she looked at her feet.

'My lady? The court waits upon your answer.'

She turned to stare into Beauceron's face. Beauceron met her eye and raised his eyebrows.

'My apologies, sir. Beauceron said to me that he no longer had patience with King Fanrolio, and that he would instead be pursuing matters with King Tardolio.'

Davanzato looked around the table at the Lords of Equity before swinging his gaze to Fanrolio. 'Beauceron explicitly admitted to intending to work with King Tardolio?'

Isola's voice dropped to a whisper. 'Yes, sir. Beauceron announced his treasonous designs to me. He had approached a Knight of the Summer Court to act as his intermediary. On several occasions he went to meet him in the evenings.'

Isola was now weeping. Beauceron tried to catch her eye, but she looked away. For a second he felt sympathy: she was only trying to navigate waters into which he had brought her. He shook his head as if to clear a fog and leaned over to Mongrissore. 'Destroy her,' he said in flat quiet voice.

Davanzato had sat down after recapitulating the main points of Isola's testimony. Mongrissore stretched himself erect.

'My lady, I too wish to extend my sympathies at your fate, not one that any observer would wish upon a fair maid.' He paused. 'You are a maid, are you not?'

Isola flushed. 'Of course, sir; although it is no business of yours, or the court's.'

Mongrissore raised a placatory hand. 'You lived under Beauceron's roof in all propriety, then?'

She set her jaw. 'Yes, sir.'

'His motives in offering you his protection were not, then, lewd in nature?'

'It appears not.'

'You have earlier advanced the theory that he felt guilt for having kidnapped you.'

'Yes, sir.'

'Perhaps you can clarify this for me: if he felt so repentant at having taken you from your home and your future, why did he not simply release you?'

Isola's face brightened. 'That was no longer his option, sir. He had given me over to Davanzato's custody on behalf of King Fanrolio.'

Mongrissore raised his eyebrows. 'You were – and indeed are – not in the power of Beauceron, but of the King and Davanzato?'

Isola's face fell again. 'If you wish to think of it in those terms.'

'We have established that you lived for a while at Beauceron's expense. I understand that arrangement ceased with his arrest. Who pays your lodgings?'

'The crown, sir.'

Mongrissore shook his head and gave an avuncular smile. 'That is not strictly accurate, is it, my lady? Davanzato, as your ransom agent, bears the costs of your bed and board.'

'Yes, sir,' she mumbled.

'I did not hear your answer, my lady. You must speak more distinctly.'

'You know full well that Davanzato pays my expenses!' she thundered.

Mongrissore put his hands over his ears. '*Thank you*, my lady,' he said. 'I have established, I think, that Davanzato, who in somewhat irregular fashion is prosecuting the case, exerts a potentially undue influence over you. Now, will you tell me of your feelings towards Beauceron?'

'I have already told Davanzato.'

'Frankly, I did not believe your account. You would have us believe that your anger with Beauceron was spent, and that you felt gratitude and even friendship at his generosity.'

Isola dabbed her nose with a handkerchief. 'You emphasize the matter strangely. Beauceron was more generous than he needed to be, but he remains my abductor.'

'I have several witnesses – we shall hear from them later – that you had promised to see Beauceron hanged in the market square at Croad.'

'I may have said something to that effect.'

Mongrissore raised his hands. 'Perfectly understandable, my lady. I doubt that I would view kidnap favourably. It does create a problem with your evidence, however. You can see that?'

'I am not clear as to your meaning, sir.'

'You have exhibited a justifiable desire to be revenged on the man who kidnapped you. You would have every motivation to testify as to his treasonous activities whether that testimony were true or not.'

Tears again rolled down her cheeks. 'I have spoken the truth, sir.'

'Has Davanzato promised you any reward for your testimony, my lady?' Mongrissore continued with iron in his voice. 'Or was the simple matter of revenge enough to persuade you to betray a man who was attempting to make amends to you?'

'There – there was no – inducement but truth.'

'My lady, you are a liar and a dupe. Your only consolation is that you lie badly, the sign of a Harmonic soul, they say. I know Davanzato's methods well. He has threatened that your captivity will be less pleasant if you do not co-operate with his schemes. No doubt he has also promised you a share of the attainder on Beauceron's conviction: enough, perhaps, to pay your own ransom. That will never happen: can you imagine Davanzato parting with coin in that way? You must now tell the truth. It will not free your person, but it will free your soul.'

Isola sank to the ground.

'Clear the court!' called Davanzato. 'Can you not see the lady is faint?'

'No,' said Isola weakly. 'I must speak.'

There was silence. Beauceron was willing to guess nobody knew what she was going to say.

She rose unsteadily and turned to face King Fanrolio. 'My apologies, Your Puissance. I have perjured myself today. Davanzato said to me that he did not have enough evidence to be certain of convicting Beauceron, who was surely guilty. I knew that he would do anything to raise an army against

Croad, so I was not lying; I was telling a truth which I had not heard.'

Beauceron prepared to interject but Mongrissore silenced him with a gesture.

'I know that this was wrong,' she said. 'I wished to see Beauceron punished for his acts, and I also wish to see my home again. Davanzato assured me that my testimony would secure both ends.'

She sat down. Beauceron said nothing but looked across at her. This time she looked up and met his eyes. He nodded at her and for a brief instant his expression could have been interpreted as a smile.

'Excellent!' said Mongrissore, springing once more to his feet. 'There is clearly no more to be said, unless we want to consider laying charges against Davanzato today.'

'A moment,' said Davanzato languidly. 'Lady Isola is much distraught, and who can blame her? She has said to me throughout the proceedings that she was aware of his guilt. Imagine my shock at learning now that her "knowledge" was mere hearsay! I admit I should have probed her more deeply before bringing her before the court, but any man would have hesitated before tyrannizing such a lovely and unfortunate lady.

'The fact remains that the court has heard testimony not only from Sir Goccio but also from fourteen of his associates. The case against Beauceron remains strong.'

He turned to the Lords of Equity. 'What do you say, my lords?'

Lord Ulrado shook his head in disgust. 'You are no efficient prosecutor, Davanzato, but there remains a case to answer.'

Lord Gionardo nodded. 'Only a fool fails to prepare a witness, but the King must have the chance to decide on

Beauceron's guilt. We shall reconvene tomorrow, His Puissance willing, and set the farrago of today behind us.'

Fanrolio raised a liver-spotted hand. 'So shall it be. The trial continues tomorrow.'

Beauceron sat waiting for the guards to take him back to his cell; he looked across to Isola and tried to attract her attention, but she rushed sobbing from the chamber, alone with her shame.

10

Glount

I

Arren awoke the next morning with a sore head and a foul taste in his mouth. None of the pleasures of Glount, it seemed, were without cost.

Duke Panarre and Lord Thaume were closeted away with whatever business occupied them. Since Master Coppercake was also involved, Arren surmised it concerned either Panarre's share of the Mettingloom ransoms or, more alarmingly, betrothals and dowries.

Oricien and Guigot decided to spend the morning in the tilt-ring, where they could impress Lady Helisette and Lady Genevieva with their martial prowess. Arren could sense that their incipient rivalry would be certain to be piqued as they vied to impress the ladies, and was not sorry when Lady Cerisa arrived to ask him to escort her and Siedra into the city for their visit to the Molo.

The Molo was a tall lighthouse on the end of the spit which marked one boundary of the Bay of Glount. It was from here that Eleanora had cast herself into the waves at the end of *The Masque of Louison and Eleanora*, on learning that her father had treacherously slain her lover.

'Imagine!' cried Lady Cerisa as they climbed aboard the

cariolo which was to take them to the esplanade. 'We shall see the very spot where the tragedy occurred! We shall all sense the emanations, the very presence of doom – even you, Arren, although by and large you are insensitive to such matters.'

'I was under the impression, my lady, that *The Masque* was a work of fiction.'

'Arren, you are so literal-minded,' said Cerisa with that air of disappointed melancholy she had made her own. 'The bard Noevart has invested the tale with his own imaginings, adding his own exquisite sensibility to events, but who can doubt the eternal verities of his tale?'

Arren was little the wiser. Was the story true or not? Lady Cerisa had been teaching them history and literature for the past three years, but at times her grasp of the distinction between the two seemed imperfect.

'What Lady Cerisa means,' said Siedra, 'is that in seeing the Molo we will gain a greater appreciation of the story Noevart has given us.'

Arren felt that they were likely to see little more than a lighthouse, but decided it was best to keep his own counsel.

The Molo lay outside the city walls and the cariolo deposited them some way from their destination, still inside the town.

'We are not yet at the Molo,' said Lady Cerisa.

'This is as close as a cariolo will take you, my lady,' said the coachman. 'You would not thank me for juddering your arses over the track between here and the Molo.'

Siedra sniggered as Cerisa drew back from the affront. 'Come, Cerisa, it will be an adventure. Surely Eleanora herself walked to the Molo.'

Cerisa assented with poor grace and the trio alighted from the cariolo. The esplanade was crowded by the wall-gate. Evidently some kind of market was in progress. Arren was mindful of Coppercake's strictures and resolved to keep the ladies away from the depredations of grasping merchants.

The inhabitants of Glount, with their olive skins and grey eyes, would have been pleasing to look on were it not for a certain superciliousness in their bearing. They carried themselves with a fastidious sense of their own worth, in garments which tended towards the luxurious. From a fried food stall came the smell of sausages, reminding Arren that he had skimped breakfast. Lady Cerisa would clearly regard sausages as beneath her dignity, and since he was in any event disinclined to haggle with the merchants, Arren resolved to go hungry.

Once they left the city through the gate the crowds thinned. The wind whipped in off the sea, leaving perky white wavelets in its train, and finding a route under Arren's cloak and shirt to the skin beneath. Siedra shivered and leaned into him a little.

The road down the spit towards the Molo became increasingly rutted. Neither Siedra nor Cerisa had appropriate footwear, and Siedra began to grow fretful.

'How much longer?' she complained. '*The Masque* did not mention this infernal wind, and neither did Eleanora appear to risk turning her ankle with every stride.'

Lady Cerisa beamed. 'Does this not add to your conception of her tragic destiny? Can you not imagine her rushing to the Molo, desperate to warn Louison he has been betrayed, only to be slowed by the couch grass, grasping with its envious strands?'

'Louison could look to his own rescue were it down to me,' grumbled Siedra. 'She would have been better advised not to have trusted her father in the first place. It should have been obvious to a child that he would kill Louison.'

'You have no poetry,' said Lady Cerisa. 'Come, step out now! Ouch! Oh! Arren, my ankle is broken!'

Arren slowed his pace and looked to where Lady Cerisa had fallen to the ground amidst the tussocks. He doubted that her injury was serious.

'Oh!' she wailed. 'Oh, what misfortune! The pain!'

Arren had no desire to examine her thick ankles at close quarters but saw no other way of assessing her injury. 'Lie back,' he said. 'I will need to scrutinize for myself.'

'Siedra! Hold my hand, dear Siedra!'

Siedra removed her look of bored disdain and limply gave her hand to Cerisa as Arren palpated the ankle to cries of dismay. He rapidly concluded there was no serious damage, although convincing Lady Cerisa might not be straightforward.

He stood up. 'You must wait here a while, my lady. I will take Siedra with me to fetch help.'

'No! Siedra must remain with me! What if ruffians approach? Those fishermen look coarse fellows.'

'My lady, if ruffians are intent upon mischief, Siedra will not be the most effectual protector. She is Lord Thaume's daughter, and I must protect her at all costs, even at a theoretical risk to your own dignity.'

'Siedra! Do not leave me amidst the dunes!'

'Come now,' said Arren. 'Stout heart is called for. We shall only be an hour, or at most two. Say three to be absolutely safe. In such a romantic locale the time will surely pass quickly.'

'I find the pain is beginning to pass,' said Cerisa with a doleful wince. 'Help me up, and I think I may be able to hobble.'

'You surprise me,' muttered Siedra.

'If you are truly sure, my lady,' said Arren, and with some difficulty levered her to her feet.

From the quay wandered one of the 'coarse fellows' Lady Cerisa had so abominated.

'Sir, Mesdames, may I be of assistance? I am Delippe.'

'Thank you,' said Lady Cerisa, bridling. 'I stumbled but am now recovered.'

'Ah!' said Delippe with a smile. 'The accents of Croad! You are perhaps visiting the Molo?'

Lady Cerisa looked carefully at the man. Tall and slender, with a twinkle in his eye, Delippe wore his shabby pantaloons and patched shirt with an insouciant swagger.

'Yes, indeed we are,' she said. 'How much further?'

Delippe shrugged. 'A few hundred yards only, but the ground is uneven . . .'

Lady Cerisa looked downcast; Arren felt rather more hopeful.

'What if I were to take you on the *Glauticus*, my boat?' asked Delippe. 'Even with my crewmen aboard, there would be room for us all to sail out into the bay. You would see the Molo from a most unusual angle, and have a day to remember.'

'You are too kind!' exclaimed Lady Cerisa. 'Siedra, we are in luck!'

Siedra smiled weakly.

'A moment, sir,' said Arren. 'What would your tariff be?' He was mindful of Coppercake's warnings.

Delippe raised his hands. 'The amount would be nominal. I lose a certain amount of fishing time; shall we say a silver florin?'

Do not part with coin under any circumstances. Arren remembered Coppercake's injunction. Delippe seemed to sense his hesitation.

'The folk of Glount have an undeserved reputation for avarice,' he said with a wide smile. 'Shall we say that you pay nothing in advance? We will complete our tour on the *Glauticus*. If you are satisfied you will pay me a silver florin – and maybe a small gratuity! – but if you are unmoved you need pay nothing. I leave the matter to your own honour. What do you say, sir? I see from your cloak and sword that despite your youth you are a seasoned man of good judgement. Will you not climb aboard?'

'Come, Arren,' said Lady Cerisa. 'The fellow clearly means well, and we need pay nothing if we are not content; and once again I feel my ankle begin to throb.'

Arren was mistrustful but could see no dignified escape. 'Very well,' he said. 'Let us travel on the *Glauticus* for one silver florin.'

Delippe's crewmates helped Lady Cerisa aboard with efficiency if little ceremony; Siedra was treated with a more ostentatious consideration, while Arren was left to clamber over the boards as he might.

'Cast off!' called Delippe. 'Let us make for the Molo!'

To Arren's eye, the Molo seemed no more than a few hundred yards distant, but Delippe's helmsman set off at a seemingly indirect angle and the destination loomed further away before it hove back into view.

'Must we take such a circuitous route?' he asked.

Delippe dismissed the objection with an easy gesture. 'The currents of the bay are perplexing to the tyro,' he said. 'Lubo has sailed these waters for twenty years; he can sniff the ebbs and flows as one tomcat sniffs the spray of another. You must all sit back and enjoy the view of Glount from the sea.'

Arren had to admit that the city, rising up towards the hills, was a spectacular sight. On top of the walls he could pick out the patrols of the Cavalieres. Lady Cerisa appeared to be enjoying the ride less; to a close scrutiny her complexion revealed a greenish tint. Siedra, meanwhile, showed every sign of relishing the experience.

Eventually Lubo turned the *Glauticus* back towards the Molo, which was certainly an impressive structure, reaching tall and spare into the sky, delineating the location of the city for sailors approaching.

Lady Cerisa struggled to her feet. 'Look, Siedra! You can scarcely see to the top, but that is where Eleanora cast herself down onto the rocks below. How cruel, how envious they are! Can you not hear them calling out to her?'

Arren could hear no such thing; he was more concerned that the envious rocks would take a dislike to *Glauticus*'s hull, although Lubo appeared competent in the management of the boat. Siedra, too, evinced little interest in the matter.

'Can we not go closer, good Delippe?' asked Lady Cerisa. 'I would see better the balcony from where Eleanora fell.'

Delippe jerked his head towards Lubo, who ostentatiously swung the tiller, although *Glauticus* appeared to move no closer to the rocks. The third crewman pulled on a rope controlling the sail; *Glauticus* lurched to the side, and Lady Cerisa sprawled into Siedra with little dignity.

'Tasolle!' called Delippe. 'Work the sail with more finesse!'

Tasolle gave no visible acknowledgement. Lady Cerisa said: 'I think we have seen enough. Those of us with sympathetic dispositions will have absorbed the essence of the place. Delippe, kindly return us to the shore!'

Delippe nodded. 'You have seen the Molo in all the detail you require,' he said. 'I feel sure that we have earned our fee.'

Arren nodded and reached into his pouch and brought forth a silver florin. 'Thank you, Delippe. It seems I was wrong to suspect all the folk of Glount of avarice.'

Delippe looked at the florin with a chagrined expression. 'Be that as it may, your humour is poorly defined.'

'Humour?'

'You appear to be presenting this single florin as our fee. As a jest it is misconceived.'

'That was our arrangement,' said Arren with a flush. 'One florin. Lady Cerisa, Siedra: you will confirm this.'

'Young sir, do not try to make liars of the ladies! Let me present my reckoning: one silver florin each for use of the boat, making three florins. A further florin each for the expert commentary—'

'What "commentary"?—'

'—bringing the grand total to six florins. Let us add a further three florins hazard money as a result of Lady Cerisa's demand to bring the *Glauticus* imprudently close to the rocks: nine florins. Add in a single florin as a gratuity and we arrive at a round ten florins.'

'Monstrous!' stormed Lady Cerisa. 'No such sum will be payable: in fact, no sum at all will be payable. You may return us to the shore on the instant!'

'There is much you fail to understand, my lady,' said Delippe with a bland smile. 'There is a concept known as "bargaining position": essentially it states that in any transaction, one party will hold the other at a disadvantage. In this situation, you are on a boat which I control. Your return to the land, put bluntly, is entirely at my whim.'

'Not so,' said Arren, grim of face but flush with embarrassment at being played for such a fool. 'You must reckon with my sword, which wreaks its own kind of advantage.'

Delippe displayed no concern. 'Once you have killed not only me but Lubo and Tasolle, how do you propose to return to the shore?'

'You will find the matter of academic interest only,' said Arren in a level tone.

'In addition,' said Delippe, 'you will observe that Tasolle is up the mast, out of your reach, and has his bow trained on your heart. Both he and I would regret being forced to use it.'

Siedra spoke up at last. 'All the while we are on your boat, you cannot go about your business. In a sense, you are as much our prisoners as we are yours.'

Arren looked at her in admiration, for the point was well made.

Delippe smilingly shook his head. 'You will notice that we are heading not for the shore, but for the small island ahead. It harbours no noxious beasts, but you will not wish to remain there for too long a period. The most convenient outcome for us all is for you to pay over my ten florins. This is business, and we can all depart content.'

Lady Cerisa and Siedra looked at Arren. He shrugged; he could see no alternative. He reached into his pouch and counted out the coins. Delippe gave an ironic bow. 'You will see that Lubo has already set our course for the shore.'

'Do something, Arren!' cried Lady Cerisa. 'This rogue has made dupes of us! Some escort you have proved to be. Lord Thaume will hear of this, in full detail!'

Siedra had been sitting quietly on her wooden bench. Now she rose to face Lady Cerisa. 'You stupid, prating, selfish ninny! You have dragged us along on your ludicrous errand that was of interest to no one but yourself. You insisted on coming aboard this boat against all sense and advice, and now you have the audacity to blame Arren! Be sure that if you mention this to my father, all aspects of the affair will be laid bare.'

'Oh! To be spoken to in such a way! I have nurtured a viper! Viator Sleech was right: you should all have been compelled to attend the Viatory daily, instead of wasting your time learning mathematics and thaumaturgy.' She sat down heavily on her bench and said nothing else until they arrived at the wharf.

'We have reached our destination,' said Delippe. 'I hope that, if you are lighter in coin, you are least richer in wisdom and experience. Ten florins is cheap at the price. Tasolle, what are you thinking of? Lay on a plank for the ladies and the boy.'

Arren gritted his teeth. Retribution would soon find Delippe.

The grizzled Lubo assisted Siedra and Lady Cerisa down the gangplank with an exaggerated delicacy which in other circumstances Arren might have found amusing. As he stepped onto the plank he stumbled and fell against Delippe, who laughed with a patronizing bonhomie. 'Careful there, lad! Don't let that sword pull you off balance.'

Arren shot him a look of detestation and walked slowly towards the ladies. Cerisa looked away; Siedra gave him a half-smile. Without a backwards glance he led the way back to the city gates.

'Cheer up, Arren,' said Siedra. 'Events have not gone to plan, but at least I have not had to spend the day with Trevarre or his brother. It is hard to know which of them is viler. Ten florins of my father's money is not too high a price.'

Arren's gaze flicked up to her face. 'Keep walking,' he said, 'in fact, speed up, and do not look back.'

'Arren?'

'Lady Cerisa, you too must step out.'

'Hmph. Have a care for my ankle, you oaf.'

'Bugger your ankle, my lady. Dawdle or step out, the choice is yours.'

From behind them came a call. 'Hoy! Wait up there!'

'The gate – run!' called Arren, taking Siedra's arm. Lady Cerisa bolted with seemingly no care for the condition of her ankle.

Fortunately they were nearly at the gate, and while Arren spoke to the watchmen, Lady Cerisa and Siedra slipped through. He looked back to see Delippe slinking away back to the *Glauticus*.

'Would you care to explain yourself?' asked Lady Cerisa. 'And to account for your language?'

Arren reached under his cloak and brought forth a purse. 'This belonged to Delippe: I know it contains at least ten florins, and I hope rather more.'

'Arren!' cried Siedra in delight.

'A pickpocket as well as a knave!' thundered Lady Cerisa. 'I should call the constable, and tell Lord Thaume.'

'Do as you please, my lady. No doubt every listener will give you the attention you merit. Siedra, shall we count what we have?'

And as he tipped the coins out on to her palm he gave thanks for those days in Croad market when he and Eilla had vied to see who could take the most plunder. He was, for today at least, King of the Raiders.

2

Arren had expected that there would have been considerable scrutiny of his exploits during the day, especially as Lady Cerisa was hobbling around the guest quarters with plentiful sighs. The matter was relegated to insignificance, however, because Oricien and Guigot had quarrelled at the tilt-yard over Lady Helisette's favour and been banished to their own quarters. After a light supper Lord Thaume convened a council in his chambers, to be attended by his wife and children, Guigot, Arren and Masters Coppercake and Guiles.

Arren could tell on entering that Lord Thaume was not in a good humour. He was dressed again in the black breeches and shirt that Guigot called his 'hanging attire'.

'Sit,' said Lord Thaume. 'If you require refreshment, you must serve yourselves: this is not talk for servants to overhear.'

There was a pause while the group chose the beverages best suiting their needs. Arren settled for a tisane, and felt that Guigot was perhaps ill-advised in choosing the rough red wine grown in Duke Panarre's own vineyards.

'First,' said Lord Thaume when they were all seated, 'I wish to express my strong displeasure with you, Guigot, and especially you, Oricien, for this afternoon's display. What can you have been thinking of?'

'Guigot attempted to unseat me,' said Oricien with a scowl. 'It was ill-done in front of Lady Helisette.'

Lord Thaume shot his son a penetrating look. 'Unseating is the purpose of tilting,' he said. 'It is unreasonable to complain.'

'We had finished the pass,' said Oricien. 'We were at rest.'

'False!' declared Guigot. 'After one inconclusive pass we were entitled to another. Oricien erred in assuming I would call for a cessation. He has learned a valuable lesson.'

Lady Jilka interjected. 'The tilt-yard is not a place for sharp practice. In belittling Oricien you belittle us all.'

Guigot looked back levelly. 'Whatever fate befell Oricien, he brought it upon himself. If he appeared a fool, it was of his own making.'

Oricien rose from his seat. 'You whelp! You wanted to cut a fine figure in front of Lady Helisette!'

'Enough! Sit down, Oricien,' said Lord Thaume. 'The facts are these: in brawling in the tilt-yard you will both have created unfavourable impressions on the ladies. Oricien, you should have shown greater self-control; Guigot, you should not have provoked Oricien. Most importantly, the notion of "impressing the ladies" is misconceived.'

'How so?' asked Oricien. 'I understood that we were partly here to discuss betrothals.'

'Just so,' said Lord Thaume. 'However, your own inclinations, and indeed those of Panarre's daughters, are of little relevance. Understand, Oricien, that if I choose to marry you to Panarre's scullery maid, you will do so.'

'Yes, sir,' said Oricien.

'You both fought at Jehan's Steppe. I imagined this kind of childishness behind you. Arren shows greater judgement than either of you.'

Arren gave silent thanks that Lord Thaume was not aware of this afternoon's events at the Molo. He might have turned a profit on the affair – four florins, in fact – but his mastery of events had been less than absolute.

'You raised the question of betrothals, Oricien,' said Lord Thaume. 'I have spent the past two days, assisted by Master Guiles and Master Coppercake, in negotiation with Duke Panarre and his advisers.'

'Without our knowledge!' said Guigot.

'Naturally,' said Lord Thaume. 'As I explained, your inclinations are irrelevant.'

Siedra, who was sitting next to Arren, said in a quiet voice: 'Have discussions reached a conclusion?'

'Patience!' said Lord Thaume. 'I have made Duke Panarre three offers. It is for him to decide which, if any, is acceptable.'

Siedra looked at her mother, whose expression was unreadable. 'You need have no alarm,' said Master Guiles, brushing crumbs from his doublet. 'Any alliance into the House of Glount can only be advantageous to your family, and illustrious to yourselves. We can only hope that Duke Panarre is receptive to our proposals.'

'They are in suspense, my lord,' said Coppercake. 'Will you not tell them the state of affairs?'

Lord Thaume nodded. Arren thought he did not seem disposed to rejoice. 'My initial proposal, and the one which represents my best hope, is for a betrothal between Oricien and Lady Helisette. As Panarre's eldest daughter she would be a suitable match for my heir, and bring a sizeable dowry to boot.'

Oricien shot Guigot a look of barely concealed triumph. Guigot did not meet his gaze. 'Such a match,' continued Lord Thaume, 'would unite our families in a strong bond of amity. It remains to be seen whether Duke Panarre wishes to be so closely associated with a vassal. As to my other offers: I have also proposed a union between Guigot and Lady Genevieva.'

'A second daughter!' cried Guigot. 'My lineage must entitle me to better.'

'On the contrary,' said Master Guiles. 'The advantage in the match would lie with us. Your lineage may be noble, Guigot, but your prospects are not strong. Lord Thaume would have to settle lands upon you to avoid a misalliance.'

Guigot opened his mouth to argue.

'Enough, Guigot,' said Lord Thaume. 'Your observations are not to the point.'

'What of me, father?' asked Siedra in a trembling voice.

'I have proposed a match with Lord Dinarre,' said Lord Thaume. 'Much as I would have liked you to marry Trevarre, it is inconceivable that Panarre would give his heir away to a vassal. Dinarre remains an excellent match, especially as Trevarre's health is not robust.'

'No!' cried Siedra, the colour draining from her face. 'He is unspeakable.'

'His pedigree is flawless,' said Lord Thaume. 'He is also a handsome young man with agreeable manners.'

'Mother!' appealed Siedra. 'He tortures kittens!'

Lady Jilka gave her a minatory stare. 'Do you like kittens, Siedra?'

'No, but—'

'Then you have no grounds for complaint. It is a harmless peccadillo, and in any event probably no more than malicious rumour.'

'I despise him! He makes my flesh crawl.'

Lord Thaume gave her a not unsympathetic glance. 'We are not all able to choose our partners,' he said with a rapid flick of his eyes towards Lady Jilka. 'Your maidenly modesty does you credit, but your objections in this case are over-heated and hysterical.'

'In any event,' said Coppercake, 'these are proposals, not firm betrothals.'

Oricien leaned forward eagerly. 'I for one am content with my match. We may proceed instantly, or sooner at your pleasure.'

Lord Thaume held up his hand. 'You are premature. Duke Panarre has rejected the match. We continue to negotiate, but I find it unlikely he will give away his eldest daughter. He has made a counter-proposal: Lady Genevieva.'

'But I thought—' said Guigot.

'We will come to you in due course, Guigot,' continued Lord Thaume. 'Needless to say, I have rejected the proposal. The only second daughter I would give my heir to is the King's. For now, Oricien, we continue to negotiate.'

'I express a clear and unequivocal preference for the Lady Helisette,' declared Oricien.

'You may prefer as you choose,' said Guigot with evident satisfaction. 'Panarre will not give her away to you unless your father waives the dowry.'

'I do not require a dowry!' said Oricien. 'The lady's beauty is its own bounty.'

'Do you value our house so low, Oricien, that its heir should marry undowered? We should be the laughing-stock of the Emmenrule. I would marry you to Lady Helisette, but only in accordance with our dignity. You have been reading too many of Lady Cerisa's romances, to spout such drivel.'

Oricien lapsed into chastened silence.

'As for you, Guigot, you may infer that Duke Panarre has

rejected my proposal with regard to yourself. However, he has suggested Lady Klaera in Genevieva's stead.'

'Infamous!' shouted Guigot, leaping from his seat. 'She is a halfwit and drools when she eats. No doubt she soils herself hourly.'

Lord Thaume raised an eyebrow. 'You exaggerate the scope of her afflictions. Granted, her wits are not of clearest water, but with well-trained attendants her condition is manageable.'

'This is intolerable, that I should marry a lackwit!'

Siedra leaned across and whispered to Arren: 'A good match.'

'She comes with an excellent pedigree,' said Lord Thaume. 'I have not rejected the matter out of hand. Remember, Guigot, that for all the excellence of your lineage, you are heir only to the kingdom of your imagination.'

'Panarre mocks us!' shouted Guigot. 'He would not offer her to anyone he wished to conciliate.'

'Negotiations continue,' said Lord Thaume. 'That is all there is to be said for the present.'

'I sense a pattern,' said Siedra. 'Naturally Duke Panarre has also rejected your proposals with regard to myself.'

Lord Thaume grimaced. 'In a sense, Siedra. He considers the dowry I am offering to be inadequate. He invited me here on the strength of the ransoms I expect to collect from Jehan's Steppe. As a result he considers my wealth higher than Coppercake feels to be accurate. The sticking point therefore remains the size of your dowry. That aside, I feel we may have reached agreement in principle.'

Siedra began to sniffle. 'Duke Panarre is so avaricious. Surely his price will be too high.'

'The match would be strongly advantageous to me,' said Lord Thaume. 'I am hopeful that we will reach an understanding.'

Siedra burst into full-fledged sobs and dashed from the room.

'Jilka, go with her,' said Lord Thaume. 'She must be brought to see matters from a broader perspective.'

A firm knocking at the door brought a startled silence.

'I gave orders that we were not to be disturbed,' said Lord Thaume testily. 'Who is there?'

'It is I.' Seneschal Tourmi bustled into the room. 'I apologize for the intrusion, my lord. Duke Panarre requests your presence in the Great Hall immediately, with all your party. There are grave tidings to convey.'

3

By the time Lord Thaume had led his household to the Great Hall, it was thronged with people of all degrees. Seneschal Tourmi led them to places of honour at the front of the hall, and Duke Panarre mounted the speaking platform with measured grace.

With a sombre expression he cleared his throat.

'My thanks to you all for assembling so quickly,' he said. 'I have news from Emmen which will keep no longer. King Arren is gravely ill: his life is in the balance.'

Arren was conscious of his heart thudding. He had always felt a bond with the King because of their shared name.

'A herald has arrived from the court,' continued Panarre. 'His Puissance suffered a seizure as he sat at his meat. One side of his body does not move, and he cannot speak. The apothecaries call such a seizure a Disharmony, since one half of the body is at variance with the other. The viators explain it in terms of the body's final struggle to achieve Harmony, an area where I will not venture an opinion.'

'When did this occur?' came a voice from the hall.

'Something around a week ago,' said Panarre.

Master Guiles looked across at Lord Thaume. By now the King could well be dead.

'Much remains to be understood,' said Panarre, 'and many of the certainties of our existence are removed. Those of us engaged in negotiations on matters of state—' here he looked at Lord Thaume '—will naturally wish to consider these new verities. All must understand that conditions are not as they were.'

Lord Thaume rose, and with a bow addressed Duke Panarre. 'My lord, these are ill tidings indeed. Our thoughts are with the King and his family, and through the viators we beseech Hissen and Animaxia to hasten his recovery. Nonetheless, my lord, I must beg your favour to return north. At such a time my place is with my people.'

Duke Panarre bowed in return. 'Naturally I grant your suit. We can proceed no further with our negotiations as things stand: we will resume them at an appropriate time. Tourmi, kindly assist Lord Thaume and his party in their preparations.'

Lord Thaume strode from the hall. Siedra was sobbing once again.

'Do not despair, Siedra,' said Arren gently. 'All may yet be well.'

She looked at him with incredulity. 'Can you be so dense, Arren? I am crying with joy: my betrothal cannot proceed under these conditions. I regret the King's misfortune, of course, but he is an elderly man. He must die at some point, and if it brings good fortune to me I give thanks for it.'

'But—'

'Arren, do not be so block-headed. You remind me of Oricien, which is not always a compliment.'

As they packed their goods Arren realized that he was the only person who seemed to feel any concern for the old man.

Oricien showed considerable irritation, but largely because his betrothal to Lady Helisette receded yet further; Guigot manifested utter indifference, while Lord Thaume discussed matters of high policy with Guiles and Coppercake. Only Lady Jilka, who had rushed to the Viatory with Lady Cerisa to supplicate for the King's recovery, showed any kind of response Arren could understand. A curious ally, he thought.

That night, under a full moon – for Lord Thaume would not wait until morning – the Croad delegation rode out from Glount. The death of a king was a great evil, but not nearly so great as a crippling illness, for in the doubt of his recovery uncertainty grew like a plague. None wished him to linger at life's boundary as he made his final reckoning with Harmony, and if he was not to recover, his immediate death was the wish of all those who desired peace and concord in the realm.

4

Lord Thaume's party made more rapid progress on the journey home than they had in visiting Glount, and within five days were back in Croad. Sir Langlan's welcome was tempered with a grim smile, for the news of King Arren's illness had already reached the city. Lord Thaume paused only to hand his gallumpher to a groom before striding off to his audience room to pool information with Sir Langlan. Arren had not been formally dismissed from the party and consequently saw no reason not to follow along with Masters Guiles and Coppercake, and Oricien and Siedra.

Lord Thaume flung himself into a stuffed chair. 'Well, Langlan, what matters do you have for report?'

'I have suppressed no ancient liberties, closed no temples,

punished no heretics. In that sense, my regency has been uneventful.'

'I am glad to hear it,' said Lord Thaume, pouring himself a goblet of wine. 'My last absence was marred by altogether too much incident.'

'It would be wrong, nonetheless, to suggest that affairs have gone entirely according to plan.'

Lord Thaume sat forward in his seat. 'The King is on his deathbed; Panarre is grasping at my ransoms; my marriage alliances go awry. I hope you refer to nothing further.'

Sir Langlan pursed his lips. 'Raugier.'

Lord Thaume gave him a quizzical glance.

'I should more properly say, Lord High Viator Raugier, King Arren's Commissioner for Orthodoxy. He is presently lodged, with his entourage, in The Patient Suitor.'

'What is his business?'

'He will speak only with you, my lord. The title "Commissioner for Orthodoxy" is pregnant with meaning.'

'Arren has no truck with such nonsense,' said Lord Thaume, his words falling into an empty silence. 'The post is surely no more than a sinecure.'

No one responded for a moment. Then Master Guiles said: 'The King lies ill, my lord.'

'Jehan is no viator's puppet.'

'Jehan is not yet King,' said Guiles, 'and yet Arren is less than a king.'

'Already they gather. What do we know of Raugier?'

Sir Langlan shrugged. 'He is not a man negligent of status. Sleech tells me he was close to being elected Consort last time around. A Commissioner of Orthodoxy will stand well in the lists next time.'

'An ambitious man, then?' said Lord Thaume. 'A worldly one, perhaps?'

'You must meet him for yourself, my lord.'

'Very well,' said Lord Thaume. 'We will invite him to our hall tomorrow. For now, you are all dismissed.'

Oricien filed out with Arren and Siedra. 'I am hungry,' said Siedra. 'Let us go and find Mistress Eulalia.'

Soon the three were sitting at a table laden with the best Lord Thaume could offer. Arren pondered the events which had unfolded so quickly over the past months: Jehan's Steppe, marriage negotiations, the King's illness, and now the arrival of the Lord High Viator.

'What are you thinking, Arren?' asked Siedra, leaning close enough that he could smell the fresh soap from her morning ablutions.

Arren gave a half-smile. 'That we are no longer children. Can you imagine us learning multiplication with Master Coppercake now? Those days are past. We must now make our way in the world.'

Siedra looked down at her plate. 'My "way in the world" would appear to involve Lord Dinarre: I see no cause for satisfaction or optimism. You and Oricien may play soldiers as you choose.'

Arren said: 'Your marriage to Dinarre may never happen. Panarre will be throwing his children at the new court. He will be hoping to marry Helisette to some Emmen lord. They will have no care for us up here.'

Siedra gave a wan smile. 'It is easy for you to be sanguine. You will not have to share a bed with that depraved lummox.'

'It could be worse,' said Oricien with a chuckle. 'You could be like Guigot, marrying a lackwit.'

'Which reminds me,' said Siedra, 'not that I wish his company, but where is Guigot?'

'He said he was going to the Viatory,' said Oricien. 'The matter struck me as unusual but I did not pursue it.'

'"Unusual"?' said Arren. 'Guigot hates the viators, and

has little care for the Way. We can assume indirection of some sort.'

'Perhaps he has gone to find a wench or a doxy,' said Oricien. 'He will wish to brag of his deeds in Glount.'

Siedra laughed with unaffected glee, leaning back in her seat. 'Poor Guigot! The only people who will listen to him are the ones he pays!' She flung her arms wide and sent a flask of wine crashing on its side, where it gushed ruddily onto the fine damask cloth.

'Oh! Maid! Maid! Hurry forth with a cloth!'

Nobody appeared. Siedra bellowed again: 'Quickly, if you want to avoid a whipping! The damask is ruined!'

From within the servantry issued a maid to mop up the spillage.

'About time,' snapped Siedra. 'What kind of buffoon is Mistress Eulalia employing?'

Arren turned to look at the maid. His mouth fell open in astonishment. 'Eilla!'

The maid turned scarlet. 'Arren . . . Seigneur . . . I . . .'

'What is going on here? Wipe up this mess,' said Siedra.

'Sorry, my lady,' said Eilla, flapping ineffectually with the cloth.

'Hopeless,' said Siedra. 'You are new, and Mistress Eulalia will hear of my dissatisfaction. And who are you to address Seigneur Arren in such a familiar way?'

'My lady,' gasped Eilla. 'I—'

'I know Eilla from when we were children,' said Arren. 'Before I came here we were playmates.'

Siedra turned to look at Eilla and caught hold of her wrist. 'Hold still, girl – Eilla. That is a low name, and you have a low, cunning face.'

'Siedra—' said Arren.

'Do not intercede for her, Arren. Oricien and I overlook your origins, but you cannot afford to be sentimental about serving girls. If you want to be taken as a gentleman, you must always be conscious of place and station. If you hobnob with the likes of this, folk will never fail to remember where you came from.'

Oricien said: 'Siedra, leave the girl alone. She is new, she does not know our ways.'

Siedra let go of Eilla's wrist. 'You may go. You have made a poor impression on me. Oricien may be deceived by your peasant looks but I am not. If I hear you addressing Seigneur Arren so freely again I will have you turned out. Do you understand me?'

'Yes, my lady.' Eilla slunk out with her chin almost touching her chest.

'Well!' said Siedra. 'I cannot imagine what Eulalia was doing to engage such a girl. She looks old to come into our service; she will never learn proper docility.'

Arren could hold his tongue no longer. 'That "girl" has been my friend since we could barely walk. You had no business speaking to her in that way.'

She gave him a sharp look. 'Can you not see I was helping you?' she said. 'Your prospects are good, if you will only take care to avoid such errors.'

'How can it be an error to acknowledge an old friend?'

'Because, Arren,' she said softly, 'you are become a man of consequence. You fought well at Jehan's Steppe, and my father makes much of you. Through his favour, and your merits, you may call yourself "Seigneur". You are a man to reckon with in Croad. Do not insult yourself – and my father – by holding yourself cheap.'

'Our views on the subject are likely to remain at variance,' said Arren.

'Who is she, anyway?' said Oricien in a conciliatory tone. 'As Siedra says, she is old to appear in service: she must be sixteen.'

'Do you remember Master Jandille, the mason?'

'Of course,' said Oricien with a grimace.

'Eilla is his oldest daughter.'

'Ah!' said Siedra. 'All is now understood. She is a charity case. A mason with one hand can no longer work, and no doubt Sir Langlan has induced Eulalia to engage her. She will be surly and resentful throughout her employment. I predict she will be discharged within the month.'

'Siedra, Oricien; will you excuse me? I am no longer hungry.' Arren bowed and left the room.

He stalked into the corridor, his head spinning. That proud, spirited Eilla should be reduced to tears by Siedra's cruelty! Poor Eilla had gone from the daughter of the city's master mason to a castle servant in only a few weeks.

He went into Mistress Eulalia's pantry. 'I am looking for Eilla,' he said.

'I have let her off duty early, Seigneur Arren. She was most distressed; I could not follow her account, which was somewhat disjointed.'

'Siedra abused her horribly,' said Arren. 'It was not a pleasant spectacle.'

'Lady Siedra is Lord Thaume's daughter,' said Eulalia. 'She may be quick-tempered, but I am sure you do not mean to take a servant's side against her. I do not misunderstand your words, but others who do not know you so well might not be so perceptive.'

Arren looked at her coolly. 'I am grateful for your clarification. Perhaps you will tell me where I can find her.'

'She is on the ground floor of the East Wing: her cubby is the third along. If anyone asks how you found out, I did not tell you.'

Arren bowed. 'Thank you, Mistress.'

He stepped along into the servants' part of the building. It was an area in which he rarely found himself, and he had never before noticed its meanness, the narrowness of the corridor and the frowning proximity of the ceiling. He knocked on the door. There was no answer; he knocked harder.

'Go away.'

'Eilla? It's Arren.'

'That applies particularly to you.'

'I am worried about you.'

There was silence, then a noise of soft footsteps within. The door opened to show a cramped chamber with a rough wooden bed, a spindly chair and a candle. Eilla stood in the doorway, her raven hair askew and her dark eyes red.

'I saw little sign of concern in the dining room,' she said.

'May I come in? I should not be seen here, for your sake and mine.'

She briefly held the door wide. As soon as Arren had passed through she closed it.

'I realize how much you are demeaning yourself by coming here, Seigneur.'

'I—'

'Yes? I am keen to hear any further insults you may wish to offer me.'

'Siedra should not have spoken to you as she did.'

Eilla gave a bitter smile. 'We agree on at least one point.'

'She has a hot nature, and she is concerned about her betrothal. I am sure she meant nothing by it.'

Eilla sat down on the bed. 'I did not imagine you had come here to defend her conduct: indeed, I should have imagined defence impossible. You saw how she spoke to me, how she touched me. But maybe I misjudge you; maybe you are already one of them, and the feelings of a servant do not matter.'

Arren perched on the chair. 'I would not be here if I felt that. I know that Siedra was wrong.'

'She does not.'

'No. That is why I am here. If I thought she would apologize you would not need me.'

'I do not "need you" now.'

'Eilla, I was mortified to see you treated so.'

'Your mortification cannot be one-hundredth part of my own.'

'I do not know what to say, Eilla.'

Eilla paused a moment. Her expression approached a smile. 'You do not have to say anything, Arren. What hurt me were not the insults; it was thinking you saw no wrong in them. I do not care what Lady Siedra thinks; but we have been close for so long. I could not bear to think that you had come to be like them: I could not bear to think of you as Seigneur.'

'Eilla, I will never be "Seigneur" to you. When we were in Glount I picked a villain's pocket and I thought of you.'

Her eyes sparkled as she laughed. 'Not every woman would take that as a compliment, but I understand. If only we could go back to those days, Arren,' she said with a soft smile.

'Eilla,' he said. 'I am so sorry for everything that has happened to you. You must know that whatever happens, we will always be friends. However bad things are for you in the castle, I will always look after you. If I must endure Siedra's scorn, so be it.'

She put her arms around his neck and kissed him. Arren was shocked but did not pull away; instead he responded with vigour. She disengaged herself and stepped back. 'I do not know why I did that,' she said, with a return to something like her old insouciance. 'But the experience was enjoyable, and I may care to repeat it in the future.'

'Now, perhaps,' said Arren.

'I think not,' she said. 'The past days have been turbulent

enough without adding an extra set of confusions and complexities.'

Arren grinned. 'No doubt you are right.'

'You should go now, Seigneur. Mistress Eulalia will discharge me if she finds you here.'

Arren bowed, kissed her hand, and slipped from the room. For a woman who wished to avoid confusion and complexity, Eilla was acting in an irrational fashion.

5

Lord Thaume's castle had several reception rooms, and he had selected with care the one he would use to receive Lord High Viator Raugier. Ultimately he had chosen the Amber Room, next to his private viatory, and sent a note to Raugier inviting him to wait upon him at ten bells the next morning. His attendants were chosen with equal care. The notoriously irreligious, such as Sir Langlan, were kept well away, as were those of exaggerated piety, such as Lady Jilka. Lord Thaume instead chose to be attended by Viator Sleech, Master Guiles, Master Coppercake, Oricien and, to his own surprise, Arren. Guigot, despite his visit to the Viatory the previous night, was not included in the party.

The Patient Suitor, where the Lord High Viator was staying, was on the other side of the river, and Arren watched from a tall tower as the party made its way across the bridge, accompanied by a fanfare of heralds. At the head of the procession rode the standard-bearer, the banner of black and white check snapping in the strong breeze. Next rode Raugier himself, his black robes trimmed with ermine. Behind him rode attendants and soldiers in the white livery of Harmonic Perfects.

The bells began to ring ten, and Arren clattered down the

stairs into the spartan reception chamber. He was concerned that he might be late, but neither Lord Thaume nor Viator Sleech was yet in attendance.

Lord Thaume's seneschal Cyngier – once a renowned warrior but never noted for his adherence to the Way – escorted Raugier and two attendants into the chamber. Raugier did not look enchanted to find the lord's seat before him empty. He was a man of mature years, his thin hair arranged to cover a balding pate. The belly straining at his doublet suggested that here was no ascetic, and his lips set themselves into a half-smile which contained little mirth or agreeability. His brown eyes took in the scene with a cool appraisal.

'My apologies, my lord,' said Cyngier. 'Lord Thaume has been unavoidably detained.'

Raugier raised his eyebrows a fraction. 'I am interested to know of the matter more important than presenting himself before the Lord High Viator, who speaks with the voice of both King and Consorts.' His voice was crisp, well-modulated, chill.

From the side of the room a door burst open and Lord Thaume strode in, Viator Sleech trailing in his wake.

'Lord Raugier,' he said with a bow, a little out of breath. 'I must apologize for my unpunctuality. I was making my devotions in my viatory with Sleech. My laxity is inexcusable.'

Raugier's half-smile twitched upwards. 'It is no part of my commission to deny you the counsel of the viators,' he said with a hint of ill-grace. 'Naturally I would not wish to impede your progress along the Way.'

Lord Thaume bowed. 'I am grateful for your indulgence. Please, be seated while we discuss our business.'

Raugier introduced his attendants, Flassille and Erlard, and set out his programme to Lord Thaume.

'I am in Croad on the simplest of business, my lord,' he said. 'As Commissioner for Orthodoxy I must establish that throughout King Arren's realm the Way of Harmony is followed to the Consorts' satisfaction. Nothing could be more straightforward: I examine the devotional practices of the city, and form my conclusion as to orthodoxy.'

'I can assure you of the fact in two minutes,' said Lord Thaume. 'I am sorry we have detained you unnecessarily awaiting my return.'

Raugier smiled and shook his head. 'A pleasant fiction! What such an approach gains in convenience, it loses in rigour,' he said. 'I will go among the people, as will Flassille and Erlard. We will reach our conclusions, and with luck achieve a rapid consensus.'

'May I see your writ?' asked Lord Thaume. 'It would be best if we all shared an understanding.'

Flassille, a thin young man of earnest countenance, reached into a valise and brought forth a paper, which he handed to Lord Thaume.

'There are two contingencies,' said Raugier. 'Ideally I find that all is as it should be, and issue a Statement of Orthodoxy on the spot; conceivably my researches reach a less happy conclusion. In this case I set forth a programme of remedial action, although of course in cases of gross turpitude I am empowered to remove from office any person from the lord of the city down.'

Lord Thaume summoned a servant to fetch wine. 'Let us be candid from the start,' he said. 'You have been here several days, and no doubt have formed preliminary views.'

Raugier leaned back in his seat. 'There are certain areas which cause me concern. Frankly, the tolerance shown in the city for the heretics of the Wheel is surprising and disturbing. I find the Gollains all too prevalent.'

Thaume ran a finger around the top of his goblet. 'We are

far from Croad, and far from the Consorts. The Wheel is well established here. If the Gollains do not make trouble for me, I do not make trouble for them.'

'They are heretics, my lord. There is no middle ground.'

'The Northern Reach is less than a day away. I expect the men of this city to fight and die to defend it: already this summer many have done so. In return I allow them to die with whatever beliefs they choose. I cannot compel orthodoxy.'

Raugier looked into Lord Thaume's face. 'Perhaps not. But you can make heresy – unappealing. That you choose not to is a powerful statement, and it is not in your favour.'

'I am no theologian. My own leanings are unashamedly orthodox, as Viator Sleech will aver. If others' are not, I am inclined to lay the blame at the feet of the viators, since they clearly fail to make a compelling case.'

Raugier gave a thin smile. 'Do you refer, perhaps, to Viator Dince?'

'In part.'

'Do not think I am ignorant that Viator Dince suffered an outrage, one ordered by you.'

'I am the lord of this city,' said Thaume. 'Dince flouted my authority. He was fortunate to escape so lightly.'

'You are lord of the city today. Tomorrow, matters may go differently.'

'I am interested in how you might go about deposing me.'

Raugier swatted the point away. 'Let us not discuss such unpleasant contingencies. How did Viator Dince come to be whipped?'

Lord Thaume pursed his lips. 'During my absence in the North, he persuaded Lady Jilka to close the Temple of the Wheel, and to mutilate one of their elders, a subject of unimpeachable loyalty. In this he set his own authority above my own.'

'Let me understand,' said Raugier in a soft voice. 'Viator Dince chose to extirpate a heretical worship. For this you had him whipped. Am I correct?'

Lord Thaume took a pull at his drink. 'Viator Dince imagined himself above my authority. If his intention was to make heresy unpopular, he failed. Had I not been on hand, the mob would have lynched him.'

'I have much to consider,' said Raugier. 'Where is Lady Jilka, so pious in her bearing? And indeed, the fine young man I met in the Viatory last night?'

'Lady Jilka is in her quarters. I did not wish to weary her with such an audience today. As to the "fine young man"—' Lord Thaume looked around quizzically.

'He may refer to Guigot,' said Oricien.

'Guigot! That was his name,' said Raugier. 'A virtuous and well-governed youth. There are many folk in this city who Follow the Way as the viators guide them. It is a pity that a minority – and the culpable laxity of their ruler – allows a reputation for heresy to be fostered.'

'I was not aware,' said Lord Thaume, 'that any such reputation existed. Neither Duke Panarre nor King Arren has expressed any adverse opinion.'

Raugier set his goblet down. 'The commendation of Duke Panarre is scarcely a matter for pride: I shall be stopping at Glount on my way back to court to assess conditions for myself. As for King Arren, regrettably his grasp on affairs is no longer what it was, and he has fallen prey to grasping favourites. Prince Jehan adopts a more militant line.'

'At such time as Prince Jehan ascends the Emerald Throne, I will be the servant of his every whim.'

Raugier rose from his seat, beckoning his attendants. 'I do not find you as humble as I had hoped, my lord. I have outlined serious reservations about your management of spiritual affairs, but you have chosen to meet them with glib evasion and outright defiance. We shall be inspecting affairs in the city. Next time we speak, I hope to find you of more compliant disposition.' He bowed to a fractional extent.

'You will find, as ever, my lord, that I seek to do what is right for His Puissance King Arren and the people of Croad. That is my own Way of Harmony. If you wish to confer with Viator Sleech as to my Equilibrium, you may of course do so.'

Raugier was already stalking from the hall and Thaume's final remarks were addressed to his back.

11

Mettingloom

On the second day of proceedings the small courtroom felt inadequate to the weight of business. The tension of the previous day's scenes still crowded the space. Today Isola was not on hand; Sir Goccio, however, remained in court, his presence a reminder of his faltering testimony. Once the court was convened, Davanzato rose slowly to his feet.

'Your Puissance; my lords. We all well remember yesterday's great drama in our courtroom. I acknowledge my own sorry contribution; like us all, I was beguiled by Lady Isola's melancholy beauty, and I did not examine her story as I should have done. Do not let this negligence, my lords, soften your hearts towards the rogue and traitor Beauceron. His guilt has been attested by many; men of honour, all. Let me set out once again the scope of his guilt.

'Beauceron came into this city many years ago, a man friendless and banished from his homeland. Every man's hand was turned against him. All he had to commend him was the power of his strong right arm. What did the world hold for such a man? Nothing, except what he could extort from it.

'He fought for our brave field captains who have so long

tyrannized the northern plains of the Emmenrule, and earned a reputation for terror and brutality. There was no deed at which he would scruple. In due course his company came to Mettingloom, and by now his deeds had elevated him to its captain, and he had acquired a sinister sobriquet: the Dog of the North.

'In his ambition he realized that he had reached the apex of the raider's career. There was nothing more for him to achieve. For a man who, as we all know, nurtured a hatred of the city of Croad in his heart, the situation was intolerable. He came to the city in winter, and before him he saw the mighty King Fanrolio. To Fanrolio he pledged good and true service. He became a man of the Snowdrop, and from that day on fought under Fanrolio's banner, even in the summer campaigns. Fanrolio had the right to expect the utter loyalty of the man who fought under his banner.

'As we have seen, Beauceron's loyalty is to no one but himself. When he raided and campaigned, he hoisted aloft his own red standard. Fanrolio had rescued him from the life of a rootless raider, but how did Beauceron repay him? He desired the King to provide him with a mighty army to bring Croad to its knees. The King's respect for the great warrior was so high that he allowed the matter to be debated in his council, despite the much-cherished peace that Mettingloom and the Emmenrule enjoy. The King ruled that no such invasion could take place.

'Did Beauceron accept the word of his sovereign lord with the meek resignation he owed his King? He did not. He continued to campaign, importuning the King's Under-Chamberlain, myself, for further audiences. I made it clear that no such audience could be expected, and that the subject had been settled last year.'

Beauceron caught his breath as it hissed out. Mongrissore shot him an admonitory glance.

'All those who knew Beauceron's proud temperament knew also that he could accept no check or rebuke. It came then, as no surprise, to find that he had approached the noble Sunflower Knight, Sir Goccio, with a proposal to change his allegiance to the Summer Court, in exchange for the chance to lead an army against Croad. Who was this baseborn man, an exile like so many who find their way to Mettingloom, to think to treat and dicker among kings, to barter his allegiance like a fishmonger haggling over his wares? Such thoughts of due place never occurred to Beauceron, a man who carried himself as a prince in defiance of his birth.'

From the gallery came a few mutterings, outweighed by many nods of approval.

'Instead Beauceron persuaded Sir Goccio, a brave knight but no statesman, that his honour was best served by indulging in a treasonous scheme and one, we can but suspect, the Summer King himself would have opposed once he knew of it. Fortunately, this false treachery came to light at an early stage. The invasion had been planned, but Sir Goccio repented of his treachery and drew the facts to the attention of those who would act upon them.

'I have set out, in summary form, the crimes of the treasonous Beauceron. I call for the ultimate penalty: execution as a common criminal, the noose and not the block. Attainder of all his goods must also follow, in the customary allocation: three parts to the King, and one to the person who brings him to justice: namely myself. Your Puissance, my lords, I await only your pleasure.'

Fanrolio nodded and blinked slowly. 'Davanzato, we all know how much I regret the continuing indisposition of my Chamberlain, but in your calm eloquence today I see much of Osvergario. Legulier Mongrissore, do you wish to add any final remarks?'

Mongrissore raised himself slowly, as if his joints pained

him, his eyes raised to the painted ceiling. 'I am grateful, Your Puissance. There is one important question I would wish to resolve first. Davanzato has pressed for Beauceron's execution as a common criminal; as your sworn man, he is entitled, if convicted, to the block.'

Davanzato leaped from his seat. 'At your advanced age, Legulier, I am sure it can be difficult to retain all the details of the case. The court will remember that I specifically petitioned, at the outset, to try the case under the Old Law, rather than the Code of Justice introduced by King Metrio. This permission was graciously granted.'

He sat back in his seat with a smirk.

'My apologies, sir,' said Mongrissore with a gentle nod of his head. 'The case has been somewhat protracted – partly through your oratory – and the occasional detail may, indeed, not be at the forefront of my mind. I now fully understand: the case is being heard under the Old Law. It is fortunate that my client's innocence will render the question moot.'

Davanzato simply smiled and looked down at his papers. Beauceron shot Mongrissore a quizzical glance. He was not as old as all that, and his wits had shown no tendency to addle thus far.

Mongrissore continued. 'With that procedural question settled, I have nothing further to say other than to assert my client's innocence. Davanzato's travesty of a summation of Beauceron's career deserves rebuttal, however. It is indeed some time since he journeyed north to join us in Mettingloom, a journey that many have made before him. Few, however, have contributed as strongly as Beauceron to the glory of his King. He has struck terror into Emmen as the Dog of the North, and served with exemplary loyalty.

'Such success, and the riches thus accrued, naturally provoke envy in the hearts of lesser men, and here I must include Under-Chamberlain Davanzato, a notoriously avaricious man.

Long has the court turned a blind eye to the increasingly elaborate and expensive presents demanded by this over-mighty servant. Avarice grows by what it feeds on: whatever it has, it must have more. So it has been with Davanzato. He has blocked again and again Beauceron's great scheme – one which would, incidentally, bring glory to the Northern Reach – solely to frustrate Beauceron. His hope, of course, was to drive Beauceron into treasonous discourse with the Summer Court. In this he reckoned without the captain's loyalty to his sworn word. His attempt to secure one-quarter of Beauceron's wealth by prosecuting a successful case must surely have fallen, had he not chosen to fabricate Beauceron's involvement.

'Consequently he suborned Sir Goccio, and here I second Davanzato's opinion of that knight as a soldier rather than a statesman. His debts are well known, and Davanzato was swiftly able to reach agreement with Sir Goccio. It was Sir Goccio, of course, who approached Beauceron, and not the reverse. Beauceron naturally rejected the overtures, so the foolish Sir Goccio was forced to perjure himself. This was not enough for Davanzato: a non-existent crime can be difficult to prove. So he also used his malign influence over Lady Isola to secure her warped testimony. Poor Lady Isola, naturally resentful against the man who had kidnapped her, and desperate to secure the funds to return to her home, was all too easily manipulated by a man as ruthless as Davanzato. I may only yesterday have turned the heat of my questioning against Lady Isola, but I do not blame her. She made an error – and which of us has not? – and then repented of it. No, I do not blame her: I salute her!

'It gives me no pleasure to expose Under-Chamberlain Davanzato as a scoundrel and a rogue: no doubt a degree of moral flexibility is essential for a man in his position. Nonetheless, Davanzato has committed a great fraud, not only against Beauceron but also, Your Puissance, against you and the Lords of Equity. What action to take against such a man is not for me to decide; my interest in this whole sorry matter ends when, tomorrow, you discharge Beauceron as an innocent man.'

He sat down almost apologetically. There was silence, broken only by the slow, mocking applause of Davanzato. 'Bravo, old man! The mummers lost a recruit when you chose the law.'

Beauceron looked at Mongrissore in admiration. The legulier had entwined the truth of Davanzato's avarice and ambition with a favourable portrait of the Dog of the North so compelling that Beauceron almost believed himself to be innocent.

2

That evening, Beauceron shared a joint of salt ham in his cell with Mongrissore and Monetto.

'I am filled with admiration for your performance this afternoon,' said Beauceron to Mongrissore. 'I am only sorry that Monetto could not have been there to hear it.'

Monetto paused in his assault on the ham. 'No doubt the scribes will soon release the speech for all to enjoy. Davanzato can only have harmed himself.'

Mongrissore shook his head. 'It is all for naught. Beauceron, you must prepare yourself for a guilty verdict tomorrow.'

'What?' said Monetto. 'I thought all were agreed that Mongrissore had trounced Davanzato.'

Mongrissore gave a sad smile. 'So I did, good Monetto. But I needed not only to destroy his case, but the man himself. Davanzato stuck to his points, and for good reason: he knows the Lords of Equity favour him. The Winter Court wants to punish Beauceron for intriguing against their King; the Summer Court hates and fears him. They will counsel the King to convict.'

Monetto scowled. 'And does the King not have a mind of his own?'

The silence which followed this question indicated that all three realized the fatuity of the remark.

Beauceron rose and shook hands with Mongrissore and Monetto. 'I thank you, Mongrissore, for your spirited defence and for your honesty. I will regret going to my death with Croad unavenged, but I can blame no one but myself.'

'Do not speak of your death,' said Monetto. 'You have survived conviction for great crimes before.'

Beauceron gave a crooked smile. 'It is many years since we have spoken of Lord Thaume,' he said. 'I was unjustly condemned on that occasion too.'

'Justice may vary depending on where you stand. Just or not, here you stand today. If there is a lesson from those days so long ago, it is that while there is life there is hope.'

'You will be calling for the viators next,' said Beauceron. 'They will tell me that the Way of Harmony is almost at its end. Lord Thaume died without acknowledging the wrong he had done me. I would not have Oricien and Siedra escape so lightly.'

Mongrissore made a gesture to attract their attention. 'You are not dead yet, Beauceron. The law has many twists and turns. Have you been exercising as I suggested?'

'Of course,' said Beauceron. 'If your expedient is for me to outrun my guards, it can best be characterized as desperate.'

'Tomorrow will bring what it brings.'

Unlike the trial, the verdict was to be delivered in front of the whole court. The Lords of Equity had rendered their advice to the King the previous night, and all that remained now was for Fanrolio to pronounce Beauceron guilty or innocent, and to impose whatever penalty he deemed appropriate.

The Great Hall of the Occonero, which Beauceron had last encountered at the Midwinter Ball, was packed to capacity. At the back stood dignitaries who might have expected deference; but today their needs were not paramount. The Hall was already full when Beauceron entered at the back, his polished boots echoing on the marble floor. At his side hung his rapier, and his decorations were sewn to the chest of his black jacket. Mongrissore walked alongside him with more vigour than he had evinced during the trial, and he had even broken out a new suit of broadcloth for the occasion. Despite the cold outside, in the Hall the dimonettoes and the closely packed bodies combined were more than ample to heat the vast space.

Although he looked ahead as he marched towards the front of the Hall, his peripheral vision took in many familiar faces as he walked. General Virnesto was there with an impassive face; Prince Brissio at the front surveyed Beauceron with a cool appraisal. On the other side of the hall were the courtiers from the Summer Court. It would not have been appropriate for King Tardolio to be present, but in the front row sat Prince Laertio, who gave a barely perceptible twitch of the head as Beauceron walked past; by the Prince's side was his sister Princess Agalina. A couple of rows behind Laertio, Beauceron noticed with a glimmer of amusement, was Lady Cosetta. She too had seen the expediency of throwing her lot in with the Summer Court. Prince Brissio's passion was destined for disappointment.

At last the long walk was over. Beauceron stood before the King and the Lords of Equity, set on lower seats at his side. Davanzato, a further level lower, sprang from his place.

'What *lèse-majesté* is this!' he cried. 'For any man to bear arms before the King, let alone this felon!'

King Fanrolio raised his eyebrows. 'Yes, Mongrissore,' he said. 'What do you mean by presenting your man for judgement in this way? No man may carry steel in this hall.'

Mongrissore bowed. 'My apologies, Your Puissance. You will recall that only yesterday we established that the trial had been conducted under the Old Law. Under this Law, a man accused of treason is permitted to retain his arms until such time as his guilt is established. He is not a "felon", as Under-Chamberlain Davanzato styles him, until your judgement is rendered.'

Fanrolio looked at the Lords of Equity uncertainly.

'Your Puissance,' said Lord Gionardo, 'Mongrissore's point may be over-legalistic, but his quibble is accurate enough. Beauceron is entitled to bear a sword until your verdict is reached.'

'Very well,' said Fanrolio querulously. 'The byways of the law can be hard to trace at times.'

'Indeed, Your Puissance,' said Mongrissore. 'Soon your judgement will be revealed and uncertainty banished.'

Fanrolio's expression brightened. 'Just so, Mongrissore.'

Davanzato shot Mongrissore a glance of glassy dislike. Score your petty triumphs while you can, his expression seemed to say.

A footman brought the King a sealed parchment: the judgement Fanrolio himself had written the previous night. He broke the seal and unrolled the paper. He squinted in an attempt to read his handwriting. Beauceron looked on in contempt. Whatever the outcome, Fanrolio was in his dotage: he had been fully justified in pursuing alternative strategies. Why had he not thrown his lot in with Laertio?

'I have been nobly advised by my Lords of Equity,' said Fanrolio, 'in deciding this difficult and painful case of conspiracy against my own authority. My lords are unanimous in their thoughts, and I cannot demur from their conclusions.

'Beauceron, the evidence before us leaves only one conclusion. You are guilty of grand treason, and tomorrow you shall die.'

4

The sentence of death was hardly unexpected, but Beauceron nonetheless felt an almost physical blow in the base of his stomach. He had faced death many times, but never in this impersonal way, a man in front of him reading from a script. He had never lacked the opportunity to fight back.

Mongrissore rose languidly from his seat. 'Your Puissance, a moment for further consideration, if I may.'

Fanrolio blinked more rapidly than usual. 'My judgement is fixed and decreed, Mongrissore.'

'I would not dream of disputing your right of judgement, Your Puissance. My concern relates to a point of law only.'

'Sit down, old man,' said Davanzato. 'The race is run, and you have lost. Let us now proceed with dispatch: a traitor cannot die a day too soon.'

Mongrissore's voice deepened. 'You will listen to me, Under-Chamberlain Davanzato. Your Puissance, you can confirm that you have sentenced Beauceron under the Old Law.'

'Must we revisit this tedium again, Mongrissore?' asked Fanrolio with a fretful scowl. 'My wits are not what they were, but I remember an extensive clarification of this point yesterday. Beauceron has been tried and condemned under the Old Law.'

'Exemplary clarity, Your Puissance. Ah, Lord Gionardo, you have a point to make?'

Gionardo looked back at him sourly. 'You have us, you rogue.'

Mongrissore nodded and smiled. 'The Lords of Equity know the law, which is encouraging. Under the Old Law, which we are all agreed pertains here, I invoke the right of my client to trial by combat.'

Beauceron stared at Mongrissore. The hall had already been silent, but now even that silence seemed quieted. Beauceron had had no idea of Mongrissore's intention; hardly surprising, then, that everyone else was stunned.

Lord Gionardo shook his head with a rueful grin. He might have lost, but the legulier in him could not but admire Mongrissore's skill. 'Mongrissore has this right, my lord. Beauceron may challenge the material witnesses against him – in this case, Sir Goccio.'

From further along the row came a clatter; Sir Goccio had dropped his papers to the floor.

Beauceron uncoiled himself and stood. 'May I not challenge Davanzato instead?'

Ulrado gave a wintry smile. 'The approach has much to commend it, but it is not sanctioned by the law. If you wish to have your right of trial by battle, it is with Sir Goccio or no one.'

Beauceron smiled softly and sought Sir Goccio's gaze. 'If that is how it must be, I claim my right.'

From the far side of the room came the sound of one person clapping. Beauceron looked to see Prince Laertio, and smiled. His hand dropped to the hilt of his rapier. Now he understood why Mongrissore had enjoined him to keep his fitness up.

5

After a stunned pause and a period of frantic activity during which Sir Goccio was furnished with a rapier, a space was cleared in the Great Hall. The courtyard was too cold for spectators, and this was an administration of justice which required witness.

The perimeter of the Hall was ringed with dignitaries, leaving the centre free for the combatants. There was ample room for manoeuvre on the chequered black and white tiles.

Both Beauceron and Sir Goccio had removed their jackets and stood ready for action in crisp white shirts and black breeches. Sir Goccio looked at Beauceron as if to say something; Beauceron merely shook his head. No doubt Sir Goccio was disinclined to fight, but he had no way of withdrawal that did not make him appear both coward and perjurer.

Each man gave a perfunctory bow to his opponent and the King, and then they began to circle cautiously. Beauceron was in no hurry to make the first move: he had a reputation as a formidable duellist, and he preferred to let that reputation work in Sir Goccio's mind; not that the Sunflower Knight was to be taken lightly. He was a professional soldier, and in good condition.

It was Sir Goccio who moved first, a feint and lunge combination which Beauceron easily parried. He riposted, as much to feel Sir Goccio's defence as with any aggressive intent. Sir Goccio was light on his feet, his body sideways-on to Beauceron to provide the minimum target area. Head and feet, head and feet, thought Beauceron. Swordplay was a simple activity made over-complex through fear. He felt himself moving almost into a trance: he was aware of his weight transferring through the balls of his feet by infinitesimal movement, his head still, alert. He could hardly sense Sir Goccio at all, a bobbing figure at the edge of his perceptions. The figure came towards him, Beauceron adjusted his feet, flicked his wrist and Sir Goccio retreated again. With a sudden surge of movement Beauceron skipped aside, ducked back in, flashed his blade forward. There was a gasp from the crowd, a stifled cry from Sir Goccio, a patch of red on his shirt. Sir Goccio danced back out of range.

Sir Goccio disregarded the nick with a grimace. He stepped back towards Beauceron, flicked again, and Beauceron moved his head aside; the blade whistled past his face by a whisker.

Beauceron was unaware of the crowd, barely aware of the lunging, parrying Sir Goccio: he knew only himself, the tautness of his sinews, the crispness of his steps, the occasional blinding movement and the more usual self-contained watchfulness. Eventually, as Beauceron had known it must, Sir Goccio's frustration, his guilt, his impatience, goaded him into a lunge a fraction too aggressive, his defence left open an instant too long; before he had consciously assessed the situation, Beauceron had reached out with his sword arm, the point slicing through cloth, skin, heart. Sir Goccio coughed and a bubble of blood came from his mouth. Before any chance of regret or last words, he slid dead to the floor.

Beauceron turned away. Sir Goccio would not be rising to threaten him. With a final backward glance, he handed his sword to Lord Gionardo. He breathed heavily as he said: 'I have exercised my right to trial by combat. If there are others who would speak against me, let them come forth.'

Lord Gionardo took Beauceron's sword. 'You are vindicated under the Old Law. You are innocent, and a free man.'

Beauceron bowed to the Lords of Equity and the King. He donned his coat, shook hands with Mongrissore and strode out past the marvelling crowd.

6

Kainera had ensured that Beauceron's house was kept clean and aired in his absence, and his heart lifted when he finally shut his door. It had been many nights since he had slept under his own roof. Lady Isola had vacated her apartments, and although they had kept apart while she lived there, the house seemed empty without her. This small occasion of melancholy was not enough to sour his mood, although he thought with regret of Sir Goccio. He had been a good man, and largely honourable; as much a victim of Davanzato as Beauceron had been. He could not afford to dilute his rage against Croad by wasting time settling his score with Davanzato; but nonetheless the Under-Chamberlain remained a grave danger, and not a man to let one failure end his designs. Davanzato would have to be dealt with, not from vindictiveness, justifiable as that would be, but from simple prudence. He would speak to Mongrissore tomorrow.

There was various correspondence awaiting his attention; one letter stood out: the envelope had the Sun Seal of the Summer Monarch. Could Laertio be starting his overtures already? Surely he would have more sense than to commit his thoughts to paper. He reached for his dagger and slit the seal.

Captain Beauceron,

Allow me to express my admiration for your skilful and courageous defence of person and reputation. Your acquittal will come as a relief to all who believe our

*strong realm needs every man of vigour and enterprise
to fight for us.*

*I am conscious that our paths have rarely crossed
during your time in Mettingloom, a loss more to me
than yourself. I hope that your complete vindication
will allow you to accept the social invitation of the
Summer Court without fear of envious tongues and
ill-informed speculation.*

*I pray, therefore, that you will wait upon me at your
convenience,*

Your cordial admirer,
   Agalina
     Princess of the Summer Court

Beauceron set down the letter in puzzlement. He knew
Agalina by sight – they had even exchanged words on occasion – but as she said, their paths had rarely crossed. Agalina
was a young woman not only of charm, but intelligence. She
was not a naive girl, regardless of the gushing letter she had
written. If she requested his company, it was not for the pleasures of sharing sweetmeats or wine. Something underlay this
cordiality, and he could not fathom it. The easiest way of
finding out was to accept the invitation, although that might
not be an advisable course. But if he went openly, his recent
acquittal surely made him proof against further plot.

The sensible course still remained to stay at home, to continue to work upon Fanrolio. Davanzato's reputation could
not have been helped by the treason trial, and an audience
with the King was not out of the question. On the other
hand, the days were lengthening; the air had not the chill it
had held before his incarceration. No one could deny that
spring was coming. If Fanrolio did not act soon, there would
be no chance of raising the Winter Armies before Tardolio

reascended the throne. It would be perverse not to understand what, if anything, the Summer Court had to offer.

He reached for his quill, wrote a brief letter to Princess Agalina and a longer one to Mongrissore. He was a gambler; he would throw the dice once more.

7

Beauceron called on Princess Agalina the next day; spring was drawing ever closer and there was no profit in delay. He had never visited the Summer King's palace – the Printempi – which was set back among a scattering of isolated islets to the north of the Fins.

He presented himself to the Chamberlain at the appointed time, determined to avoid furtiveness. He had been invited openly by the Princess, and he would attend in the same spirit. He was, after all, a celebrated figure in the wake of his remarkable acquittal.

He was shown into the Princess's reception rooms, furnished with the same quiet good taste which characterized Agalina herself. Beauceron put her age in the mid-twenties, old to be unmarried, especially for such an attractive woman. The number of men suitable to marry a princess of Mettingloom was not high, however. It was inconceivable that the royal house of Emmen would wish to ally itself with what it saw as renegade blood, so Tardolio's choices in finding a husband for Agalina were limited to his own nobility or the royal houses of more distant realms. The former possibility risked raising a rival to himself, and while in the latter case there was a sufficiency of princes from Garganet, Gammerling or even Paladria, those who were available did not necessarily wish to invoke the full implications of an alliance with the Northern Reach. When added to Agalina's notoriously haughty temper it was perhaps unsurprising that she remained a spinster.

'Captain Beauceron,' she said, rising from her seat to shake his hand, 'I am honoured by your visit.'

'And I by your invitation,' replied Beauceron, unwilling to be outdone in empty formality.

Agalina gave a half-smile. She understood the game. Her dark hair, which would normally have cascaded in a gentle wave, was confined in a fillet behind her head; her equally dark eyes knew no such restraint, and took in Beauceron's person with a look of frank appraisal.

'Please, take a macaroon cake,' she said, proffering a plate. 'I find in the winter I crave sugar to keep my mood sanguine.'

Beauceron accepted with an inclination of his head. 'The time for sweetmeats will soon be past, my lady; spring can be only a few weeks away.'

'My father's thaumaturge suggests less than a month,' she said. 'How I hate the cold.'

'King Tardolio maintains a weather-wizard?' he asked in surprise.

'Of course – and not just to foretell the weather,' she said. 'When the first green shoot is seen in the garden at the Occonero, it is spring, and the Summer Court steps forth. My father would be negligent if he did not attempt to speed the event. Pintuccio is not simply a thaumaturge but a horticulturalist.'

'I had never considered the matter,' said Beauceron. 'No doubt King Fanrolio employs a similar device.'

'Just so. His thaumaturge attempts to bring on the first snows, of course.'

Beauceron furrowed his brow. 'I was not aware that he maintained a thaumaturge.'

'Of course not. You are out in the field in the autumn, trying to clip the last Emmen heads before the winter comes.'

'How we are all run by the seasons,' said Beauceron with a smile.

Agalina sipped at her tea. 'You are right, Captain. No doubt there are good reasons for our customs in Mettin-gloom, but they lead to some curious outcomes. There cannot be a King who has not considered uniting the crowns.'

'By force, necessarily.'

'Since the sole other option would be my marriage to that buffoon Brissio, I can only hope so.'

'Your brother has a similar conversation technique of alluding to the unthinkable to assess the listener's attitude. Let me state unequivocally I have no interest in over-throwing King Fanrolio; and I would make the least apt marriage-broker imaginable.'

Agalina gave a high tinkling laugh. 'I have in mind nei-ther of the schemes you suggest – although I confess I would raise an army myself to avoid marrying Brissio. It may also interest you to know that Laertio departs for Niente on the morrow.'

'Far Niente? How so?'

'Candidly, my father does not trust him. At times his con-duct goes beyond headstrong.'

Beauceron cast his mind back to Laertio's schemes and grimaced.

'I see you take my meaning,' she said with a chilly smile. 'My brother's position prevents him facing the full conse-quences of his acts; that does not apply to his associates.'

Beauceron inclined his head.

Agalina smiled as she sipped her tea. 'I had not been sure what manner of man I would find today. I admit that your intelligence is at the upper end of my expectations.'

Beauceron rubbed his ear. 'I would have been distressed to find it otherwise.'

'Tell me,' she said, leaning forward, 'is your rage against Croad as extreme as is portrayed?'

'I suffered a great wrong from the rulers of Croad in my youth. My pride does not allow me to forget it.'

'Will you not tell me of this slight?'

Beauceron gave an ironic smile. 'I have not spoken of it thus far; I see no reason to change my policy today. I would not wish to impugn you with the vice of vulgar curiosity, but if I were to tell you of my feelings, you would regard them as trivial, overstated or even – worst of all – pitiable. I am always conscious that an air of mystery sits well upon a man.'

Agalina's round cheeks dimpled. 'You are more adroit than I had expected. Are there any lengths you would not take to reach your goal?'

'I prefer not to deal in hypotheses.'

'Very well,' she said, her eyes flashing. 'Let me be more explicit. You have been acquitted of conspiring with Sir Goccio to lead the Summer Armies against Croad. Legal processes being what they are, acquittal and innocence need not be one and the same.'

Beauceron said nothing.

'If my father were keen to avenge Jehan's Steppe, he would not use a reed like Sir Goccio. You should perhaps have realized this.'

Beauceron nodded.

'I am going to make an assumption,' continued Agalina: 'that you would not, in fact, be hostile to involvement in my father's army if he chose to move against Croad.'

'If you have followed my recent trial you will be aware that such an intent on my part would be treasonous.'

'Pah! We are alone. Talk of treason is irrelevant in this context.'

'I have enemies in the Winter Court. I cannot treat treason in the cavalier fashion you suggest.'

'I am the King's daughter. If I say that I know Tardolio wishes to avenge Jehan's Steppe, you can believe me.'

'Your brother said the opposite,' said Beauceron with a frosty smile.

'For reasons we both understand, and which we need not explore here. My father wishes to avenge Jehan's Steppe, and he wishes you to help him. He understands your unique constraints; at this stage, an agreement in principle will be sufficient.'

'What you ask is not trivial. I have been approached twice before with the selfsame offer.'

Agalina gave him a haughty look. 'These men were Davanzato's agents. You may be sure that the Summer King's daughter is not.'

'Will the invasion go ahead without me?'

'Candidly? I do not know. You have special information which will make any assault more likely to succeed; you have a troop well used to fighting in the South and a lust to take the city. Without that, I do not know.'

'Special information?'

'Do not fence with me, Beauceron. You grew up in Croad. Indeed, I think you grew up in the lord's household.'

'You veer into the realm of speculation,' said Beauceron with a tight expression.

'I am a student of history,' she said. 'I spend much time in my father's excellent library. It occurred to me to wonder what could cause a man to hate the ruling family of Croad with such a passion. It would have to be a matter of great moment. Lord Thaume did more than whip your kitten; he took something from you which haunts you to this day.'

Beauceron stared back at her wordlessly.

'Perhaps he took the future you imagined for yourself. Or

perhaps he took your birthright, and gave it to his son. Am I right, my lord?'

Beauceron rose from his seat, his mouth a thin line. 'I am Beauceron: who I was before I came here is of no consequence. If your father wishes to destroy Oricien, and take Croad, all he needs to know is that Beauceron understands that passion.'

'Sit down,' said Agalina softly. 'I did not mean to pry. I have great admiration for what you have achieved; and any man who comes to Mettingloom has the right to be judged on his deeds. Be assured I will never speak of the question again, if it displeases you.'

Beauceron set his jaw. 'Tell your father to call on me when he needs me,' he said. 'I will be there.'

8

A week later Beauceron presented himself at the Occonero. 'I am here to see Davanzato,' he said with a calm assurance to the guard, who was a stone heavier and three inches taller than him.

'The Under-Chamberlain does not see anyone without an appointment.'

'Then make me one. Perhaps you would like to make us tisane as well.'

The guard stepped closer to Beauceron. 'Already I dislike you. I am a good judge of Davanzato's perceptions. I don't think he will like you either.'

Beauceron permitted himself a smile. 'When you are discharged from this post, a calling as a clown awaits you. Davanzato fabricated evidence to have me tried for treason; does that not already suggest dislike?'

The man drew back. 'You are Beauceron?'

'And you are?'

'Ferliccio. Davanzato said if you had the audacity to present yourself I was to whip the hide from your arse.'

Beauceron sized Ferliccio up. He was a big man, well-muscled, but he did not look quick. 'I bear you no ill-will,' he said. 'I will not suggest we put the matter to the test. Let us treat Davanzato's remark as a jocularity. You may allow me admittance.'

Ferliccio nodded to his colleague on the other side of the corridor; both he and Ferliccio drew their swords.

'Go now,' said Ferliccio. 'We will pretend you have never been here.'

Beauceron shrugged and turned away. With a rapid motion he turned back and smashed his elbow into the second man's nose. Ferliccio moved towards Beauceron with his sword but it was too late: Beauceron's rapier had skewered his wrist to the heavy wooden table. He uttered a low-voiced curse.

'I do not know,' said Beauceron, 'why Davanzato does not pay the rate necessary to secure competent guards. One would think he had learned by now.'

He pulled Ferliccio's sword from his nerveless fingers and tossed it over the balcony to the marble floor below, where it rang with a discordant clamour. He flicked his rapier out of Ferliccio's wrist and stepped into Davanzato's doorway. 'You are a fool. Do you think I became Dog of the North through insipidity? Threaten me again and you die.'

Ferliccio did not meet his gaze.

'Davanzato,' called Beauceron as he stepped through the doorway. 'Your new guards are inept.'

Davanzato looked up from his desk, where he had been poring over a ledger. He half rose, reached for a rapier lying at his side.

Beauceron grinned. 'Carry on. If you wish to fence, let us

proceed at once. I have long imagined the outcome of such an encounter.'

Davanzato returned to his seat, a pallor discernible through his olive skin. 'What do you intend? I warn you, I am not friendless.'

'I intend no impudence; although naturally my feelings towards you are not cordial. You cannot find that surprising.'

'You are a brash, coarse man, to threaten the King's Under-Chamberlain thus in his own office.'

Beauceron sheathed his rapier and sat down. 'You mistake me. I have threatened nothing.'

'You have arrived, uninvited, in my office, with your blade drawn. Is that not a threat?'

Beauceron leaned forward. 'You should see me when I truly mean to intimidate. I needed my rapier only to discountenance your guards.'

Davanzato had recovered something of his composure. 'What, then, do you want?'

'Nothing could be simpler: my audience with the King.'

Davanzato gave an incredulous smile. 'The King you purposed treason against?'

'You may recall that I was acquitted.'

'Only through the agency of a quibbling legulier.'

'We both know that the evidence was fabricated.'

'Equally we both know that you were guilty. Will you take a drink? Langensnap, perhaps?'

'I think not.'

Davanzato gave a negligent gesture. 'You still expect an audience with Fanrolio?'

'Of course. My plans remain unchanged: to lead the Winter Armies against Croad. The extent of your duplicity surprised me, but I cannot afford either scruples or squeamishness. I am even prepared to overlook your offences against me if you deliver what I require.'

'You are in no position to do anything else.'

'You have misread the situation, Davanzato. I offered you significant bribes to arrange an audience. For your own reasons you chose to oppose me instead. Now you are out of pocket and the King's favour. Your prosecution made the Winter Court a laughing stock.'

'My only concern throughout was His Puissance's welfare. I believe your obsession can only end in disaster for Mettingloom. I acted honourably in obstructing it.'

'And in taking my gratuities while you did so?'

'Your "gratuity" included Lady Isola's ransom agency. A more expensive present I have never received.'

'You have your grievances; I have mine. All can be laid to rest if you provide my audience with Fanrolio.'

'Why should I, given my opposition to your schemes?'

Beauceron stood and walked towards the door. 'Because I will kill you if you do not. I am beyond – well beyond – the point of rational calculation. You have two days to arrange the audience. Without it you will end the week with a still heart.'

He walked out of the room without a backward glance. He no longer cared if Davanzato carried out his commission, or which King approved his scheme. But if Davanzato was worried about his own safety, he would have that much less time to plot against Beauceron. If the audience came to pass, that could be turned to advantage; if not, Agalina's offer remained in force. When dealing with men as slippery as kings, it was always as well to retain several options.

9

Beauceron returned home to find a visitor in his parlour

calmly drinking tisane: Lady Cosetta, whom he had not seen for some while.

'My lady, you are most welcome, and looking lovelier than ever.'

Cosetta was arrayed in a gown of the richest red silk, but set against her complexion it shrank away to insignificance, merely a foil to display her animate perfection. Her blue eyes sparkled with unquenchable vigour, her cheeks suffused with her ruddy health and youth. Her blonde hair, drawn back from her face and pinned up, set off her cheekbones to their best advantage. Beauceron thought back to the frightened spiritless girl cowering under an oilskin who had first seen Mettingloom. The transformation was barely to be under-stood without thaumaturgy.

Cosetta seemed to divine something of his thought. 'I have been here only four months,' she said. 'Already it is hard to remember anything else.'

'The time has been eventful – and not just for you.'

'I was glad,' she said, 'to see you elude death as you did. You are a rogue, but Davanzato is far worse. I would have hated to see his plot succeed.'

'Lady Isola no longer believes I will live to be hanged in Croad,' he said, 'or so I surmise, given her testimony against me.'

Cosetta shook her head sadly. 'You must not think ill of her. She is friendless, and desperate. She was an easy victim for a man like Davanzato. But I forget your vengeful dis-position. You will wreak a horrid retribution upon her.'

Beauceron bit back a smile. 'I do not take vengeance on ladies.'

Cosetta pursed her lips. 'Your dismay on finding we were not Lady Siedra when you kidnapped us suggests otherwise. Do not tell me you planned a surprise ball for her.'

'Lady Siedra is a special case,' said Beauceron. 'I admit to bearing her a particular animosity. I am conscious that I have wronged Isola more than she ever hurt me.'

Cosetta looked into his face. 'Is that remorse? I never thought to hear it from the Dog of the North.'

'Do not mistake me, Cosetta. I can accept that I have mal-treated her; that does not mean I regret it. Regrets are for those who can no longer take action. I look only forward.'

Cosetta appeared to be suppressing a laugh. 'The words "forward" and "Croad" would appear to be all but inter-changeable in your vocabulary.'

'My plans are no secret.'

Cosetta gave him a searching look. 'They should be; that is your difficulty. I know about the conversation you had with Agalina.'

'What conversation?'

'Beauceron, do not play me for a fool. I have connections at the Summer Court. There is little I do not know.'

'I understood Laertio had been banished to Far Niente.'

'So he has; but Tardolio is too late. What man will slight Laertio's friend, when he knows Laertio will be King?'

'Friend?'

'I use the term in its broadest sense. The Prince would be most displeased were anyone to offer me discourtesy. The result is that I retain all the influence I had when Laertio was here; and he will be back soon enough.'

'Laertio and Agalina take different views of the King's attitude to the invasion. They cannot both be correct.'

'No, they cannot.' Her blue eyes fixed Beauceron's gaze. 'And?'

'The situation is simple. Tardolio's defeat at Jehan's Steppe was so crushing that he will never take the field against Croad again. He knows that Oricien, backed by Tre-varre's troops, would destroy him.'

'In that he is wrong,' said Beauceron harshly. 'Oricien has

never been put to the test. I know how to take Croad; I need only the chance.'

Cosetta shook her head. 'You will not get it; not from Tardolio, at least.'

'I do not believe you. If you know of my conversation with Agalina, you will know her opinion of Tardolio's intent.'

She said nothing for a moment. 'Sometimes you are not as clever as you think,' she said. 'Agalina's only interest was in assessing the scope of your obsession. You are a dangerous and influential man, and the Summer Court hoped you could be persuaded that your cause was hopeless. Your conversation with Agalina convinced them that such persuasion would be futile. I could have told them as much, had anyone asked.'

'I do not understand.'

'No. Tardolio is desperate to avoid the assault on Croad; the only possible outcome, whether you fail or not, is an army of Emmen coming north, perhaps led by Enguerran himself. You can be sure it would not campaign in winter. Tardolio would be forced to defend a siege of Mettingloom while he sits the throne. He would take any steps to avoid it. His best hope was to persuade you of the futility of your scheme. Now that has failed, he has only one recourse.'

Beauceron looked steadily into her face. 'Assassination.'

She nodded.

'Why are you telling me? And why should I believe you?'

'Believe or not, I have done my duty. I feel a curious gratitude to you, which is why I am warning you. My life in Mettingloom is good; I hope it will improve yet further. You brought me here, even if not for my benefit. Add that I like and admire you. I cannot force you to believe me; but if you do not, and neglect your safety, you will be killed. What harm can a little vigilance do?'

Beauceron sat in thought. 'I am grateful,' he said, 'but

I am much vexed to find the Summer Court closed to me. I should have listened to your paramour.'

'I do not want to know what Laertio said to you. He has not told me, and I have not tried to learn. I know that he respects you, and hopes to make you an ally in future: I suspect your plans may have gone further.'

'I will not convey information you do not wish to hear.'

She leaned forward. 'You have two choices, Beauceron. Give up your scheme; or persuade Fanrolio.'

'The first option is naturally impossible; the second was always my preferred strategy.'

'You will need to overmaster Davanzato.'

'I am aware of that.'

'Your man Mongrissore is delving deep to learn more of Davanzato.'

'He is a determined man.'

'Undoubtedly; but he is looking in the wrong place.'

Beauceron gave her a quizzical stare. 'You speak with great certainty.'

'I know much that I never wished to know. May I send a man to Mongrissore?'

Beauceron weighed her up for a second. He had no real reason to trust her; her beauty made her veracity if anything less plausible. She could have no real reason to help him, unless it was that she hated Davanzato more.

'How much of my conversation with Agalina were you privy to? I will not embarrass you by asking how you came by your information.'

Cosetta gave an airy wave. 'Oh, Laertio has excellent sources. I know the whole of the conversation.'

'Including her speculation as to my original identity?'

'"Speculation"? Her hypothesis seemed to me highly plausible.'

Beauceron pursed his lips. 'The subject is displeasing to me. I would not have it the tittle-tattle of Mettingloom.'

'Gossip is not amenable to control. It works its way through the cracks like water. No one will hear your secret from me.'

'If you know as much as you say, you will be aware that I did not confirm Agalina's guess – and it was no more than a guess.'

'It is of no consequence. Now, may I send my man to Mongrissore? I think he has information about Davanzato he may find interesting.'

Beauceron narrowed his eyes. 'Very well.'

Cosetta rose. 'Excellent. Now, if you will excuse me, I am required once again at court. Do not trouble to call Kainera; I am adept at finding my own way out.'

12

Croad

I

Arren slipped out from the hall and went to find Eilla. She was alone in the servantry, polishing the silver plate: that evening there was to be a banquet in Lord High Viator Raugier's honour.

'Arren,' she said softly, 'you should not be here.'

'Come outside,' said Arren. 'I need to speak to you.'

'Mistress Eulalia will be vexed if she finds me gone.'

'Tell her to speak to Seigneur Arren if she has complaints.'

She followed Arren out into the Pleasaunce. A breeze ruffled the branches on the overhanging trees.

'I have been with Thaume and the Lord High Viator. You know why he is here?'

Eilla looked away. 'They say he has come to stamp out heresy.'

'He is a cruel and dangerous man. This morning he threatened to depose Lord Thaume for allowing the Wheel to flourish.'

A flash of concern ran across Eilla's eyes. 'He cannot do that.'

'He says he can, and has a writ to prove it. Thaume and

Guiles seemed to believe him. He rebuked Thaume for having Viator Dince whipped.'

Eilla sat down on a bench under the shade of a dappling tree with a controlled dignity which wrenched Arren's heart. 'What will it mean for the Gollains?' she asked.

'I do not know,' said Arren. 'It must depend on how Thaume reacts. He may close the Temple, as Raugier wants, but I think he will resist. That will call Raugier's bluff.'

'I was sent over to The Patient Suitor when he was staying there. I would not like to play bluff with him.'

'What can he do? I cannot see how he can depose Thaume in practice, whatever his writ says.'

'He can come back with an army. The viators' faction is dominant at court in Emmen, they say. King Arren is in no state to stop him, and Prince Jehan is by all accounts a pious man, willing to follow the Consorts.'

'I do not think it will come to that,' said Arren. 'But you must be careful. That is why I came to see you. I am sure he will want to make an example of somebody. Your father must stay away, and you must be invisible.'

A smile briefly animated her face. 'I am wearing the servants' livery,' she said. 'There is no better cloak of invisibility.'

Arren took her hand. 'I am sorry it has come to this. Things were so simple when we were children.'

'I do not object to complexity,' she said with a sharp smile. 'I object to being a servant.'

'You could be a farmer's wife,' said Arren.

She kicked him. 'Do not mention that lummox Chandry. My choices are not immediately promising.'

'My mother always thought we would marry,' said Arren with a sideways glance. 'She predicted it from the cradle.'

'So did mine,' she laughed.

Arren frowned. 'The contingency is remote, but surely not inherently ludicrous.'

'You don't understand, do you? You are Seigneur Arren, a favourite of Lord Thaume and an intimate of Lord Oricien. I am peasant girl Eilla, maid.'

'I am no more Seigneur Arren than I am King Arren,' he said. 'My status is both illusory and irrelevant—'

'Arren! Someone is coming!'

Arren too could hear footsteps along the gravelled path. 'Stay sitting,' he whispered. 'Leave matters to me, and let us hope it is not Lady Siedra.'

In this Arren was in luck, for around the corner walked Guigot with Raugier's attendant Erlard. They did not see the pair sitting on the bench.

'. . . Your observations interest me,' said Erlard, a portly young man of pleasant appearance. 'I feel sure they will interest the Lord High Viator equally.'

'I am always guided by the viators,' said Guigot. 'Naturally I abominate the Wheel, and seek only to Follow the Way. It surprises me that so few folk see matters with such clarity.'

'You must not concern yourself with the progress of others along the Way, my lord. Cleave to your own path, and take the counsel of the viators to heart. You will soon reach Equilibrium, and thence Harmony.'

Guigot inclined his head. 'Your wise words soothe my spirit, Viator – Arren! What are you doing here?'

'Guigot; Viator. Please do not let us intrude upon your discussion.'

Guigot coloured. 'I had thought the garden was unoccupied; I was merely showing Viator Erlard around.'

'So it seemed,' said Arren with a slight smile. 'I am glad to find your advance along the Way so smooth. You never showed such leanings in our classes with Viator Sleech.'

'Do not judge a man on where he begins his journey, young Seigneur,' said Erlard. 'Harmony is achieved at the road's end, not its start.'

'And anyway, Arren, what are you doing in my uncle's private garden with a serving wench – if I need to ask?'

'Your thoughts are callow,' said Arren. 'Eilla had been overcome by the smell of the silver-polish. I thought some fresh air might help.'

Guigot smirked. 'No doubt you would have been equally eager to assist one of the more elderly servants.'

'Your remarks do you no credit,' said Arren. 'Viator Erlard will come to doubt your piety.'

Erlard leaned forward to look at Eilla's dress.

'Is that a brooch of the Wheel I see, girl?'

'Yes, sir.'

'You are a Gollain?'

'Yes, sir.'

'And you flaunt it in Lord Thaume's household?'

'My lord allows us to wear favours.'

Erlard pursed his lips. 'Lord Thaume is a most tolerant master.'

'May I go, sir? I am needed in the castle.'

'For now. You may be certain I will comment on this matter to the Lord High Viator.'

'You may assure Lord High Viator Raugier that the girl will be discharged,' said Guigot. 'Such flagrant heresy is inappropriate for Lord Thaume's household.'

Arren rose from the bench. 'How will you achieve the dismissal, Guigot? You are neither the Lord of Croad nor his seneschal. I am sure Viator Erlard is too wise to be impressed by your bombast.'

'Such wrangling is not on the Way of Harmony!' said Erlard. 'Lord Guigot, I have many interviews to conduct today, but I have enjoyed our conversation: I hope it is of profit to us both.' He bowed and followed Eilla from the garden.

'What game are you playing, Guigot?'

Guigot spat into the flowerbed. 'I did not know you were here, mooning over some servant girl. It is no secret that there will be changes ahead; it does no harm to sit well with the viators.'

'You hate them and their cant.'

Guigot shrugged. 'What if I do? Prince Jehan holds them in high esteem. I may attend the Viatory more frequently in future. I advise you to do the same, rather than dally with heretic servant girls. Lord Thaume has given you a great gift by bringing you into his household; it is nothing to me if you squander it.'

'You are unscrupulous.'

Guigot grinned. 'In my position I cannot afford scruples. What of the servant girl? Was she a good tumble?'

Arren tensed; but Guigot wanted a response, and Arren was not going to oblige. With an easy laugh he said: 'Why don't you ask her yourself, preferably when I am absent? The sight of violence distresses me.'

2

The evening saw Lord Thaume host in his Great Hall the banquet for which Eilla had been polishing silver plate. Arren did not imagine that Thaume was displaying any cordiality towards the Lord High Viator, but protocol insisted that the dinner be held, and that those who might more prudently be kept away would be in attendance.

At the head of the great table sat Lord Thaume and Lady Jilka, displaying no discernible amity. The Lord High Viator was seated to their right. Cyngier's seating plan had placed caution ahead of all else: Oricien sat close by, as did Master Guiles, with Viator Sleech opposite. Viator Dince, who might have expected a place of honour, remained in his quarters with an ague. Sir Langlan was seated well away from the head of the table, as was Guigot, despite his cordial relations with Raugier's attendants. In this group also sat Arren and Siedra.

Lord Thaume had insisted upon a well-set table, with venison, boar and fish fresh from the River Croad supplementing the fowl, beef and lamb more common to the board. He had judged Raugier willing to indulge his stomach, and the gusto with which he attacked the early courses seemed to bear out the judgement.

'I trust you have had a productive day, my lord,' said Lord Thaume as the meat courses drew to a close; by all understanding it would have been indecorous to raise such matters of business any earlier.

Raugier chewed the last of his perch with deliberation. 'I have learned much of interest. I have encountered many folk well along the Way, and yearning for the viators to help them yet further.'

Lord Thaume sipped at a crisp white wine from his own vineyard. 'We may live a spartan life in Croad,' he said, 'but there is always scope for folk to Follow the Way.'

'As they see fit, of course.'

'Naturally,' said Lord Thaume, setting his goblet down. 'Since the alternative is to proceed in a way they find unfitting, this is surely uncontentious.'

'Your views interest me,' said Raugier, dabbing his lips with a damask napkin. 'Candidly, I have seen too much of folk thinking they can choose their own path along the Way. Such an approach does not, ultimately, lead to Harmony.'

'I take it you refer to the Gollains.'

'All are agreed that the Wheel constitutes a pernicious

314

heresy. If all followed their own inclinations, who would need the viators?'

'My lord fully agrees with you, sir,' said Viator Sleech, blinking rheumily.

'Thank you, Sleech. I am able to articulate my own opinions,' said Lord Thaume. 'My own beliefs are strictly orthodox. If a minority of my people chooses to follow the Wheel, that is a matter for their own judgement.'

'The minority appears to me sizeable, my lord. Some estimate that fully a quarter of the population of Croad are heretics.'

'My lord, the estimate is grossly exaggerated,' said Lady Jilka, who had scarcely spoken during the meal. 'I would be surprised if one in twenty follows the Wheel.'

Raugier inclined his head. 'I would be churlish to challenge the opinion of a lady so noble, pious and beautiful. My own calculation would be materially higher, but that is by the by. Even one heretic would be too many, especially when the lord of the city connives at their practices.'

'"Connivance" is a strong word, my lord,' said Lord Thaume.

'You may wish to supply another,' said Raugier. '"Encouragement", perhaps?'

'My lord!' said Jilka. 'My husband may display a tolerance some deplore, but he, and our entire household, are wholly orthodox in their persuasions. I challenge anyone to say otherwise.'

'I understand your view was somewhat different during Lord Thaume's absence at Jehan's Steppe.'

Jilka flushed. 'Tales of our disagreement were exaggerated. Lord Thaume has now explained the basis of his policies.'

Raugier leaned forward with a quizzical glance. 'I am

315

intrigued. Has he explained them to your satisfaction? Your devotion to the Way is legendary.'

Jilka's mouth sagged. 'Lord Thaume – naturally has his own perspective. As his consort my duty is to obey.'

'If so upright a lady endorses her lord's orthodoxy, how can I do otherwise?'

Lady Jilka gave a nervous smile.

'Let me ask you one further question, my lady.'

Jilka looked back dumbly.

'Were your husband to leave you Regent of Croad again, would you permit free worship at the Temple?'

'I – I would take the advice of Viator Sleech and Viator Dince.'

Raugier narrowed his eyes. 'Viator Dince might think twice about offering candid advice, my lady. I suggest that you would not in conscience allow the Temple to remain open.'

'It – it would not be a comfortable sight for me. I cannot say I would close it again.'

'I thank you for your candour, my lady. Lord Thaume, let me ask you a hypothetical question.'

'I do not believe there can be such a thing from a Commissioner of Orthodoxy.'

Raugier shrugged. 'Hearing Lady Jilka's response as you have, would you leave her as Regent again? On the last occasion you chose Sir Langlan who, to be blunt, suffers a reputation for dissipation and irreligion.'

'That is not "suffering"; it is a boast!' called Sir Langlan from away down the table.

'Thank you, Sir Langlan,' said Lord Thaume with a reproachful glare. 'I chose Sir Langlan merely because I travelled south, leaving a potential northern army to my rear. That, and the fact that I wished to take Lady Jilka to

Glount, explained my decision. I would have no hesitation in appointing my wife as Regent in the future.'

'You paint a pleasing picture of domestic felicity and mutual trust,' said Raugier. 'This will weigh – to an extent – in my conclusions.'

'Lord Raugier,' called Erlard from towards the base of the table. 'I find that Lord Thaume's household is not as orthodox as he claims. You, girl, come here.'

Arren saw with horror that he was summoning Eilla from her duties clearing the plates away. She stepped forward. 'This girl was wearing a Wheel brooch this morning.'

'Come here, girl,' said Raugier. 'Let me examine you.'

Eilla looked helplessly at Arren. She walked over to Lord Raugier and curtsied.

'Are you wearing a brooch now?'

'No, my lord.'

'But you did this morning?'

'Yes, my lord.'

'You are a heretic?'

'I said to Viator Erlard this morning that I followed the Wheel.'

'You admit as much, in front of Lord Thaume, and the Lord High Viator?'

'I was always brought up to be truthful, my lord. I do not regard it as occasion for shame.'

'You are forward, for a servant.'

'I merely answer the questions you ask me, my lord.'

'Is that so? Answer me this: why should I not have you whipped?'

She looked down levelly into his face. 'Because it would do no good. I should still follow the Wheel.'

'You are highly impertinent.'

Lord Thaume intervened. 'She is only responding to your

inquisition, my lord. No doubt you would be equally critical were she struck dumb.'

'Enough. You can go, girl.'

Arren felt a surge of sympathy for Eilla, blotted out by a tight-lipped rage. He could see Eilla was on the verge of a sharp retort, and he could not blame her.

Her face scarlet, she said: 'Until a month ago I cared nothing for the Wheel. I could hardly have told you the difference between the Wheel and the Way. It was only when Viator Dince cut my father's hand off that I realized it was important. If I follow the Wheel, it is the viators who have shown the way. Is that not what they are supposed to do?'

Raugier rose from his seat. He kicked Eilla twice. 'Impudent hussy! Schismatic harlot! You shall not only be whipped but hanged! I command it!'

Lord Thaume spoke quietly. 'In my hall, you command nothing, my lord. Eilla, your provocation has been extreme, but you have gone too far. Leave us now. Lord Raugier, you may reach whatever conclusions you choose about practices in Croad, but while I rule you shall not pass sentence on any of my servants.'

Raugier collected himself and performed an immaculate bow. 'I hear and understand fully, my lord. I thank you for your hospitality and frank insights this evening. I hope you will now excuse me: I have eaten my fill.'

Not even pausing to wait for his attendants, he strode from the hall.

Siedra leaned across to Arren. 'She does not know her place.'

'I am glad of it,' said Arren. 'She only spoke the truth as she saw it.'

Guigot chuckled. 'Truth? It is a truth that will cost Thaume his head. Raugier's pride will not tolerate that rebuke. He will have his revenge, and it will not be on the servant girl.'

'Arren, listen to me,' said Siedra. 'She is bound for destruction, and soon. Do not let her take you with her.'

3

A short while later Arren pleaded fatigue and slipped away from the table. He was not the only one to make an excuse; Guigot had disappeared as soon as Lord High Viator Raugier had departed, and Sir Langlan's increasingly elevated spirits had driven away most of his immediate neighbours.

Arren made his way to the servantry; on seeing his entrance Mistress Eulalia beckoned him outside. 'You cannot keep coming in here, Seigneur. You do not help Eilla, or yourself.'

'I am sorry, mistress. You may have heard something of this evening's incident.'

Eulalia gave a wintry smile. 'Eilla has not been discreet. If you have any influence over her, you may wish to enjoin her to restraint. She has been disruptive ever since she arrived here.'

'How could it be otherwise?' said Arren. 'She has suffered greatly.'

'She is drawing too much attention to herself – including your own. It does not speak well for her.'

'Where is she?'

'In her room, I should imagine. I do not want you to see her there.'

With a barely perceptible shrug he turned and left the servantry.

He strode through the mean corridors, his boots ringing on the stone floor. He found himself at Eilla's door and knocked. Wordlessly she opened it. Her eyes were red and swollen.

'Let us go somewhere more private,' he said. 'I undertook to Mistress Eulalia not to visit you here.'

'Your scrupulous sense of honour does you credit,' she said with a flicker of a smile. 'You may yet find favour with the Lord High Viator.'

'The Pleasaunce became a little crowded this afternoon,' he said. 'I am sure Lord Thaume's own viatory will be more private.'

'Arren!' said Eilla. 'What if we are discovered?'

'We will not be,' he said. 'Lord Thaume will not wish to visit the viatory tonight. In any event, who could condemn us for drawing solace in such a place?'

Eilla gave a half-shrug, and they set off up the stairs.

Lord Thaume's viatory was a small room with panels of coloured glass at either end. Set into the wall opposite the altar was an alcove concealed behind an arras. In the flickering candlelight of the viatory it was scarcely visible, and by unspoken consent they stepped behind the arras into the alcove's veiled obscurity. Eilla sat down on the single wooden chair and Arren leaned against the wall. 'You were unwise to speak to Raugier in such a fashion,' he said.

'Perhaps I was, but I could not have kept silent,' she said with a quiet intensity. 'My father has always said the viators were wicked corrupt parasites. I never much cared; even if he was right, the viators were hardly alone in their vices. But then I saw what Dince and Jilka did to him, and on top of all Raugier comes here and says we cannot worship the Wheel, and threatens to depose Lord Thaume. Who is he to threaten us?'

'He is the Lord High Viator, and Commissioner for Orthodoxy. He carries the weight of the King's words, and the Consorts'.'

Her voice throbbed with emotion against the cold stone walls around them. 'We have all lived our own lives in Croad for as long as I have known. Why do they suddenly have to turn everything upside down?' she asked, with a renewal of tears in her voice.

'Eilla—'

She leaned away from Arren and wiped her sleeve across her face. 'I should not be so pitiful. I am alive, healthy and I have people to care about me: many cannot say as much.'

'You have suffered a lot, Eilla, and so quickly. It is only natural that you find it hard.'

'We are still at war, Arren. You marched all the way north and beat Tardolio, and then you come back here and find that he was not the enemy at all. Raugier is far more dangerous, and he can take Croad far more easily than Tardolio ever could.'

'It is not a war I know how to fight,' said Arren. 'I cannot see an enemy with a sword. Raugier is the King's man.'

Eilla gave a brittle laugh. 'Do you believe that? Raugier is no more the King's servant than he is mine. He and his faction are manipulating a sick old man and a stupid younger one.'

'Eilla! It is treason to describe Prince Jehan so.'

'And a lie not to. The Gollains are not only in Croad: men follow the Wheel in Garganet, in Gammerling, even secretly in Emmen itself, they say. All the while the King permits it, no harm is done to anyone, but once he tries to stamp it out, he will have war. The King's counsellors should tell him so – but they are all viators.'

'I do not think deeply on such questions,' said Arren, 'but I am concerned for you. If you do not make your sympathies less obvious, Thaume will not be able to save you. Raugier needs to make an example of someone, and I cannot imagine he thinks to challenge Thaume himself. Make sure you are not the scapegoat, Eilla.'

She rose from her chair and stroked his cheek. 'I am touched at your care for me, Arren. I know how easy it would be for you to leave me behind.'

'I will never do that, Eilla. We have always meant too much to one another.'

'Shh!'

Arren could hear a faint creaking from outside the alcove. It could only be the viatory door opening. He beckoned Eilla to the back of the alcove and gingerly peered through the tiny gap where the arras met the wall.

He could dimly make out a lantern and two indistinct figures obscured in its shadow. He was conscious that Eilla was at his shoulder, but he could not risk moving to send her further back. Arren could only hope that whoever had entered would not want to enter the alcove. But instead the figures went to stand before the altar. Neither man was tall: Lord Thaume was not visiting his own viatory. So who were they?

'I hope this is worth the subterfuge, Lord Guigot,' said the clipped voice Arren recognized as Lord High Viator Raugier. This could not be an innocent meeting, and for a moment Arren considered the consequences of being discovered.

'I believe you will find it so, my lord,' said Guigot, the lantern casting a vast shadow on his face. 'It is late, and the viatory is chill. I will be brief and candid.'

'Please proceed.'

'I have seen your progress, and that of your attendants, around Croad today. I might not be hazarding too much to suggest that you have been disappointed in my uncle's conduct.'

Arren's eyes had become accustomed to the light, and he

saw Raugier purse his lips. 'There is a tolerance for the Gollains I find unsettling. The episode with the servant girl showed Thaume in a poor light.'

'All true-minded folk must think as much. Thaume panders to a minority, at the expense of those who follow the true Way.'

Raugier nodded briskly. 'Just so.'

'May I ask how you intend to proceed?'

'You may not.'

'Let me outline my own understanding. You have come to assess Croad's orthodoxy, and have been dissatisfied with Lord Thaume's intransigence. You see no way of restoring a proper tenor while Thaume remains lord; yet equally you lack a ready means of removing him. An Instrument of Deposition would be a waste of paper, unless you had the method of enforcing it.'

'Continue, if you must.'

'Suppose I offered you a solution which would nullify the power of Lord Thaume and assure Croad's orthodoxy?'

'I am unclear as to how such a situation might occur.'

Arren felt Eilla grip his arm.

'I am the nephew of Lord Thaume,' said Guigot. 'In strict lineage, my claim to the lordship is better than Thaume's, since my father was his elder brother. And unlike Thaume, I have no tolerance for the Wheel.'

'It is fortunate we are alone. You are offering yourself as Lord of Croad if I depose Thaume?'

'I am already Lord of Croad, in all but title. I was cheated of my birthright by my age. Thaume should have been my regent, but he cozened Arren into making him Lord outright.'

'The legitimacy of your claim is of no interest to me,' said Raugier with a touch of flint, 'except in so far as it has a veneer of plausibility. I am more concerned as to the practicality of your approach.'

'I have considered the matter in some detail,' said Guigot. 'Sign the Instrument of Deposition; send your Harmonic Perfects to his chamber at dawn; proclaim me Lord of Croad. You will need, I think, to kill Thaume. Imprisonment, possibly with gelding, will be sufficient for Oricien, and I shall marry Siedra.'

'And would the people of Croad accept you?'

'I will make them. The Guard are loyal to their paymaster. Since I will control the Treasury, and you speak with Arren's voice to make me lord, they will do as they must.'

Raugier nodded slowly. 'There is much to ponder.'

'Think fast, my lord. Such words should not hang in the air too long.'

Raugier nodded. 'Very well; it is the Way. But remember, Guigot: I am making you, and I can break you.'

'I understand, my lord.'

Without a further word they turned on their heels and walked in unison from the viatory. Arren, his heart pounding, signalled Eilla to silence and waited until long after the plotters' footsteps had died away.

4

An hour before dawn the next morning, Lord High Viator Raugier was awoken by a deputation of Lord Thaume's Guards, led by Captain Fleuraume, with Arren prominent among them.

'You must awake now, my lord,' said Fleuraume, his sword at Raugier's throat.

'What is this?' said Raugier blearily through narrowed eyes. 'I do not take kindly to your tone.'

'Lord Thaume wishes to see you immediately. Your choice in the matter is limited.'

'I have the full authority of King Arren. You will regret treating me in this fashion.'

Fleuraume shrugged. 'My orders come from Lord Thaume. That is sufficient for me.'

Raugier was escorted unceremoniously to the Amber Room to find the Lord Thaume dressed in his black livery. Two guards pinioned Guigot's arms; Sir Langlan and Seneschal Cyngier sat at Lord Thaume's side, and Oricien had his back to the company as he stared from the window.

'Lord Raugier,' said Lord Thaume quietly. 'I am glad you could join us at this early hour. I have important decisions to make.'

'Indeed you do, my lord,' said Raugier with a steely grin. 'I suspect your conduct in the next hour will determine your fate and that of Croad.'

'Let me go!' roared Guigot. 'This is not fitting treatment for a man of noble blood.'

'Release him,' said Lord Thaume. 'If he makes a move to attack or escape, kill him.'

'You may wish to explain the purpose of this early-morning drama,' said Raugier. 'I can barely see my accusers in this light, let alone rebut their lies. Am I under arrest?'

'Cyngier, turn up the lanterns,' said Lord Thaume. 'We will have light in every sense. You were overheard, with Guigot, plotting in my own private viatory, of all places, to depose me and set my nephew up as Lord of Croad.'

'The notion is nonsensical,' said Raugier. 'Let my accuser stand forth.'

'I heard you, my lord,' said Arren, stepping forward from among the Guards. 'I was in the alcove opposite the altar tonight while you and Guigot decided not only to depose but to kill Lord Thaume.'

'Lies!' bellowed Guigot.

'So this is my accuser?' said Raugier. 'May I ask what you were doing in your own Lord's viatory at such an hour?'

'Your question is irrelevant,' said Arren.

'Answer him, Arren,' said Lord Thaume. 'I would not have it said that I denied Raugier the chance to speak.'

'I was talking to Eilla. I thought to do so in a private location,' said Arren.

'The heretic girl! The lad's motive is all too plain. He was honeying up to his sweetheart – who I planned to see whipped today. He saw Guigot and me in the yard, and they fabricated this confection to save the girl. It is Arren who should be punished.'

'You do not deny being in my viatory?' asked Lord Thaume.

'No, we were there, but the idea that we were purposing your deposition is ludicrous.'

'How so? You have flaunted your writ ever since your arrival.'

'Can you not see, my lord, that the boy is making a mock of you? Would you not have gone to great lengths at his age to impress your sweetheart?'

'To the extent of fabricating baseless capital charges against the Lord High Viator? I think not.'

'There is no evidence other than Arren's word; and presumably that of the girl, which is worthless.'

'Your defence, if I may summarize, is that Arren and Eilla concocted false accusations to prevent you having her whipped for heresy?'

'Essentially so.'

'Eilla's father was my master mason until Viator Dince had him mutilated for supposed treason. No act of mine can make up to him, or to his daughter, for what they have lost. Eilla knows that as well as I; she knows that under no circumstances would I allow her to be punished by you. Fleuraume, chain the Lord High Viator, if you please.'

Raugier attempted to shake off the restraint; Fleuraume applied a hold to his elbow and within seconds the chains had been secured.

'Guigot, do you have anything to say?'

Guigot glowered. 'The conversation was in the nature of a joke.'

'You do not deny that you discussed my deposition, and your own elevation?'

'The conversation took place broadly as Arren described, but it was a late-night fancy, not a genuine plot.'

'I did not realize that you regarded my viatory as at your disposal. Do your 'late-night fancies' take the form of my deposition?'

'Not in that sense, my lord.'

'In what sense, then, Guigot?'

'It is no secret that there are circumstances under which I might have been Lord of Croad.'

'They do not include the present ones.'

'I cannot deny that on occasion I allow myself to think how events might have gone differently.'

Lord Thaume shook his head. 'That is the great misfortune of your life, Guigot: not that you failed to become Lord of Croad, but that you cannot forget it.'

'In this case I was merely expressing frustration to Lord Raugier. Neither of us meant the matter seriously.'

'May I ask a question?' said Sir Langlan, lounging back in his seat. 'Guigot, it is fair to say there is almost nothing I like about you, but one aspect of your character I relished was your adamant hostility to the viators. Suddenly I find you are going to the Viatory every day. Is this not strange?'

Guigot shrugged. "We must all Follow the Way at our own pace.'

'Lord High Viator Raugier would scarcely have elevated a rogue like you to the seat of Croad unless you showed greater piety than you had heretofore. You set out to display yourself to Raugier as a man who would bring orthodoxy to Croad. You might even have succeeded if Arren had not been by.'

Guigot shot Arren an automatic glance of hatred. 'You would take a baseborn boy's word over mine?'

'Arren's father is Captain of my Guard,' said Lord Thaume. 'I vouch for both of their characters. Guigot, you are every bit as guilty as Raugier. I must decide how to deal with you both.'

'I have recommendations on that score,' said Sir Langlan with a wintry smile.

'Fleuraume, take them both to the dungeons. I will announce my decision tonight.'

5

Lord Thaume had designated the Amber Room, where he had first received Lord High Viator Raugier, as the place where he would render his judgement. When Arren slipped in at the back of the room, Raugier and Guigot stood in chains before Lord Thaume's seat, but Lord Thaume himself was not yet present. Arren wondered if, once again, he was detained in the viatory.

Instead Lord Thaume strode into the room from his chambers, flanked by Sir Langlan and, surprisingly to Arren's eyes, Master Pinch. Pinch had a habit of vanishing and re-appearing at irregular intervals, and he had slipped away before Thaume's visit to Glount. How the thaumaturge occupied himself during such interludes, nobody knew.

Lord Thaume seated himself with an expressionless countenance.

'Lord Raugier, I have debated your fate for much of the day. I have no doubt that you have plotted with my nephew to depose and murder me; naturally I look upon your actions with disapproval. Were I to inflict a penalty proportionate to my displeasure, you would now be hanging from the marketplace gallows.'

He paused. Raugier looked back unflinchingly.

'I make no secret,' continued Lord Thaume, 'that several of my counsellors recommended this course. If I were to act in accordance with my personal feelings, I too should have followed this approach. I am aware, however, that my animus is not to the point. As Lord of Croad, I must look to the welfare of my city. I must also take account of the respect due to your office, however treacherously you have discharged it. My ruling, then, is this: you are to be expelled from the city tonight, with your attendants, on pain of death. Should you ever return, with or without the King's writ, be assured you will be hanged.'

Raugier permitted himself a half-smile. 'You would not dare, now or later, to kill me. You would bring a terrible retribution upon yourself.'

'I have treated you with considerable leniency,' said Lord Thaume, 'largely at the advice of my thaumaturge Master Pinch. It is not too late for me to revoke my clemency.'

Raugier bowed ironically. 'If you wish to turn every man's hand against you, and to declare your city sanctuary for every heretic in Mondia, I cannot stop you. Since you have the wisdom to listen to the counsel of Master Pinch, I am confident as to my survival.'

Sir Langlan rose from his seat. 'You may be assured, my lord, that I was among those who advocated, most strongly, your immediate execution. I have not given up hope that Lord Thaume chooses to make such an example of you.'

Raugier's eyes glittered. 'You are a drunken, irreligious fool, Sir Langlan. You have no more concept of statecraft than a baboon. Every man in the room knows that Lord Thaume dare not touch me. This fanfaronade is designed only to disguise his impotence.'

Lord Thaume rapped his fist against the heavy oak table. 'Enough. You seem intent on proving the hypothesis that my patience is inexhaustible and that you may treat the Lord of Croad with contempt within his own hall.' He paused. In his cheeks were spots of red. 'You are correct that I do not judge it prudent to hang you out of hand: nonetheless, I now decree that the whipping you so richly deserve, and which so improved Viator Dince's character, shall be imposed.'

Raugier's face blanched. 'You intend to whip the Lord High Viator?'

'Can you be surprised?'

'This is treason!'

'If you can persuade the King so, come back with an army. Now, will you disrobe, or must I order Serjeant Fleuraume to intervene?'

'You make a grave mistake, Thaume,' hissed Raugier, licking his lips. 'I am an old man. Your barbarity will return to haunt you.'

Lord Thaume made a dismissive gesture. 'Take him away. I have no desire to witness the matter.'

'My lord, if I might—' said Master Pinch, as Raugier was dragged kicking from the hall.

'Yes, Pinch.'

'This falls outside the line of conduct we discussed.'

'What more do you want, Pinch? I spared his life, which he deserved to lose. Rather than being grateful for my mercy, he continued to fleer and mock.'

'His rage will be the greater at a whipping than a hanging.'

Lord Thaume gave him a puzzled look. 'His emotions after being hanged would be of hypothetical relevance only.'

'You leave a dangerous man alive to hate and fear you.'

Lord Thaume shrugged. 'Hate is a destructive and self-consuming passion. The man who hates is too hot of head to plan with competence.'

'As you say, my lord,' said Pinch.

'In addition, he will be able to display the scars the next time he seeks to be elected Consort. He should thank me for providing him with such an electoral advantage.'

The close of this speech was drowned out by howls from the next room. Lord High Viator Raugier was not submitting to his novel method of professional advancement with docility.

'We turn now to you, Lord Guigot,' said Lord Thaume over the cries from the ante-room. 'You have no powerful protectors or venerable office to protect you.'

Guigot's eyes were coals as he glared back at Lord Thaume. 'You have always been a cruel and unjust lord.'

'Now is not the time for a litany of your grievances,' said Lord Thaume.

'I am not allowed a statement of defence or extenuation?'

'Your guilt is manifest,' said Lord Thaume from behind tense lips. 'Have you no remorse for your acts?'

Guigot gave a harsh laugh. 'Remorse? For a conversation? You are over-sensitive to criticism.'

Lord Thaume raised one eyebrow. 'Your "criticism" took an unreasonably direct form.'

Guigot shrugged. 'Whatever decision you have arrived at, my intervention will not change it. It would be as well if you pronounced it now.'

Lord Thaume shook his head. 'I am giving you a chance at repentance. I cannot show mercy without it.'

'Very well,' said Guigot in a flat voice. 'I heartily repent my acts.'

The thin line of Lord Thaume's self-control snapped. 'Your father was my brother. No man could have loved and esteemed him more than I. Were it possible for me to spare you for his sake, I would do so. I am clear, however, that your character is irredeemable, and as long as you live, you remain a danger to me. You have plotted my murder, and in this game of high stakes you have failed. Tonight you shall be taken out and hanged.' Arren noticed that his hand was shaking as Cyngier presented the warrant for signature.

Guigot looked back at Lord Thaume a long second. There was only silence in the room. 'I demand to make a final statement.'

Lord Thaume nodded. 'I cannot deny you the right.'

Guigot drew himself up. His face was unusually pale but otherwise he seemed composed. 'If I die tonight,' he said, 'I die as the only true Lord of Croad. When Lord Gaucelis died at the hands of the Northerners, with Borel at his side, the true heir to Croad was Borel's son: namely, myself. Instead of ruling in my stead until I came of age, Thaume arrogated to himself the lordship of Croad. I had always wondered if he was conscious of the great wrong he had done me. Then I found he proposed to marry me to Duke Panarre's lackwitted daughter Klaera, the embarrassment of one house united with that of another. If I chose to consider alternatives with the Lord High Viator, who can blame me?'

'Lord Guigot,' said Master Pinch. 'You have used your last speech unwisely. Do not die with this bitterness on your lips. I am no advocate of the viators, but you are preparing to die in Disharmony.'

'Thaume,' said Guigot, 'I intend to exact a terrible

vengeance on you and your house. Since I will find this easier alive than dead, I prefer to avoid execution by any method. If you persist in the treacherous folly of murdering your own just lord, however, I demand my right as a nobleman to die by the sword rather than the rope.'

Lord Thaume looked at Guigot from behind hooded eyes. 'My regrets at your fate are too numerous to list,' he said. 'That I must order the death of my brother's son . . . even for Borel's sake I could not spare you; but for his sake I grant you death on the block. It must proceed immediately.' He nodded to Fleuraume.

Guigot looked around the room. 'Will none of you speak for mercy? Thaume will take my head in any event, so your intervention will cost nothing. Oricien,' he said with a harsh smile, 'will you not intercede for your cousin? Siedra?'

Siedra said nothing. In a thick voice Oricien said: 'You richly deserve your fate.'

'Master Pinch,' said Guigot. 'You have been wont to present yourself as a voice of moderation in Thaume's counsels. Will you not speak a gentle word?'

'I have counselled Lord Thaume as to his most prudent course,' said Pinch. 'In this case it is hard to demur from his judgement.'

'Sir Langlan?'

'If I catch a fox raiding the chicken coop, do I appeal to its better nature to desist, or do I put it to immediate death? Why spare you to wreak yet more mischief?'

'Ah, Seigneur Arren, skulking at the back, always skulking. Had you not hidden in the viatory with that trollop, I would be Lord of Croad tonight. Do you not feel guilt at your agency in my fate? Surely a counsel of mercy would become you.'

Arren's lips twitched. 'I saw you at Jehan's Steppe,' he said. 'You stood by to let Oricien die. There is justice in the end.'

'So be it,' said Guigot. 'I go to my fate a wiser man, and I need no viator to bring Harmony.'

The doors burst open and Lady Jilka rushed in.

'Jilka! I told you to keep away. I will not hear remonstrances about the Lord High Viator.'

'My lord,' she cried. 'The King is dead! Jehan is King of Emmen.'

6

The Amber Room fell into a shocked silence at the news of the King's death. Arren, despite having known that the old man was unlikely to recover, felt a hollowness in his stomach.

'How do you know, Jilka?' asked Lord Thaume.

'A messenger from King Jehan has come,' she said. 'King Arren died in his sleep nearly three weeks ago.'

'Where is the messenger?' asked Lord Thaume. 'We must all pledge fealty to His Puissance. Fleuraume, make sure that the Lord High Viator is not on hand when the King's messenger comes: in fact, I will receive him in my personal chamber.'

'What of Guigot, my lord?' asked Sir Langlan.

Lord Thaume's mouth was a thin line. 'Arren's death changes nothing. The execution proceeds immediately.'

'May I at least prepare myself in the viatory?' asked Guigot in a calm voice. Lord Thaume looked at him with a raised eyebrow.

"Execution"?' asked Lady Jilka. 'You mean to proceed, then?'

'The matter was extensively debated in your absence. My sentence, though harsh, is irrevocable. On this occasion, Guigot, you have my permission to use the viatory next door.'

Guigot sneered. 'Thank you, my lord. If, as it seems, I must die, I would do so with the comfort of the viators. I will await Sleech in the viatory.'

Arren wondered at this sudden access of piety from Guigot. There was no doubt that he had manufactured his recent attendance for Raugier's benefit, and Arren was sceptical that the prospect of death had brought about a late conversion. He slipped into the viatory behind Guigot. There was no chance of escape: the only door led back out into the Amber Room; the altar stood against one wall, the alcove in which he and Eilla had overheard Guigot set into the other, and the other two ends of the room were taken up with coloured glass panels, a green one depicting Hyssen facing the sunrise, and an orange representation of Animaxia the sunset. The sun caught this latter panel to flood the chamber with an intense radiance.

Guigot, looking around the viatory, seemed to have little of Harmony on his mind. He saw Arren and his mouth curled.

'I should take you with me,' he said. 'If I were armed, be assured I would.'

Arren stepped closer. 'Bare hands make as good a weapon as any. You may try if you wish.'

'If it were not for you, I should be Lord of Croad this minute. I do not fear death; it is the failure of my plan I regret. To have come so close . . .'

'You should perhaps prepare yourself for what is to come.'

Guigot gave a bark of laughter. 'I never reckoned you among Sleech's flock, Arren.'

'You know I am not. Nonetheless, the imminence of death must surely elevate your thoughts.'

'Imminence? You are pedestrian, Arren. I am not about to die, by blade or by noose.'

He rushed at Arren, knocking him from his feet, and threw himself head-first into the Sunset Window of Animaxia. The glass shattered and as the orange glow vanished, Arren had a sight of Guigot spiralling out towards the ground below. He scrambled to his feet and looked through the shattered opening: by accident or design, Guigot's fall had been arrested by the sloping roof of the refectory below. Guigot eased himself down the slope of the roof, jumping the last ten feet to reach the courtyard. Immediately he scampered away.

'I will be revenged on the whole pack of you!' he called up.

Arren shook his head ruefully. Guigot's grievances were real enough, but his indulgence of them had always tended to the melodramatic. He turned and ran back into the Amber Room to tell Lord Thaume what had happened.

'Quickly! Find him!' shouted Lord Thaume. 'He cannot be suffered to escape.'

While Fleuraume drew up a squadron of troops, Arren and Oricien slipped back into the viatory and dropped down to the ground using the same route as Guigot.

'Where would he have gone?' said Oricien, looking around him in frustration.

'He cannot hope to evade capture,' said Arren. 'Unless – the stables!'

'Of course!'

Together they ran towards Thaume's private stables. 'Cornelis!' Oricien called to the stable-boy. 'Is Lord Guigot within?'

'Yes, sir. He came but a minute ago.'

Oricien grinned. 'We have him. Guigot! Give up. We have found you.'

From within the gloom of the stable rushed a huge black gallumpher, charging straight at them. Arren and Oricien jumped aside to avoid being mown down.

Oricien scrambled to his feet. 'That's Black Butz!'

Arren could not resist a smile. Not only had Guigot cheated the block, he had stolen Lord Thaume's prize gallumpher to do so.

'Cornelis! Saddles!' called Oricien. Within a minute both he and Arren were mounted on their favourite gallumphers.

'Where will he have gone?' said Oricien, reining in his mount.

'He cannot afford to dally. It will be the South Gate,' said Arren, and they pelted through the streets, where walkers were forced to jump aside to avoid being ridden down.

Soon Guigot was in their sight. He was already at the gate, which the guards were opening to let him out.

'Stop!' called Oricien. 'In Lord Thaume's name, shut the gates!'

The guards stared back blankly.

'The gates!' shouted Arren. 'You fools!'

From the castle came the long mournful note of the herald's horn. The guards looked on in puzzlement as Guigot rode through, then they shut the gates after him. By the time Arren and Oricien arrived, the gates were proof against an army. But Guigot was outside them. He had made his escape.

7

Later that evening Lord Thaume reviewed matters in his chambers with Oricien, Arren, Sir Langlan and Master Pinch.

'I have been awake since before dawn,' said Lord Thaume. 'In that time I have suppressed a plot against my life, scourged the Lord High Viator, sentenced my nephew to death, seen that nephew escape, and learned the King is dead. We shall not readily forget today.'

'Long live King Jehan,' said Oricien.

'Indeed,' said Lord Thaume. 'I must, of course, go to make my obeisance on the instant. Delay would be disrespectful.'

'You need not travel immediately,' said Pinch. 'News takes time to arrive, even tidings so grievous.'

'I would rather be in Emmen before Raugier,' said Lord Thaume. 'I cannot imagine his report of events will represent me in a flattering light.'

Sir Langlan smiled. 'There are many circles in which beating that hypocrite would speak strongly in your favour.'

'King Jehan's court is not one of them.'

'I knew him as a youth,' said Sir Langlan. 'He is not the milksop he is portrayed, nor the viators' puppet.'

'He lacks his father's warlike temper.'

'Nonetheless,' said Pinch, 'a man can be peaceable without being a puppet of the viators. He will wish to make peace with Gammerling, if Gundovald will sign a treaty. Such a move can only please the viators.'

'How so?' asked Oricien.

'The Consorts' power is increased if there is peace in Mondia. It spreads Harmony and – more to the point – makes it easier for the Viatory to exact alms. Men will be free to travel from Emmen to Vasi Vasar, paying dues and tolls wherever they go. Wars only make the smiths and the corn-factors rich.'

'Be that as it may,' said Lord Thaume. 'I will leave for Emmen the day after tomorrow. Oricien, you will come and swear your own fealty.'

'Yes, Father. What of my mother and Siedra?'

'They will remain here. Sir Langlan and Arren, you too will stay behind. Darrien can captain my retinue.'

Sir Langlan chuckled. 'I have little choice. There is still a price on my head in Emmen, unless Jehan chooses to lift the ban.'

'That was long ago, Langlan. I am sure Jehan will soon offer a pardon. In any event, I require you to remain behind as Regent. I need a man I can trust to catch Guigot.'

Sir Langlan looked coolly ahead. 'The hunting dogs are out tonight, and Fleuraume with them. Guigot has only a single gallumpher. He will be caught by morning.'

Lord Thaume stared into the fire. 'Do not be so sure, Langlan. The boy may embody Disharmony but he is no fool, and he has luck – and spirit. He will not yield easily.'

'Do not worry, my lord.'

Lord Thaume shot him a sharp glance. 'I do – and so should you. Oricien will not sit safe after me if Guigot is not brought to book. He is spite incarnate.'

'You should see the dogs when they are roused. Guigot will wish he had settled for the block.'

8

One morning, a week after Lord Thaume and Oricien had left for Emmen, Siedra came upon Arren reading in the gardens.

'Will you take a stroll with me, Arren?' she said. Her golden hair shone in the sunlight.

Arren was always suspicious of Siedra when she was friendly. Nonetheless, it would have been churlish to refuse, so he offered his arm and they walked in the mid-morning sun. Arren had to admit that she was looking more than usually becoming, and his book, *Applied Principles of Fortification*, by Urald of Taratanallos, had not made stimulating reading.

'Have you been avoiding me, Arren?' said Siedra with her cheeks dimpling. 'I have hardly seen you since my father went away.'

'Our pursuits are dissimilar,' said Arren mildly. 'My interest in needlecraft and fabrics is insignificant, and I cannot imagine my exploration of siegecraft with Cyngier is any more stimulating to you. The censorious might even regard our meeting privately in the garden as injudicious.'

'The company of my mother and Lady Cerisa rapidly becomes wearing,' she said. 'In the circumstances I am prepared to risk the disapproval of gossiping old women.'

'I was thinking specifically of Master Guiles.'

'As I said: gossiping old women.'

Arren grinned. 'In truth I do not much care either.'

'Good! We can enjoy the sunshine without fear or guilt.'

They strolled in companionable silence for a while, the birds in the background and the freshness of Lord Thaume's flowers making a pleasant solitude that no one could disturb.

'Where do you think Guigot is now?' asked Siedra.

Arren grimaced. 'Wherever he is, he is alive. That is all that matters.'

'How could he have evaded capture?'

Arren shrugged. 'He has always been a rogue, but a resourceful one. Most likely he is hiding out in the hills somewhere.'

'He said he would return and take vengeance – specifically on our family.'

'He was always given to large pronouncements. Since he has no means of making good his threat, I should not worry, either for you or Oricien.'

'I have been meaning to ask you: I never understood what you said at his trial about Jehan's Steppe and letting Oricien die.'

Arren paused and looked into her deep blue eyes. 'There is little to dwell on.'

'Enough to make you call for his death.'

'I thought he stood back when a Northman came on

340

Oricien unawares. Fleuraume stepped in, and no harm was done.'

'Are you sure?'

'I spoke to Fleuraume afterwards; he said I was wrong to be so certain. But I had no doubts then and I have none now.'

Her eyes narrowed. 'You never told Oricien?'

'I had no proof; and Oricien never trusted him in any event.'

'Let us sit here,' she said, as they came to a bench. 'My father thinks highly of you,' she said.

'It was always his intention that Oricien should have a counsellor when he grew older.'

'It easy to forget that you come from nowhere,' she said with a half-smile, her cat's eyes shimmering.

'I have never sought to disguise it.'

'Your address is that of a gentleman, aside from your prowess on the field. And I do not forget the way you fleeced those rogues at the Molo.'

'I should never have allowed that situation to develop as it did.'

Siedra plucked a leaf and crushed it between her fingers. 'You are more of a gentleman than Lord Dinarre.'

'That is a minor compliment. Dinarre shows every sign of growing into one of the most depraved and dissipated men of Glount.'

Siedra threw the pulped leaf aside. 'You are talking, perhaps, of my future husband.'

'Then I pity you. But your father's plans may be changed with the accession of King Jehan.'

Siedra shook her head. 'If he had intended me to captivate the court at Emmen, he would have taken me. He still wishes me to marry Panarre's son, to bind them closer and to save gold by merging my dowry with his tribute to Panarre from Jehan's Steppe.'

341

'You should not be so pessimistic,' said Arren after a pause. 'Many things can happen between now and a betrothal. Panarre may marry him to another bride, perhaps at Emmen.'

'You are thoughtful to offer such hope. You do not know how I have petitioned Animaxia for Dinarre's death.'

'I did not know you visited the Viatory.'

'Of course not! I Find the Way in my chambers: the viators oppress me with their sermons.'

'Technically that is the Gollain Heresy. I could denounce you for following the Wheel,' said Arren with a grin.

'Arren! You know that I do not care in the least for such nonsense. Wheel, Way, it is all nonsense. The viators fleece everyone and the Gollains have not the courage to reject the whole notion of the Way of Harmony.'

'Now that is heresy. To deny the Way altogether . . .'

Siedra laughed. 'You are shocked!'

Arren frowned. 'I am sure we all question the Way at times; deep down some may indeed feel it is false. But I have never known anyone admit it.'

'In some places my views would be unremarkable. They say that Garganet is a haven of free-thinking.'

'Overt heresy will not increase your chances of a good match.'

'My arse to a good match. You are not repelled beyond measure by my views?'

'No, but others—'

'I am more concerned by your good opinion.'

'You have it,' said Arren. 'But there are other, better judges you may wish to impress.'

She leaned against him on the bench. 'At this moment there is no one else around, nor any prospect of there being. If you look upon me as I look upon you . . .'

'Siedra – I do not understand . . .'

'Or you choose not to.' She ran her hand across his chest. 'If I must marry Dinarre or some dissipated old lecher, first I would know something of how men and women should be. Am I not beautiful, Arren?'

Arren looked into her eyes. 'Beyond a doubt, Siedra. You are fated to a higher destiny than me,' he said with a catch in his throat.

She stood up and pulled him from the bench by his shirt. 'Let me worry about that, Arren.' She pushed her face into his and kissed him.

9

That afternoon Arren lay on his bed staring at the ceiling. Sleep would not come. The morning's events with Siedra had been extraordinary, sudden and unexpected. He had no idea that she had such feelings, or was willing to express them with such abandon. He should be delighted, he thought. Siedra was ardent, passionate, delicious. No man could fail to be flattered by her attentions. He did not delude himself that he was ill-favoured: he was already a warrior of repute, with a quick intellect besides. Nonetheless, he was uneasy.

There was no possibility that a dalliance with Siedra could have any happy outcome. She was destined for a political match, if not to Dinarre then to some other lord of her father's choosing. He had already shown Thaume considerable disrespect by consorting thus with his daughter. Lord Thaume's temper had always been quick, and recently he had been more ready than ever to decree flogging or hanging for those who displeased him. It would be wrong to call Thaume a tyrant, but his keen sense of justice took a mordant slant. It would be better for him never to find out about this morning's episode.

Arren realized that even this, bad as it was, was not the whole nor even the worst of his malaise. If he truly cared for Siedra, he would be less concerned about Thaume. The truth was, flattered as he was by her attention, and overcome as he had been by her allure, he did not regard her with any true ardour. She had the character of a cat, charming and malicious by turn, and never motivated by anything other than self-interest. Unbidden, the image of her as a child blackmailing Sir Langlan after Illara's performance in The Hanged Raider came to his mind. She was a young woman now, but her beauty concealed a warp in her heart. She was not a safe associate, particularly in a situation as secret as theirs would have to be.

He pursed his lips. The matter would have to stop here. Alluring as Siedra was – and he could not deny that his heart beat faster at the thought of being alone with her again – he could not allow their intimacy to continue. He puzzled for a moment. Surely a short diversion could not do any real harm – at least until Lord Thaume returned.

He jumped from the bed and shook his head. More resolution was necessary. He barely had the willpower to keep away from her now; if he became more accustomed to her favours it might become impossible. Then there was the prospect of quickening: if he thought the situation was complex now, imagine the horror if he got her with child. Thaume would hang or geld the man who made his unmarried daughter pregnant. There was nothing for it: he would have to keep away from Siedra. The risks and the rewards were simply incommensurate.

He stalked from his room, out through the castle gates and into the streets. He did not want to be caught alone, by anybody.

It was market day and by some unseen force he was pulled towards the marketplace. He remembered the day Eilla had stolen a cow. How long ago it seemed, although it could only have been five or six years.

'Arren! Ignore me if you choose!'

He looked around guiltily. Surely Siedra could not have found him in the market. But it was Eilla herself. He embraced her before he realized what he was doing.

'Seigneur, you forget yourself,' said Eilla with a grin, her cheeks red from the sun.

'Sorry,' said Arren. 'I had just been thinking about the cow, and there you were.'

'I am not sure I understand what you mean. Eulalia has sent me for some fish. There will be nothing decent left at this time of day, and she will berate me for slackness and incompetence.'

'Let her fetch her own fish.'

'You may say as much to her; I cannot.'

Arren rubbed his chin. 'She is unreasonable.'

'I am learning nothing new.'

'I will speak to her on my return to the castle.'

Eilla paused and inspected Arren. 'You seem distracted,' she said, 'unsettled in some way.'

'Shall we walk down to the wharf?' said Arren. 'We might yet pick up some fresh bream.'

They turned and walked the short distance to where the last of the fishing boats was unloading.

'Will you not tell me what is troubling you?' said Eilla gently.

'You would not thank me,' said Arren with a wry grin. 'The matter is trivial, especially compared with your own concerns.'

'Arren . . .'

'If I mention the Lady Siedra, that should be sufficient.'

Arren saw Eilla tense. She spoke to one of the fishermen unloading his wares. 'Is that your best catch?'

'Depends what you have to pay,' grunted the fisherman.

Eilla spoke again to Arren. 'There can be no tale involving Siedra which makes good hearing – You there, I am buying for Lord Thaume's table, so I'll thank you for some civility.'

'Thaume's silver is as good as any, but I'll not part with my goods on the cheap.'

'Siedra has conceived something of a fancy for me,' said Arren in a quiet voice.

'How much for your five best bream? – You are deluding yourself, Arren. She has a fancy for no one but herself.'

'Two and a half florins.'

'My lord will have you whipped for insolence. Twenty-five pennies is more the sum I have in mind.'

'I have all the proof you could ever need,' said Arren.

Eilla paled. 'Would I care to know the nature of this "proof"? – No, even a florin is too much. Let us say forty pennies and be done with the matter.'

'We should discuss this elsewhere,' said Arren with a meaningful glance at the fisherman.

'As you wish – No, forty or nothing. Thank you. That need not have been as difficult as you made it.'

Eilla took the bream which the fisherman had wrapped and followed Arren over to the wharfside railing.

'Are you going to tell me about Siedra? Are you trying to tell me you—'

'Yes.'

Eilla jerked her gaze away and stared down at the turbid water.

'Eilla?'

'You are a – Arren, do you love her?'

'Of course not! She is Siedra!'

Eilla shook her head. 'Then why, by the Wheel – Do you even like her?'

Arren looked down at his feet. 'She is not as bad as you may think.'

'Perhaps not, since I see her as spite and selfishness incarnate. Have you forgotten how she treated me?'

'No, of course not. It's just—'

'No further, Arren. You have not forgotten how she treated me?'

'I have just said that I had not.'

'In that case, you clearly regard it as inconsequential.'

'Eilla,' said Arren miserably. 'It was not like that.'

Eilla folded her arms and looked him in the eye. 'You have a choice to make, Arren. You cannot be her friend and mine. I will say nothing about how ludicrous the notion of any kind of match between you is. I hate Siedra second only to Lady Jilka. She has behaved abominably to me. You may disport yourself with that hussy to your heart's content, and I do not care.'

Arren too looked down into the murky water. .

'Eilla, there is no one as precious to me as you.'

'Do not continue. I cannot hear your voice without hearing it honeying up to Siedra. I will judge your acts, not your words.'

'Eilla—'

'I must return to the castle. Mistress Eulalia will not thank me for bringing back stinking fish.'

Arren leaned against the railing and watched Eilla's straight back as she marched back towards Lord Thaume's castle. He should have known better than to raise the topic with her.

13

Mettingloom

I

The King's Council met by tradition on the first day of the week. On one morning in late winter a cariolo drew up before the Occonero with four occupants. The first of them, Beauceron, alighted on paving damp from melted frost. Monetto leaped down immediately behind him, and Mongrissore clambered down more slowly. The fourth figure, a man of middle years, carried himself with a stiff and watchful gravity. He licked his lips and surveyed the scene. Beauceron, in his crispest black coat and starched white breeches, gave the man a wolfish smile.

'You can relax, Quinto,' he said. 'No harm will come to you in the Occonero. Soon you will be free of your burdens. Are you a religious man? Think of today as a long march on the Way of Harmony.'

Quinto climbed gingerly down from the cariolo. 'I have never taken much notice of the viators,' he said. 'I make my own way in the world.'

Monetto said: 'The approach has brought you neither wealth nor happiness thus far. Speak true today, and you may start afresh.'

Quinto narrowed his already thin eyes. 'Neither of you

seems to me a man of the Way. Your concern is not with my welfare.'

'Naturally not,' said Beauceron. 'Nonetheless, what helps us helps you.'

'But Davanzato will be present.'

'Allow us to worry about Davanzato,' said Monetto. 'Your safety is assured. You have Mongrissore for company.'

Mongrissore bared his crooked teeth in what might have been a reassuring smile. 'I have been present at many confessions,' he said. 'The penitent always feels a lightening of spirit as a result.'

'And on occasion a lightening of his neck, by the weight of his head,' said Quinto with a morose glare.

'Where did Cosetta find such an avatar of joy?' asked Monetto.

'Tush, Monetto,' said Mongrissore. 'You too might tend to the lugubrious if you had Quinto's crimes at your account.'

Monetto gave a rueful smile. 'If only you knew,' he said.

'Enough,' said Beauceron. 'We must be ready soon. Mongrissore, you are sure Lady Cosetta will be here?'

Mongrissore nodded. 'For whatever reason, she feels she owes you a debt. She will be on hand when she is needed.'

'Good. Shall we step inside?'

Beauceron and Monetto strode along the marbled corridor, their boots echoing against the plastered walls. Mongrissore and Quinto made their own soft-footed way along some distance behind.

King Fanrolio's Council at this time consisted of a small group of influential figures: General Virnesto, responsible for the Winter Armies; the Lord of Equity Gionardo, the Chamberlain Osvergario (represented during his indisposition by the Under-Chamberlain Davanzato) and, for the development of his statecraft, Prince Brissio. As groups of advisers went, it was not considered either unusually corrupt or unusually inept, a judgement perhaps as telling on expectations of probity and competence as on the capabilities of the persons involved.

Beauceron and Monetto were escorted before this group by two footmen, and made the necessary obeisances. Beauceron looked around the room and saw little sympathy for his projects. Davanzato was an enemy, Brissio both stupid and malicious. Virnesto was fair-minded but not a man to wink at a treason trial, and Gionardo had not looked on Mongrissore's legalisms in good part. Still, he was at least here before the King.

Fanrolio cleared his throat. 'Welcome, Beauceron. Davanzato, can you remind us why the captain is before us this morning?'

'He wishes to raise again the topic of the invasion of Croad, Your Puissance.'

Fanrolio peered at Beauceron. 'You were accused of treason against us less than a month ago.'

Beauceron inclined his head. 'All present will remember that I was acquitted. I desire nothing more than to bring glory to the Winter Court by taking the city of Croad for Mettingloom.'

Fanrolio frowned. 'Did we not consider this very matter last year?'

'Your Puissance is acute,' said Davanzato, sitting back and steepling his fingers. 'On this occasion Beauceron has additional arguments to deploy.'

'Is that so, Beauceron?' asked the King, coughing into a lace handkerchief.

'Your Puissance, my reasoning remains essentially the same as last year. However, I have been fortunate in my plunder during the summer season, and propose to finance the invasion myself, in the hope of recouping the sum from pillage of the city.'

'Captain,' said Virnesto, 'Prince Brissio did not sit on this council last year. Perhaps you would care to outline your proposals.'

'With pleasure, General. The prevailing wisdom within Mettingloom is that the city of Croad is impregnable. This assumption is rarely challenged and is based, in so far as it can be said to have a basis, on the defeat suffered by the Summer King at Jehan's Steppe, an event which took place thirteen years ago.

'It is my contention that the popular view is wrong. The ability of Croad to withstand a siege is untested; Tardolio's army never reached the city walls.'

Lord Gionardo interrupted. 'Is there any reason to believe that your army would be able to forge so far south?'

'Tardolio's army made significant tactical errors, most importantly in dividing its cavalry. This meant that Thaume's smaller force never had to withstand a full cavalry onslaught. Lord Thaume was also fortunate in the exceptional quality of his commanders: Thaume himself, Artingaume, Langlan, Darrien. Only Langlan survives. Oricien has not the flair of his father. My belief is that he will not ride out to meet an army. He will prefer to sit behind the walls of Croad and wait for aid to come from either Trevarre or Enguerran. His policy has been to build alliances, not armies. He will not commit his forces to a battle in the North when defeat would leave Croad unprotected.'

Virnesto nodded. 'Your analysis is not implausible. However, Croad is a walled city. If it expects relief from the South, it will not fall easily.'

'I know the fortifications of Croad well. They are not impregnable. We will have weeks rather than months before help arrives, but I am confident that the city will fall in that period. Monetto has brought diagrams for improved siege engines which will throw larger rocks faster and more accurately.'

'The cost of such machines will not be trivial,' said Gionardo.

'It is a cost I meet myself. There will be no drain on the Treasury.'

Virnesto scratched his chin. 'You are an unparalleled field commander, Beauceron. Your reputation is well earned. However, you have never, to my knowledge, commanded a siege. The discipline is different to the harassment and bravado which characterize your raiding strategy.'

Beauceron gave a harsh smile. 'You speak to me of discipline, sir? I have waited long years for this opportunity; I have denied myself the pleasures of my wealth, the softness of easy living, the favours of beautiful women. Do you think I would waste my toil in an assault on walls before they were broken? My lust for revenge is strong, but it is cool. You may have no fears on that score.'

Prince Brissio broke in. 'I say you are not to be trusted. You schemed and plotted against my father the King. What is our guarantee that you will hand over the city once it falls? You may shut yourself behind its walls and call yourself the Lord of Croad.'

'My lord, only an imbecile would consider such a course. The walls of the city will have been compromised and a sizeable army from the South will be on the way. No adventurer could hold the city.'

Davanzato spoke for the first time. 'Prince Brissio's observations bring us to a profound point. Your plans are based solely on the events leading up to the city's capture. Virnesto will be best placed to advise on the robustness of these plans. No attention, however, has been given to outcomes following the city's fall.

'How, for example, will you hold the city once Enguerran marches north? And what of his inevitable reprisals as he brings his army to Mettingloom? Next summer, at the latest, the army of Emmen will sit on the shore of our lagoon. Or is your prowess so extreme that you expect to destroy the flower of his army in the field with your own invasion force? You still have many questions to answer.'

'Do you believe,' asked Beauceron, 'that any force marching from the Emmenrule can take Mettingloom? Enguerran will not come in winter; there will be no food for his gallumphers, or his men. If he comes in summer, he can harry the shore as he chooses, but he has no means of taking the lagoon.'

'What if he allies with the Garganets?' asked Brissio. 'Their galleys are strong.'

'Galleys are ineffective in our choppy northern waters. Our cogs would destroy them; and Garganet will not wish to boost Enguerran's pride.'

'Do you suggest,' asked Virnesto, 'that Enguerran will sit at home and bear the loss of Croad with equanimity? If so, you are a poor judge of character.'

Beauceron smiled and shook his head. 'I think the opposite; Enguerran cannot accept the rebuke. He will march north with all the men at his command. He may come next summer, or he may wait and come the year after, once he has prepared. I think he lacks the patience to wait. When he finds Croad has fallen, he will move north with his relief army, and think to deal with Croad on his return.'

Lord Gionardo frowned. 'You present the certainty of invasion as a boon.'

'Exactly so, my lord. Enguerran's pride, his folly, his over-confidence will send him forth with his Immaculates to chastise our city. He will arrive in the summer, and find Tardolio before him. How will Tardolio deal with the threat?'

There was silence as the Council tried to assess how Tar-dolio would respond.

'He will sally forth!' declared Prince Brissio.

'I think not,' said Beauceron. 'He lacks the stomach for a fight.'

'In his position,' said Virnesto, 'I would wait Enguerran out. He cannot starve us, for he lacks the fleet to blockade the lagoon; he cannot take the city by assault, because once again he lacks the naval power to do so. Enguerran will ride up and down the shore, harassing the lords' estates until it occurs to him that he cannot win. Then he will turn south to set about reducing Croad.'

Beauceron beamed and nodded. 'You show potential as a strategist, General. Tardolio will not ride out to meet Enguer-ran, because it would be folly to do so.'

Fanrolio frowned. 'I do not understand the point you are making.'

'Simply this: Prince Laertio will wish to fight; the Lords of the Shore will be vexed, to say the least, at the devastation of their estates. Tardolio will be correct not to fight, but he will look timid, and his stature will sink. When the winter comes around, who will be the beneficiary?' He paused. 'The Winter Court, of course. Tardolio will be isolated within the Summer Court and Enguerran will have slunk away in frus-tration. How you follow up that advantageous situation is a question for your own judgement.'

Fanrolio smiled slowly and nodded. 'Your points are most interesting, Beauceron. We will need to reflect on them a while.'

Beauceron bowed. 'I ask no more, Your Puissance. There is, however, another matter I wish to bring to your attention.' From the corner of his eyes he looked at Davanzato. 'I have recently engaged the services of an excellent apothecary, who I hope will travel south with us. However, I have heard of the travails of your own health, and wonder if I might send the man to recommend a regimen for your chest. Such things should not be neglected.'

Davanzato looked at Beauceron with raised eyebrows and a flush to his cheek. 'Surely, Your Puissance, your own apothecaries cannot be improved upon. Carledo is skilled and seasoned.'

'I grow no younger, Davanzato. Beauceron, let your man wait upon me. If he is a charlatan, I shall send him back.'

Beauceron bowed again. 'As you say, Your Puissance. He waits outside, if it pleases you.'

Fanrolio nodded. 'Very well. Monetto, will you bring him in?'

Monetto looked at Beauceron. Davanzato caught the glance. 'Your Puissance—'

Fanrolio waved an irritated hand. 'Not now, Davanzato. I wish to hear no further objections. May I not seek health?'

'But—'

'Enough.'

Seconds later Monetto stepped back into the room, followed by Mongrissore and Quinto in his green and white apothecary's cape. Beauceron, who was watching intently, saw Davanzato sag in his chair. His olive complexion blanched. 'Your Puissance,' he said. 'I am indisposed. You must excuse me.'

Beauceron gave a wry smile. 'Fortunately an apothecary is on hand. You need not depart.'

Fanrolio peered at Quinto. 'You are welcome, sir. Beauceron speaks highly of your healing skills.'

Quinto looked at the ground and mumbled.

Beauceron interjected. 'Your Puissance, matters would go more expeditiously if the good Quinto were allowed to make a statement before we proceed to a consultation.'

Fanrolio's expression of puzzlement deepened. Quinto

gave Beauceron a plaintive look. Davanzato made as if to rise; Monetto moved towards the door to prevent his exit.

'I am come before the Council,' said Quinto in a faltering voice, 'to confess to my wicked deeds. I have been suborned from my oath of healing to do great wrong.'

Davanzato gave a brassy laugh. 'What buffoonery is this? The man is clearly addled in his wits. If every man who had beaten his wife confessed before the King, he would have no time to rule the realm.'

'I think we must hear this,' said Lord Gionardo. 'I sense this is more than a casual blow against a pert wife.'

'Thank you, my lord,' said Quinto. 'I am the apothecary who has been treating the indisposition of the Chamberlain.'

Fanrolio's eyes rose in surprise. 'How does good Osvergario?'

'My lord, his malady was never as severe as you had believed. At the instigation of Under-Chamberlain Davanzato, I administered herbs which kept him prostrated. Sirs, in simple language I poisoned him.'

Virnesto rose from his seat. 'This cannot be!'

Brissio's hand went to his belt, before he remembered that swords were not worn in the King's presence.

'The man is a lunatic!' cried Davanzato. 'He should be whipped for his impudence.'

King Fanrolio spoke slowly. 'Davanzato, we will hear no more from you for now. Master Quinto, please continue.'

'The Chamberlain fell sick four years ago, and Davanzato asked me to attend him. I confirmed that his illness, a griping of the guts, was transitory and brought on by simple gluttony. This news did not please Davanzato. By one indirection and another he insinuated that he would be grateful if Osvergario's recovery were deferred, perhaps indefinitely. There was talk of money and, good sirs, my affairs were not well-placed.' He stood slightly taller. 'I said that under no circumstances would I kill the Chamberlain. Davanzato said that was very well, since he did not wish him dead. "Chronic incapacitation" was the term he used. I came to understand that by this method Davanzato would enjoy all of the powers of the Chamberlain's post; if Osvergario died, the King would appoint a new Chamberlain, who would not be Davanzato.'

He fell silent. The weight become oppressive for Quinto, who added: 'I am most heartily sorry, my lords. I never imagined that I would need to continue for four years. I asked Davanzato to stop long ago; he told me that exposure would mean my death, and he was not yet minded to change his policies. You may do as you will with me.'

'Where is the proof!' said Davanzato in a flat rapid voice. 'This is the rambling of a halfwit.'

'My lords, there is proof aplenty,' said Mongrissore. 'We know the herbs Quinto acquired, and the uses to which he put them. We have found the medicines he keeps for Osvergario, and tested them upon an unfortunate dog, now dead.'

'My agency cannot be inferred!' shouted Davanzato.

'If it please Your Puissance,' said Beauceron, 'I would bring another man before you.'

Fanrolio scratched his pate. 'The room is scarcely big enough for your drama, Beauceron. Nonetheless, proceed if you wish.'

Beauceron nodded at Monetto, who stepped from the room once again. There was an audible gasp – from Davanzato perhaps – as he re-entered, with Lady Cosetta and, leaning on her arm, a frail-seeming elderly man.

'Osvergario!' exclaimed Fanrolio.

The Chamberlain essayed an inflexible bow. 'Your Puissance, I have been away too long. I am ready to resume my duties.'

Davanzato gave a tinny laugh. 'Osvergario, I am delighted to see you in such good health. I had been given to understand your condition was grave. I gladly relinquish my temporary duties!'

Mongrissore stepped quietly forward, with his legulier's skill of commanding attention with the most understated gestures.

'My lords, one week ago we ceased to dose Osvergario with the medicines provided by Quinto. The result is the remarkable recovery we see before us. My own apothecary says that with a month or two of proper care, the Chamberlain's recovery will be complete.'

Fanrolio turned in his chair to look at Davanzato. 'You have much to explain.'

'And so I can, Your Puissance!'

'Not today. Virnesto, bring guards and Tintazzo. Davanzato will be a guest at Darkstone tonight.'

'No!' roared Davanzato. 'My service, my loyalty! This is intolerable! All the while you fawn and flatter the traitor Beauceron.'

Guards had appeared as if from nowhere. Davanzato was dragged off, still bellowing in his outrage.

'Lord Gionardo,' said Fanrolio mildly. 'Please see that Davanzato is brought before me for trial in short order.'

'Yes, Your Puissance.'

2

The next day Beauceron was summoned back to the Occonero before a specially convened King's Council. Chamberlain Osvergario had taken his rightful place, although Beauceron noticed an unhealthy pallor. The other members of the Council were also present.

'I apologize for summoning you in this way, Beauceron,'

said Fanrolio. 'The spring draws ever closer, and decisions must be made.'

'I am at your disposal, Your Puissance.'

'I was favourably impressed by your proposals yesterday,' said Fanrolio. 'I am an old man, and disinclined for the business of war, but the pressures of state are paramount. I will this day issue the orders for the Winter Armies to be mobilized and to march on Croad: nothing less is consistent with the dignity of the Northern Reach.'

Beauceron felt a surge of exultation. Fanrolio had approved the plan: Croad would feel his vengeance.

'Nonetheless,' continued Fanrolio, 'there are certain aspects of your plan which require modification.'

Beauceron narrowed his eyes. It would be easy for compromises to undermine the scheme altogether.

'First, and most importantly, I do not consider you the most suitable candidate to lead the army. Your counsel and your martial prowess will be invaluable, of course, but – for several reasons – you are not the best choice for leadership.'

Beauceron looked across to Captain-General Virnesto, whose face was blank. The old soldier had outmanoeuvred him.

'We must all learn to take our just place in the world,' continued the King. 'This applies to great and humble alike. The time has come for Prince Brissio to assume the mantle of leadership, and the Winter Army will march under his banner.'

Brissio's eyes shone. He shot Beauceron a glance of sly triumph. Virnesto remained expressionless. Beauceron merely shook his head.

'Your Puissance,' he said, 'with all due respect, such an assault must be led by an experienced commander. Prince Brissio's valour is not in doubt—'

'Enough,' said Fanrolio in a stronger voice than Beauceron remembered. 'Who is King here?'

Beauceron bowed his head at this presumably rhetorical question.

'Prince Brissio will one day – alas, too soon! – become Winter King of Mettingloom. I would have him a seasoned battle commander on that day, the more so given the somewhat bloodthirsty leanings of Prince Laertio. He must have around him advisers of sound judgement, and his orders will include the requirement to consult both the Captain-General and yourself: nonetheless, command rests with my son. In addition, Prince Brissio will command the cavalry, Virnesto the infantry. Beauceron, you will be responsible for the siege engines. If you find these terms unacceptable, you may withdraw without prejudice.'

Beauceron looked around the table. Brissio stared back with a malicious grin; Virnesto gave a quizzical glance, while Lord Gionardo looked bored. Chamberlain Osvergario's guileless blue eyes danced; it was here, Beauceron realized, that Fanrolio's decision had originated. Beauceron's scheme was sound, but the Council did not trust him. The credit for any success would go to Brissio.

He set his mouth. He cared nothing for credit; Brissio could claim to have invented the moon. What was more alarming was Brissio's certain incompetence. He was capable of leading the entire army to destruction, or of sitting outside Croad until Enguerran appeared and obliterated the northern force. But there was no choice. He went with Brissio, or he did not go at all.

'Your Puissance, I accept your commission. I will follow the Prince to Croad and give my best counsel and battle to ensure its fall.'

Fanrolio beamed. 'Excellent! With such a harmonious command, how can we fail? Virnesto, see to it that the fleet is ready to sail within the week. I will not be cheated of my victory by the spring.'

'Brissio is a dangerous man: vindictive, stubborn, stupid. It is an unfortunate combination.'

Beauceron stood on the dockside where Virnesto super-intended the lading of his fleet of cogs.

'He lacks experience, for sure,' said Virnesto, rubbing a hand across his grey hair. 'He will have need of good advice.'

'You are too generous. We both know he will not take advice, and in addition he nurtures a resentment against me.'

'You cannot expect my sympathy,' said Virnesto. 'If you had wished to secure Brissio's good opinion, you should not have conspired against his father.'

'I was—'

'Acquitted, yes, I know. That is scarcely to the point. You have courted Brissio's enmity: now you are under his com-mand, and wish you had been more tractable.'

'He will wreck the invasion.'

'I think not,' said Virnesto. 'You have the siege engines, I have the infantry. There is little damage Brissio can do to himself with the cavalry.'

'What if Oricien sallies forth from Croad? Brissio could not command a battle.'

Virnesto peered at him intently. 'You have assured every-one who will listen that Oricien is of timid disposition, and will sit behind his walls. I hope you did not say that for simple advantage.'

'I am affronted,' said Beauceron mildly. 'Oricien will be disinclined to fight; but if it is forced upon him, an army com-manded by the Prince will not shine.'

'What use is cavalry in a siege? His role will be periph-eral.'

'That will not stop him trying to settle scores with me.'

'That is a problem of your own making. Do not expect me to be interested. If your personal safety is of such concern, you may remain in Mettingloom with the King.'

'You know I care nothing for my safety; but I do not wish to die either through Brissio's malice or his incompetence.'

3

Beauceron broke early one afternoon from supervising the drilling of his men and walked over to that part of the Occonero where Isola was lodged. The sun was beginning to generate warmth as well as light, and spring could not be far away. How ironic it would be if his plans were ended by green shoots.

He had not seen Isola since she testified against him at his treason trial. She had been Davanzato's dupe, and he had to acknowledge that he had no claim on her loyalty. Her attitude was harder to read: her initial resentment had softened and at times she had seemed almost to show a regard for him.

Isola had been reinstalled in her old suite and Beauceron was escorted up the stairs by a servant. 'You must be careful, sir,' said the maid. 'Her humour is unstable.'

'This is not a new situation,' said Beauceron. 'She has always been an unpredictable woman.'

The maid shook her head. 'This is something different. I hope you can bring her some comfort.'

The maid took Beauceron into Isola's parlour. 'Captain Beauceron, my lady.' She bowed and withdrew as rapidly as consistent with her dignity.

Lady Isola looked up from her couch with bloodshot eyes, her hair straggling and her skin pasty.

'Beauceron,' she said in a quiet voice. 'You have come to gloat at my misfortune.'

'Isola – my lady – you know that is not the case. I was simply concerned that we should not part on bad terms.'

'"Part"? Am I going home?'

Beauceron grimaced. 'It is I who am leaving,' he said. 'The invasion against Croad proceeds. We sail the day after tomorrow.'

Isola gave Beauceron a long unfathomable look. 'You are remorseless, and implacable. I should not like to be Oricien. I think he will not live to hang you after all.'

'That was always my intention,' said Beauceron, sitting on a couch opposite her, since Isola did not seem inclined to offer.

'I no longer care,' said Isola heavily. Beauceron noticed a new puffiness to her cheeks. 'Oricien does not deserve my loyalty, and it may be you do not deserve my enmity. I have found little enough kindness here: does it matter if you all kill each other?'

'My lady, your perspective is unduly gloomy.'

A flash of the old Isola appeared in her dark eyes. 'I fail to see the benefits of my situation. I am forgotten in this garret, no one will pay my ransom, I have been kidnapped by you and threatened by Davanzato, and there is no chance I will ever go home. If it were not for my good friend langensnap life would be intolerable.' She reached for the flask at her side and filled her glass.

With a sudden burst of energy, Isola sprang from her couch and knelt before Beauceron, taking his hands. 'Take me with you, Beauceron! When you march south, return me to Croad. You no longer have any need to worry about ransoms, or flattering Fanrolio.'

Beauceron pulled his hands away. 'You are not mine to take. Fanrolio holds your ransom in his gift.'

'You kidnapped me once! Can you not do so again?'

Beauceron pursed his lips. 'The course is inadvisable; in

any event, I should hardly be helping you by returning you to a city I intend to sack.'

'The risk is mine,' she said. 'From Croad I can make my way to Glount, and thence to Sey.'

Beauceron stroked his chin. Isola would not be an ideal travelling companion; she might even cause mischief at Croad. Her value as a hostage would be negligible, since Oricien did not care enough to raise a ransom. Now was not the time for sentiment.

'I will raise the question with the King,' he said. 'I see no reason to be optimistic.'

Isola looked at him with brimming eyes. 'You must help me! I will die here!'

'You must not overdramatize the situation. I am more likely to die than you; I am off to war.'

'Loneliness and misery kill every bit as effectively.'

'I can only speak to the King. If I do not see you again, you must know that I bear you no ill-will for your testimony. It is all policy, and you are a victim.'

Isola seemed to have difficulty speaking. 'Go now,' she said in a thick voice. 'There is no more to say.'

4

The ice on the aquavias had thinned and in some places thawed. It was no longer possible to walk safely upon it, nor yet possible for the wherries to navigate the waterways. Beauceron therefore took a circuitous route from the Occonero to the Printempi, the last stage of the journey undertaken in a small boat across the deeper water separating the Summer Court from the rest of the city.

The great lobby of the Printempi was all but empty. In winter few had reason to visit the Summer Court. Beauceron approached a factotum and asked if Lady Cosetta was on hand; the man scurried away to find out. It was by no means a foregone conclusion; Cosetta maintained a formidable social schedule in her enthusiasm to extract the maximum advantage from her situation.

Beauceron looked from a nearby window into a court-yard where a patch of bare earth was on display. This was the home of Tardolio's horticulturalists, where every effort was made to cause plants to bloom, and thus prove spring to have arrived. At the centre of the effort was a man of inde-terminate age with a shock of white hair. Beauceron looked on in astonishment, for it was a face he recognized. His first impulse was to shrink back behind a pillar; this was hardly consistent with the Dog of the North, and instead he stepped out boldly into the courtyard.

'Good afternoon to you, sir.'

The man turned and bowed. 'Good afternoon.'

'I know you, do I not?'

'My identity is no secret. I am Pintuccio, King Tardolio's thaumaturge.' He scrutinized Beauceron's face. 'I know you of course; although not the name that you presently use.'

'I am Beauceron, called by some the Dog of the North.'

'Ah! Your life has not taken the path I might have expected.'

'My title is all part of the menace necessary to a success-ful brigand. I would prefer you not to advertise the name under which you originally knew me.'

Pintuccio made a negligent gesture. 'The subject holds little interest for me; I have no appetite for casual gossip. If you wish to cultivate an air of mystery, it is of no concern to me.'

'Your own name is now different.'

Pintuccio shrugged. 'Here I am Pintuccio; in Emmen I am Pinch. Neither is my true name. I go where I will.'

'I did not expect to find you in Mettingloom, nor a horticulturalist. Is this not a demeaning calling for a man of your
learning?'

'You never understood the way of the thaumaturge in
Croad; neither do you now. In the winter, the blooms lie dor-
mant; dead even. Yet come the spring and they burst forth in
such abundance that no power can check them. What is the
source of such wonder, the birth of life itself? It is hard to see
such study as "demeaning" or trivial. The thaumaturge must
always follow his own way.'

Beauceron stroked his chin. 'My own motivations are less
complex.'

'We approach existence in a different way. I myself find
little to commend brigandage, yet it clearly exerts an endless
fascination for you. The viators would tell us we all Follow
our own Way.'

'I have long lost any respect for the viators.'

'As you will,' said Pintuccio, brushing earth from his
hands. 'If you are concerned that I will upset your plans,
whatever their nature, you may be assured. Your goals are
a matter of utter indifference to me. You may wish to know
that in the abstract I disapprove of the course you have taken,
but I do not pretend to understand your provocations; or
indeed to have any interest in them.'

'Do you not intend to protect Croad from my depredations?'

'Croad, Mettingloom, what is the difference? Such loyal-
ties as I had were to Thaume; he is now dead.'

'My own feelings with regard to Thaume are somewhat
different.'

Pintuccio made an impatient gesture. 'I have much work
to achieve before nightfall. No doubt you too have other
business.'

Beauceron bowed. 'Good day to you, Master Pinch. I wish you success in your inquiries.'

He turned and walked back into the lobby to find a footman waiting to take him to Lady Cosetta's apartments.

5

'Beauceron! How good of you to call,' said Cosetta, offering him a seat with a gracious smile.

'The least I could do is to thank you for your assistance,' he said. 'I am indebted that you alerted me to Davanzato's use of Quinto to poison the Chamberlain, and for presenting Osvergario at the Council.'

Cosetta's cheeks dimpled. 'There is no real need for gratitude. I view Davanzato with scorn and hatred. For whatever reason, I do not look upon you in the same light.'

'I should also thank you for warning me of Agalina's scheme.'

'My generosity is on occasion inexplicable.'

'You have saved my life and brought my enemy to ruin. Your actions have also helped to spark the invasion. Thanks are insufficient. It is a bizarre and perverse place to arrive, but if you require your ransom paid . . .'

Cosetta gave a peal of delighted laughter. 'The ransom which you set yourself, and then transferred to the King? Is this not a wonderful irony?'

Beauceron did not respond.

'Your offer is most generous. In fact, Laertio has already made the same offer, which I declined. I do not care if I am ransomed or not, since I am not intending to leave the Northern Reach. I have no desire to see Fanrolio – and by association Brissio – enriched, so I am content to remain upon my parole. My ransom is 10,000 florins, and I am suitably awed at your gesture.'

'I do not need the money. The King is financing the invasion after all, as he must if he requires Brissio to command the army.'

'I had heard that rumour,' said Cosetta. 'It is scarcely credible. I detected no latent military genius in my acquaintance with the Prince.'

'Were it not for Virnesto the situation would be impossible. As it is, he will have to listen to his captains.'

'Are you not worried that he will take some kind of vengeance against you?'

'I have no doubt he will try. If he can outwit me I deserve my doom.'

'You should not be so cavalier.'

'I prefer to think of it as negligent grandeur.'

Cosetta grinned. 'I should be sorry to see you hurt. So too would Laertio: he is most keen to welcome you to the Summer Court on your return. I assume you have no particular attachment to Fanrolio once your plans are complete.'

'You are pleasingly unscrupulous,' said Beauceron. 'Perhaps that is why we avoid recriminations. I have no loyalty at all to Fanrolio. I do not know if I will return to Mettingloom after the fall of Croad, but I appreciate Laertio's good wishes.'

'There is a theory that you will not return because you intend to rule the city yourself. There is a rumour as to your identity—'

'You would oblige me by discountenancing it whenever you hear it. It serves no purpose, and I have no desire to rule Croad or any other city.'

'Not everyone would believe your protestation,' said Cosetta with a soft smile. 'Your ambitions are your own affair.'

Beauceron nibbled on a sweetmeat which had been set before him. 'I have been to see the Lady Isola.'

Cosetta's eyes widened. 'I hope you thrashed her roundly.'

'That was not my intention. Her condition is pitiable.'

'She is largely to blame. She prefers self-pity to activity.'

'I was not quite so direct, but I suggested that certain remedies were within her own hands. As her kidnapper I was not entirely comfortable in recommending this robust self-help policy. It would be well if you looked in on her.'

'Me? Whatever for?'

'She is alone and friendless. She even welcomes my visits, and I will be gone.'

Cosetta set her mouth. 'I owe her nothing.'

'You were her companion; you were kidnapped together.'

'When you offered her freedom at my expense, she took it. And no doubt when you recommended my methods for surviving captivity to her, she characterized me as a harlot.'

Beauceron made an evasive gesture. 'She does not find your approach suitable for her own personality. It does not mean she abuses you.'

Cosetta shrugged. 'She thought nothing of my situation when we came here. It is she who drove me to my present expedients. She cannot expect any sympathy or support from me now. It is too late.'

'You are a harsh woman, Cosetta.'

'Now, Beauceron, do not play such a game with me. You are a brigand, kidnapper, traitor; and you reprove me for failing to pay social calls. If I thought you meant it, you would be a deep-dyed hypocrite.'

Beauceron smiled and shook his head. 'You are right, Cosetta. I am in no position to lecture you. Visit Isola if you choose: I shall not try to compel you.' He rose to leave. 'I wish you well.'

She came closer and kissed him on the cheek. 'And I you,

Beauceron. You will always have one friend in Mettingloom. Goodbye, Captain.'

'Goodbye, my lady.'

6

It was early evening when Beauceron returned to the Occonero. He was conducted immediately to Lady Isola's apartments. Isola's maid woke her from a gentle slumber on the sofa.

'My lady,' said Beauceron. 'Gather up by tomorrow evening whatever effects you require. You are coming with me to Croad.'

'But—the King . . .'

'Leave the King to me. We sail the day after tomorrow.'

7

So it was that on a morning in late winter, the army commanded by Prince Brissio embarked on the fleet of cogs moored outside the Bay of Mettingloom. Once under way, they were no longer subject to recall by King Tardolio should the spring arrive: they remained under Winter Orders for the duration of their commission.

Beauceron had ensured that he was on a cog far from Brissio and, for that matter, Virnesto. This was his triumph, and he did not intend to share it with anyone. Down below were all forty of his usual company. They might be forced to conduct themselves in line with Brissio's command, but he would still rather serve with these seasoned renegades than with all of Fanrolio's knights – who naturally travelled on other vessels.

Monetto was in the hold superintending the packing of the siege engines; his practical mind was eager to see the results of his modifications. On deck with Beauceron was only the Lady Isola, wrapped in a borrowed sea-cloak, a hood thrown over her head. She remained quiet and withdrawn. She might at last be completing her journey to Croad, but not under the circumstances she had envisaged.

Beauceron stood at the stern watching Mettingloom fall away behind them. The tall tower of the Occonero reached into the sky, and the wan sunlight caught the gilded dome. Mettingloom, all its seething vitality, its corruption and intrigues, was receding.

'What are you thinking?' asked Isola. 'Your face is so cruel.'

He forced a smile. 'If you must know, I was imagining hanging your betrothed. The line of Thaume deserves extinction.'

'Can you not be satisfied with taking the city? Is your rage against Oricien so vast?'

Beauceron's eyes flicked away from Isola's. 'He was not the worst of them. Thaume was more unjust; but he is dead, and poorly placed to face my vengeance. I will enjoy minimal satisfaction from desecrating his tomb. Siedra was the cruellest, the most depraved. She had great capacity to do harm, and used it to the full. She too will pay the full price, once I catch her. Oricien is fortunate: he will pay his debt by death alone.'

'I would not like to be your enemy.'

Beauceron suppressed an instinctive smile. 'Testifying against me was perhaps unwise in that context.'

Isola waved the point away. 'That is the past; that was Mettingloom. Both of our destinies lie in Emmen.'

An idea occurred to Beauceron. 'You were high in Emmen society: do you know where Siedra is?'

'I would be betraying her to a terrible vengeance if I told you. And anyway, all I know is what you know. She married Lord Dinarre of Glount; Dinarre died last autumn, lamented by no one, least of all his wife; and Siedra is to return home with her dowry.'

Beauceron shrugged. 'It is all one. If she is in Croad, I shall find her. If not, there will be another day.'

8

The plains outside Croad in times of peace were home to farmers and those who, for whatever reason, chose not to live within the city walls. In this particular late winter, however, they became the temporary residence of a new population. Prince Brissio's host encircled the walls just out of bowshot, and opposite the weakest point of the walls, two giant trebuchets grew instead of wheat.

Brissio dismounted from his gallumpher and stepped with measured dignity to where Beauceron and Virnesto superintended the loading of the giant machines. His scarlet uniform was frogged with cloth-of-gold, and epaulettes sprouted from his shoulders like wings on a stag beetle. A four-cornered hat sat atop his head.

'Virnesto,' said the Prince. 'Are you convinced this is the best way?'

Beauceron scowled and kicked at a loose stone. 'This debate is not fresh. Oricien will not—'

Brissio turned with petulant gesture. 'I was addressing the Captain-General. Your views are well understood. We need not rehearse them again.'

Virnesto leaned back against the trebuchet. 'Beauceron is correct, my lord. Sending Oricien a challenge to bring his army forth will be unsuccessful. Let him feel the weight of our stone.'

Brissio shrugged. 'Very well. I suppose it is unreasonable to expect men of your stamp to have the grandeur of vision of a prince. Fire your catapults.'

Beauceron made a gesture to Monetto. The first trebuchet creaked as the rope was wound one last turn tighter. 'Release,' said Beauceron in a level voice.

With a whoosh and startling speed, the arm of the trebuchet swung over. A sizeable flint, once part of a farmer's cottage, seemed to hang in the air. Then it plunged towards the ground at high speed, disappearing over the top of the city wall. Cries of outrage floated across from the city.

Brissio raised an eyebrow. 'That is the marvel of the trebuchet? How will you demolish the walls if you cannot hit them?'

'The equipment is delicate,' said Beauceron. 'Already Monetto is recalibrating the second engine.'

'Hmmph,' said Brissio. 'This is hardly the blood-stirring glory of warfare I had been led to expect.'

Virnesto spoke softly. 'We have time, my lord. Every moment that passes depletes Oricien's food.'

'And brings Enguerran closer.'

'I thought you wanted battle,' said Beauceron with a tart smile.

'You are a cross-grained man, Beauceron. Combat with Oricien's army with his city at stake is fit and seemly for knights of renown. To face King Enguerran's entire muster is a different matter.'

Beauceron turned away to signal Monetto once more. The second trebuchet released: another stone flew above the sun as it sank low in the sky. This time it crashed into the upper section of the wall. There was a puff of dust and a small section of the wall toppled back. Beauceron clenched his fist. 'Well done, Monetto!'

Brissio gave a measured nod. 'Impressive,' he said through tight lips. 'Let us launch another.'

'My lord,' said Monetto. 'Reloading the trebuchet requires much time and effort.' He indicated the crew straining to tighten the winch. 'It will be at least half a glass before we can fire again.'

Brissio snorted. 'I might have expected sustained action to be beyond your powers. I will return to my quarters. Send to me when matters require my attention.' He turned and stalked away from the trebuchets.

Virnesto clapped Beauceron on the shoulder. 'You must ignore the Prince—'

'—I do—'

'—and you should avoid provoking him. He hates you as it is, and he is a vindictive man.'

'And a stupid one. We have ample masonry: the walls will be down in a matter of days. Then Brissio will have his battle, unless Oricien surrenders.'

Virnesto nodded. 'They cannot stand.'

'And Trevarre will not get here in time, let alone Enguerran.'

9

Beauceron returned to his tent with a brisk stride. On impulse he stepped across to Isola's pavilion. 'Good evening, my lady.'

Isola rose to greet him. 'You appear in a rare humour, Beauceron.'

'Today we begin,' he said. 'Come outside. You will see the walls already beginning to crumble.'

Isola pulled at her lower lip. 'This is not a sight I care to see.'

'In that case, you should have remained in Mettingloom. All you will see over the next days is the destruction of the city. You should take pleasure in the humbling of the man who did not care enough to pay your ransom.'

Isola looked at the roof of the pavilion. 'I am betrothed to Lord Oricien. I take no satisfaction in his humiliation. I should have been the Lady of this city.'

Beauceron poured himself a goblet of wine, and another for Isola. 'Life in Croad would not have been to your taste, my lady.'

A spot of colour appeared on her cheek. 'You are offensively certain of my tastes, for a treasonous brigand.'

Beauceron raised a hand. 'I was acquitted, if you remember, despite your testimony. As to your tastes, I suspect I know you better than your betrothed.'

Isola said nothing for a moment as she sipped her wine. 'Lord Oricien is a true and noble knight,' she said. 'He is a glorious match for any woman in the Emmenrule. You are – my powers of invention falter at characterizing you. You may think you know me; well, I understand you no better than the day you kidnapped me, whatever suspicions I may have as to your identity.' She looked at him from under lowered lids.

Beauceron gave a half-smile. 'Your suspicions are your own, and unlikely to be correct.'

'Princess Agalina believed otherwise, so I heard. She felt your relationship to Oricien was more than casual: indeed, that this whole affair might be a blood feud.'

Beauceron started. 'And how would you be in a position to know Princess Agalina's speculations?'

Isola laughed. 'Brissio told me. He is keen to know more of you, and was eager to regale me with what he had heard.'

Beauceron set his goblet down with a thump. 'Brissio is a buffoon, a farmyard animal in the vestments of a prince. His theories should be evaluated in that light.'

Isola gave a quick harsh peal of laughter. 'You are piqued.'

'The matter of my identity is not germane,' he replied. 'Come, the hour is late: let us take dinner.' He put his head outside the pavilion.

'Rostovac!' he called. 'Kindly set up the tables. We shall be dining al fresco tonight.'

Rostovac, a gnarled veteran of many previous campaigns, gave an uncertain smile and bustled off to carry out his errand.

Beauceron offered Isola his arm and they walked outside. Once Rostovac had set up the tables, he said, 'Sit down. What better prospect could we have for our meal?' He gestured with a sweep of his arm to take in the city of Croad immediately before them.

'Are we not in some danger?' asked Isola. 'This close to the walls, might we not be killed by arrows, or fall victim to a sortie?'

Beauceron shook his head indulgently as Rostovac positioned the table and spread a heavy cloth. 'Oricien will not dare to sally forth. His safety lies in his walls. And if he did choose, the watch on the North Gate would alert us in high time. As to arrows, my experience allows me to calculate their range with exactitude.' He pointed to a spot some fifty yards towards the walls. 'That is their maximum extent. You can relax. Tonight we will have a memorable meal.'

Lady Isola looked unconvinced. Campfires burned all around against the chill of the twilight. Behind them stood Beauceron's trebuchets, eerily reminiscent of giant grasshoppers, and now quiescent for the night.

'The occasion is unconventional,' said Beauceron with a

smile, 'but all the more noteworthy for that. You will be able to tell your grandchildren you dined before the walls of Croad, during their destruction.'

Isola grimaced. 'Grandchildren presuppose a husband. You have made your intention to kill mine clear.'

Beauceron waved the point away with an airy gesture. 'You are not yet married, and many other prospects await you. But this is not the time for such talk. Look at the sun setting behind the walls, feel the warmth of the burgeoning spring. All over Mondia, folk toil for their meagre bread: behind the walls, they wonder how long they will be able to eat at all. And look! Rostovac approaches bearing a noble roasted capon, and that is merely the start of our repast. Rejoice in the privileges that you enjoy: do not complain of imaginary woes.'

Isola gave him a steady look. 'You lack empathy for the suffering of others.'

Beauceron acknowledged the point with a nod. 'Empathy is not a helpful quality for a man in my profession.'

'Your profession as soldier, or monomaniac?'

Beauceron poured two goblets of wine from the flask Rostovac had set before them. 'You shall not provoke me, my lady. And you mistake me if you think feasting before the walls of a starving city denotes a lack of feeling. The opposite is true: my effect is precisely calculated. All along the walls Oricien's soldiers will see us eating the finest viands: their bellies will grumble, their spirits will be sapped. Word will reach Oricien; the capacity of the city to resist will be correspondingly diminished.'

'I imagined you had invited me to dine for the charm of my company,' said Isola.

'And so I have. My illustration to the people of Croad could have been carried out as well on a table laid for one.'

'May I ask where the food has come from?'

Beauceron smiled. 'This is an additional irony, although not one which will be apparent to Oricien. Our victuals have come from the kitchen of The Patient Suitor inn, on the south of the river, which is now our command headquarters. The people of Croad have furnished our meal tonight, and I salute them!' He raised a goblet high towards the wall. Some seventy or so yards off an arrow thudded into the turf.

'Poor,' said Beauceron, shaking his head. 'Both accuracy and range are below the optimum.'

Isola picked at the food before her. 'I am not sure that I have a great appetite this evening.'

'As you will,' said Beauceron. 'The lesson for Oricien may be even more compelling if I feed the leftovers to my dogs.'

'Does Prince Brissio countenance your behaviour?'

'We have arrived at an arrangement of sorts,' said Beauceron. 'He has allowed me to deploy the trebuchets as I choose to the north of the river. He retains the bulk of the troops to the south, shuts himself away in The Patient Suitor and sends daily challenges to Oricien.'

'How so?'

'He characterizes my siege tactics as "throwing stones". He disdains anything so base: he wishes to win his victory on the field of battle, and demands that Oricien bring his army out to fight like men. Oricien, of course, has more sense. He stays where he is, and gambles that a relief force will reach him before his food runs out. In his position I would do the same.'

'Brissio does not see the siege as real battle?'

'Exactly. He wants to fight a second Jehan's Steppe, before the walls of Croad. In this he is destined for disappointment.'

'What if your trebuchets breach the walls?'

'Either Oricien will surrender, or we shall have our battle, but it will be in the streets of Croad. A dirty, bloody business, taking a city by storm. There is little honour, and much bloodshed. Brissio would not enjoy it.'

'And you?'

Beauceron shrugged. 'It is effective. Once we are in the city, we will win. That is enough for me.'

Isola sipped reflectively at her goblet. 'If the city surrendered, the garrison would be allowed to march out, would it not?'

'That is the normal way of war.'

'Oricien would be able to negotiate a safe-conduct with Brissio. He would escape your vengeance.'

'Be assured, he will escape nothing of what he is owed.'

'You would still be unsatisfied if he surrenders.'

'Perhaps. But I do not think he will surrender. He will fight before he concedes his city.'

'Why then does he not do so now, while he has food and strong soldiers?'

Beauceron laughed. 'You have the makings of a strategist. A battle can only end in defeat, either glorious or inglorious. It can be seen as "dynamic surrender". His best, his only, hope is the arrival of Trevarre or Enguerran, and he will cling to that to the point of starvation, and even beyond.'

'Will you excuse me?' asked Isola, rising stiffly. 'I find this chilly calculation enervating. I will be in my pavilion if you wish to see me later.'

Beauceron raised his goblet and helped himself to another portion of ragout.

He walked around the northern perimeter of the city, until finally he found himself at the Traitors' Gate by the river bank. He gave a rueful smile as he looked up. How long it had been since he stood on the other side of the wall! He thought of the faces of his youth, so many of them now dead: Lord Thaume, Sir Artingaume, Darrien. He hardly knew what had happened to many of the others. Had Sir Langlan ever returned to Emmen? He would no longer be a young man. What of the virtuous Lady Jilka? He doubted that age would have improved her temper, if she still lived. Rarely was Beauceron this introspective: it must be the proximity of his great goal. He knew for certain that Oricien was there: and it was Oricien, as the Lord of Croad, who must pay the price for his family's misrule.

By the time he returned to his tent, the moon stood high in the sky. The campfires blazed and, on the walls of Croad, lanterns burned. There was a glow from within Isola's pavilion: she had not yet settled herself for sleep. She seemed preternaturally aware of his presence, for although he made no sound she came out to meet him.

He bowed. 'You are abroad late, my lady.'

'I do not find it easy to sleep.'

'I will send to Brissio to dispatch you another mattress from The Patient Suitor.'

'It is not the mattress which keeps me awake.' Her eyes were dark and full in the moonlight. Her deep green velvet dress held a curious lustre. Beauceron fought down a pang of sympathy: she was about to bemoan her fate again, an experience no more agreeable for extensive repetition.

'Is there any help I can offer?' he said.

Her mouth compressed into the involuntary sneer which had become all too common of late. 'The time is late to make amends,' she said. 'You have shown the man I was to marry to be not only a niggard but a coward, hiding behind his walls until death finds him. There is no restitution you can make for that.'

Beauceron felt an obscure motivation to support Oricien against so absurd a charge. 'He has no real alternative. To come out is to invite defeat and the destruction of his city.'

Isola looked at him in astonishment. 'You ride to his

rescue? He is as far from the gallant lord of popular repute as can be imagined.'

'In that, at least, you are correct,' said Beauceron. 'But as a commander and lord of his city, he takes the only course open to him.'

'A man of spirit would ride forth with every man at his call, to gain a mighty victory or heroic defeat.'

'It would be the latter,' said Beauceron. 'He is outnumbered four to one. Then a city of women and children would fall to the sack. Be assured, that is not good lordship.'

She paused as they walked and turned to look at him, a shaft of moonlight falling across her face. 'You speak without conviction,' she said. 'You, for all your faults, are a man of spirit. You would not perish in such a timid way.'

'I am not the lord of a city; nor would I wish to be. I am responsible for no one but myself. Such a situation allows me the occasional rash gesture.'

She stopped and looked up into his face. Her eye met Beauceron's. 'Had we met under different circumstances, matters might have gone differently between us.'

'Differently from kidnap, you mean?' said Beauceron with a smile. 'It is perhaps not the best introduction.'

'I am serious,' she said, looking down. 'You have a warped nobility, but a nobility nonetheless. It would not be hard for a woman to – You know, of course, that Cosetta greatly admired you.'

Beauceron stared gravely into her face. This was not one of her occasional forays into flirtation.

'Cosetta admired nothing more than her own advancement,' he said. 'I do not condemn her for that. Her feelings towards me must be viewed in that light. Prince Laertio will make a far more suitable patron.'

'You underestimate – either yourself, or Cosetta's feelings, perhaps both.'

'Cosetta's feelings are of little interest. She is far away.'

Isola's voice dropped. 'But I am not, Beauceron. I am here, now, one foot away from you. If you touched me you would feel the warmth of my body.'

'I am warm enough,' said Beauceron. 'I need no additional heat.'

'Must I beg you?' she said softly. 'For six months we have ranged the steppes of fate together. You have been cruel, you have been indifferent, on occasion you have been tender. I can never return to my old life. Beauceron—' She broke off and her eyes searched his face.

Beauceron stepped back a pace. He looked over her shoulder to the glowering city walls beyond.

'Isola, this is not wise,' he said.

'Am I not beautiful? I have been in your power, and you did not touch me. What you could have taken, I give to you freely.' She put her hands on his shoulders, moved her face forward.

Beauceron tried to look away. She was undeniably an attractive woman, if highly strung. But she was brittle, vulnerable, damaged. A flicker of a grin reached his lips as he recognized the irony that he had no compunction about plotting to bring down a city, with perhaps hundreds of deaths, but he scrupled to take advantage of a lone woman.

She sprang back. 'Are you laughing at me?'

'Nothing could be further from the truth,' said Beauceron. 'I honour and admire you. But I will not exploit you.'

'Exploit me! You were happy enough to kidnap me and give my ransom away to win favour. But you will not "exploit" me!' The moonlight highlighted the pink flush of her cheeks.

She turned and ran back to her pavilion. At the threshold she looked back. 'I thought you had given me every insult imaginable. I was wrong.'

*

In the morning, when Beauceron went to her pavilion to check on her, Lady Isola was gone.

Beauceron cursed as he looked around Isola's pavilion. He had brought her against his better judgement, and now he had managed to mislay her. At the very least, with her ransom standing at 45,000 florins, this was careless. Irritably he saddled up a gallumpher and rode across the pontoon bridge to Prince Brissio's camp.

He strode past the guards and bounded up the stairs to Brissio's suite on the top floor. 'Good morning, my lord,' he said, bowing as well to Virnesto, who was poring over a series of charts on a table in the corner.

'Beauceron,' acknowledged Brissio stiffly. 'We rarely see you south of the river. Have you come to notify me of a breach in the walls?'

Beauceron scowled. 'Regrettably I must inform you that Lady Isola has absconded from my company. I had hoped to find her over here.'

'Absconded? The woman has been nothing but trouble since her arrival in Mettingloom.'

'I take it she has not been found?'

Virnesto rose and walked to the window. 'If you want to find her, that is where you look.' He gestured to a queue of ill-dressed figures shuffling across the bridge; in the main, country folk who thought to find safety in the city. 'She will be trying to get inside Croad, I would have thought.'

'Send men to detain her,' said Beauceron.

Brissio raised a hand. 'Let her in; let them all in. They all eat Oricien's bread. I am sure Beauceron is too wily to have shared valuable secrets with her.'

Beauceron shrugged. 'She will not be safe inside the walls when the city falls. It would be advisable to secure her now.'

'Her fate is of no interest to me,' said Brissio. 'She has

ruined Davanzato and been a drain on the Winter Court. If she wishes to take her chances with Oricien, let her.'

Beauceron shook his head in impatience. 'Her father will yet pay for her return. You are throwing away silver.'

'Enough, Beauceron. I have spoken. I told my father you show nothing but insubordination. Do not forget who commands here: if I must take stern measures, I shall.'

14

Croad

1

After a poor night's sleep Arren rose early and took a dismal breakfast of flat beer and a haunch of bread left over from the servants' supper. He looked out through the window; as the early sun spread into the courtyard he saw Sir Langlan stepping crisply through a series of drills with his rapier. He got up and went to join him.

'Good morning, Sir Langlan!'

'Why, Arren, you are abroad early! At your age I would sleep until noon, if indeed I had gone to bed yet.'

Arren grinned ruefully. 'I could not sleep.'

'You are young to have worries. I have the excuse that I am Regent in Lord Thaume's absence. I find a pass or two with the rapier keeps me calm. The apothecary tells me it is better than ale.'

'Shall we spar a little?' asked Arren, reaching down a rapier hanging on the wall.

Sir Langlan bowed his head. 'Why not, although you are becoming too proficient for me.'

They fenced with vigour for a quarter-hour. In real combat Arren would have been dead three or four times over.

'Sit down, lad,' said Sir Langlan. 'We all have troubles

from time to time: I have surely had my share. The important thing is never, ever to have troubles in your mind when you have a sword in your hand. The blade is a mistress who shares her favours with nobody.'

Arren sat on the bench. 'It is not always so easy.'

'No,' said Sir Langlan. 'But it is possible. I killed two men in Emmen, both in fair duels. That is bad, is it not?'

'Well, I—'

'King Arren had banned duels at court: he had lost too many nobles from petty vendettas. So what I did was all but treasonous. How could things have been worse?'

'It seems they could not.'

'You are wrong,' said Sir Langlan. 'In the duels, it could have been me who died. I was under sentence of death for the second, but I could not let that enter my mind. I killed the man they sent to take me, and King Arren spared my life. If there is a moral to the story – other than not to fight a duel when they are banned on pain of death, which is self-evident – it is that your mind must be empty when you fight.'

Arren nodded.

'At your age, I will wager your concerns are, if not trivial, at least of a nature you will look on with greater proportion when you are my age. Let me guess: a girl?'

Arren flushed.

'Aha! In this matter, at least, I can speak with the authority of considerable experience. Women are the most important aspect of life, as long as you realize that they are the least important. A lovely woman is a spectacular diversion from the travails of the day, so potent that your concerns vanish to less than nothing. All is delight, until you make the mistake of believing that her charms are real or enduring: it is like trying to grasp a dream, doomed to failure, and destroying the phantasm you once enjoyed.'

Arren frowned. 'Your view is somewhat cheerless.'

'Nonsense! I am exhorting you to enjoy your frolics at face value, and not to delude yourself looking for deeper meanings. Under such circumstances no lasting harm can ensue.'

Arren frowned as he tried to apply this precept to his dalliance with Siedra. 'Your precepts are perhaps simplistic for all situations.'

Sir Langlan gave an airy wave. 'Maybe so, although if a contingency more complex arises I swiftly remove myself from the scene! Think of the dog in the yard as he mounts the bitch: does he concern himself with illusions of imperishable love? Of course not! He seeks only to ease his needs in the most convenient way.'

'I do not view my own relations in quite the same light,' said Arren stiffly.

Sir Langlan smilingly shook his head. 'You are young, you are young. Look, here comes Siedra. As long as you keep away from her, you cannot go too far amiss.'

Arren smiled wanly. 'Good morning, Siedra. You are awake early.'

Her eyes passed slowly over Arren's face. 'I could not sleep.'

'I had a similar experience: I found that a bout of swordplay with Sir Langlan answered very well.'

'The expedient is not open to me,' said Siedra. 'I would be as like to skewer myself. Besides, I am sure that Sir Langlan's duties as Regent will soon take him about his business.'

Sir Langlan rose. 'That moment has arrived. The merchant Graix complains that his neighbour has blocked his sewage pipe and I must give a ruling. The life of the lord is not all wine and ladies, unfortunately.' He bowed and walked across the courtyard to Lord Thaume's reception room.

'I did not see you last night,' said Siedra. 'I had hoped to find you.'

Arren shrugged. 'I had to exercise my gallumpher, and I took some ale with Fleuraume.'

Siedra scowled. 'Your implicit assessment of my company is not flattering. Still, today will do as well.'

'Siedra—'

'If you have energy to repeat yesterday's exertions, of course.'

'There is something I must say.'

Siedra tilted her nose in the air. 'Nothing introduced with such a portentous tone can be worth listening to. Either you propose a sentimental declaration which cannot be germane to the situation, or you advance some feeble reason why my plans for the day will be overset. I will tolerate neither possibility. You are to be light, cheerful and attentive, without puppyish scampering. The task surely cannot be too challenging.'

Arren drooped. This was going to be even more difficult than he had expected.

'Well, Arren? You surely cannot think your drab demeanour represents my wishes.'

A voice interrupted them as a liveried servant burst into the courtyard. 'My lady! Seigneur Arren! Lord Thaume is at the gate!'

Arren gave an inward sigh. 'Thank you, Maussay. We will repair to meet him immediately.'

Siedra shook her head in vexation. 'Am I always to be thwarted? Perhaps we can slip away after supper tonight. The Pleasaunce in the moonlight will be suitable for an assignation.'

Arren refrained from mentioning that the moon was at its smallest phase. Time enough to deal with the matter later.

Supper was a more convivial occasion than the last time Lord Thaume's household had eaten together. 'Welcome, one and all,' said Thaume to the select group he had chosen to assemble around him for his first night back in Croad. On either side he had seated Lady Jilka and Oricien, who carried himself with greater confidence than six weeks earlier when they had departed for Emmen. Ranged around the table were Sir Langlan, Master Pinch, Master Guiles, Viator Sleech, Master Coppercake and, at the foot of the table, Siedra and Arren.

'I have much to report,' said Lord Thaume. 'I have paid homage to King Jehan, as has Oricien, against the day when he rules Croad.'

'What manner of man is Jehan, Father?' asked Siedra.

'He is in the prime of his life, perhaps thirty-five years of age. He is fair-spoken, pious without over-religiosity, and displays no overt vices. He desires peace with Gammerling, and while we were there he invited King Gundovald and his sons to visit Emmen at their pleasure.'

Sir Langlan sniffed. 'A milksop, then?'

'He desires the good of his people. And he displayed no intention to invite either of the kings of Mettingloom to wait upon him. He will do well enough, I think.'

'A good king considers the welfare of his people above glory,' said Master Pinch. 'The view is unfashionable, particularly among the gallant, but such a man should command our respect, if not the adulation of balladeers.'

'I told him of our wars in the North,' said Lord Thaume. 'The King was much interested in your dimonetto, Pinch – as was young Prince Enguerran. You will find a ready welcome at the court whenever you require it.'

Pinch assumed an expression half-smile, half-grimace.

'The honour is one I neither merit nor desire. Thaumaturgy and princes do not mix. Much as I have valued your company, my lord, this world of affairs is not for me. These questions are all distractions from my study of the Unseen Realms.'

'And how were you received at the court, my lord?' asked Master Guiles.

Lord Thaume smiled at some private amusement. 'I was fortunate to arrive half a week before Lord High Viator Raugier, and was able to explain the matter of his expulsion without interruption or misdirection. By the time Raugier arrived His Puissance had formed his opinion, and Lord Raugier's complaints fell on indifferent ears. The King has required Darrien to remain as a hostage until the question is officially settled, but the matter is a formality. I do not flatter myself if I say that the King formed a positive impression of our party. If I were minded to spend half the year at court, I might exert some influence.'

Siedra spoke up. 'Are our prospects enhanced, sir?'

Lord Thaume stroked his chin. 'In a manner of speaking, I suppose.'

'Perhaps you will find it less necessary to conciliate Duke Panarre now that our standing is so high in Emmen?'

'Duke Panarre remains my overlord; in addition, his troops are a week away in time of need, unlike the King over the mountains.'

'Surely,' continued Siedra, 'you no longer need to pursue the idea of marriage into the Duke's house with such enthusiasm. Are there no suitable matches at court?'

Arren noticed that Siedra was not so interested in his own attractions tonight now that the court in Emmen beckoned.

Lord Thaume said: 'The idea of a match at court must be pursued. However, Oricien made such a favourable impression that it is he who shall be returning. Since Guigot is no longer available in my marriage plans, it remains expedient that you marry a connection of the Duke's. Indeed, we may now be able to press for Lord Trevarre: I should like to see my grandson Duke of Lynnoc.'

Siedra's eyes narrowed. 'I am no more enthusiastic to marry Lord Trevarre than the unspeakable Dinarre. Do my wishes count for nothing?'

'You have at last appreciated the truth. I naturally hope for every happiness in your marriage, but it would be in the nature of a bonus rather than the purpose of the match. Granted, Lord Trevarre tends to the effeminate at times, but I am assured he can father children. All else is froth.'

Arren excused himself and slipped out to the privy, although his main aim was to see Eilla. On his way back he saw her in the corridor bringing dishes to Lord Thaume's table.

'I hope that is not yesterday's fish,' he said.

Eilla, trim in her crisp white livery, shot Arren a look of incredulity. 'Have you spoken to Siedra yet?'

'Not as such.'

'Then you have nothing to say to me.' She bustled past into the dining room. Arren returned to his seat with a heavy tread.

Siedra leaned over and whispered to him. 'Where have you been?'

'I have drunk half a flask of wine. Where do you think?'

'I noticed you came in behind that Eilla, and she does not look in a good humour.'

'Neither would you be if you had been running up and down from the kitchen all evening.'

Siedra narrowed her eyes. 'I have suggested before that it is unwise for you to associate with the servants. It lowers your cachet.'

Eilla appeared on her round of the table with a flask of strong red Garganet wine. 'More wine, Seigneur?'

'No thank you, Eilla.'

'My lady?'

'I think I shall,' said Siedra, holding out her goblet. As Eilla moved to pour the flask the highly polished silver slipped from her grasp and in an instant disgorged its contents all over Siedra's honey-silk dress.

'Oh! My lady!' cried Eilla, with a quarter-glance at Arren. 'How could I have been so clumsy!'

Siedra sprang erect. 'A cloth! Water!'

Eilla dabbed at Siedra's dress with a napkin, grinding the wine ever deeper into the fabric. Siedra's face was the colour of the wine. Eilla would pay a high price for her prank.

'Eilla, enough!' said Siedra. She took a slow and deliberate look at Arren. 'Come now, it was an accident. I am sure Mistress Eulalia knows a thousand methods for leaching a wine-stain. Do not fret yourself.'

Arren looked on in astonishment. The dress was ruined, and everyone knew it. On past experience she would have demanded Eilla whipped and the cost of the dress deducted from her wages.

Eilla too looked dumbstruck. She bowed tamely. 'I am very sorry, my lady. I will be more careful in future.' She walked from the room, her head down.

'You must excuse me, Arren,' Siedra said. 'I will need to change my dress.' She leaned forward so no one else could hear. 'And when I have changed I will meet you in the Pleasaunce. I will be no longer than thirty minutes.'

'You were surprisingly temperate with Eilla,' said Arren.

Siedra shrugged. 'The girl is slow and clumsy. It is not her fault. Perhaps in due course she will be moved to less demanding duties, but it is wrong to berate her.'

'Indeed it is,' said Arren carefully.

'I know, you are thinking of when I abused her last. Perhaps you are a good influence on me,' she said with a surreptitious squeeze of his knee under the table.

Arren sat and finished his wine thoughtfully. He listened as Oricien told the company about his experiences at court; Arren would not have recognized the diffident young man of a season back. He had hunted with Jehan's son Prince Enguerran and danced with his daughter Princess Melissena, and gave favourable reports of many of the young ladies of the court: Ladies Misiana, Reute, Isola, Nolmina. He was growing into the next Lord of Croad.

Arren still had a while before his rendezvous with Siedra. Her restraint when Eilla had spilled the wine had surprised him. Was Siedra perhaps capable of better than he had imagined? She had always been spoiled and indulged at every turn. For whatever reason, she seemed to regard his good opinion as important, and perhaps she was willing to improve her behaviour to secure it. Eilla had not shown to such advantage: the spillage had surely not been accidental. It might be precipitate to break with Siedra when they met in the Pleasaunce. Did he not owe her the chance to prove that her conduct had improved?

With a sigh he rose from his seat and set out for the Pleasaunce. Why could affairs not be more straightforward?

His reverie as he walked along the corridor was interrupted by a soft voice. 'Arren.'

He turned to see Eilla half-hidden in the shadow of an alcove. The torch flickered and cast a grotesque distorted shadow.

'I thought you were not talking to me.'

'I assume you are going to meet Siedra.'

'You have left me in no doubt that the matter is irrelevant to you.'

'You are angry with me about the wine.'

'It was not a sensible action.'

Eilla shrugged. 'I did not plan it. But she gave me such a vile look.'

'You are imagining things. I saw no "look".'

Eilla shook her head. 'Of course not.'

'You have to admit that her behaviour afterwards was all one could wish of a lady.'

'Arren,' she said in exasperation, her small hand bunching into a fist and hitting the wall. 'Can you not see what she is about?'

'I saw her the victim of a misconceived and damaging prank, responding with grace and dignity.'

'You are a fool, Arren,' she said in a thick voice. 'If you cannot see she was feigning composure, your judgement is at fault.'

'She is not used to governing her temper. Why should she feign now?'

'Why do you think?' she snapped. 'To make her appear to advantage and me to disadvantage.'

'You managed that on your own.'

Arren thought to see a glimmer of a tear in the flickering light of the candle. 'When you spilled the wine,' said Arren with a sudden certainty, 'you were not just aiming to spoil her dress, were you?'

Eilla set her mouth. 'What do you mean?'

'You wanted her to abuse you, to strike you, to call for you to be whipped, didn't you? You wanted to destroy her character in my eyes and earn my sympathy for yourself.'

Any tears in Eilla's eyes were gone now. Her voice was flat yet somehow throbbed with emotion. 'Why do you see through my schemes so easily and yet see no wrong in Siedra? She is far more manipulative than I.'

'Can you not trust the strength of my regard for you,

Eilla? You do not need to resort to scheme and plot to recruit my sympathy.'

Eilla's face curled into a harsh smile. 'Do I not? You seem to find great difficulty in breaking with Siedra. You should not blame me for presenting the facts in a way which illustrates her character.'

'It may be that you have done that, Eilla; but not in the way you have imagined. If you will excuse me, I do not wish to keep Siedra waiting.'

He turned on his heel and strode off towards the Pleasaunce. In the background he could hear Eilla's sobs which she could no longer contain.

3

The sliver of moon was high as Arren stepped into the Pleasaunce. Under the benevolent canopy of the nottar tree stood Siedra, her honey-silk dress replaced by one of deep burgundy. He looked around to make sure that no one else was around: he was all too aware of how easy it was to be overheard in the gardens.

Siedra showed no such concern and met him with a melting embrace. 'I thought you were not coming.'

'I could not get away,' said Arren. 'Oricien was expanding on his experiences at court.'

'Pah! He has been away for a month and he thinks he is the King's boon companion. "Prince Enguerran this", "Princess Melissena that". He is still a man of Croad.'

Arren gave her a surprised glance. 'If he stands well at court we all profit. He expands your prospects as much as his own.'

'Hah! My prospects are expanded from Dinarre to Trevarre.'

'Siedra, this is fruitless. Besides, you are yet young to marry.'

'I am sixteen, and well developed. I will be married within the year.'

Arren knew this for the truth, and he declined to insult either of them by denying it.

'Have you no false comfort to offer?' she said. 'You bear the matter with indifference.'

Arren shrugged. 'It is pointless to fight what cannot be changed.'

Siedra shook her head ruefully. 'I do not know if you are as stolid as a stone, or you have Master Pinch's grand perspective. Perhaps it is all one.'

'I know you are unhappy. It hurts me to see it.'

'Dear Arren – you at least I can rely on. Come, let us forget the future.' She took his hand and led him deeper into the trees. Arren thought of Eilla: he should not be doing this, and he had already resolved not to. Then he remembered the incident with the wine, and Eilla berating him afterwards. She would have to take care of herself; he could not be responsible for every injustice in the world.

4

Arren was woken by the first glimmers of sunlight infiltrating through the leaves. By his side Siedra continued to sleep. He levered himself up onto an elbow. This was insanity: to be caught in this situation by anyone at all would mean the information proceeding instantly to Lord Thaume. Arren's certain knowledge faltered at that point: Thaume would be enraged, and he was a man who imposed justice in the heat of the moment. Hanging, gelding, exile: it was difficult to imagine the penalty falling outside that range. Siedra's punishment had already been decreed: marriage to the man of her father's choice. In a sense, she had no more to lose; indeed, the more wantonly she behaved, the greater her chances of being considered unsuitable for a political marriage. Lady Cerisa's history lessons had more than once involved well-born young ladies who had forfeited the respect of their husbands through wantonness. These had been intended as cautionary tales, but in the circumstances Siedra might be taking them as exemplars.

Beside him on the ground she stirred and looked up at him with a smile. 'After exercise, sleep,' she said with a glint in her eyes.

'Do you know what time it is?'

'I am governed by my impulses, not the hourglass.'

'You will not say that if your father stumbles over us at his morning constitutional.'

She waved a hand in dismissal. 'He never walks in the Pleasaunce in the morning. Besides, does the risk not set the heart beating?'

Arren sat up abruptly. 'Not in any way I wish to encourage.'

'I took you for a passionate gallant. It seems I may have been mistaken,' she said with a studied curl of the lip.

'This is futile, Siedra. The whole notion of our intimacy is a mistake.'

She flushed and stood up. 'What do you mean?'

'I have been uneasy from the outset,' he said. 'It is rash, foolish, insane: it cannot continue.'

'Can you deny your feelings for me?' she said, her cheeks flushed.

'There are no feelings,' said Arren through gritted teeth. 'I have been flattered and captivated, but I can own no deeper feelings.'

'It is that little bitch! Did you not see how she tried to

humiliate me last night? She is desperate to turn you against me.'

'It is nothing to do with Eilla,' said Arren in as level a tone as he could muster.

'You cannot refute her jealousy of me. She is bitter at the constriction of her prospects, and she cannot bear to see you with anyone else.'

'The description would appear to fit you at least as well as her,' said Arren.

She slapped at him, and although the blow was obvious and easy to avoid, Arren let it take him on the cheek.

'Does that make you feel better?'

'You have not heard the last of this, Arren – neither you nor that trollop. You will live to regret the day you spurned Lady Siedra.'

She spun on her heel and ran from the glade. Arren watched her go with foreboding.

'Arren!'

In alarm he turned to find the voice. 'Over here.'

It was Oricien. Had he heard the scene in the glade?

'I have scarcely seen you since our return,' he said. 'There is much I would tell you about Emmen. You must return with me.'

'Would your father spare me?'

'The court greatly respects martial prowess. You will soon become a great favourite. That alone will be enough to gain my father's support. Besides, who knows when your father will return? The King may even choose to keep Darrien with him permanently.'

'When do you return to court?'

Oricien shrugged. 'A month, two months. And the ladies, Arren, you would not credit the loveliness! Even the ladies in waiting carry themselves like princesses. We had a tourney and I wore the favour of Lady Isola.'

'Who is she?'

'The daughter of some lord, Sey, I think. A handsome girl, if a touch haughty.'

'Do I sense a match?'

'She is too young for marriage. In truth, I preferred Lady Helisette, but the choice will not be mine. Come, let us take some breakfast.'

Oricien put his arm around Arren's shoulder and they walked back towards the castle. Arren wondered again about Oricien's access of confidence. Perhaps it was down to the absence of Guigot, a disconcerting presence and always a challenge to the legitimacy of Thaume's rule. Still, the idea of a sojourn in Emmen had much to commend it, not least distance from Siedra.

'Good morning, Master Pinch,' said Arren as they met the thaumaturge approaching the castle. 'Would you care to join us for breakfast?'

'I thank you, no, Seigneur Arren. I find it bloats me for the day and distracts the mind from its studies. I had hoped for a word in private with you.'

Arren raised his eyebrows. 'I am always happy to oblige you, sir.'

'Good. Perhaps we will repair to my workroom.'

Oricien continued towards the dining room and Arren followed Pinch up a narrow writhing staircase to his room at the top of the tower. The space was not large and every available inch was crammed with retorts, basins, books, with a small bed wedged into one corner. The thaumaturge clearly did not put a premium on luxury.

'Sit down, if you can find a space, yes, yes, the bed will be perfectly satisfactory.'

'I am at a loss as to why you wished to see me, sir.'

'All will become clear soon enough,' said Pinch, leaning against a table which appeared inadequate for the additional weight. 'Of all the youngsters of Lord Thaume's household, you have been the most exasperating. Your release of my dimonetto was highly vexing, and put me to great effort.'

'I can say no more than my apology at the time.'

Pinch raised a placatory hand. 'I am not reproving you. Your curiosity always commended you to me. Had you shown the slightest trace of thaumaturgical talent I should have taken you as a famulus. Lord Thaume would not have prevented me. Compared with Guigot's brazen self-interest, Oricien's polite boredom and Siedra's inattention your own attitude was refreshing.'

'I am glad to have secured your good opinion,' said Arren, 'although I am still unclear as to the purpose of our conversation.'

'I am merely establishing my good will before my warning. I had resolved not to become involved in the day-to-day life of the castle.'

'Warning?'

'You are playing a dangerous game, Arren.'

'I do not understand, sir.'

Master Pinch pushed against the table – which groaned alarmingly – to stand to his full modest height.

'Do not insult us both with tedious evasions. Can you tell me in truth that there is no area of your life where you are not conscious of acting in the most rash and perilous of fashions? Remember, I am a thaumaturge: I see much.'

Arren coloured.

'Good. You are at least conscious of my meaning.'

'I believe so.'

'A man who is familiar with snakes may handle them with impunity. He may even drape them around his neck if he chooses. You or I, watching him, may think the trial of little consequence; we may even try the feat for ourselves. Of course, we are instantly bitten, and if the snake is venomous we die.'

'I do not—'

'You are handling a viper, Arren, and you do not have the charm of snakes.'

Arren pursed his lips. 'You are telling me little I do not already know.'

Pinch raised his eyebrows. 'Your conduct then is even more inexplicable. Ignorance of your folly was the only conceivable excuse.'

'I have broken – I have set the snake down, only this morning.'

Pinch nodded. 'Unless you have the skill to draw a snake's venom, it still remains dangerous.'

'If I may ask, how have you come by your information?'

'I have cautioned you in the past that asking a thaumaturge such a question is, aside from its impoliteness, usually fruitless.' He nonetheless spoke with a smile. 'The thaumaturge can open many doors closed to others: farseeing, the agency of the dimonetto, a hundred charms and enchantments.'

'Of course,' said Arren.

'In this case,' said Pinch, 'you may also care to look from the window.'

Arren rose from the bed and walked over to the slit in the heavy stone wall. Below him, he could see the Pleasaunce, and look down directly into the glade.

'Fortunately for you,' said Pinch, 'no other room commands this view. No one else will have seen your assignations.'

Arren sat down again. 'For that I am grateful.'

'However, anyone else can have observed your demeanour in a certain lady's presence, and in this you have not been subtle. Both you and the lady have been indiscreet in the way you have carried yourselves. I am glad to hear you have called a halt to the affair.'

'Why have you warned me?' asked Arren.

Pinch gave an avuncular smile. 'It is the lot of the thaumaturge that human society is by and large uninteresting to me. The pull of the Unseen is greater. But I am soon to leave Croad, perhaps for ever. I would not leave behind me a situation which inevitably will play out to disaster. I am well disposed towards Lord Thaume, yourself, and Eilla, who has carried herself with great dignity and kept my room tolerably ordered.'

'I thank you, sir.'

'You may wish to leave now: a favourable conjunction of dimensions is about to occur, and I would take advantage. And Arren – do not think you are safe yet.'

Arren was about to reply, but Pinch was already reaching for a sheet of parchment crowded with his cramped script. He turned and left the room.

5

Arren was at a loss how to proceed, but the morning was still young. He collected his practice sword and went over to the exercise yard and for an hour drilled himself to exhaustion. Several of the grooms who had made up his mounts joined him and ended the session with sore heads, but Arren felt no guilt. Such harsh lessons bred alertness, and better that their heads should be cracked with a wooden sword than split asunder with sharp steel.

The sun was high in the sky by the time he had finished and the sweat was standing out on his forehead and sticking his shirt to his back. Feeling unpleasantly damp, he walked down to where the city walls abutted the river and out on to the river bank. There was no one around and he took off his shirt and boots before plunging into the water. He swam to the other bank with slow easy strokes, before returning, dripping but much refreshed. He picked up his boots, slung his shirt over his shoulder and went back inside the castle. The exercise had cleared his mind and he felt better able to deal with whatever events might occur.

He returned to his chambers to change into some dry clothes and poured a glass of ale from the pitcher by his bed. He lay down and stared up at the ceiling. Master Pinch had confirmed Eilla's judgement with regard to Siedra, and he reluctantly admitted that he had known all along they were right. She was cruel, selfish, manipulative: to that list Arren now had to add vindictive. He did not think she would crawl away to lick her wounds in secret. She would need to score some kind of actual or symbolic revenge. He realized that her spite would be as likely to comprehend Eilla as himself, and Eilla had fewer resources with which to respond. Disagreeable as the interview might be, he owed it to her to set out the latest events and his conclusions. It would be helpful, too, for Oricien's awareness to be heightened, but his inventiveness palled when he tried to think of how he was to make Oricien aware that he had debauched his sister. He doubted that he would have Oricien's unequivocal sympathy. It was out of the question to throw himself on Lord Thaume's mercy: Thaume might look kindly upon him now, but he had a keen sense of the value of his family and its connections; Siedra was the only daughter he had to bestow, and the notion of her deflowered, or worse yet with child, would not commend Arren in his eyes.

It was nearly lunchtime, he realized, and he levered himself from his bed to walk down to the servants' refectory in the hope of finding Eilla. He was in luck; he saw her immediately sitting by herself in a corner dipping a hunk of bread into last night's reheated stew. He slipped into the space beside her.

'I need to talk to you,' he said.

She looked up with dull eyes. She did not appear to have slept well. 'Can you not see I am taking my lunch?'

'You need say nothing, merely listen.'

'We exhausted the last of our conversational topics last night. As far as I am concerned there is nothing further to be said.'

He took hold of her wrist as it conveyed bread to her mouth. 'This you will listen to, Eilla: I insist.'

She laid her hand back down on the table. 'It seems I will get no peace until I consent.'

'I have broken with Siedra.'

Eilla shrugged. 'If you recall, that is the course I advised. You need not have interrupted my meal to bring the matter to my attention.'

'She did not take the news calmly.'

'If that surprises you, your knowledge of her character is slighter than mine. I imagine she spat curses and vituperation, implicit and explicit threats, and dire promises of vengeance.'

'Well, yes. That was exactly her response.'

'You will have observed that the front of reasonable and balanced conduct she displayed last night was not in evidence.'

'No.'

'I take it you are no longer in the slightest doubt as to her true nature.'

'No.'

'Good. But all this could have waited until this evening.'

'She gave me to understand that her retribution will include yourself.'

Eilla picked up her bread again. 'There is a difference between a threat and the means to carry it out.'

'Do not underestimate her, Eilla.'

She gave a harsh laugh. 'I have been telling you that consistently. I do not need to hear it from you now. You have been here long enough; you should leave now.'

'Shall I see you this evening?'

'I finish at nine bells. I may take a walk over to the Temple. If you are on hand you may accompany me.'

As Arren left the room he was conscious that Eilla had not been as pleased to see him as he had expected. Could she not be satisfied that she had beaten Siedra? The female mind could be difficult to follow.

6

'I am sorry I was so cross-grained at lunchtime,' said Eilla as they walked through the quiet streets of Croad under a moonless sky.

'I am the one who should be sorry,' said Arren. 'I should never have succumbed to Siedra so easily.'

'She is beautiful and lively,' she said. 'I am sure men with more experience would have been equally pliant.'

Gingerly he slipped an arm around her waist; she made no effort to shake it off.

'I will never argue with you again. You have always been right, as long as I can remember.'

'It does not seem so to me,' said Eilla. 'If I had been as wise as you say, I would not be a servant with no prospects at the mercy of every lord's ill-humour and every lady's tantrum.'

'That was not a fault of yours, Eilla. The only solution for you and your family would have been to forswear the

Wheel. Such questions have never interested me, but I understand their importance to some.'

Eilla shook her head. 'The irony is that it never mattered to me either, until the proscriptions. At the Temple they say "Make one martyr today and you make a dozen tomorrow."'

Without conscious intent, they made their way to the Pleasaunce, and Arren steered them away from the view commanded from Master Pinch's window.

'I have not helped you as I might have done,' said Arren. 'It has been a cruel time for you, and I have been too busy with other affairs. Can you forgive me?'

They came upon a pond and Eilla sat on the ground in front of it. 'Can you see the fish?' she asked.

Arren peered at the murky water. Under the black sky no fish were in evidence. 'They are too far below the surface.'

'The fish have their own world. Only on occasion can we see them; the rest of the time their affairs take them away from us. Even the most ardent fish-lover would not reprove the fish for their absence. Each of us lives in our own pond, Arren. The wonder is that we ever come together . . .'

'The Wheel is a most individualistic creed,' said Arren.

'I am not speaking specifically of the Wheel,' she said, 'although yes, it does imply a greater sense of responsibility than the Way. But we are all alone, Arren, even if sometimes we are alone together . . .'

'I am unclear as to whether you have forgiven me,' said Arren. These lurches into the spiritual were not part of the Eilla he knew.

'I am trying to say that I recognize that you have concerns other than me. I am sure no one regrets your dalliance with Siedra more than you.'

'You are right there. I was foolish ever to trust her, foolish not to trust you, and most foolish of all for not seeing you in front of my eyes all this time.'

Even in the dark he could see her cheeks flush. 'I am not sure what you are saying.'

He took her hand but continued to look down into the pond. 'Eilla, I have been blind not to see from the start that my feelings have been for you. We were children together before such things could have entered our hearts, and I had not noticed the change in mine.' He glanced up into her face to see a glimmer of tears in her eyes.

'Oh, Arren,' she said. 'Why does this happen too late?'

Arren felt a tremor run through him. 'Too late?'

'There must have been a time that would have been right for this,' she said. 'But it cannot be now. Surely you see that?'

Arren looked back down into the pond. A ripple broke the surface. Out of sight, the fish went about their business.

'It was too much to hope for; too much to deserve,' he said. 'I am sorry to have upset you again. I will pay for Siedra for ever, and I cannot argue against the justice of it.'

'Siedra? This is not about Siedra,' she said quickly.

'But you said it was too late.'

'I did not mean because of Siedra. There was a time when I was the daughter of a respected man in the city, and you were a humble member of Lord Thaume's household. A match between us would have been suitable. Now I am disgraced, and you stand high in Thaume's favour. You will live to be Sir Arren; you cannot consort with a servant girl, and I could not settle for secrecy.'

Arren scanned her face for hidden meanings and found none. 'Is that what you mean by "too late"?'

'Is it not enough?'

'Eilla, I care nothing for such things. Siedra seduced me with consequence and status. If I had to choose between becoming Sir Arren and being with you, can you imagine I would hesitate?'

She took both of his hands. 'It is easy to say in the empty

night with no one around. Do not say it unless you know you can say the same in front of the world.'

Arren leaned forward and kissed her. 'Hissen take them all. I have listened to them for too long. We both know this is right.'

Eilla returned his kiss and further conversation became both redundant and impractical.

7

'I need to get back to the servants' quarters,' Eilla said. 'For now, at least, affairs must proceed as usual.'

'Can you not stay a little longer?' asked Arren with a grin. 'I can offer inducements.'

She stood and pulled Arren to his feet. 'And very compelling inducements they are, but we must be careful for now.'

'You were the one who forswore secrecy.'

'The time for openness will come. It is not yet.'

'It is up to you, Eilla. You have been right so far.'

'Do you want to know what I think?'

'Of course.'

'We should leave Croad altogether. Your prospects will be irredeemably blighted if you stay here, and I have no reason to love the city.'

'Where would we go?'

'There is a whole world for us to choose. Glount, Garganet . . .'

Arren thought for a moment. It would be hard to leave the city, but without Lord Thaume's patronage, and with the perpetual enmity of Siedra, it would be a less comfortable place. He had been well-schooled in warfare, and he knew he could find employment wherever he went.

'What about my family? What will my parents do?'

'I must leave my father too, Arren. If they care for us, they will not begrudge us our happiness. Matten will look after your parents, Clottie mine. We can write to them when we are safe.'

Arren pondered a moment. 'My father would prefer my death to offending Lord Thaume in any event,' he said. 'We will go. I did not care for the folk of Glount. Let us proceed to Garganet.'

She flung her arms around him. 'Thank you! You will see I am right! If we leave, it should be soon. There is no profit in awaiting Siedra's revenge.'

Arren nodded pensively. 'You are right, of course.'

'And if you are wise, you will not tell anyone where you are going. Once we are away you can write a full justification, although you may wish to gloss over Siedra's role in events.'

'Tomorrow night.'

She kissed him. 'I will meet you in the courtyard of The Patient Suitor at midnight,' she said. 'Can you bring a gallumpher and provisions?'

'Of course.'

Hand in hand they walked back to the castle. Once more they kissed and Eilla said: 'Until tomorrow.'

8

Arren had undertaken to spend the next day hunting with Oricien, and soon after dawn they set out for the hills to the north.

'My father has agreed to allow me to go to court next month,' said Oricien. 'You will be coming with me, won't you?'

Arren was tempted to tell Oricien everything – or nearly

everything, at any event. He would have preferred not to lie about his intentions, but Eilla had counselled silence in this case.

'Do you really want me to come? It is a long journey, and I am not going to make any spectacular match.'

'Nonsense, Arren, you must! It is gratifying to see how the people of Croad are regarded in Emmen, and our recent victory over Tardolio has only improved matters. Your father may be a hostage, but already he will have forged a great reputation for himself! There are many tales at court of men who have made good marriages after carrying all before them in tournaments. Why should you not do the same?'

'I am sure the men you refer to are of more illustrious lineage than me.'

'Remember, you will be under the sponsorship of the heir of Croad. No one will dare fleer at you. I should not say this, but Siedra thinks you are rather gallant!'

Arren involuntarily twitched on his gallumpher's reins and the beast stumbled in its stride. 'I am sure you exaggerate,' he said.

'My revelation does not find you indifferent!' cried Oricien. 'I am sure my sister will laugh to hear it. If she has overlooked your birth, you may be doubly certain that the ladies at court will do so.'

'You are mistaken. Nippet stumbled because of the terrain, not my beastcraft.'

'As you will, Arren. Siedra will be in Glount soon enough, whatever she may say.'

'Let us race to the top of the hill,' said Arren, digging his heels into Nippet's side.

Both Oricien and Arren were skilled hunters, but today all the life of the hills seemed fled. The gallumphers enjoyed their exercise, but neither stag nor boar did they see.

'Arren, what do you think happened to Guigot?' asked Oricien as they rode home.

Arren shook his head. 'He was always wily. Maybe he joined the hill bandits, maybe he even struck north for Mettingloom. He may have gone south to Glount and taken passage anywhere.'

'My father worries that he has not been captured.'

'He is one man,' said Arren. 'He can never come near the city without being taken and recognized. For all we know he perished in the wilderness.'

Oricien shook his head. 'Guigot has too much spite to allow himself to die in obscurity. For my money, if we ever see him again, it will be with Tardolio's army.'

Arren laughed. 'Even less reason to worry. By the time Tardolio has gathered the men and the spirit to come back, you will be an old man. With a sister married into the Duchy of Lynnoc, you will always have an army to call on. There are plenty of more pressing matters to dwell on than Guigot.'

'No doubt you are right, Arren. Come, if we press the heels we can be back for dinner.'

9

Arren stabled Nippet and went back to his quarters to change and make his final preparations for departure. Lord Thaume did not take a late table, and he would have time to dine before stealing into the night. He looked around his quarters for the last time. He knew that he was not being fair to Thaume, who had spent time and money educating him in the arts of statecraft and war: his intention had clearly not been to fit him for a clandestine marriage with a dowerless servant. He had every reason to expect that Arren would be a strong support and counsel for Oricien. Perhaps in time he would be able to return; but if not, he had no doubt that he was following his only real course in eloping with Eilla. What was a seat at the lord's table compared with that?

On his pillow he noticed an envelope addressed in a feminine hand, 'Seigneur Arren'. He ripped it open.

> *I need to see you urgently, and in secret. Meet me in Lord Thaume's viatory at eleven bells: we know that he does not use it at night-time.*
>
> *If you value my safety do not try to see me beforehand. I will explain all when I see you.*
>
> *E.*

Arren's heart beat faster. What could be so important that it could not wait until midnight?

He read the letter again. Eilla wrote in a fair lady's hand: he realized that he had never seen her handwriting before. The Gollains put a great premium on reading and writing. Eilla was a credit to whoever had taught her.

Arren was not convinced that the viatory was the best place to meet. Lord Thaume had rebuked him for using it as a meeting place at Guigot's condemnation and would not be pleased to learn of them visiting it again. On the other hand, there were few locations to meet in secrecy, and in the Pleasaunce it was clearly impossible to be secure against eavesdroppers.

Arren sat back in his chair. Of course, Eilla would have thought the question through: she had as much to lose as him if they were caught together. Tomorrow it would not matter – they would be away from the city. Until then, a modicum of caution was appropriate. He chose a fresh set of clothes, and went down to the table.

Arren forced himself to eat although he had no appetite.

It might be a while before he had anything more than the barest rations. He did not drink the wine at all; a clear head was a necessity in what was to come.

In his mind he had already left, he realized. The conversation rumbled on around him but it was as if he were watching a play. Lord Thaume was in a genial humour, ribbing Oricien about his failure to bring anything back from the day's hunting trip; Oricien responded with a sober analysis of the conditions and made occasional appeals to Arren, who gave only perfunctory responses. Master Guiles regaled the company with an anecdote of some lapse of etiquette during his days at court; it would have been tedious even had it not been a story everyone present had heard many times before. Master Coppercake, as was his way, said little. His favoured companion, Master Pinch, was not present, and Arren suspected he had slipped away for good to carry on his researches elsewhere. Sir Langlan, who always enlivened the company, was not present: tonight he was commanding the Guard in their unceasing vigilance for threats from the North.

Arren realized with a touch of regret that he would never be part of this company again. There was no other way for it, and it was a small price to pay to be with Eilla, but he had spent many years among these men, and for some of them he had real affection. One day, he promised himself, when the notoriety had died down and he had established himself in his new life, he would return, and they would see what he had made of himself. Maybe then they would all be easy together again.

'Arren, you are quiet tonight,' said Lord Thaume.

'I am sorry, my lord. I am feeling a touch unwell.'

Lord Thaume's brow furrowed. 'Do not let us keep you, Arren. There are plenty more feasts. Take yourself off to your bed, now.'

Arren nodded. 'Thank you, my lord. I am sure I will be restored tomorrow.'

He walked from the hall for the last time, feeling guilty at taking advantage of Lord Thaume's solicitude, with only a single backward glance. On his way back to his room he picked up some provisions from the pantry. The less they had to forage until they reached Glount, the better.

He left the pantry and then, stepping boldly to deter any questioners he might encounter, made his way to Lord Thaume's viatory. What could Eilla want? Surely she could not be postponing their departure – or might she have changed her mind altogether? He would know soon enough.

He slid the door open, wincing at the creak, and slipped into the room. There was a chill draught: the window through which Guigot had jumped had still not been repaired. He looked around in the dim candlelight but there was no sign of Eilla. He was a few minutes early: Eilla was timing her arrival to a nicety.

He gently moved the arras aside and settled down to wait. He would hear Eilla arrive and no doubt she would think to look behind the arras in any event.

There was a sudden rapping on the door, as if with a sword hilt. 'My lady! Will you open the door?'

It was Fleuraume's voice. What could he possibly want? And who did he think was inside?

While Arren was deciding what to to, the door flew open and Fleuraume crashed in, with three other guards; all had swords drawn. Arren came out from behind the arras. It could not be him they were looking for.

'Fleuraume! What is this?' asked Arren.

'Arren, this grieves me greatly. I had hoped the reports were false.'

'Reports? What are you talking about, Fleuraume? There is a misunderstanding of some sort.'

'Conceivably not,' said Fleuraume. 'Please do not attempt to leave; you would not wish to be restrained.'

Unarmed, with four men facing him, Arren knew he had no choice for now. What would happen when Eilla appeared?

'Heray, fetch Lord Thaume; Gildier, see if you can intercept Lady Siedra.'

The two guards marched off. The odds were still not good, thought Arren, and anyway, what was his crime? How was Siedra involved?

'Fleuraume, will you tell me what this is about?'

'The less you say, the better, lad. You will have your chance soon enough.'

From along the corridor Arren could hear the sound of boots. Lord Thaume came in, his face thunderous. In his wake trailed Oricien and Master Coppercake.

'Bring him outside,' said Lord Thaume. 'And when Siedra appears, bring her too. Send also for Sir Langlan.'

Flanked on either side, Arren stepped out into the Amber Room. Almost immediately another guard appeared with Siedra at his side.

'Arren!' cried Siedra. 'What is happening?'

'We will now learn the truth,' said Lord Thaume, taking his place in his judicial chair. 'Gildier, where did you find Lady Siedra?'

'She was in the corridor outside, my lord. She appeared to be on her way here.'

'Siedra? You were supposed to be at Lady Cerisa's soirée.'

'I had the headache, father.'

Lord Thaume raised his eyebrows. 'A coincidence. Arren too was indisposed, although he appears hale enough now.'

'My lord—'

'Silence, Arren! I will hear you in due course. Siedra, all is known: your scheme has been betrayed.'

'What – How?'

'You will not improve matters for yourself or Arren by feigning girlish ignorance. You have been caught at the most foolish intrigue. A full account is your best course.'

'But—'

'Did you not hear me, girl? One of your ladies has betrayed you, and the proof is Arren's presence awaiting you in my viatory.'

Siedra began to sob. 'I am sorry, Arren, my love. It is too late to dissemble. Father, forgive us!'

Arren looked on in astonishment.

'Arren, will you not tell my father of our love?'

Arren remained dumbstruck.

'Please,' she sobbed. 'Do not deny me now! You said you would be true to me through all.'

'Siedra, this is lunacy!' cried Arren.

'This is the worst blow of all! I can bear my father's fury, but not your indifference. Be brave, my love!'

'My lord, I do not know what Siedra is saying.'

'Enough whimpering, from you both,' said Lord Thaume. 'Siedra, continue your account.'

She knelt before her father. 'My lord, it was not our fault. We tried to hide our feelings from ourselves and each other, but it was no use: they would not be denied. Arren and I have been lovers these many months. We would send each other messages through the servant girl Eilla, and he would come to my chambers with such ardour. We knew it was wrong, but our love was so strong. Arren wished to tell you, but I knew your wrath would be terrible. We have been so foolish, but I cannot regret a second of it! Please forgive us.'

Lord Thaume's face had taken on a purple tint which seemed to threaten an apoplexy. Oricien's jaw hung loose; Sir Langlan, who had slipped into the back of the room, slowly shook his head. Coppercake looked down at his feet.

'Your account at least tallies with my information,' said

Lord Thaume after a pause. 'That does not make your conduct any more excusable, but it helps me to establish the facts. I will consider your punishment later, and indeed that of Eilla, from whom I would have expected better. Meanwhile, I must turn to Arren. What have you to say, boy?'

Arren swallowed hard. 'It is all lies, my lord.'

'Lies? You call my daughter a liar?'

'Yes, sir.'

'Your evasions only magnify your offence. My daughter has admitted this shameful misalliance in front of us all. It is she who is degraded. Can you not be a gentleman and confess your own deeds?'

'The account is false, my lord.'

Lord Thaume's mouth pinched into an almost invisible line.

'You have not deflowered my daughter? Such matters can be verified with ease, if little dignity.'

'No, my lord,' said Arren, conscious that he was forked in an inescapable trap. The truth would not save him either.

'Mistress Eulalia will be brought forth to assess Lady Siedra's virginity. I hope you are man enough to deny her this ordeal.'

'If she is not pure, my lord, the fault may not be mine.'

'Impudent whelp!' roared Lord Thaume, rising from his seat and striking Arren in the face. 'You deflower my daughter, debauch her repeatedly, deny that you have done so, and seek to portray her as a wanton. And to think that I took you into my home, raised you from your miserable birth, gave you every advantage and education. This is how you repay me. Be assured that no one mocks Lord Thaume in this way! Your punishment will be swift and harsh.'

Master Coppercake stepped forward. 'My lord, may I speak?'

Lord Thaume looked at him in surprise. 'Your counsel is always to be valued.'

'In my lore of mathematics we speak often of proofs. One fact is laid upon another in such a way that deeper truths are revealed, and that which we may only suspect is proved.'

'This is not the time for a mathematics lesson, Coppercake.'

'My point, my lord, is that notions of proof apply to life as well. You do not, in this case, have what I would consider a proof. You have two sets of "facts", Lady Siedra's account, and Arren's. They are contradictory, and at most one set can be true. You have no means for distinguishing which is correct.'

'Have I not? I find Arren waiting in my viatory, which I have explicitly forbidden him; my daughter pleads illness and then trips forth to meet him; her maid coming to me with the tale of what I would find, and her suppositions being borne out. The evidence is strong.'

'But not conclusive, my lord.'

'Arren, if your account is true, can you explain Siedra's motives?'

Arren looked back gloomily. If he said that it was spite and jealousy because he had thrown her over, it would go no better for him than Siedra's fabrication. The essential offence was that he had deflowered her; she had simply arranged events so that Lord Thaume would learn of it.

'Perhaps, my lord, she thinks that if she is held to be no maid, Duke Panarre's family will not wish to pursue the match.'

'Panarre is not so choosy, especially where dowries are concerned. I give Siedra credit for more sense, and more honesty. Everyone seems to have an opinion: Sir Langlan, what of you?'

Sir Langlan shrugged. 'Truth is hardly to the point here.

Tonight you must judge your daughter a liar, or Arren. You cannot do anything but believe Siedra, since otherwise you ruin her. That is "truth".'

Lord Thaume looked at him sourly. 'You do not credit my integrity highly.'

Sir Langlan gave a half-smile. 'Think rather that I esteem your statecraft.'

'Oricien, have you any light to shed?'

Oricien looked hard at both Siedra and Arren. 'I have observed recently a partiality on Siedra's part for Arren. I thought it nothing but a fancy. Today I mentioned it, almost in jest, to Arren, and his reaction was extreme and alarmed. Now I understand why.'

Lord Thaume shot his cuffs. 'I have heard enough. Arren, there can be no doubt of your acts, and your lack of shame and remorse. Siedra is equally guilty; however, she has at least acknowledged her acts, and the range of sanctions I may take against my own daughter is limited. As far as your own culpability goes, gelding is the most appropriate punishment. Clearly you have not forced Siedra against her will, so the noose goes too far. Your immoderate lusts, however, demand suppression.'

'No!' bellowed Arren. His bowels turned to water. 'I beg you, not that!'

Lord Thaume rose from his seat and his hand dropped to his sword-belt. Arren looked around in desperation. Lord Thaume drew his sword.

'My lord!' cried Arren. 'Have mercy!'

'Silence,' said Lord Thaume in a clipped voice. 'Your father would not beg so.'

He put his sword on the floor and spun it on the hilt boss. The sword circled three or four times, coming to rest with the point facing the altar.

'I am mindful of the great service your father has given

me; also of your own valour on the battlefield, and your role in uncovering Guigot's treachery. On this occasion, I am inclined to mercy. Your sentence, then, is exile, on pain of death. You see that the sword points north. You will be taken from the Traitors' Gate, with a gallumpher and provisions for three days. You are required to ride in the direction of the sword until you quit my territory. Any man of Croad who sees you has my leave to kill you on the spot.'

Arren's legs felt weak. He was not to be gelded, but exile was a cruel blow. He thought of Eilla, even now waiting at The Patient Suitor.

'In addition,' said Lord Thaume, 'I must judge the case of the girl Eilla, whom I defended against the Lord High Viator at the jeopardy of my own rule. Words cannot express the depth of her betrayal. I will spin the sword again, and she too must follow it to exile: and lest Arren should be tempted to follow her, I will not carry out the sentence until tomorrow.'

'My lord,' said Coppercake. 'You rule in defiance of the evidence, and surely Eilla has a right to speak in her own defence.'

'Enough, Coppercake. I heard your counsel, and have given it weight. Nonetheless, my sentence stands. Arren and Eilla are both clearly guilty of the offences in question, and further debate will not alter the nature of their betrayal of their true lord.'

'I cannot serve such a lord,' said Coppercake. 'Good and bad are mingled in you to an unusual degree. The viators have much work to bring you to Harmony.'

'You may leave my service at any time, Master Coppercake. I am no tyrant.'

'I used to think not, my lord.'

There was a silence as Lord Thaume considered his options. All present were aware that violence was one of them.

'You will know best whether your wages are in arrears,' he said in a tight voice. 'Apply to Cyngier for any shortfall before you leave.'

'I have always ensured I was paid in advance, my lord. I can no longer with dignity serve you; by your leave I will accompany Arren.'

Lord Thaume raised his eyebrows. 'So be it.' He rose from his seat. 'Fleuraume, accompany Arren yourself, with ten of your best men. I will not have a repeat of Guigot's escape.'

'Yes, my lord.'

As Arren was led away by the guards he passed Siedra. She looked him in the eye and her mouth twisted into a sneering smile. She pursed her lips into a kiss as he was marched past. She had her revenge: not just on Arren, but on Eilla too.

15

Croad

I

Beauceron heard sounds below and looked out from the window of The Patient Suitor across the river. Virnesto heard the noise and walked across to join him.

'What is happening?' asked Virnesto.

'It sounds like a battle-horn,' said Beauceron steadily. 'Surely Oricien cannot mean to fight.'

Brissio leaped from his seat and ran to the window. 'At last! He will fight like a man and die like one! Quoon! Saddle my gallumpher! Lorin – my armour! Rouse the Winter Knights!'

'This is premature,' said Virnesto. 'We must assess Oricien's dispositions.'

Beauceron pushed past both men and took the stairs two at a time on the way down. Whatever the Croadasque were planning, they would not be coming across the bridge – and that meant any fight would be to the north of the river.

He leaped onto his gallumpher and galloped for the pontoon bridge. He had chosen his men with care, and he would not wish to fight anywhere but alongside them. As he crossed the bridge the angle of his travel allowed him to see a column of cavalry charging from the North Gate. It was not an army;

Oricien had not resolved on a decisive battle. Instead he had unleashed a cavalry charge: no more than fifty or so men. What was he planning?

Beauceron spurred his gallumpher the harder. The Winter infantry milled around in confusion. Rather than form a square to oppose the cavalry they dived aside. Not for the first time, he cursed the inferior quality of the Mettingloom troops. His own men would fight better, but they were only forty. Until the infantry's officers could instil some order, the Croadasque cavalry would have a free rein.

Into the air went a volley of fire arrows, arcing up into the sun until they were lost from view, and then dropping back into sight. Beauceron realized what they were doing: the trebuchets! Beauceron cursed; his gallumpher snorted under him as his spurs drew blood. Why could the Winter Army not see what the cavalry were intending?

Beauceron knew he was too far away to affect the skirmish's conclusion. The cavalry would either have destroyed the trebuchets or been routed before he was on the scene.

Even as he rode towards the scene he saw a flash of fire as one of the varnished tarpaulins took light. Half of his siege power was gone in a single arrow. He put his silver horn to his lips, and saw that fifteen or so of his men had saddled up: the others were gathered around the surviving trebuchet.

Beauceron's cavalrymen charged into the Croadasque. They were outnumbered but had the advantage of taking their opponents in the flank. In addition, they were proficient at skirmish warfare: they spent most summers doing little else. Five Croadasque went down, ten: they were on the point of flight. The lead rider, who was past the Mettingloom assault, turned and went back to the aid of his men. Beauceron nodded in admiration: this was a brave man, and a good commander. His armour was polished to a high sheen and his helmet dinted from previous combats.

Even amidst the melee, another fire arrow flew out, and flew true. The second trebuchet took fire like its cousin. Beauceron had lost both expensive siege engines in half an hour's inattention. It was no one's fault but his own.

The Croadasque commander saw that he had been successful. There was no point in engaging in further combat. He pointed back to the city and wheeled his gallumpher around.

The remaining Croadasque fled for the city, Beauceron's riders on their heels. Beauceron turned his gallumpher to the right; he could join the fight before they reached the city walls.

The Croadasque spread out to baffle the pursuit. The commander was at the rear of the group, trying to draw the chase after him.

You have to die, thought Beauceron. *You are too brave to be suffered to live.*

He set his own gallumpher at the man. The commander saw him coming and wheeled to face him. Beauceron continued his momentum and ducked under the blow aimed at his head, twisting as he did so to thrust his own sword at the vulnerable point under the arm. The movement was too violent and he toppled from his gallumpher to fall heavily on his side. The Croadasque commander had also been unseated and the two men lay on the ground. Beauceron could see blood seeping through the knight's armour.

He pushed himself erect with his sword hilt. The prudent act was to skewer the man past his gorget before he could rise. Shaking his head at his weakness, he stepped back. 'Stand and fight,' he said. 'Or you may yield.'

Beauceron could see nothing of the knight's face behind the grille of his helmet. His armour was considerably heavier than Beauceron's chain mail, and it was only with difficulty that he raised himself to his feet. 'I yield nothing,' he said in a voice muffled within the helmet. 'If you want my life, you must take it, boy.'

Beauceron's eyes narrowed. He feinted once, lunged at the knight, who parried at the last second and stepped forward inside Beauceron's swing, confident that his armour made him proof against all but the shrewdest thrust; Beauceron skipped back. Trading blows at close range with a fully armoured man would be fatal. 'Stand and fight, boy!' called the knight. Blood was still oozing from the side of his armour, staining his white surcoat. He stepped towards Beauceron again, and Beauceron edged away, to feel his gallumpher at his back. He had nowhere to go. The knight raised his sword, prepared to bring it down on Beauceron's head; then his knees buckled and he sank forward to the ground. Beauceron moved in towards him: this time there would be no chivalry. But the knight toppled forward. 'You dog,' he hissed as he fell. There was a thud as his armour hit the turf; his helmet, loosened in the fall from his gallumpher, slid off his head. He lay still in the dirt, his long grey hair matted with sweat, and a pool of blood grew at his right-hand side.

Beauceron kicked the sword from the knight's mailed hand, and gingerly turned him over. The eyes were cloudy, but he was still alive. His beard was greyer than Beauceron had remembered. 'Sir Langlan,' he said softly. 'You die well; I salute you.'

Sir Langlan looked up, his eyes glassy. He coughed and a bubble of blood rose in his mouth. 'You!' he hissed, and sank back. The long and eventful life of Sir Langlan was over.

The other riders reached the sanctuary of the North Gate. Sir Langlan lay dead along with the others who had been killed earlier in the skirmish. Beauceron pulled his mail hood back from his head and wiped his brow. Sir Langlan might have died, but his mission had been successful: the Winter Army no longer had trebuchets to raze the walls of Croad. The city could now survive until its food ran out.

He walked over to where the trebuchets continued to blaze. The varnish of the tarpaulins had ensured the conflagration was complete. It would not be possible to salvage or repair the equipment. Monetto leaned against a provisions wagon while Rostovac applied a bandage to a deep cut on his forearm.

'Are you hurt?' Beauceron asked.

'Nothing too daunting,' said Monetto. 'But the tre-buchets . . .'

'I have much to explain to Brissio,' said Beauceron. 'If I had not been chasing after Lady Isola, things might have gone differently.'

Monetto gestured to the ring of infantry surrounding the city. 'Fifty men should not have got close,' he said. 'They are buffoons led by buffoons.'

'It may not be possible to convince Prince Brissio of that.'

Monetto looked quizzically at Beauceron. 'It is unlike you to be downcast after a minor reverse.'

Beauceron gave a half-smile. 'You do not know who led the assault.'

Monetto laughed. 'Not Oricien, I'll wager.'

Beauceron paused a moment. 'It was Sir Langlan. He was too old to fight and he died for it.'

Monetto was silent while he took in the news. 'Langlan was an indifferent knight, but a good man. There was a sadness that never left him.'

'I had no quarrel with him,' said Beauceron. 'He did not set out to do me harm.'

'I have no truck with the viators,' said Monetto, 'but his death was better than his life. By any standards he reached the end of the Way of Harmony.'

Beauceron thought back to the drinking, fighting and

wenching which had characterized Sir Langlan's life. It was hard to see how he would have derived satisfaction from dying a moral exemplar. And satisfied or not, he was dead nonetheless. His vitality, one of the greatest Beauceron had known, was extinguished as thoroughly as a timid old woman's. If there was a meaning here he was at a loss to understand it.

2

'Your presence is requested at The Patient Suitor, sir. Immediately.' The soldier in Prince Brissio's silver-grey livery bowed and withdrew from Beauceron's tent. Beauceron carefully set down his goblet. The interview was likely to be marked by recrimination, much of it justified. The loss of the trebuchets marked a potentially decisive shift in the balance of the siege. A seasoned commander would be able to assess the situation with discrimination, but Brissio lacked the qualities of sober reflection. It was hard, however, for Beauceron to represent his own capacities in a favourable light when he had managed to lose both Lady Isola and his trebuchets in less than a day. His revenge was not yet going to plan.

Beauceron climbed aboard his gallumpher, rode across the pontoon bridge and soon found himself at The Patient Suitor and conducted to the rooms on the top floor.

'My lord; General Virnesto. I await your pleasure,' he said.

Brissio leaned back in his chair and put his feet on the table. 'Lord Oricien rides to meet us under a flag of truce this afternoon.'

'So soon?' said Beauceron. 'He cannot mean to surrender yet.' *Particularly with our trebuchets gone.*

'He is surrounded,' said Brissio. 'Our forces overwhelm him. His provisions may be low.'

'He will not surrender yet,' said Beauceron. 'He awaits relief, and he will believe it to be coming. The glorious ride of Sir Langlan was not the gambit of a demoralized army.'

Virnesto rose from his seat and looked from the southern window.

'Their bellies are shrinking. Relief: that is the key, is it not? If relief does not come, he is beaten. Even if we cannot raze the walls, he knows he cannot match us in the field, or he would have fought before he let us take the Voyne. How certain is his knowledge of relief?'

Beauceron paused. 'For all his caution, Oricien is no coward; neither is he a fool. I can only assume he has reasonable assurance that a relief force will arrive.'

'Enguerran or Trevarre?' asked Virnesto.

'When I was in Croad, relations were better with Emmen than Glount,' said Beauceron. 'On the other hand, Enguerran has never shown any interest in the North. If I were gambling, I would expect a modest relief force from Glount – and I doubt that Trevarre can field a large enough force to worry us.'

'We should have been in the city tomorrow if we had retained the trebuchets,' said Prince Brissio.

'Perhaps; perhaps not,' said Beauceron. 'It is possible to exaggerate their effectiveness. In any event, I thought you disdained a victory achieved by throwing stones.'

'What I disdain,' said Brissio with narrowed eyes, 'is no victory at all. What I disdain is watching the spring turn into summer while I sit here in idleness. What I disdain is sitting like a rat in a trap waiting for Enguerran to bring his Immaculates north.'

'If we must take the city by storm,' said Beauceron, 'we may yet do so.'

Virnesto frowned. 'The stratagem is heavy in blood. The walls are sound. Many men would die.'

'We have escaliers,' said Beauceron.

'So we have. But we still need to climb them, and put men in the city. It is a last resort.'

Brissio looked at them through squinting eyes. 'If ladders are the only way to take the city, we will do so. On this occasion Beauceron is right, although the expedient becomes necessary only through his negligence.'

'I will be at the head of the assault, my lord,' said Beauceron. 'No doubt you will wish to hearten your own troops in the same way.'

Brissio stood abruptly from his seat. 'If you can show me how my cavalry may ride up the siege ladders, I will gladly take your counsel. Otherwise, a commander has more important duties.'

'As you wish, my lord. I merely thought to pre-empt any potential innuendoes regarding your appetite for combat. Naturally you will feel that such whispers are not worth the effort of discountenancing.'

Brissio's hand dropped to his sword hilt. 'You speak with dangerous latitude to the man who will be your King. Once the city is taken I will ensure you show me the respect due to a prince.'

'On another matter, my lord,' said Beauceron with a shrug. 'It would be better if I were not present when Oricien arrives this afternoon. I will wait in my tent.'

A crafty smile spread across Brissio's face. 'I assume that you do not wish Oricien to recognize you and reveal your identity. This is foolish vanity.'

'I assure you, my lord, that the sight of me will only stiffen

Oricien's resolve. If he is coming to discuss the terms of his surrender my presence will not help.'

'He is right, my lord,' said Virnesto.

Brissio grunted with ill-grace.

'You are both old women, afraid to fight; but if this is your counsel, so be it.'

3

The mid-afternoon bell rang in Croad as Lord Oricien rode out from the River Gate on a white strider. Beauceron, who was concealed in an ante-room next to Brissio's reception chamber, was surprised to see that he came alone. He could not accuse the Lord of Croad of lacking courage.

Oricien was preceded by the clatter of his boots on the wooden stairs. Beauceron slid aside the small grille allowing him sight of the reception room. It would be interesting to assess Oricien's demeanour, and to see how Prince Brissio conducted himself.

Oricien stepped into the room and bowed to the Prince. He was unarmoured, garbed only in a black cape, a white shirt and black breeches, with a sigil at his breast. At his side hung his rapier.

'I am Lord Oricien,' he said in a level voice.

Beauceron noted the easy assurance of his address. His fair hair had receded to a widow's peak and his cheekbones were more apparent than he had remembered, but the main change in the intervening years was a self-possession he had never previously commanded.

'You are welcome. I am Prince Brissio; Captain-General Virnesto commands my infantry; these are my aides Isello and Capedralce. Please be seated. Will you take refreshment?'

Oricien gave an infinitesimal nod.

'We have not yet dined. Perhaps you will join us for dinner,' said Brissio in a hearty voice.

Oricien held up a hand. 'I thank you, but no. I will eat nothing which is not available to my soldiers – unless you wish to extend your invitation to my entire fighting force, in which case I accept with pleasure.'

'This will not be possible,' said Virnesto. 'Although if you were to invite our army to sup in Croad, we might share a banquet of good fellowship.'

Oricien permitted himself a wintry smile. 'I doubt that our hospitality would be to your suiting. We will each keep to our own provisions and territories, which is perhaps for the best.'

'As you will,' said Brissio. 'Let us at least sit while we discuss our business. I take it you are familiar with these surroundings.'

Oricien raised his eyebrows. 'The Voyne falls under my rule, but The Patient Suitor is a low tavern: I have never set foot in it until today.'

'Be that as it may,' said Brissio. 'You requested an audience with me, and I am happy to oblige. Do you care to state your business?'

Oricien crossed his legs. 'The presence of the northern army is naturally inconvenient to me. A relief force is on its way, and we would all benefit were you to depart before its arrival. The destruction of your siege engines makes it unlikely you can take the city by force.'

Virnesto gave a soft chuckle. Brissio was nonplussed. 'My Lord Oricien, the course is impractical. We have sailed south with the express intention of capturing the city. We do not fear the forces of Glount, and you have admitted that your food supplies are low. We will not depart until we have the keys to the city.'

Oricien nodded as if to himself. 'I suspected you would

say as much. You are the dupes of one "Beauceron" who pursues a scheme of his own. There will be no benefit to you in taking a city you cannot hold.'

'Allow us to be the judge of our own good,' said Virnesto. 'We have come for the city, and we shall have it. All that remains is to discuss the terms of your surrender.'

'Name them,' said Oricien. He looked Brissio directly in the eye.

Virnesto said: 'If you yield up the city, no harm will come to the inhabitants. The soldiers will be suffered to march out bearing arms, on their parole not to return for a year and a day.'

'And if I do not?'

'The normal rules of plunder will apply. Our soldiers will sack the city: the men will be killed, and the women violated. This is not pretty, but it is war. You may act to spare them.'

Oricien sipped at his tisane. 'You must take the city before you can make good your threats. Our walls are strong and, as I noted, you no longer have trebuchets.'

Virnesto stood up and walked to the window overlooking the bridge. 'Trebuchets do not take cities; hunger does.'

'An assault on our walls, starving defenders or no, can only cost lives you would rather preserve.'

'You cannot beat us in the field,' said Virnesto. 'Your only hope is that we leave, either through hunger, disease, or defeat. We are supplied by boat from Hengis Port and health in the camp is excellent. We can only be defeated in battle by a large and well-led relief army. Do you concur?'

After a pause Oricien nodded. 'Essentially.'

'If your relief does not arrive, Croad must fall.'

Oricien said nothing.

'Your food is running out,' continued Virnesto. 'Are you eating the cats yet? The day cannot be far away. Let me make this offer: you need not surrender today, but if your relief army has not arrived in a week, your doom is sealed. You may surrender with honour at that point, and march out under the rules of safe-conduct.'

'Alternatively,' said Prince Brissio, 'you may bring out your army tomorrow and we shall fight.'

Both Virnesto and Oricien looked at the Prince with ill-concealed contempt.

'Thinking of realistic outcomes,' said Virnesto, 'what do you make of my terms?'

Beauceron could see in Oricien's face the realization that he had no choice. If Trevarre did not arrive, there was no hope. Oricien nodded quickly.

'Very well,' he said, 'subject to two conditions.'

'They are?' said Virnesto.

'First, I require a fortnight, not a week. Our supplies are not so low as you believe.'

Virnesto gave a brisk acquiescence.

'Second, you will know that I have Lady Isola in the city, formerly one of your party. She is of course my betrothed.'

'Just so,' said Brissio.

'She speaks at length of one "Beauceron", the animus behind your invasion. He is the infamous Dog of the North and, Lady Isola believes, a renegade lordling from Croad.'

Virnesto gave a half-smile. 'He is not accustomed to view himself in those terms.'

Oricien continued. 'I am given to understand that your camp is not a garden of universal amity. Specifically, Beauceron is not popular within the Winter Court. Prince Brissio, I believe there is considerable ill-will between you.'

Brissio said nothing, but a nerve in his cheek twitched.

'My second condition is this: Beauceron has long plundered the land around Croad as the Dog of the North. This is an offence which cries out for stern punishment. Since he is an encumbrance to the Winter Court, you may hand him over to my justice.'

'You wish us to hand over the Dog of the North?' asked Virnesto in astonishment.

'Exactly so. It is a small enough price.'

'No,' said Virnesto.

'Yes,' said Brissio. 'When you march out of the city I will deliver him to you myself.'

Behind the screen Beauceron gave a grim smile to himself. *We shall see who faces justice.*

'Then we have agreement,' said Oricien. 'If my relief has not arrived within the fortnight, I shall march out of the city with my men under a safe-conduct, and you will give me Beauceron. If my relief arrives, our arrangements are void, although if you wish to hand over Beauceron nonetheless I will take him.'

Brissio rose. 'We are grateful for your wisdom, my lord.'

Oricien bowed. 'I must observe that should you take Croad, you will never hold it. Your best course remains withdrawal; but if you do not perceive that for yourself, the dice will fall as they must. The Way of Harmony is followed regardless.'

He turned and left the room.

Immediately Virnesto said: 'You will not give him Beauceron?'

Brissio gave a wide grin. 'Naturally. He betrayed my father and escaped death; he fleers at my high birth; now we shall have our revenge. He will die as the common criminal he is.' He held up his hand to forestall Virnesto's objection. 'I am resolved. Do not attempt to deflect me.'

Prince Brissio and Virnesto went outside to review the dispositions of their troops and inform the captains south of the river of the new realities. Beauceron gave them a few minutes to depart and slipped out of The Patient Suitor via a back entrance. Brissio's decision came as no surprise, but it changed the situation significantly. Brissio had not needed to agree to Oricien's stipulation: the Lord of Croad was in no position to bargain, for his food ran ever lower. Brissio's agreement was determined by malice. Beauceron felt a ripple running his spine: one thing he understood was vengeance, and he resolved to settle with the Prince when circumstances permitted. He wondered whether Virnesto would attempt to warn him of Brissio's treachery – but he knew the general had sworn fealty to the Winter Court, and owed Beauceron no particular loyalty.

He had himself rowed over the river and walked back around the camp to allow his thoughts to settle. The guard on the city wall lacked animation, and there was a palpable air of slackness around the Mettingloom troops. Clearly the concord between Brissio and Oricien had become common knowledge. Why fight when in two weeks all would be resolved peacefully? The treasures of Croad, such as they were, would be available to all without the need for bloodshed.

Beauceron shook his head in dissatisfaction. There would be blood shed, and it would be his, unless he could contrive an escape. He expected in due course to meet a violent death, but how galling it would be to be undone by the lubberly Brissio!

He walked back to the section of the camp where his own men were stationed. They lay around in attitudes of negligence, Monetto among them.

'What is happening here?' asked Beauceron. 'Why are you not drilling? My orders to Monetto were clear.'

Rostovac laid down the stick he was whittling with his knife. 'There seems little purpose in risking death or injury when Oricien is packing to leave. If Emmen troops come, we will fight them, but there is nothing else for us to do.'

'False!' said Beauceron. 'Prince Brissio plans to hand me over to Oricien when he marches out of the city. If we do not take it in advance of surrender, I am betrayed.'

Monetto sat erect from his lounging posture. 'This is infamous!'

'Just so. New expedients are necessary.'

'We cannot construct new trebuchets in a fortnight, even had we the materials. You must storm the city.'

Beauceron rubbed the stubble on his chin. 'Virnesto cavils at the cost in lives. Brissio cares nothing for the lives of his men but he will not risk a repulse when he can gain the city through a fortnight's indolence.'

Monetto grimaced. 'We cannot take Croad with forty men.'

'I will not be thwarted, Monetto. It is my destiny to take the city, with only one man if necessary. What I cannot do by force I will do by guile.'

5

Soon after sunrise towards the end of the truce, Prince Brissio presented himself at Beauceron's tent. Beauceron was already awake and taking breakfast.

'Good morning, my lord,' he said, not troubling to rise. 'It is rare to find you north of the river. Will you take a kipper?'

Brissio sat heavily on a field chair designed for a smaller

frame. 'Thank you, no. I have come to discuss dispositions with you.'

'Dispositions?'

'Come, man, do not fence. Lord Oricien surrenders tomorrow! Croad is mine! I would not have the event lacking in ceremony.'

'This is not a palace ball.'

'Do not be so prickly, Beauceron! We have not always enjoyed complete concord, I agree, but the time for pettiness is past! There is glory enough to go round. I will have avenged Jehan's Steppe, you will have whatever satisfaction you seek. Now is the time for cordiality.'

Beauceron carefully conveyed a piece of bread to his mouth. 'Such statesmanship augurs well for your future and Mettingloom's, my lord.'

'Excellent!' Brissio beamed. 'I have sent to Oricien to arrange for his surrender at sunset. It is my wish that you and Virnesto are on hand for the moment, for who has earned the right more? I would not have you sulking away in your tent.'

Beauceron permitted himself a slight smile. 'You prefer to have me where you can see me, my lord.'

Brissio frowned. 'Have I not spoken of our new mood of amity? Come, I will let you into a secret, although I had intended it as a surprise for the morrow.'

Beauceron raised his eyebrows.

'I intend to honour you in accordance with your merits, before the very walls of Croad,' he said, with a glint in his eye.

'You do me too much honour, my lord.'

'Both you and Captain-General Virnesto will be knighted,' he said. 'How does the name of Sir Beauceron sound? You will be a Snowdrop Knight.'

'You are a most magnanimous lord.'

Brissio nodded in a private reverie. 'The matter is settled, then,' he said. 'I will be taking Oricien's surrender at The Patient Suitor as the sun goes down.' He rose and stalked from the tent.

From outside came a hubbub of hoofs and voices. Beauceron rose, brushed the crumbs from his shirt and ducked under the flap.

'What is the meaning of this?' cried Brissio. Before him, on gallumphers, were Captain-General Virnesto and a soldier in Beauceron's livery. They dismounted.

'My lord, all is changed!' said Virnesto in voice tight with tension. 'King Enguerran is on his way!'

Brissio looked all around as if to see the King's army. 'What is this? Enguerran? Where?'

'Half a day's march south,' said Virnesto. 'He has brought much of his strength.'

Brissio paled. 'What is the source of this information?'

Virnesto jerked his head towards the soldier. 'It seems some of Beauceron's men were plundering the countryside. This fellow ranged south, and saw troops.'

Brissio stepped close to the man. 'What is your name? Could you be wrong?'

The soldier rubbed a long chin. 'I am Tocchieto, my lord. There can be no error. I have ridden with Beauceron these past eight years, and I know troops. Enguerran's personal standard flies high. He has many infantry and cavalry – more than we have here.'

Brissio looked at Virnesto, who said nothing.

Beauceron asked Tocchieto: 'How closely were you able to scrutinize the forces?'

'Well enough. Since I imagine I will be fighting them, I took care to glean as much information as possible.'

'Is this man reliable?' asked Virnesto.

Beauceron nodded briskly. 'He is one of my best men, if over-fond of the pleasures of the field.' He frowned at

Tocchieto, who responded with a gap-toothed grin. 'Did he have any siege engines?'

Tocchieto thought for a moment. 'No, my lord. He had baggage wagons, of course, but for certain there was no trebuchet.'

Brissio licked his lips. 'King Enguerran is a bloodthirsty man. His wrath is best avoided.'

'Do you suggest lifting the siege, my lord?' asked Beauceron with a sardonic smile.

'Can we not keep the information from Oricien?'

'He will be here in half a day. It will be hard to disguise his presence at that point.'

'We have only one choice,' said Beauceron. 'We must storm the city.'

Virnesto frowned.

'Consider, my lord,' Beauceron said to Brissio. 'If we are caught on the plain, we will be trapped between Enguerran's larger army and Oricien's men behind the walls. Once we take the city, Enguerran cannot extract us without siege engines.'

'We will be trapped!' said Brissio in a high voice.

'Better to be trapped behind the walls than on the plains. The Summer Armies can relieve us.'

Brissio looked around. 'We will starve as Oricien's men starve.'

'We can keep men in the field. My men can live off the land, and they can ravage the countryside. Enguerran will soon come to terms.'

Brissio ran his hand through his hair. 'Virnesto?'

'Either we raise the siege now, my lord, in which case Enguerran may drive us into the sea; or we assault the city today.'

Brissio straightened his doublet. 'So be it, General. Sound the assault!'

6

Beauceron stood at the foot of the ladder looking up at the walls. Never before had they seemed so tall. From high above, Oricien's archers fired down into the press of men. He signalled to his own archers, who set up a concerted fire at the men on the city walls. With curses the defenders drew back, and Beauceron pulled on a steel cap and dashed up the ladder with his own men, including Tocchieto and Rostovac behind him. Something clattered off his helmet. From above he heard cries of 'Oil, oil!' and shuddered. He was no stranger to battle, but this was something new. He tensed his shoulders.

'Come on, lads!' he cried. 'Before they burn us.' He looked down for a vertiginous moment: he had thought only to climb a couple of rungs, but he was almost at the top of the ladder. Tocchieto pressed at his heels. Above him a soldier in a ragged leather hauberk drew back a battleaxe: before he could complete his stroke, an arrow from the ground sent him plunging forwards over the wall. Two more rungs!

The press of men defending the walls grew thicker. Beauceron's ladder was the one closest to a breach, but the defenders jostled so thickly they did not have space to bring their own weapons to bear. All that was preventing him from entering the city was the sheer bulk of men before him. From below, Tocchieto saw what was happening and levered his cupped hands under Beauceron's boot. He was thrust upwards, propelled into the air and headfirst over the wall. He rolled as he landed on the walkway; then he was on his feet, his sword in his hand. The defenders turned to face him: before they could realize their error, Beauceron's men surged over the wall and fell upon the disorganized Croadasque.

Beauceron's men were armoured, battle-hardened, ready

to fight: their opponents wore whatever had come to hand, and had been expecting to hand the city over by nightfall. By the time they had realized the changed situation, the wall had been taken in several places along the western boundary. He watched as the West Gate swung open, taken by Virnesto's men from another ladder. The broad street leading to the market square offered no barrier to the troops. Virnesto's herald blew a triple call. From his vantage point atop the walls Beauceron could see Brissio's cavalry assembling. Once they were in the city they would be unstoppable.

From the market square came Oricien's cavalry with his own banner flying at the head: a pitifully small force. A gallumpher drew a rattlejack containing a cauldron of oil alongside. It was too late to pour it on the ladders now: the attackers were already in the city. The cart trundled its futile course ahead of the cavalry. Oricien, on his white gallumpher, rode alongside it. Would he surrender? The city would be sacked in any event: he had little to lose by fighting on.

Beauceron looked down to where Brissio's gilded armour rode at the head of his cavalry. His right hand was high in the air: he dropped it and spurred his gallumpher forward, leading the triumphal cavalry charge. Beauceron shook his head in disgust: he had left no reserve at all, but chosen to charge with his entire cavalry. In the circumstances it would make no difference, but it was the mark of an amateur – an amateur who intended to see him dead, he reminded himself with a start. He could not stop his heart thrilling at the sound of the gallumphers' hoofs as they clattered across the cobbles of the street, the cries of the knights and the snorting of their mounts.

Oricien signalled to two of his men, who pulled on a rope and positioned the rattlejack athwart the street. It would hardly delay the cavalry charge, but it might give Oricien's men a chance to escape and fight again. Brissio's cavalry continued their charge, howling with bloodlust. As he watched, one of the gallumphers slipped and fell to the ground, bringing another with it. Beauceron noticed that the cobbles were darker here, and he realized – Oricien had pulled the plug from the oil container. At the speed Brissio's cavalry were moving they had no chance. One gallumpher after another hit the spreading patch of oil: on the slick surface of the cobbles they fell before they realized what was happening. From the houses on either side of the streets archers fired from the windows into the prone cavalrymen. Oricien's men dismounted and waded in among the fallen knights as they scrabbled to rise in their heavy armour. The sun glinted on the bodkins of the defenders as they stabbed the knights through their gorgets and visors. The oil mixed with the slick of blood leaking from the knights' armour.

It was slaughter. Beauceron, too far away to intervene, watched as Brissio scrambled to his feet, surrounded by a phalanx of knights who had managed to rein in before they reached the oily cobbles. Brissio was hauled aloft and skittered back down the road with the few knights who had stopped in time: no more than ten in total. Brissio had managed to destroy his entire cavalry in less then ten minutes. Beauceron shook his head. *I hate you, Oricien, but that was magnificent. Your father could have done no better.*

Beauceron removed his helmet and dashed towards the fray, his men at his heels. He had to find Virnesto and launch a counter-attack. With Brissio's cavalry lost, Oricien could yet win the battle.

Virnesto had managed to secure the northwest quadrant of the city, which contained houses but few fortifications. They were cut off from the bulk of the army outside, which Brissio was trying to bring into order. There was a real danger, Beauceron realized, that Virnesto would be killed or captured before a larger force could rescue them. The

Mettingloom officers were not generally of a high standard. Without Virnesto they would surely be beaten.

He gave Monetto orders to rally the troops outside and plunged into the press of fighting in the streets. He needed to find Oricien: he might have to take any vengeance which presented itself to him. But where had the Lord of Croad gone? He had not yet conceded defeat, that much was sure. Oil, that was the key. It had beaten the cavalry, and it could yet hamper the infantry. And where was the oil stored? He grinned to himself: the viatory.

The shrieks and howls of the fighting reached his ears as if damped by cloth. They could have been from another city, and in a sense they were. He ran through the market square, noting as he did so one gibbet set away from the others, with his own wolf's-head standard flapping limply above it. Isola had not exaggerated: Oricien had built him his own gallows. He smiled. The gallows would only be effective if Oricien could capture him.

By the time he reached the Viatory the city could have been deserted: the fighting was all on the western side of the city. The tower of the Viatory reached for the sky above him. It was many years since he had listened to Viators Dince and Sleech inviting the folk of Croad to Find the Way: one a sadistic hypocrite, the other a feeble reed. Little wonder that he had fallen away from the Way.

He cautiously opened the heavy wooden door. If he was right, Oricien would be within, and whoever he had commandeered to help him. In the gloom of the cavernous interior, at first he thought to see no one. Then, in the Arch, an elderly stooped figure: Beauceron fought back a laugh, for it was surely Viator Sleech, a decrepit character even when Beauceron had been growing up. By now he must be in his dotage.

As his eyes became accustomed to the dark, he saw

another man on the steps to the tower. It was Oricien. Beauceron regretted for a moment leaving behind his bow; but it was no part of his plan to kill the Lord of Croad from a distance. He crept along the walls until he stood within touching distance of the Arch. Oricien turned the spigot which released the flow of Harmonic Elixir from the tower. The glutinous liquid gurgled irritably into a long low trough.

'Quickly, Sleech, the buckets!' called Oricien from the ladder. 'We must fill as many as we can.'

Sleech inched towards the front of the Arch and picked up a bucket, moving with even greater slowness towards the channel. '—no care for my old bones – at my age – retire—' he grumbled as he moved.

Suddenly he turned his head. Something had alerted his rheumy suspicion. Beauceron cursed, for Sleech was looking straight at him. 'Oh!' he cried in a scratchy voice. 'My lord—'

Beauceron struck the old man across the face with a mailed fist. *Old fool*, he thought. *Lucky I do not kill you.*

'Sleech?' called Oricien. 'Sleech, is anything amiss?'

He jumped from the ladder, turned to see Sleech's form slumped before him. His broadsword was in his hand even as he took in the scene. Beauceron would have had no compunction about settling with him whether he were armed or not, but maybe it was better this way.

He stepped from the shadow. 'Oricien,' he said softly. 'Turn slowly, or die now.'

Oricien took a step away from Sleech and turned to look into the flickering sconce. 'Arren,' he breathed.

Beauceron gave an infinitesimal bow. 'I now use the name Beauceron or, colloquially, the Dog of the North.'

Oricien raised his sword. 'Isola said the Dog of the North was Lord Guigot.'

Beauceron shrugged. 'Such was the rumour in Metting-gloom. I saw no reason to discountenance it.'

'Either way, you were banished upon pain of death.'

'Guigot's exile was deserved. Mine was not.'

'Now is not the time to rehearse your grievances. My city is under attack.'

'Everyone is fighting on the West Walls,' said Beauceron. 'No one will come, and no one will save your city. We may talk a while, if you choose.'

'I choose to pour burning Elixir upon the northern raiders. I have already shattered your cavalry,' said Oricien. 'If you try to stop me I shall kill you.'

'You have the chance now,' said Beauceron with a slow smile. 'Although I would know why you betrayed me first.'

Oricien shook his head impatiently. 'There was no "betrayal". You abused my father's favour by defiling Siedra. He was merciful – to excess, as events have turned out – in allowing you to live.'

'Siedra trapped me. She was jealous of Eilla, for whom I had made my preference clear.'

Oricien waved the point away with a swat of his hand. 'The question is of little relevance. It was many years ago.'

'It is rather less academic to me,' said Beauceron. 'There has not been a day when I have not sworn revenge on all who betrayed me: your father, your sister, and you. My father died in your father's service, at his side. I never saw him or my mother after that night. Eilla, the sweetest and truest lady of all, was torn from me and exiled. Your family destroyed her life and mine.'

Oricien raised his eyebrows. 'You have not used your time profitably. You could have made an honourable career for yourself in this time.'

'There is nothing dishonourable in repaying debts,' said Beauceron. 'Your father eluded me by squandering his life chasing hill bandits; Siedra has yet to be found. Only you remain, the perfidious boy and also the Lord of Croad. You will do.'

'Siedra is in Glount,' said Oricien, licking his lips. 'Why do you not take your army there?'

'Glount, eh? For now, you may wish to apologize for your oafish mendacity,' said Beauceron. 'This is a question for your own judgement, since it will not prolong your life, which I intend to conclude in the near future. Sadly Viator Sleech is insensible, and can offer little guidance on the matter of Equilibrium.'

'Enough!' cried Oricien, springing forward. 'I will do what my father should have done twelve years ago.' His blade rose high over his head and crashed down towards Beauceron's head. Beauceron held his own sword with two hands and turned the blow aside. In the emptiness of the Viatory their blades rang shrill and tinny. Oricien caught him with a mighty blow to the shoulder and knocked him spinning across the floor, his mail winking crazily in the torchlight. Beauceron scrambled onto the steps leading to the top of the tower containing the Elixir. He chopped down from the higher point, buffeting Oricien from his feet. There was little delicacy or subtlety in fighting with such heavy swords. Oricien surged onto the steps and forced Beauceron ever higher, towards the top of the tower where the steps ended.

'Why did you come back?' said Oricien through gritted teeth. 'You have destroyed us all.'

Beauceron smiled as he forced aside another lunge. 'It is the Way of Harmony,' he said. 'You lived in Disharmony, spurning the truth. This is your reward. It is almost enough to make me return to the Consorts.'

Almost before he had realized it, Beauceron was at the top of the steps. A narrow perimeter ran around the edge of the tower: he looked into the hollow centre of the tower to see a mat of rough fibre which covered the huge vat of Harmonic Elixir lying below. In the dim light, illuminated only by a single torch, Beauceron stepped carefully onto the perimeter stones: it would not do to fall into the vat of Elixir.

'I have you now, Arren,' said Oricien. 'We will not both survive today.'

Beauceron edged back against the wall. Other than circling the perimeter he had few options. He reached for the torch on the wall behind him and pulled it from its sconce. At least he could control the light.

'Are you not going to kill me, Arren? Surely the Dog of the North does not fear to fight a single man.'

Beauceron rushed forward, hoping to catch Oricien off guard. Oricien stepped aside, swung his sword down to catch Beauceron's mailed forearm. The torch in Beauceron's hand skittered away to the stone perimeter, and as both men watched mutely, toppled onto the mat below.

'No!' cried Oricien. 'The flames – the Elixir!'

But even as he spoke, the mat took fire. It would burn for a while, but once the flames reached the Elixir below, only disaster could ensue. Beauceron knocked him aside and scampered down the steps.

'Oricien, you have destroyed your own city. No army will be able to put out the flames once they take hold.'

'I will kill you yet, Beauceron,' Oricien called, as he dashed down the steps after him.

'Unless you want Sleech to burn, you will wish to leave your pursuit of me,' said Beauceron at the bottom of the steps.

Oricien paused irresolutely, then darted across the room to where Viator Sleech lay motionless against the wall. He could not attend to Sleech without leaving his back exposed. Beauceron grinned and ran for the exit. Oricien turned with a shrug and lifted Sleech's stick-light body over his shoulder. With a sideways look at Beauceron he dashed from the building. Beauceron gave his head a brisk shake: Oricien had risked his life to save the old fool. Some things were incomprehensible.

Beauceron gained the street. Neither Oricien nor Sleech was anywhere to be seen. As he looked around he heard a vast roar from the Viatory and he was thrown from his feet. A single immense gout of flame shot up through the wooden roof of the Viatory. Flaming shards flew high into the sky, where the wind carried them in all directions. Even as he staggered to his feet, he saw them fall to the ground and, in some cases, onto the thatched roofs of the houses, where they immediately ignited. There were too many fires: Oricien's city was lost.

The stone walls of the Viatory remained intact: the flames had been trammelled by the tower and forced upwards. From the shell of the building crawled a figure in a black cowl. It was neither Oricien nor Sleech. Who could have been taking refuge in the Viatory? It was unlikely to be anyone well-disposed towards him, and Beauceron stepped smartly across to the Viatory and administered a sharp kick to the figure on the ground.

A muffled scream from within the cowl surprised him: a woman! He reached out and pulled the cowl back to reveal a mess of blonde hair. His stomach lurched and he reached down to brush the hair aside from the face it concealed. Looking into the blue eyes, he held the face steady by the jaw for a long second before standing up.

'Get up, Siedra,' he said. 'We have much to discuss. How I have waited for this moment.'

7

Siedra looked at the ground before her. 'Arren,' she gasped. She pulled her gaze to his face. 'My father should have hanged you.'

'You picked the wrong hiding place, my lady. You are the last person I would have expected to put her trust in the viators.'

She spat in the dirt. 'Circumstances have changed,' she said. 'You have left few refuges in the city. Even the viators have their uses.'

Beauceron laughed. 'Your last refuge is gone. Your father should have killed me when he had the chance, if he chose not to believe me. Now his city is in ruins.'

He dragged Siedra to her feet and gestured around at the roofs already now well ablaze. Her eyes kindled with the fire he recalled from long years past. Her skin still had the translucence he remembered, but he wondered how he could ever have found her beautiful. Her face had grown pinched; lines of ill-temper were etched around her mouth. Increasingly she resembled her mother.

Siedra sensed something of Beauceron's thoughts and stared back with defiance kindled in her blue eyes. 'Do not look at me with pity, Arren,' she said. 'I am still far too clever and far too dangerous to pity.'

'You mistake me, Siedra,' said Beauceron in a level voice. 'My only emotion now is hatred. It has never ceased since the day of my exile, and it will never cease until my vengeance is complete.'

Siedra's mouth convulsed into a sneer. 'Vengeance? You are burning Croad to the ground. What more can you want?'

'Oricien's death,' said Beauceron. 'Your continued life – for a while, at least.'

Siedra looked around her. There was nowhere to run. She licked her lips. 'What – what do you intend?'

Beauceron leaned back against the wall behind him. 'The most appropriate revenge would be to debauch you in the way you convinced Thaume I did all those years ago.'

'You were guilty,' she said, her eyes flashing. 'The events I described took place.'

'Not in the way you presented them.'

'Perhaps not,' she said. 'You should have thought more carefully before you chose that trollop over me. Do you think you are the only one who can nourish hatred? Your actions led to my marriage with Dinarre, a torment you cannot possibly imagine.'

'I find it unlikely you wish to revisit the events in detail,' said Beauceron, taking a step towards her. 'In any event, my recollection is that your fate had already been decided. Do not attempt to make me feel remorse. Your fate cannot arouse any pity.'

For a fleeting moment a smile flashed across her face. 'I was right about you, Arren. I always thought you were stronger than Oricien or Guigot. You could have been a great man.'

Beauceron smiled. 'I am a great man.' He indicated the buildings flaming in the distance. 'I am the man who destroyed Croad.'

'You have not told me what you mean to do with me.' As the Viatory burned in the background, she seemed to draw strength from the flames. Something of her old hauteur kindled in her face.

'I no longer have the taste for your flesh,' he said. 'I will bestow you where you are more appreciated. My men will play dice for you tonight. The winner may use you as he chooses. It is unlikely to be what you are accustomed to.'

She stepped forward and spat at his face. 'You are unspeakable.'

Beauceron shrugged. 'My own opinion of you remains equally unflattering.'

He took two lengths of rope from his belt. With the first he bound her arms behind her back. The second hobbled her ankles together so that she could take only a half-stride. 'As you say, my lady, you remain clever and dangerous.'

By the time he was back amidst the fighting, Siedra stumbling behind him, the wind had driven the flames ahead of him. Houses burned and women and children huddled together in the centre of the roads, away from the flaming buildings. There was no doubt about it: the whole city was on fire, and there was no way to put it out. Yes, it had been better to spare Oricien; he would have to live with this day always. Any attempt Oricien might have wished to make to rally his troops was clearly futile as the city burned around them. Siedra sobbed quietly as he led her through the streets.

Beauceron hauled her more roughly as they approached the Temple where his men remained clustered. He raised his hand above his head and rotated his finger: the signal to disengage. Monetto nodded, blew his horn. The men retreated in a disciplined phalanx and slipped out through an untended sally port.

'Why are we leaving?' panted Monetto.

'Do you want to roast?' said Beauceron. 'The city is lost.' He led his men back to their camp at an easy lope, Siedra keeping pace as best she could. A stream of fleeing civilians poured out of the West Gate as the fire took hold.

'Ride for the ridge,' he said as his men reached their gal-lumphers. Beauceron slung Siedra across the back of his own gallumpher. The troop spurred up out of the valley towards the selfsame path where they had looked down into the city half a year earlier: where Isola had begged to walk down into Croad. Well, she was there now. He wondered, with a brief pang, if she would survive the conflagration.

<h2 style="text-align:center">8</h2>

They tethered their mounts in a copse and stood looking down at the pall of smoke rising from what once had been the King's stronghold in the North. The walls, being made of stone, should survive with minimal damage, but the wooden buildings within must be consumed utterly.

Monetto examined Beauceron's prisoner, who still lay sprawled and tethered across the gallumpher's back. 'Another kidnap?'

Beauceron grinned. 'Look carefully.'

Monetto rubbed the soot from her cheek with a callused thumb. 'My Lady Siedra! I thought never to see you again.'

Siedra twisted on the gallumpher's back to see Monetto's face. 'Master Coppercake.'

'None other.'

'You have come far from your multiplications.'

Monetto raised an eyebrow to comprehend her undignified pose. 'No further than yourself, my lady.'

'What about our plunder?' interjected Rostovac with a truculent frown.

'Much of value will have been burned,' said Beauceron. 'The rest, I suspect, will have been appropriated by Virnesto's men. Look, his standard flies over what is left of Croad.'

'So we have fought for nothing?' There was a muttering from within the group.

'Croad has slim pickings,' said Beauceron. 'Think on this: Duke Trevarre has dispatched all force north to relieve Oricien. He arrives too late, of course: but think of the riches of Lynnoc with all Trevarre's troops in one place. The merchants will not stay at home. The caravans from Glount to Emmen will still roll. If you are game for a summer in the field, you will learn the meaning of plunder.'

Rostovac grinned in understanding. The muttering from the men took on a more approbatory tone.

'You never wanted to occupy Croad at all, or you would still be down there now,' said Rostovac.

'A moment,' said Dello. 'We are entitled to our share of the spoils, regardless of what we may gain later. We risk our lives; we are entitled to a share.'

'He is right,' said Monetto. 'That is always the bargain we make.'

Beauceron nodded to acknowledge the justice of the point. 'If I must deal with Brissio, so be it. Monetto, in the circumstances perhaps you would like to accompany me back to Croad.'

Monetto gave a half-smile and mounted his piebald gallumpher.

'Wait!' called Siedra. 'Do not leave me with these brutes!'

'They are not such fiends once you get to know them,' said Beauceron. 'Still, the sight of your tearful farewell from Oricien – if he still lives – will be an affecting and edifying spectacle. Tocchieto, untie the Lady Siedra; set her on one of the spare gallumphers.'

Siedra composed herself, looked around. 'Do not try to flee, my lady,' said Beauceron. 'There is nowhere to go.'

Below them Prince Brissio had set up the field-throne which he had brought from the North in his baggage train. He intended to take the surrender of the city with full pomp. Since the surrender was that of an empty shell, the ceremony appeared exaggerated to Beauceron's eyes.

*

Beauceron and Monetto rode slowly down the path to the field outside the smouldering city, Siedra's mount a pace behind them. The inhabitants milled around, some staring into space, the children either sobbing or playing with complete unconcern – there was no middle ground – and others seemingly fixated on the tower of the Viatory, which flamed long after the rest of the city had burned itself out.

Huddled by the destroyed West Gate was what was left of Oricien's army. Their casualties did not seem to have been excessive: they had been beaten more by demoralization at seeing their homes go up in flames.

As they rode through the newly homeless, Monetto asked: 'Are you now Arren once more?'

Beauceron shook his head wryly. 'I can never be Arren again. I have had my revenge. Oricien's city is destroyed and he lives to witness it. That does not make me who I was, or give me what I have lost. What of you, Master Coppercake?'

Monetto looked around at the devastation he had helped to cause. 'I left Coppercake behind when I rode out with you,' he said. 'I never imagined it would come to this.'

Beauceron turned in the saddle to look into Monetto's face. 'I am sorry, old friend. Would you have come if you had known where it would lead?'

He gave a harsh smile, bitter with the weight of hindsight. 'How could I? Lord Thaume had misjudged you, and I could not stay. But if you had told me that night that you proposed to destroy not only Thaume's family but his city, to cast all of Croad to the wolves, to roam the steppes with a band of vagabonds – indeed, to be a vagabond myself – well, I think I would have taken myself back to Glount.'

'I did not know myself,' said Beauceron quietly. 'On that night, I knew only my rage, my pain, my loss: I did not know where it would take me. We came here by degrees. Perhaps that is how we all come to wrong.'

'"Wrong"? You acknowledge error?'

Beauceron laughed. '"Error" is perhaps not the term. I have achieved a kind of Harmony, albeit a dark one. Viator Sleech or Lord High Viator Raugier might not have approved, but I have followed my own Way. I cannot delight in what I have done, but I cannot regret it.'

'How touching is your remorse,' called Siedra from behind them. 'I never imagined you so maudlin.'

Beauceron turned in his saddle. 'Do not mistake me, Siedra. My revenge is not yet complete. I will not set it aside through softness of heart.'

They rode over to Brissio's throne. 'Good afternoon, my lord,' said Beauceron politely. 'Allow me to present my prisoner, the Lady Siedra.'

Brissio gave a moment's incredulous stare. 'You are cool, and no mistake. You flee the field, and return as if nothing had happened.'

'I did not "flee",' said Beauceron. 'I chose not to burn my troops. Since you are here, and there has been no formal surrender, you evidently made the same choice: although, in keeping with your slow perceptions, later than me. And if you had not thrown the cavalry away with your rashness, the city need never have been burned.'

'Be assured you will account in Mettingloom for your conduct,' said Brissio. 'I hear a rumour that you started the fire.'

'It is not rumour, but fact.'

'You freely own to destroying the city?'

'It was never worth the expense of garrisoning. Better to remove the presence of Emmen in the North altogether.'

Brissio rose from his throne. 'The cost of the army was underwritten by the city's revenues. The Winter House will be bankrupt! How will we repay our loans?'

Beauceron shrugged. 'That is not my concern. Davanzato

may suggest some weaselly expedient, if your father has not yet hanged him.'

'I will have you hanged in his place! Guards!'

'My lord,' said Captain-General Virnesto. 'With all respect, this is not the most opportune time to settle your scores with Beauceron. Lord Oricien approaches with his party. We must accept his surrender with fair grace, then consider how we will defend the city against King Enguerran's approach.'

Beauceron and Monetto both uttered caws of laughter. 'King Enguerran!'

'I fail to see the joke,' said Virnesto.

'My man Tocchieto may have been mistaken,' said Beauceron. 'He is fond of a tipple on occasion.'

Brissio rose. 'There was no army?'

Beauceron shrugged. 'Conceivably not.'

'I might have taken the city without losing my cavalry?'

'Time will tell.'

Virnesto said: 'Why, in the name of the Consorts? Your own men have died along with mine, to no purpose.'

'You disappoint me, Virnesto. You were present when Brissio and Oricien made their compact to dispose of me once the city had surrendered. You did nothing to stop it. In such circumstances I was entitled to look to my own deliverance.'

Virnesto looked at the ground. 'My lord,' he said to Brissio. 'There is nothing to be gained from further wrangling. Oricien is here.'

Brissio sat back on his throne with heavy emphasis. 'My crown!' he called.

Virnesto and Beauceron, as the senior captains, flanked the throne, mounted on their strong gallumphers. Before them approached Lord Oricien on a white gallumpher, its coat stained with smoke and soot; on a smaller black strider at his side rode Lady Isola, who was once destined to be the

Lady of Croad. Beauceron tried to catch her eye but she stared only at the ground.

Brissio rose from his throne. 'Halt before me, the master of the North!' he said in a ringing voice. 'Why do you approach me?'

Oricien reined in his gallumpher. He removed the golden chain from around his neck. 'I am come to make surrender of my city,' he said in a thick voice. 'The ruins you see behind me are yours now.'

A retainer took the chain and placed it around Brissio's neck.

Oricien looked around. 'Siedra!' he cried. 'Are you hurt?'

Tears streamed down her cheeks. 'Arren has kidnapped me,' she said in a thick voice.

Oricien addressed Beauceron. 'Can you not release her? Is the destruction of Croad not enough? I have nothing: you have taken it all. Would mercy not be a greater demonstration of your power?'

Beauceron laughed. 'My plans for Siedra are not yet complete. If you wish to have her back, go to the slave markets at Taratanallos in a year's time. You may buy her, if you have the money. She is unlikely to command a great price unless my men use her with unusual care.'

'Arren, I beg you!'

'As I once begged Siedra to tell the truth to your father? Say your farewells while you may.'

'Enough!' bellowed Brissio. 'This is a solemn moment, my great investiture. All other matters are subordinate. Tell me, Oricien: were you at Jehan's Steppe?'

Oricien blinked slowly. 'I was – as was he.' He pointed at Beauceron. 'Arren is the son of Darrien, the Captain of my father's Guard.'

'We shall come to "Arren" later,' said Brissio. 'For the

nonce, it is necessary that you make apology for Jehan's Steppe, where so many good knights died.'

'My lord! This is unprecedented! Tardolio invaded us: we merely defended our lives and our property. You may not do this!'

'I now decide what may and may not be done,' said Brissio. 'I am Prince of Mettingloom by right, and Lord of Croad by arms. If you do not comply with my wishes, the folk of my new realm shall suffer.'

Oricien hung his head.

'Good my lord,' said Isola, her voice barely audible. 'Such vindictiveness is not the mark of a great prince.' She swivelled her eyes sideways to Beauceron's face at the mention of vindictiveness. 'Can you not show compassion?'

Brissio scowled. 'Now is not the time for your importunities, woman, especially as you have broken your parole in fleeing to Oricien. I am the master of the field, and all must acknowledge it.'

Oricien slipped from the saddle of his gallumpher and knelt before Brissio, his face expressionless.

'I kneel before the new Lord of Croad.'

Brissio permitted himself a look of satisfaction. 'Your obeisance pleases me. Still, you must abase yourself further, and beg pardon for the crimes of Jehan's Steppe.'

Beauceron looked around the group. Virnesto stared stolidly ahead; Isola's face was crimson. He had yearned to see Oricien humiliated, so where was his satisfaction? Brissio was a man so far below Oricien in dignity, honour and courage that the scene before him was an abomination.

'Come, man, a prince must not be kept waiting. When we return to Mettingloom, while you await your ransom, I will teach you something of due respect.'

Beauceron gave Brissio a marvelling stare. What was the point of taking Oricien for ransom? There was no one left to

pay it: his city was a smoking wreck, Siedra his only surviving relative. Once again Brissio had proved himself a
buffoon.

Oricien dropped to his second knee. 'I beg the pardon of
your lordship for—'

'No!' came a sudden scream from Isola. In a moment
Beauceron was never able to recapture, she leaped from her
strider to Brissio, full length, without touching the ground.
Her arms were outstretched, and there was a glint of metal.
Brissio staggered back with a cry, Isola on top of him.

'She has pricked me, the dimon!' cried Brissio. 'Oh, but I
am hurt!' He pushed Isola aside and from his belly came an
ooze of red. 'Treason!' Blood bubbled thickly from his
mouth. Attendants rushed to his side.

'Detain her!' shouted Virnesto as the guards looked on in
horrified wonderment.

Beauceron weighed up the situation. Brissio was sorely
wounded: there was no hope for Isola. Treason it might not
be, for Isola had sworn no fealty to the northern kings, but
she had wounded – perhaps mortally – the royal Prince. He
hesitated for a moment. He could not rescue Isola and extract
Siedra from the fighting. Could he let her off so easily? Isola
climbed to her feet, looked around in desperation. Her eyes
met Beauceron's, shining with glorious defiance. He spurred
his gallumpher forward, scooped Isola up in one arm. 'Monetto, ride!' he called and with his free hand wrenched the
gallumpher's nose towards the ridge and the trees.

Brissio tried to rise and sank back with a groan. 'After
them,' roared Virnesto. But Beauceron had a crucial twenty
yards' lead, and from the hill charged fifteen of his cavalry,
firing with cool accuracy into the gap between the Dog's men
and their pursuers. Anyone who wished to catch Beauceron
would need to brave a storm of arrows.

Beauceron did not look back. It was hard enough to

control the gallumpher with one hand and counterbalance Isola's weight.

By the time he gained the ridge the pursuit had been reined in. His men were experienced in this kind of skirmish, and they knew the terrain. There was no way Virnesto would be able to bring them to book.

He set Isola down. 'You have paid any ransom you ever owed, my lady. You are free.'

Isola looked up at his gallumpher and gave a hoarse laugh. 'And so you repay me for my treacheries,' she said. 'You leave me in the wilderness without a mount, my choices the woods, or Brissio's men.'

'You mistake me, my lady,' said Beauceron. 'There has rarely been good will between us, and perhaps I have rarely deserved it. You are free to leave if you wish; otherwise you may remain with us. Our path is unlikely to take us to Sey, but we will set you down wherever on our travels you see fit. I have achieved my goals, in large measure.'

Isola extended her hand. 'Thank you,' she said. 'For my part, I repent of any wrongs I have done you. They are too many to list.'

After a moment she said: 'You left Siedra behind.'

'I could not have taken her and you as well. I had to leave one of you. I found I could not leave you to suffer for such a noble deed.'

'The "noble deed" was defending the honour of a man you had sworn to humble. And then you let Siedra go. What of your vengeance?'

Beauceron swept his arm to encompass the smouldering city. 'We have had vengeance enough for one day, my lady.'

He smiled and summoned Rostovac with a fine white strider, onto which he gently handed her.

'Shall we go, my lady? We have many miles to travel before we make camp tonight.'

As the column moved away, Beauceron looked back over his shoulder one last time. The plume of smoke, reaching skywards from the burning city, all but blotted out the setting sun.

Epilogue

Six months later Beauceron led his men back north after a summer campaigning in northern Emmen. He judged it unwise to return to Mettingloom until he had a better sense of the tenor of affairs. Prince Brissio had died three days after his stabbing by Isola, and events in the Winter Court would necessarily be febrile. It would be difficult now to return before the snow came, and Beauceron had resolved that if he returned at all, it would be when the Summer Court was in session. For now, he had decided that his men would winter in Hengis Port while he gathered intelligence of the North.

He had sent his men on ahead to secure lodgings, so when the path took him along the ridge past Croad he was alone. The sun was sinking in the sky and he fancied to see a smoky smudge across the clouds. He looked down into the valley to see signs of movement. There were even some wooden structures inside the still-intact walls, although no one had troubled to mend the West Gate through which the Winter Armies had entered. Croad was slowly returning to health and life: there had been nothing to detain the folk of Mettingloom.

He rode down the track from the hills and at the base

turned to the south, away from the city and out into the sprawling agglomeration of farms, many of which appeared neglected. As he came out through a straggly clump of trees he saw the house of Canille's old farm before him. A lad of some twelve or so years deftly broke the neck of a rabbit he had caught in a snare; rapt in his task he did not notice Beauceron's approach. His gallumpher snorted and the boy looked up and jumped to his feet.

'Have no fear, lad. Is this Canille's farm?'

The boy backed away. 'You are a raider. There is nothing for you here.'

'You need not be alarmed. I am merely revisiting the scenes of my youth. Tell me if this is Canille's farm.'

The lad pulled the knife he presumably used to skin rabbits from his belt and set his jaw. 'We have no need of you here. Go back to the North!'

Beauceron looked down into the boy's flashing dark eyes with a hint of recognition. 'You are brave, to stand against a mounted raider. I admire your courage. It is not necessary for you to prove it today: I require information, not goods. Someone – a lady, a lady who needed no title – once lived here.'

From his side came a female voice. 'Do not move! I have a bow trained on your neck.'

Beauceron turned to look, stared into the copy of the boy's face. 'Eilla! But Lord Thaume exiled you!'

The woman blanched, peered into Beauceron's face. She quickly turned away. 'Arren!' She turned to the boy. 'Run along, son, attend to the cesspit.'

'But it does not need—'

'Do as I say,' she said in a low voice which brooked no dissent. 'I do not expect to see you for an hour.'

'What of the raider?'

'He is no raider; just a traveller.'

The lad looked sullenly at the pair of them, scowling at Beauceron as the agent of his unexpected cesspit duty.

'Will you not climb down, Arren?'

Beauceron stepped down and tethered his gallumpher to a post.

Eilla brushed a hair out of her eyes. Her face was tanned from outdoor work and her hair had streaks of grey in places, but Beauceron could still see the girl he had loved the long years ago.

By unspoken agreement they walked around the farm, away from the house.

'You look well, Eilla. After Thaume exiled you, I did not think to see you here. I never thought to see you at all.'

'I was never banished, Arren. They say Sir Langlan counselled Lord Thaume to mercy.'

'I would have returned,' he said in a tight voice. 'If I had known you were here, no ban of Thaume's would have stopped me.'

'The Wheel turns as it will, Arren. I learned that long ago.'

They walked on in silence. Beauceron had nothing to say on the subjects of the Wheel or the Way.

'You have the wolf's head on your surcoat,' she said. 'You are one of them.'

Beauceron gave a steady look into her face. 'I had few choices, Eilla. If we had – I had always been going to support us through arms, you remember.'

'How long ago those days were,' she said, her voice controlled.

'There has never been a day I have not thought of that evening,' he said. 'I had always dreamed to see you again.'

From nowhere Eilla laughed. 'The Patient Suitor! You took your time.'

Beauceron gave a sad smile. 'I swore I would return, but you were not there to hear.'

'I always thought you would come back,' she said. 'I did not expect to wait twelve years to see you.'

'The boy – he is your son, of course.'

'I have three,' she said, with a shy smile.

'You are wed, then.'

She gave him a look of surprise. 'How could it be otherwise? I waited; you did not return. In due course I married Chandry.'

'Chandry?'

'Do not say anything, Arren. You were not there. He is a good man and a good father.'

'Where is he now?'

'In the city. Oricien requires the men to give two days a week to rebuilding. Do not reproach me, Arren.'

Beauceron was conscious of a heaviness in his heart. Had he expected her to wait? Eilla had always been a pragmatic girl. He smiled.

'I am in no position to reproach anyone, Eilla. I have not used the intervening years in a way calculated to secure your approval.'

She reached out and touched the wolf's head on his chest. 'You have served the Dog of the North.'

Beauceron could not control a quick high laugh. 'Eilla, I *am* the Dog of the North.'

Her jaw sagged. 'You are Beauceron?'

'To you I will always be Arren; to the world, yes, I am Beauceron.'

She shook her head and looked at him again in marvelling wonder. 'You have done this to Croad?'

Beauceron paused for a moment. 'I had much to avenge.'

'You did all this, destroyed all this – for me?'

Beauceron gave his head a rapid shake. 'For us. The rage was all mine. I did not think to make you a present of the ashes of Croad.'

'I did not ask this,' she said. 'Thaume and his family wronged you and they wronged me; but I never asked their destruction.' Her eyes were full.

'There is no guilt for you, Eilla. The responsibility is mine. I humbled the house of Thaume, not you.'

'And has it mended anything? All you lost remains lost: even me.'

Beauceron shook his head. 'Especially you. Some part of me longed to return, to claim you after so long. Instead I find you wed with three children.'

Eilla said nothing.

'And no,' he continued, 'it has mended nothing. Thaume escaped my vengeance; I let Siedra go to save a more deserving lady from a worse fate; I let Oricien live in shame rather than kill him when I had the chance. I have destroyed his city; but bringing him down has not raised me up.'

She touched his cheek. 'The Way is not always a straight road,' she said. 'You have far to go. I wish you fair speed. If you would learn from experience and my advice, do not try to find Siedra again. You will not bring yourself peace.'

Suddenly Beauceron smiled. 'Do you remember when we used to play raiders?'

Eilla laughed. 'And now you are truly King of the Raiders.'

'At least I have never stolen a cow.'

'I have enough of my own now,' she said. 'I no longer need to dare such extravagance.'

They had returned to where Beauceron's gallumpher was tethered. 'I should leave now, Eilla: my men are far ahead and I must join them. I am glad I have seen you.'

'Even though you have not found what you hoped to find.'

Beauceron leaned forward and embraced her one last time. 'I have found you safe, healthy, happy. I do not think we shall meet again: it gladdens me to think of you like this. Goodbye, Eilla.'

She reached out and took his hand as he mounted the gallumpher. 'Goodbye, Arren,' she said through a voice choked with tears.

Beauceron gently spurred his gallumpher into motion. As the track turned away into the wood he looked back to see her watching his departure with an unreadable expression. With a hand raised in salute he dug his heels into the gallumpher's side and Eilla was lost from view.

Eilla walked back to the cesspit, drying her eyes on her sleeve. She called softly: 'Arren, you can come out now. The raider is gone.'

And young Arren clambered from the pit into his mother's waiting arms, to wonder at the fervour of the kisses she rained upon his head.

Visit **www.panmacmillan.com** to read more about all our books and to buy them. You will also find features, author interviews and news of any author events, and you can sign up for e-newsletters so that you're always first to hear about our new releases.